D0864247

AWAKEN

Awaken

A SPIRAL OF BLISS NOVEL:
Book 3

NINA LANE

SNOW QUEEN
PUBLISHING

ISBN: 978-0-9887158-8-2

This book is for all the readers who love Liv and Dean West as much as I do. This is for those of you who know the courage it takes to trust your instincts and find your way. This is for the women who love being someone's girl, and for the men who are your heroes. And this is for everyone who believes in the good things—books, a cup of tea, sexy professors, interesting travels that lead you back home, warm quilts, and perfectly imperfect love.

We loved with a love that was more than love.

—Edgar Allan Poe

PART I

CHAPTER ONE

March 3

E ven from thousands of miles away, I can feel my husband. I feel his thoughts brushing against my skin, the beating of his heart in rhythm with mine. I feel him in the world, a powerful, unyielding presence who will forever be my source of safety and warmth. And because of that, the distance between us doesn't seem quite so vast, and my aloneness not quite so *alone*.

Mirror Lake is beginning to wake from the hibernation of winter. Colorful, adhesive tulips, butterflies, and robins plaster the windows of the shops lining Avalon Street. The frozen surface of the lake is starting to crack, ice floes melting under the increasingly warm sun. Piles of snow still cap the surrounding mountains and line the streets of town, but the promise of spring clings to the air.

I put a coat on over my jeans and T-shirt and pull my long brown hair into a ponytail before heading outside. I stop at a coffeehouse to get two takeout coffees, then walk to Emerald Street and the Happy Booker bookstore. Big signs in the windows read Going Out of Business Sale.

I push open the door, deflecting a pang of regret. I'd offered to try and help my friend Allie Lyons save her bookstore by applying for a small business loan, but my loan application was denied, and we couldn't bring in enough revenue to afford the raised rent on the building.

"Welcome to… oh, hi, Liv." Allie straightens from a pile of books and pushes a tumble of red curls off her forehead. Twenty-seven years old and possessing an undaunted, boundless energy, Allie hasn't let the loss of her business get her down.

"Morning, Allie." I indicate that one of the coffees is for her and place the tray on the front counter. "What can I do?"

"I haven't gotten to the children's section yet," she tells me. "The toys and stuff need to be packed up too, but let's wait at least another week or so. Brent will be here in about half an hour with his truck to load some boxes."

After taking off my coat, I head to the back of the store where the children's section is located. The bookstore is closing for good at the end of the month, and we've started packing up returnable inventory and organizing sale tables and bins. I pick up an inventory sheet and get to work.

"Hey, Liv, there's a bunch of freebies in the bin by the windows," Allie calls. "I'm going to leave them outside starting tomorrow, so take what you want now. There's something in there about medieval history that Professor Hottie might like."

"Thanks." I put a few picture books into a box and go to the bin filled with paperbacks.

I look through the books and set aside the one on medieval literature even though Dean probably already has it. I put a few more paperback novels in the stack.

"When's he coming back?" Allie asks.

"Not sure yet. This phase of the job lasts until the end of July." I try to ignore the clenching of my heart at the reminder that Dean is gone.

No, I remind myself. He's not gone. He's just *away*.

He had refused to leave, at first. It seemed as if nothing— not the dictate that he had to stay away from King's University, not the threat to his career, not the sexual harassment accusation of a vindictive student—could force my husband to leave my side.

He'd spent the few weeks after the miscarriage hovering around me, desperate to do something to make it better. I soon realized that being there for me was his way of coping with the loss and his own anger, even though I held to the belief that he needed to be away from Mirror Lake. The opportunity to serve as an advisor on an archeological dig in Italy for the next six months was waiting for him, but he wouldn't accept it, not if it meant being away from me.

Then one afternoon in mid-February, Dean went to King's University to return some books. He saw Maggie Hamilton, the girl making the false harassment claim, at the library. Though they didn't speak to each other, Frances Hunter, chairperson of the history department, came to our apartment later that day.

Frances was livid that Dean had dared set foot on campus when he'd been unofficially suspended. And she was even more upset by the fact that Maggie Hamilton's father had contacted her with threats about obtaining a restraining order against Dean if he didn't stop "stalking" Maggie.

"If you're not careful, things are going to get worse than they already are," Frances warned him. "A restraining order, Dean, for God's sake. You won't need a suspension from the university if Edward Hamilton hits you with a legal order forbidding you from going anywhere near King's University. Do you think for one second we could keep that quiet?"

Then Frances had looked at me. Dean saw that look. And I knew exactly what hard conclusion he'd reached in that one instant—if he left Mirror Lake, if he removed himself as a target for Maggie Hamilton and her father, he had a better chance of keeping the arrows from hitting me. Protecting me was the only thing that could force him to leave.

He left for the airport at dawn the following morning. I could feel the sadness and anger radiating from him, and I almost wavered in my insistence that I couldn't go with him because of my own responsibilities in Mirror Lake.

But I didn't waver. He had to leave, and I had to stay.

"I don't know where we go from here," Dean said, reaching out to touch my cheek as we stood by the front door.

"I don't know either," I admitted. "But why does either of us have to know? There doesn't always have to be a plan."

"Yes, there does."

I turned to pick up his travel bag. I know my husband. He likes plans and schedules. He needs to be in control. He's accustomed to getting what he wants. The avalanche of recent events—our separation last fall, the miscarriage, and now the threat to his career—hit us both with unimagined and heart-wrenching force.

And he hadn't been able to prevent or stop any of it.

In that moment, I thought of something I'd written in my manifesto a couple of months ago.

I will remember how it was when we first met.

How I cherished those early months of slow exploration, learning all the spaces of each other's bodies and hearts. Feeling as if the world had narrowed to us alone, as if nothing could invade our intimacy. The place of Liv and Dean.

I followed him downstairs and out into the cold, gray morning. He unlocked the trunk of his car and hefted his suitcase and travel bag inside.

I watched him—my tall, handsome husband with his dark, rumpled hair and strong features enhanced by thick-lashed, brown eyes. His powerful body and broad shoulders that looked as if they could bear any weight in the world.

"Dean?"

"Right here." He slammed the trunk closed, his shoulders tight.

"Remember the first few months of our relationship and how good we were?"

"I'll never forget."

"Me either." I stepped closer to him. "So I was thinking that when you get back, maybe we could just… date."

"Date?"

"Like we did at the beginning," I suggested. "Maybe you could court me a little."

"Court you?"

He looked as if I were speaking a foreign language. I reached out to brush a speck of lint from the lapel of his peacoat.

"On our second date, you told me you'd loved the King Arthur tales when you were a boy," I said. "Sir Galahad was your favorite. The greatest knight ever. You loved stories about the Holy Grail, Excalibur, Lancelot. Do you remember?"

"I remember."

"In addition to all their adventures, I'm sure the knights did a great deal of wooing their ladies," I continued. "Wasn't that the basis of courtly love? You must know something about that."

"I've done some research, yeah."

"Well?"

I could almost see his mind shift to the comforting ground of scholarship. The tension in his shoulders eased a little.

"The idea of courtly love dates to about the eleventh century," he explained. "In literature it was a concept of secret love usually between members of the nobility. A cross between erotic and spiritual desire. The knight has to prove himself worthy of the lady's love by undergoing a series of trials while also accepting her independence. And he does indeed court her with rituals, songs, gifts, elaborate gestures."

"Sounds promising," I remarked. "For the lady, anyway."

"The lady was called the *domina*," Dean said. "She was the exalted, commanding mistress. The knight was the *servus,* her lowly but faithful servant."

"Really?"

"Really." He reached out to tuck a lock of hair behind my ear.

"This is sounding better and better." I smiled.

"Yes, it is." Dean looked at me, his eyes warming. "I haven't seen that pretty smile in too long."

Tenderness swirled through me. I brushed my hand over his chest again, feeling the heat of his muscles through his shirt. He bent to press his mouth against mine, a warm pressure that made my blood run like melted honey.

Oh, lovely pleasure.

"Good start, faithful servant," I whispered.

"Thank you, exalted mistress." And there it was—that crinkling at the corners of his eyes, the amused twinkle that never failed to lighten my heart.

"Knights often went off on long journeys and crusades, didn't they?" I asked. "We can think of your trip like that. Except without all the pillaging or whatever."

"They did travel often," Dean said. "And always with a token from their lady. So I'll need something of yours to take with me."

"A token like what?"

"A scarf or a glove." He shrugged. "Your underwear, maybe."

"I am not sending you off with a pair of my panties. What if the airport security agent finds them in your bag?"

He grinned. "Trust you to worry about something like that."

"Hold on." I hurried back upstairs to our apartment and into the bedroom. I grabbed an item from a shoebox inside the closet, then went back outside.

"Here." I held out my hand toward Dean. "A *proper* token of my love and devotion."

He took the metal disk attached to a silver chain and ran his finger over the engraved Latin quote: *Fortes fortuna iuvat.*

Fortune favors the brave.

"Keep it safe for me," I said.

"I will." He tucked the necklace into the pocket of his jeans.

"So that's the plan," I said. "You'll court me long-distance.

And when you get back, we can go to dinner, the movies, that kind of thing. Dating. It'll be fun."

Heaven knew that after the turmoil of recent months, my husband and I needed some *fun*.

"I would love to date you all over again, Olivia Rose." Dean put his hand against the side of my neck.

"I'd love it too."

He moved closer, his deep voice rolling over me. "Give me a kiss, beauty."

I stood on tiptoe to press my lips against his, my whole being filling with love and the belief that we would soon find our way back to each other. Dean cupped my face in his hands, his lips moving over mine in that perfect way that was both familiar and always new. Then he took me in his arms and pulled me against him in an embrace so tight I felt his heart beating against mine.

When we parted, I took a reluctant step back toward the building. Although I knew he had to go, my soul still cracked a little at the realization that he was actually leaving.

We gazed at each other for a moment, an arc of energy resonating between us. I memorized the way my husband looked in that instant, standing beside the car with a slight breeze ruffling his hair, faded jeans hugging his long legs, that warm brown gaze containing a thousand thoughts meant for me alone. So different from five years ago when he'd stood on the sidewalk looking at me… and yet somehow exactly the same.

"Promise me you'll unbend a little while you're in Tuscany," I said. "Get your hands dirty. Eat good food. Enjoy discussing all things medieval with your colleagues. Laugh. Remember why you love doing what you do. Promise."

"I promise." He reached into his coat pocket for his keys. "Say it for me."

"I'm yours." I swallowed past the lump in my throat. "Say it back."

"I'm yours. Always will be."

He pressed his palm to his chest and lifted his hand to me. I gave him a little wave, then turned and went back inside so I wouldn't have to watch him drive away.

He's been in Italy for ten days now. And though I miss him terribly, I have things to do, goals to accomplish. I've been working at the bookstore every day, volunteering at the library, and helping organize a new exhibition at the Mirror Lake Historical Museum. And I need to find a new job, since Allie has lost the Happy Booker.

I go back to the children's section and continue packing up picture books. I leaf through one about a boy and his pet dinosaur. Ever since the miscarriage, I've wondered at the aching sense of loss I feel, the realization that I'd started making plans. I'd even started imagining what it would be like—a baby wrapped up in a blanket, soft and warm as a muffin. Fuzzy tufts of hair, toothless smiles, tottering steps.

I'd pictured Dean cradling a newborn in his arms, and I'd felt that certain, bone-deep knowledge that he would love and protect our child with a fiercely devoted tenderness. That our child would be indescribably blessed to have Dean West as his or her father.

And while I hadn't yet been able to imagine myself as a mother, I thought one day soon I'd be able to. I could at least see it on the horizon.

I still can.

"Liv, I'm going to label the boxes in the backroom," Allie calls, her voice pulling me out of my thoughts. "Brent and I will get those loaded up first."

I keep working on the picture books, pausing a couple of times to check my email. Dean and I exchange two or three emails a day, all wonderfully mundane messages about our work, a trip he took to Florence, a new sports shop that opened on Tulip Street, but we save most of our communication for our nightly phone calls.

After Allie and Brent head to the storage garage, I stay to help customers. At five o'clock, I start to lock up the store when my friend Kelsey March comes in, dressed in a gray pinstriped suit and heels, the swath of blue in her blond hair almost glowing.

"Hi, Kels. What're you doing here?"

"Thought I'd see if you want to have dinner. I'll even agree to go to that tearoom you like so much."

"Matilda's Teapot is closed for good now." I pull on my coat. "How about Abernathy's?"

"Whatever you want."

I steer the conversation to her atmospheric science work as we leave the bookstore and walk to Abernathy's. After we're seated and have placed our orders, Kelsey sits back and looks at me.

"And what about you and Professor Marvel?" she asks. "When is he getting back?"

"I don't know yet." Neither Dean nor I have told Kelsey about the miscarriage or the sexual harassment allegation. The pain of the miscarriage is still raw, and we're not supposed to talk about the allegation to anyone.

"Hey, since the Happy Booker is closing, I'm looking for a job again," I say. "Remember last year you said you could get me something in the atmospheric sciences department? Do you think there are any openings now?"

"Probably not, since it's midyear, but I can ask around. Sometimes there's administrative assistant stuff."

"Well, I was fired from my last administrative job at the art gallery," I admit. "I guess that's not my thing anyway. But I've applied for a cashier's position at a couple of places. I was thinking I'd like to do something with food, since I've learned how to cook."

In addition to searching the classifieds and online ads for career possibilities, I've applied for jobs at a French patisserie on Dandelion Street and a pie shop called the Pied Piper.

Though I know I want something more than a cashier's position, I need a job—*any* job—sooner rather than later. So I think it might be fun to work at a pastry shop for a while, especially since I know how to work a cash register, and I have a deep, abiding love for baked goods.

"There's also an opening at a photography studio over on Ruby Street," I continue. "They're looking for a marketing agent, whatever that is. I don't know anything about marketing or sales, though."

"I think you'd be a great marketing agent or salesperson," Kelsey remarks.

"Really?"

"Yes, *really.*" Kelsey sits back with a sigh of exasperation. "Liv, you're such a… a mouse sometimes. It's one of the reasons people love you, because you have this air of innocence and no guile whatsoever. You're sweet. People want to take care of you.

But sometimes you drive me nuts with your lack of confidence in your own abilities."

"I know! I drive myself nuts. I've just never been able to figure out what my abilities even are, so how can I have confidence in them?"

"Well then, instead of assuming you can't do *anything*, why don't you assume you can do *everything?*"

"I'm starting to, Kelsey. I'm trying, anyway."

"So make a list of things you like to do and can do well."

"I like to read," I say. "And garden. I can still make a great cappuccino."

"What else?"

"I'm good at refurbishing things like old furniture. I've also always liked decorating and organizing stuff. I'm helping plan the museum exhibit and editing the catalog. I'm a good cook, and I've loved working at the bookstore with Allie. Oh, and I'm a decent artist."

Saying all that aloud bolsters my ego. It's not a bad list.

"So there you go," Kelsey says.

"There I go what?"

"You're good at lots of stuff, Liv. You just need to put it to use."

"That's one of the reasons I'm looking for a job. But I'm scared it'll end up like all my other jobs. Just something to do rather than something I really *want*."

I push my plate away, no longer hungry. "My mother was always like that," I say. "Odd jobs here and there."

"What does that have to do with you?"

I stare at my plate, unable to confess even to Kelsey what I've discovered in the past couple of months—that my dependence on Dean and my lack of career or even job stability is downright frightening. Without Dean or my own financial security, it's just a few short steps to a life of constant transition and uncertainty.

"Well… I don't want to end up like my mother," I admit. "I've never wanted that."

"Does *she* have a ridiculously good marriage?" Kelsey asks. "Does *she* live in a great town and have a majestic friend named Kelsey who is willing to kick her ass when she needs it and then buy her a hot fudge sundae?"

"No."

"Then stop using your mother as an excuse for not figuring yourself out." Kelsey shakes her head. "Honestly, Liv, sometimes you have to put on your big girl panties and deal with shit."

She waves the waitress over and places an order for two hot fudge sundaes.

As my majestic friend probably intended, her scolding echoes in my head after we've finished our ice cream and parted ways.

I walk back home to Avalon Street, making a mental list of career possibilities based on my skill set. When I get home, I settle into my routine of cleaning, job searching on the Internet, and working on the museum exhibition catalog.

As the clock nears ten, I go into the bedroom and change into one of Dean's old San Francisco Giants T-shirts that I've been wearing to bed ever since he left. It's comforting, all soft and worn, the faint scent of his shaving soap clinging to the cotton. I imagine I can still even feel the heat of his body. I brush my hair and return to the kitchen to make myself a cup of tea.

I go into Dean's office, set the mug on the desk beside the

computer, curl up in his big leather chair, and pull my ragged old quilt over my legs. This is a ritual I've come to love in the past ten days, as my whole body hums with anticipation.

It's five in the morning in Tuscany, so Dean's day is starting just as mine ends. The instant the clock strikes ten, the phone rings. I press the talk button.

"Hi, professor."

"I'm Indiana Jones out here, baby."

I smile. "You're way sexier than Indiana Jones."

"Glad you think so."

"I know so." I shift to tuck my legs underneath me. "What are you doing today?"

"Missing my girl."

My chest tightens. "Your girl misses you too."

"Yeah? You talked to her?"

I giggle as the ache eases a little. "Every day. And she says you'd better not be looking at any pretty Italian women."

"You're the only woman I want to look at, beauty." His deep, affectionate voice warms me to my toes. "The only woman I can see."

I let out a breath and rest my head against the back of the chair. Even though I know Dean needs to be away from Mirror Lake right now, even though I was the one who first told him to go, there's no question that our separation still hurts. And it hurts because it shouldn't have to be this way.

My husband should be stretched out on the sofa right now, winding a loop of string around his fingers. I should be tucking my body against his at night and sliding my hand over his chest. We should be having dinner, talking about our days, making summer plans. We should be together.

"So did you find anything interesting yesterday?" I ask.

"Few liturgical things." Dean tells me about their findings, the scientific processes of the excavation, his work with another professor from Cambridge, the progress of the conference King's University is hosting in July.

I press the phone close to my ear, feeling his voice wrap around me like one of his warm, protective embraces.

"What did you do today?" he asks me.

"Worked at the bookstore, then had dinner with Kelsey. She told me I was a mouse and scolded me for being wishy-washy."

The instant the words are out of my mouth, I can almost feel Dean bristle with irritation.

"Why'd she do that?" he asks.

"For my own good. She's right in some ways, I think." I pause for a second. "Have you ever thought of me as a mouse?"

There's a brief hesitation that speaks louder than words. My heart sinks a little.

"Really?" I ask. "You think I'm mousy?"

"I've never thought of you as weak or cowardly," Dean says. "Just the opposite, in fact. But when we first met, I thought you were shy like a mouse, kind of skittish. Like you wanted to be brave, but were scared of what would happen if you let yourself. It was just one of the reasons I liked you so much."

I consider that. Objectively, it makes sense. I'd been so drawn to Dean from the beginning because I knew I could take chances with him that I'd always been too scared to take before.

"Well, at least mice are cute," I mutter.

"Maybe you could dress up as Minnie Mouse when I get back," he suggests. "Short, ruffled skirt, bow in your hair, heels…"

I laugh, though the idea is rather appealing. "Your fantasies are getting creative, professor."

"They're all I've got without you here."

Warmth tingles through me at the thought of him fantasizing about us. Though we did a lot of touching and holding in the days before his departure, this has been the longest Dean and I have ever gone without some form of sexual intimacy. Even during our nightly phone calls, neither of us has yet shifted the conversation to overtly sexy talk.

But I'm not foolish enough to think Dean hasn't wanted it. Our sex life has always been so good because, frankly, we turn each other on. Whatever animal magnetism or chemistry is responsible for driving our attraction, we have it in truckloads.

Sex is an explosive, overwhelming pleasure for me and my husband. It's an intense craving, an unabashed joy, the place where we can forget everything but each other, where everything is right and pure. It's the one place where I can surrender without fear.

I want all that again as much as Dean does. And just within the past few days, I've finally felt the awakening of my arousal again. I've even started having some rather lusty and imaginative dreams about us, and the sheer enjoyment of such dreams is most welcome.

And though I'm already anticipating getting sexy with Dean again, I can't help believing that a little bit more restraint right now will help put us back into balance, reminding us why we just *like* each other.

I close my eyes and picture my husband sitting in the chair, me in his lap, his arms strong and tight around my waist. I can smell the delicious, woodsy scent of his shaving soap, feel the scrape of his whiskers against my cheek.

"Hey, Dean?"

"Hey, Liv."

"Are you okay with us putting that on hold for just a little longer?"

"As long as you're okay with me imagining you naked and sweaty most of the time."

"I'm not only okay with that, I encourage it. Except for when you're digging up a medieval skeleton or something."

"Don't worry, I'm discreet." He pauses. "And it's not the only thing I'm thinking about."

"I know."

"Abstinence is actually part of the philosophy of courtly love," he tells me. "The knight suppresses his erotic longing in favor of exalting his lady's soul and spirit."

"Really? You think you can do that?"

"I'll exalt your spirit, but there's no chance in hell I'm suppressing my erotic longing for your body."

I smile. "I love that you love me, professor."

"I love loving you, beauty."

An intense, rich adoration floods my heart. Once upon a time, I didn't know men like Dean West existed. I certainly never believed I'd ever have someone like him in my life, and our separation only intensifies my gratitude.

"So I have a poem for you," Dean says.

"A poem?"

"Written by Guillaume de Machaut, a fourteenth-century composer of love poetry. Want to hear it?"

"Of course."

"Okay." He clears his throat.

I want to stay faithful, protect your honor,
Seek peace, obey,
Fear, serve and honor you,
Until death, peerless Lady.
For I love you so much, truly,
that one could sooner dry up
the deep sea and hold back its waves
than I could restrain myself
from loving you.

"Wow," I whisper. "That was something."

"Want to hear it in French?"

"You need to ask?" I love hearing Dean speak French.

"Je veux vous demeurer fidèle, protéger votre honneur," he murmurs in that baritone voice that I feel pulsing in my blood, *"assurer votre paix, vous obéir, vous craindre, vous servir et vous honorer, jusqu'à la mort, gente dame…"*

By the time he's finished, I'm melting. "That was the kind of poem a knight would use to woo his lady?"

"Better than 'roses are red,' huh?"

"I'll say." I smile into the receiver. "Thanks."

"Just trying to get a start on courting you."

"That's a lovely start. And you'll call me tomorrow?"

"When the clock strikes ten, my peerless lady."

We say goodbye and hang up. I sit in his chair for a while longer, then get up to tend to my houseplants that are arranged on a rack near the balcony. As I'm plucking dried leaves from the stems, I notice my peace lily has bloomed, the creamy white flower turning its face toward the sun.

I do not think I have ever owned *big girl panties*. So after cashing my last paycheck from Allie, I go to the store to buy some. Old Liv is whispering that this is a complete waste of money, but New Liv is tackling life again, and new panties seems like an unexpectedly good place to start.

The lingerie shop is a haven of lace and loveliness—flowered wallpaper, a glass chandelier, vintage chairs and vanities, open cabinets filled with neatly folded satin robes. The scent of vanilla spice wafts through the air, and a Mozart sonata plays on hidden speakers.

The saleswoman approaches me with a welcoming smile. Her nametag reads Sophia, and she's an attractive woman in her forties who looks like she knows all about the importance of what you wear beneath your clothes. After I tell her I need new underwear, she gets me measured right and explains all the various styles of panties, which I had no idea existed.

"What kind do you usually wear?" she asks.

I'm a little embarrassed by my answer. "Just cotton briefs."

"And you're looking for something different?"

"I think so." I dubiously eye the racks of V-strings and thongs, then pick up a pair of panties called "cheekies" which look like they'd give me an atomic wedgie.

I put the cheekies back. "But, uh, maybe not quite that different."

I pick up a package of briefs and study the label. I can almost feel Sophia's dismay.

"Well, briefs are comfortable," she remarks, taking my arm

and steering me toward another rack. "But you might want to try the hiphuggers. They're a cross between boy shorts and bikinis, so they offer you good coverage without being... dowdy."

"I don't want to be dowdy," I agree.

Kelsey did say *big girl panties,* not *granny panties.*

"Here, these are your size." Sophia takes a few hiphuggers off the rack and hands them to me. "They're sexy, flirty, and comfortable. Go try them on and let me know what you think. Would you like the matching bras too?"

I start to decline, but then figure I might as well try them on. Sophia gives me a pair of nylon panties to put on underneath and, with an armful of silky lingerie, I head to the dressing room.

After stripping down and putting on the nylon panties, I pull on a pair of lace-trimmed, floral hiphuggers and the matching push-up bra. I turn to look at myself in the mirror.

Well, *damn.*

I've never been thin and willowy, but... wow. My curves are a good thing. The bra pushes my breasts up into a bountiful cleavage that complements my tapered waist, and the panties look both pretty and sexy stretched around my hips and rear end.

After examining myself from all angles, I do a few squats and stretches to make sure the panties don't ride up.

"How do those feel?" Sophia calls from outside the room. "Would you like to try on the boy shorts too?"

"Sure."

"We also have baby dolls and cami sets on sale. They're very comfortable. Shall I bring you a few?"

"Why not?"

I spend the next two hours trying on more bras, as well as silk slips, teddies, and camisoles with matching shorts or little skirts.

By the time I leave the store, I have a bag filled with three hiphuggers and matching bras (on sale, three for the price of two), and three pairs of boy shorts and matching bras (on sale, twenty-five percent off), plus a camisole top and shorts, two halter-style nighties with a matching robe, and three fitted lace slips. Though the splurge cost almost my entire paycheck, New Liv is off to a good start.

As I walk home, a rush of excitement goes through me as I think about Dean's reaction when he sees me in the lacy bra and panties. And I wonder why I've never bothered buying pretty lingerie before, even for his sake.

The answer comes without any thought. Because he's always loved me exactly the way I am. Cotton briefs, plain white bras and all. Never once has my husband wanted me to be different from what and who I am.

Just the opposite, in fact. He's never wanted me to change.

But I have changed. I'm a different person than I was six months ago. Hell, *one* month ago. No, I still haven't figured out what I want to do, or how to put to use all the things I'm good at, and maybe I'm still not all that confident about my abilities—

"You're such a mouse, Liv."

Kelsey's voice in my head stops my self-defeating train of thought.

Before Dean left, I told him that I desperately wanted to find a way to prove myself *to* myself. To be self-reliant and find my own path.

I know I can do it.

I'm smart. Dedicated. Loyal. Organized. I always carry an extra pen. I'm hardworking. Reliable. I know how to get stuff done. I've made mistakes and learned from them. I'm a good student. I've been knocked down and gotten back up.

A *mouse?*

Fuck that.

CHAPTER TWO

DEAN

MARCH 8

"*D*ean, we have a problem."

"I don't like problems, Frances. I like solutions."

"Okay, perhaps it's not a problem yet. More like a wrinkle."

"Don't like wrinkles either."

I grip the phone with one hand and shield my eyes from the sun with the other. The dig trenches are organized into a grid and sectioned off with string, the façade of the eleventh-century church and perimeter walls rising from the ground like dinosaurs.

"If you don't like wrinkles, then you really won't like this," Frances warns me.

"What?" Irritation scrapes at my insides.

"Edward Hamilton is considering a large donation to King's to fund a new law school building."

"Oh, for fuck's sake." If I weren't so frustrated, I'd laugh. Maggie Hamilton's father has carried on his family's legacy of big alumni donations to King's, and he's going to dangle this possibility in front of the board like a damned carrot until they do what he wants.

And what he *wants* is for them to fire me.

"Why doesn't the board of trustees just bend over for him?" I ask Frances.

"Dean, he's considering the donation at this point. He hasn't committed."

"He'll *commit* once he sees me out on my ass." I inhale and focus on the excavation site again.

Archeologists, volunteers, and students are scattered throughout the trenches, digging for artifacts and recording finds. The hills of Tuscany roll around the site like giants sleeping under green blankets.

"What do I do?" I ask Frances, both expecting and dreading her answer.

"Nothing," she replies.

"I can't do nothing," I snap. "I'm sick of doing nothing."

"Nothing with regard to the investigation, Dean," she clarifies. "Going on that dig was the best thing you could have done. I've been reading your reports, your podcasts are brilliant, and the board of trustees has sent out a press release about the IHR grant and your contributions to the dig. Your job is to keep doing exactly what you're doing."

"For how much longer?"

"Ben Stafford has to make a recommendation to the university board of trustees soon," she explains. "If he brings your case to them, they'll have to further investigate and possibly hold a public hearing."

"When's the next board meeting?"

"End of May."

"That's almost three months."

"They can convene earlier, if needed."

"I'm not staying here another three months, Frances. No way. It's been over two weeks already. I miss—"

I stop. The sun disappears behind a cloud.

My wife. I miss my wife.

"Work," I finally say.

"You are working," Frances replies. "And it's good for your career. When you come back, you'll go right from the dig into the conference. It's an excellent move, Dean, but you need to stay there and finish the work."

After a few more comments about the job, I end the call and walk toward the trenches. I grab a notebook and camera and start recording the features of the monastery located between the church and the cloister.

I haven't worked on a dig since grad school, and I'd forgotten how much I like the work. Being outside, hunting for treasures, wearing jeans and old sweatshirts, not needing to shave. Digging in the dirt reminds me of being a kid, back when Archer and I would hunt for bugs and rocks in the garden. I like figuring out what an object is, what it could have been used for, when a structure was built.

Even missing Liv as much as I do, even wanting to be home again, it's good here. I know what I'm doing. Thinking and talking about sediment samples, structural planning, building stages… this, at least, all makes sense.

Unlike the miscarriage.

Unlike the threat to my career.

Unlike the trouble in my marriage.

None of that makes any sense. It never will.

I take pictures of the perimeter wall, then go to assist on the other areas of the site. There's a solid routine to my days here. Wake early, breakfast, shower. Talk to Liv, then get to work. Digging, cataloging, consulting, studying, recording, photographing. Sometimes a trip to Florence or Lucca. Soccer games. Dinner with my colleagues, followed by a campfire, drinking, music, or a movie.

Liv is always there, always in the back of my mind, my girl five thousand miles away shelving books, organizing a display of photographs, cooking dinner in our apartment that she's made a home with all her houseplants and decorating touches.

I don't want to be away from her, but being here, I've figured one thing out—I need to do the same thing with my marriage that I've done my entire career as a historian.

Study the data and figure it out.

I can do that. I've done it countless times before. I'll do it again.

After consulting with the site architect about the drawings of the monastery, I return to my room and spend an hour reviewing site data sheets and writing up a report about yesterday's finds.

I pick up the phone and dial my father's number for my weekly check-in to see how he's doing after his heart attack.

After he and I talk about his health, he asks about work.

"It's good," I tell him. "Still on-site."

"Helen told us she'll be attending your conference," he says.

Though the thought of seeing my ex-wife doesn't bother me the way it once did, my chest constricts at the mention of the Words and Images conference. I'm acutely aware that I could be relieved of my duties as conference chairperson if this harassment allegation isn't resolved soon.

"When are you going back to King's?" my father asks.

For a second, I'm tempted to tell him everything. Confess all that's happened. Though my father and I aren't close, he's always supported whatever I've wanted to do. He's always been proud of me, though at the expense of my younger brother.

"I'll be back soon," I finally say. "How's Mom?"

After a few more minutes of talking, my mother gets on the line. She chats about her charity work and local events, then asks me to ship her some painted terracotta from a showroom in Florence.

I promise her I'll look into it. After we hang up, I check my email. There's a message from Liv along with a scanned drawing:

Olive you berry much

I print out the picture and tack it to the wall above my desk alongside a photo I took of her a couple of years ago. I could stare at the photo for hours—the faint freckles across Liv's nose, her high cheekbones and dark brown eyes fringed with thick lashes. The top few buttons of her shirt are undone to reveal a V of pale skin and the swell of her breasts. Her straight, brown hair is loose around her shoulders, her lips curved with a smile.

Still scares me sometimes. How much I love her. All this stuff about her needing me, relying on me, depending on me… when I'm the one who can't take his next breath without her.

I fantasize about her to get off every night, but haven't told her what I think about during the day. All the things that make Olivia Rose Winter *Liv*—the way she arranges the cereal boxes in alphabetical order, always stops to pet dogs on the street, hums when she waters her houseplants, and gets emotional over sappy commercials.

And I think about the secret parts of her that no one knows about but me. The soft crease at the back of her knees. The curve of her collarbone. The crevice beneath her breasts. The small of her back where my hand fits perfectly. The ridges of her spine. The beauty mark beneath her left shoulder blade.

Mine. She's mine.

The possessiveness that grabbed me the instant I saw her is fathoms deep. It's in my bones, my blood. It will never go away. And I don't know what to do with my suspicion that it's part of the problem.

I push away from the desk and go back outside. After more work and planning for the next day, I get some dinner and go to bed early. I'm always up before dawn to talk to Liv, and it's still dark the next morning when I call her.

"Hi." Her voice is slightly breathless against my ear. "I'm excited."

"So am I." I shift the phone to rub my cock, which is still half-hard from a hot dream. "Let's talk about our excitement."

"I mean, I'm excited because I got a job," Liv says in amusement. "You know that French bakery down on Dandelion Street? I applied for a position working at the front counter, and I got a call this afternoon that they want me to start tomorrow."

The pride in her voice makes me downright happy. "That's great, Liv. I knew you'd find something soon."

"It's not what I want to do forever, of course, but it'll be a good temporary job."

"How many hours are you working?"

Liv gives me the rundown about her hours and new schedule, then tells me about the upcoming exhibition at the Historical Museum.

It's my favorite time of day—lying on the bed in my rustic hotel room, dawn breaking outside the window, listening to my wife's voice like music in my ear.

"Dean?"

"I'm here."

"I also… um, I saw Dr. Gale today."

Tension claws my shoulders at her mention of the counselor who brought up the whole "sex is a problem" bullshit.

"Yeah?" I manage to keep my voice even. "What did she have to say?"

"Well, I've seen her a couple of times, but ultimately she just verified what I already knew."

"Which is?"

"That I wanted our baby."

My heart constricts. "I know you did."

"Have you thought about it at all? About trying again someday?"

"Some." I stare out the window, where the sky is still pallid and gray from the night. "Scares the crap out of me."

"Me too, but I was anticipating it, you know?" Liv says. "And I think I want it more than I'm afraid of it."

Silence falls between us. I can't look at the black possibility of what could happen to Liv if she got pregnant again. Yet the rational, researcher part of my brain knows that I was getting used to the idea of having a baby. That I'd started preparing for fatherhood.

And the pieces were falling into place because I was with Liv, the woman who stole my heart and my breath with one look. The woman I didn't even know I was looking for until I found her.

I tighten my grip on the phone. "What if—"

"I know, but what if you hadn't been at the UW registrar's office that day?" Liv asks. "The very same minute I was? What if you hadn't decided to speak to me?"

The darkness of that thought, of what *might not have been,* lodges between us.

"What if I hadn't had a job at Jitter Beans?" Liv continues. "What if you hadn't come in that morning? What if someone else had been working at the counter? We might not be together now."

"Liv…"

"Dean, how many things in the universe had to fit together for us to have *met,* let alone fallen in love?" Liv asks. "And how many of those things changed our lives forever?"

"Every one."

"Exactly. For the better. Sometimes *what if* reminds you of *what is*."

I don't know what to say. I can't tell her I want to try again because I don't know if I do. I don't think I could stand the fear and uncertainty again. Not when it involves Liv.

"Dean, I'm just saying I want us to think about it more," she says gently. "Okay?"

"Okay. I can do that."

"I know you can, professor."

You can't control everything, Dean. Her voice echoes in my head again.

But I know there are still some things I can control. How I think. How well I make and follow a plan. Every facet of my research. How hard I work to get what I want.

And what I want most has everything to do with my wife.

"Now tell me something research-y and esoteric," Liv says. "You know I love it when you use your big, academic… words."

"Careful," I warn her. "I'm battling all sorts of erotic longing over here."

"Me too."

"Yeah?" My cock twitches a little at the thought that she might be ready for some hot talk.

"As much as I miss you, this separation has been great for my dreams," Liv remarks. "I've had all sorts of lusty, imaginative dreams about us."

"Tell me."

"Well, in my last dream you were an incredibly hot gladiator—"

"A what?"

"A *gladiator* with chest armor and a loincloth, and I was…

um, I think I was a vestal virgin or something, and we were in one of those temples with the columns… anyway, it was sexy."

Since I'm not too sure where she's going with this, I switch the topic to safer ground.

"Want to tell me what you're wearing?" I ask.

"Oh, er… hold on a sec." There's a thunk as she puts the phone down.

I wait. A few minutes later, she's back.

"Okay," she says, "Guess what I'm wearing."

"A T-shirt."

"No."

"Your white nightgown?" I ask hopefully.

"No."

"Tank top and pajama bottoms?"

"No."

"Please tell me it's not your padded bathrobe."

"Hey, you love me in that bathrobe," Liv says. "It drives you wild with lust."

"I love you in anything, and *you* drive me wild with lust, but trying to feel you up in that robe is like fondling the Stay Puft Marshmallow Man."

Her laugh warms my blood.

"I'm not wearing my robe," she assures me.

"Then you must be naked."

"No. I'm wearing a pair of navy blue satin panties and a push-up bra with lace around the edges."

Lust bolts through me. My head floods with images of Liv's curves all fitted into sexy lingerie. "Wow."

"You should see my boobs in this thing," Liv remarks. "They look amazing."

"They are amazing." I grab my dick through my boxers, picturing her full breasts pushed up into pillowy cleavage. "I'm hard just thinking about them."

"Oh." She lets out one of her breathy little sighs, and I can see her all stretched out in my office chair, skimming her hand over her body. She murmurs, "Remember that first time when you showed me how you could fuck my breasts?"

I groan. Raw talk from her gets me hot in less than a second. "I remember."

"We haven't done that in a while," Liv whispers.

"We will when I get back."

"Are you near your laptop?" she asks.

"Yeah."

"Hang up, then turn on your webcam."

I end the call and grab my laptop from my desk. Sitting back on the bed, I get the software running. After a few false starts, Liv's call comes through.

My heart crashes against my chest. Even in the small screen of my laptop, the grainy picture sends my lust skyrocketing. She's adjusting the camera, her hair all loose around her shoulders, her cleavage… *God in heaven.*

I struggle to pull in a breath.

"Can you see me?" Liv asks with a slight frown.

"Yeah." The word comes out strangled. "Christ, Liv, you look incredible. I want to see it all."

"Okay, hold on." She moves away from the desk and stands. My vision fills with the sight of her full breasts pushed together, hugged by satin and lace, the curves of her hips, a pair of satin panties cupping her between the legs…

"Turn around." I reach into my boxers and close my hand around my shaft.

Liv turns, displaying the satin stretched across her ass. My body tenses with the urge to hook my fingers into that flimsy material and pull it down slowly over those gorgeous cheeks…

"Bend over," I tell her.

"Make sure the record button is off," Liv says, but her voice is getting breathless as she pulls the chair closer and kneels on it.

She leans over the back of the chair. The panties stretch across her ass. I tighten my grip on my cock and stroke it, imagining shooting all over that smooth blue satin.

"Hey, wait." Liv turns, her hair sliding over her shoulders as she peers into the camera. "I can't see you if I'm turned around. And why are you still wearing a shirt?"

"Because I'm too busy staring at your ass. Turn around again and pull your panties down for me."

She leans closer to the camera and gives me a mock frown that makes me want to reach through the camera and kiss her senseless.

"Okay," she says. "But then you're taking your shirt off. Boxers too."

"Show me your ass, woman."

Liv turns again and tucks her fingers into the waistband of her panties. After shooting me a wicked grin over her shoulder, she pushes them slowly down until her ass fills the screen. My blood pounds. I want to kiss and squeeze those perfect cheeks, slide my cock into the valley, then down between her legs where she can tighten her smooth thighs around my shaft…

A groan rumbles my chest. I'm as hard as a rock. I take a deep breath, trying to regain some control.

Liv twists around again and sits, the panties all tangled around her thighs. "Is your shirt still on?"

I pull my shirt off and throw it on the floor, then shove my boxers down.

"Oh." Liv peers at the screen, her voice husky. "Very nice, professor. I so wish I could touch you. I wish I could *taste* you."

My erection pulses at the thought of her sliding her tongue over my chest and stomach before she takes my cock into her hot mouth. I move my hand up and down my shaft, pressure boiling through me like steam.

"Now take off your bra," I tell her.

She unhooks the front clasp, displaying her full breasts topped with hard nipples. Just the sight of them, the knowledge of how soft they are, almost makes me come. I rub my thumb over the head of my aching prick.

"Wait, I can't see you." Liv looks at the screen again, moving her hands up to her breasts. "Adjust your camera. You know how much I love watching you touch yourself."

I shift the laptop. Liv draws in a breath, her lips parting.

"Oh, God, Dean," she murmurs. "That's so hot."

"Move back." I can't take my eyes off her as she massages her breasts and plucks at her nipples.

She scoots back a little so I can see more of her, then she slides one hand down to her pussy. A visible shudder goes through her. She leans her head against the back of the chair and lets out a soft moan that goes straight to my blood.

"I want to watch you come," she whispers, her gaze on the screen. "I wish you were here, wish I could wrap my fingers around your cock, take you in deep..."

My heart pounds. I work my hand faster, pressure flooding

me. The sight of her all spread out in my office chair, one hand between her legs and the other playing with her breasts, fills me with urgency.

"Oh, Dean, I'm so… so *ready.*" Liv's breathing intensifies. Her pale skin is flushed, her eyes filled with arousal. She bites down on her lower lip, the way she always does when she's getting close.

I wish more than ever that I could feel her warm breath, taste her lips, push my cock into her sweet, hot pussy…

"I want to touch you again," Liv murmurs, her chest heaving with the force of her breath. "I want you on me, in me… I want you again, Dean, it's been too long… I'm ready for you… for *us*…"

Her throaty voice, the way she's starting to writhe in the chair, is enough to bring me to full boil. She lets out a cry, her body trembling with vibrations. I watch her as she rides out the wave, her words fading into pants and moans.

I stroke my cock faster, and then the tightness in my groin explodes into blinding pleasure, jets of semen pooling onto my stomach. Liv leans closer to the camera to look at me, her eyes dark with lust and lingering pleasure.

"You are so damn sexy," she whispers.

"It's all for you." I rub my cock until the sensations ease, not taking my eyes off my wife. I swear I can almost taste her heat, smell her arousal.

Liv pushes up from the chair and presses a kiss close to the camera. I smile and put my finger against her puckered lips, wishing I could feel them, feel her.

A stab of irritation hits me suddenly that there's an ocean between us, that we're on different continents, that she's there and I'm here.

Liv moves back from the camera. Her pretty face fills the screen, all brown eyes, thick lashes, that luscious mouth.

"I love you," she says. "Call me tomorrow?"

"Right at ten."

We exchange goodbyes, and I go to clean up. I get dressed, organize my work for the day, and put file folders in my backpack.

Before leaving, I draw a quick picture and scan it into an email:

TO: The Queen Bee
FR: The Frog Prince

Have I toad you how
much I love you?

I press the send button, then pull on my jacket and head out into the dawn.

CHAPTER THREE

OLIVIA

*M*y husband doesn't just love me. He knows *how* to love me. He knows what I need and when I need it, sometimes even better than I do. He knows how to unfold all the tight, rough parts of me and smooth them out with one glide of his hand. He knows how to prove that he—and only he—understands every crevice of my soul. He knows how to remind me that I am forever safe within his heart.

And all of this has never been more apparent to me than it is now, as Dean continues wooing me under the precepts of his own version of courtly love.

I know. Could not be more dorky. And yet, after all

we've been through, for us it is also intensely personal and beautiful.

Over the next week, Dean sends me emails at least three times a day with poems and quotes:

> *TO: Olivia West (aka exalted mistress)*
> *FR: Dean West (aka lowly servant)*
>
> *Miss you.*
> *Want to kiss you.*
>
> *(for the record, Mrs. West, I wrote this one myself)*

He attaches Internet pictures of smiling cartoon hearts and fluffy, big-eyed animals snuggling with each other. These adorable images are often followed by notes about the archeological discovery of a post-medieval building north of the transept wall or the aboveground structural analysis of a church.

Our messages never fail to make me smile, and the warm feeling lasts all day as I run errands, take walks along the lake pathways, and work at the library, bookstore, and museum.

One morning almost three weeks after his departure, I return home for lunch, taking a few letters and bills from the mailbox. There's a small box outside our apartment door with a printed label reading: *Mrs. Olivia West.*

I go inside and open the package, which contains a slender gold ring with a ruby embedded in the band. The accompanying note instructs me to wear the ring on the little finger of my left hand with the stone turned toward my palm, symbolic of our intense, secret love.

I glance at the clock and calculate that it's about nine p.m. in Tuscany. Picking up the phone, I dial Dean's cell number. He answers on the second ring.

"Good one, professor," I say.

"You like it?" He sounds pleased.

"I love it. Thank you."

"Are you wearing it?"

"Just like you told me to." I spread out my hand to admire the gold band. "It fits perfectly. How did you know the size of my little finger?"

"I know exactly how you fit into things and what fits into you."

Warmth floods my chest at the faint huskiness of his voice. "Oh."

He gives a muffled laugh. "Gotta be at a review meeting in five minutes. I'll call you later tonight."

"Tease."

"Just trying to prove my adoration for my lady."

"You proved that years ago."

And every day since.

After we hang up, I enjoy the warm fuzzies for a few minutes before I gather the mail I'd left on the foyer table.

There's an official-looking envelope addressed to me at the bottom of the stack. The return address is *Sinclair and Watson Law Offices,* based in Phoenix, Arizona.

My stomach tightens. Maggie Hamilton's father is a lawyer, but he's based in Chicago. I can't think of any reason a lawyer in Arizona would want to contact me.

I tear open the envelope and unfold a piece of paper imprinted with the law office's letterhead.

Dear Mrs. West,

I am writing to formally notify you of the recent death of Mrs. Elizabeth Winter and my role as the executor of her estate. You are named as a beneficiary in her will and trust. Under the terms of the document, the will and trust are now irrevocable, and we are required to distribute assets accordingly.

All debts have been paid, and you are entitled to receive the sum of fifty thousand ($50,000.00) dollars which Mrs. Winter bequeathed to you as part of the distribution of her estate...

The words blur in front of my eyes. For an instant, I can't make sense of them, can't process the name *Mrs. Elizabeth Winter.*

I take a breath and keep reading the letter, which informs me that as soon as I supply my social security number and sign the enclosed forms, I'll receive a check for fifty thousand dollars via certified courier.

I drop the letter onto the table. I want to think this is a scam or a bad joke. But the name *Mrs. Elizabeth Winter* is embedded in my memories.

My mother's mother.

My grandmother, whom I saw once from a distance when I was seven years old. A woman I never spoke to, never even knew. I grab the phone and dial my aunt Stella's number in Castleford. Stella is my father's sister and—before Dean—my only family outside of my mother.

Trying to keep my voice from shaking, I ask her if she knows anything about Elizabeth Winter.

"A lawyer called a few weeks ago to ask if I knew your address," Stella says. "He didn't tell me anything except that she'd died. I had no contact with her, of course."

"Did my mother ever talk to you about her?" I ask. "Or even mention her?"

"No. I didn't even know your grandmother was still alive."

Neither did I.

I thank Stella and tell her I'll call her again soon. I start to dial Dean's number, then stop. I need time to figure this out first. Instead, I call the lawyer's number.

"Yes, Mrs. Winter named you as a beneficiary of her estate," Mr. Thomas Sinclair explains. "I'm sorry to tell you that she died of cancer in January. She'd finalized her will and trust last year, after her doctors told her that her illness was no longer treatable."

I swallow past a sudden tightness in my throat. "I'm… did she ever try to contact me?"

"I don't know, Mrs. West. I had to track down your married name and address, though, which leads me to believe that Mrs. Winter didn't know you were married or where you live."

"Was Elizabeth Winter in touch with my mother? Crystal Winter?"

"I don't know that either. I did write a letter to Crystal Winter informing her of Mrs. Winter's death."

"You have my mother's address?"

"I had the letter sent to her last known address. Would you like a copy of Mrs. Winter's will and trust? All beneficiaries are entitled to a copy."

"No, that's not necessary."

"I'll have your check processed and sent as soon as I receive the signed forms."

I thank him and slowly put the phone down. I reread the letter. Fifty thousand dollars, from the grandmother I never knew. The woman I saw once.

My mother was twenty-four when she took me from my father. Tall and slender, she wore long skirts and costume jewelry. She had delicate features, blue eyes, pale skin, and thick, wheat-colored hair that spilled like a waterfall down her back.

When we left Indiana behind, she drove a circuitous route west, as if Los Angeles were a magnet pulling her through a maze. She drove fast, without a seatbelt, windows rolled all the way down. The wind pulled at her hair. Her round sunglasses concealed her eyes. Her mouth was pearly pink and shiny.

Until a few hours prior, we'd been living in a two-bedroom apartment with my father. He and my mother had had a huge fight—yelling, sounds of things crashing, crying. I'd hidden in my bedroom, underneath the covers.

My mother woke me when it was still dark and told me to pack my suitcase, the one with the wheels and pink flowers. She dragged her own big, black suitcase from her room. I'd packed my stuffed animals and two hairbands before she returned.

"Not those," she snapped. "Clothes, Liv. Underwear. Hurry."

Her car was an old Chevrolet with vinyl bench seats. She hefted our suitcases into the trunk, told me to get in the backseat, and tossed a quilt over me. Then she got in the car and started to drive.

Hours passed. We ate fast food. Listened to Madonna,

Duran Duran, Neneh Cherry. I don't remember a lot of the places I lived with my mother, but I remember the first place we stopped was a huge, two-story house at the end of tree-lined cul-de-sac.

I had no idea where we were. My mother told me to wait in the car, then she walked up the driveway to the front door and rang the bell.

The sun was high by then, burning a hole in the sky. I got to my knees and peered out the window. A tall, elegant-looking woman with sleek blond hair answered the door. She stared at my mother, then shook her head.

My mother put her hand on the door like she wanted to stop it from closing. They seemed to be arguing. My mother gestured to the car.

The woman looked toward me. I don't know if she saw me. She shook her head again. Closed the door so hard I heard the snap from inside the car.

My mother stood there for a second, then spun on her heel and stalked back down the driveway. I could tell by her tight expression, the way she slammed the car door, that she was really mad.

"Bitch," she muttered. The tires squealed.

I buried myself under the quilt. Madonna's voice drifted through the car.

Feels like home.

Home.

I can't even remember how long it took me to realize the blonde woman was my grandmother.

Dean calls at our usual time tonight. He listens as I read him the letter, the words sounding dusty and dry. There's a knot in my chest. My brain can't stop shuffling through old, unpleasant memories. Part of me thinks I should be ecstatic—who wouldn't want to receive an inheritance of this magnitude?—but instead I feel numb.

"What should I do?" I ask Dean.

"Be grateful," he suggests.

"Why do you think she put me in her will?"

"Maybe she felt guilty for not being there for you."

"If that was it, then I wish she'd tried to find me. I didn't even know where she lived, much less that she remembered me. I hardly remembered her."

I stare at the letter again, the evidence that my own grandmother knew I existed and yet never contacted me. Until she left me fifty thousand dollars.

"What should I do with the money?" I ask.

"Whatever you want. It's yours."

"It's ours."

"No, Liv. You do what you want with it."

I wish I knew what that was.

After I hang up the phone and Dean's warm, deep voice is only an echo, an unexpected wave of loneliness hits me. I reach for the phone again, then stop. I don't want to indulge in hot talk with my husband, not when there are five thousand miles between us.

I want him *here*, with me, right now. My whole body aches

with the need to feel his arms around me, to press my face
against his chest and remind myself that *he* is my home now.
He's the only real home I've ever had.

I press a hand to my chest, picturing him stretched out on
his bed in the rustic, old inn where the archeological team is
housed. Dean told me his room has whitewashed walls, worn
oak floors, a wrought-iron bed, and a window that overlooks
a little courtyard.

I close my eyes and surrender to the image. I can see him
lying there, his T-shirt ridden up to expose a few inches of his
flat, hard stomach, his long legs stretched out on the bed. I
can see his disheveled hair, his whiskered jaw, his gaze looking
out the window at the Tuscan sky streaked with dawn light.

I wonder if he fantasized about us today. Just the thought
of him stroking his cock while thinking about me sends my
heart rate soaring. I lean my head against the back of the chair,
pulling my legs up beneath Dean's oversized T-shirt. I can feel
a gentle pulsing between my thighs.

After a few more minutes of imagining, I go into the bedroom. I tumble on the bed with a soft groan and roll onto my
stomach, pressing my face into Dean's pillow that still holds
his masculine scent. His T-shirt envelops me, draping over
my hips and thighs. The pulsing between my legs intensifies.

I squeeze my eyes shut and picture Dean's gorgeous body,
his firm skin and sculpted muscles. I love smoothing my hands
over the curves of his shoulders to his chest. I love the way I can
trace the line running down the center of his torso, bisecting
the ridges of his abdomen. His skin is always so warm and taut
beneath my hand.

His body tenses with arousal when I press my mouth

against his chest, trailing a line of kisses down that center line to where his muscles form a perfect V shape near his hips. I rest my hands on either side of his abdomen and move lower, kissing his flat stomach, the circle of his navel, lower still to where his cock is already half-hard.

He tangles a hand in my hair when I wrap my fingers around his shaft and guide him into my mouth. My blood fires with heat at the salty, male taste of him, the warm throb against my tongue.

It wasn't always like this for me, wasn't easy to learn how to pleasure him this way after my first sexual experience had been so horribly shaming. Even with Dean, it wasn't easy for me to understand that I could enjoy it too. That I could even learn how to love it, to crave the feel and taste of him.

I do now, longing for the way my husband's large cock slides past my lips, the way he pushes his hips upward to fuck my mouth. I love the way his fingers tighten in my hair, the groans and soft curses that escape him as hot tension rolls through his body.

Explicit images of us flash behind my closed eyelids. I moan and press my face deeper into the pillow. I shift around, rubbing the cotton T-shirt against my stiff nipples. I inhale, drinking in the scent of Dean, then hitch the shirt over my hips up to my waist. I slither out of my panties, grab another pillow and push it between my legs. Cool air brushes against my naked ass.

In this moment, I lose all sight of the reasons Dean needs to be away from me right now. None of them matter any-more. Not now. I just desperately want him here. I want him to walk into the room and see me half-naked on the bed with my bottom bare and a pillow shoved between my legs.

I want him to stand there, hot and hard as he watches me

writhe against the pillow. I imagine his gaze burning into me as my blood flares. Desperate to ease the ache blooming through my entire body, I circle my hips and grind my clit into the pillow.

I push one hand beneath the shirt to fondle my breasts and twist my nipples. It's an erotic shock, this sudden onslaught of sensation. I press harder, imagining Dean climbing onto the bed behind me, stroking his hand over my ass, pushing my shirt up even farther. I moan again and spread my legs, empty and aching, squirming frantically against the pillow to create more sensual friction.

It's not enough. The material is too soft, too giving. With a muffled groan, I shove the pillow aside and press my hand between my legs. I keep the material of Dean's T-shirt between my fingers and my sex, as if that will somehow bring him closer to me. I rub the cotton against my clit and gasp as a wave of electricity jolts my nerves.

I close my eyes again, and there he is behind me, gazing at my ass. He's only wearing his boxers, and he shoves them off to grasp his erection. I can see it, the thick shaft pulsing in his hand, the way he strokes himself with such slick ease from the base to the head.

My body fills with urgency. He grips my hips, pulling me upward so he can push the pillow beneath my stomach. He puts his hands between my thighs to spread me open, then trails one long finger over my folds.

I twitch and moan, pressing my own finger into my body. Dean positions himself behind me, his knees pushing my legs wider. He puts one hand flat on my lower back as he rubs the head of his cock over my slit. I gasp, every part of me aflame, aching for him to impale me with one fierce thrust.

Instead, he teases me, sliding the tight knob in and out of me and over my throbbing clit. I hear his breathing, heavy and deep, feel the tension radiating from his muscular body.

"Dean!"

With a half-laugh, half-groan, he sinks into me, filling me, stretching me. I let out a cry of pleasure and shove my hips upward so he can thrust even deeper. I bury my face into the pillow and surrender, letting him stroke his cock in and out of me, his thighs pushing my legs apart, his flat stomach slamming against my ass. It's raw and hard, a fuck stripped of tenderness in the drive toward release.

I work my hand frantically between my legs, my mind filling with images of Dean sweaty and hot behind me. The intense pressure snaps the second I imagine him grabbing my hips and plunging so deep my entire body trembles.

He groans and comes inside me, the flood of semen slick and warm. Explosions fire through my blood, and I bite down on a corner of the pillow as the vibrations peak and surge.

With a gasp, I sink onto my stomach. It's a few minutes before the images begin to fade, and I become aware that I'm lying half-naked on the bed with my hand still between my legs. I push the T-shirt over my hips to cover myself and stumble to the bathroom.

I stare at myself in the mirror. My hair is a mess and my eyes look too dark, almost haunted, my skin too pale.

I splash water on my face and crawl back into bed, pulling Dean's pillow against my body. I don't sleep well, my dreams snarled and chaotic with memories of my childhood and the ever-present longing for my husband.

After I wake from my broken sleep, the dreams fade. I

take a shower and let the hot water wash away the lingering threads of unpleasantness as I think about what I'm going to do with the money.

A sudden decision spins through me, diluting the fear and uncertainty of the previous night. I call Allie and ask her to come over before the Happy Booker opens.

I get an old VCR out of our apartment storage closet and hook it up to the TV just before Allie arrives with a bag of croissants. She pours herself a cup of coffee while I get a VHS tape from a box in the closet. I'm both nervous and excited.

"You okay?" Allie takes a sip of coffee and eyes me over the rim of the mug. "You seem a little weird."

"I want to show you something." I push the tape into the VCR and hit the play button.

A fuzzy image appears onscreen of a young girl with straight dark hair tied into red ribbons. There's a Christmas tree in the background. A woman appears in the frame—long, blond hair; fine, elegant features. She adjusts one of the girl's crooked ribbons, then smiles and waves at the camera.

I can feel Allie looking at me.

"That's you?" she asks.

"And my mother. That was… that was the Christmas before we left my dad. I was six."

"Oh."

The scene shifts to a birthday party, my seventh. I'm wearing a pink party hat and eating cake. My mother is standing beside me, waving at the camera. We would be gone two months later.

"You were a really cute kid," Allie offers.

I fast-forward to the part of the tape I'd been looking for.

A grainy image appears of a cherubic blonde girl sitting at a table with a bowl and spoon, a cereal box prominently displayed beside her. The kitchen is spotless and generic. A male voice booms over the scene.

"For a great start to your child's day, serve Honey Puffs cereal all the way! These crunchy puffs are packed with vitamins and dipped in honey for a breakfast that's both nutritious and deeeelicious! Amy, how do you like your Honey Puffs cereal?"

The girl picks up her spoon, takes a bite of cereal, then gives the camera a big smile and a thumbs-up.

Jingly music filters from the speakers along with a chorus of, *"Honey Puffs cereal, crispy and sweet, full of vitamins and a tasty treat!"*

There's another shot of Amy enthusiastically eating more cereal as the camera fades into a full-screen image of the Honey Puffs cereal box.

I switch off the TV.

"Honey Puffs cereal?" Allie asks.

"That was my mother, Crystal, when she was five years old."

"Really?" Allie glances at the TV and back to me again. "That's pretty cool. She was the Honey Puffs cereal girl?"

"Just for that one commercial." I toss the remote onto the coffee table. "Apparently they offered to contract her for more, but her mother wanted more money and the producers wouldn't negotiate. I guess there was a big fight about it, and in the end they withdrew the offer." I shrug. "So that was the end of her Honey Puffs cereal career."

"Too bad." Allie seems a little confused. "So... is she still in show business?"

"No. Rumors about *her* mother spread... you know, stage

mother, difficult to work with. Crystal still auditioned a lot, but didn't get any other big offers. She was in a lot of local theater productions and beauty pageants, school plays, that kind of thing. Then she got pregnant with me when she was seventeen."

"Oh."

"Her parents were furious… their perfect little girl, pregnant. They disowned her, kicked her out, so she had to drop out of high school and move in with her boyfriend."

"Wow. Harsh."

"Yeah."

I've gone through all this with two therapists, so I understand it—the compliments heaped on my mother as a child, her parents' high expectations for her to succeed, the constant praise of her beauty and talent. All of that was ripped away when she got pregnant with me.

Replaced by a bad relationship. Fighting. Regrets. Then when Crystal was rejected for another woman, she retaliated by taking me away from my father.

She's spent all these years searching for the approval she had as a child—through sexual relationships with men and a twisted relationship with me. I was the one who had to give her the right praise and approval, to validate her, while she never stopped resenting me for being the cause of her downfall.

I get it on an intellectual, psychological level.

Emotionally, it still hurts like a bad burn.

"I haven't watched that video in ages," I admit. "But I wanted you to see it so you'll understand where this is all coming from. I've always felt that my life has been shadowed by my mother, even though she hasn't been part of my life since I was thirteen."

"When was the last time you saw her?"

"Right after I married Dean." I glance at Allie. "My father died when I was eleven. I've never known my mother's parents or any of her family. But yesterday, I got a letter from a lawyer who told me my grandmother died and he's handling the distribution of her estate."

I tell her the whole story, ending with, "So I want to invest the money in the bookstore."

Allie's eyes widen behind her purple-framed glasses. "Oh, Liv."

"You know I've been wanting to help you, to be a partner." Excitement rises inside me. "Now I can, Allie. I actually have the money to do it. We don't need to take out a loan anymore or worry about borrowing the money from Dean or your father."

I jump up and start to pace. "I mean, I don't have the check yet, but I'm signing the paperwork, and the lawyer is going to send it via courier next week. That gives us a few days to talk to the landlord and distributors, see if we can work out a payment schedule for—"

"Liv, no."

"What?"

Allie shakes her head, looking dismayed. "You're not investing your inheritance in the bookstore."

"Why not?"

"I don't want you to."

I stare at her. "But you said you'd love for me to be a partner."

"I would, but not like this. I don't want you to use *your* money to save a business that'll probably still fail anyway."

"You were fine with me applying for a business loan."

"Because I was doing it with you, Liv. And because then, there was still a chance we could succeed. But with the rent hike on the building and losing our lease…" She shakes her head again. "The business is gone. It would be a waste of money to try and salvage it now."

"But we can come up with a whole new business plan." I spread my hands out. "We've talked about adding a café, establishing a membership, holding workshops. Now we have the capital to actually implement all of that."

"I don't want to, Liv."

I can only look at her in disbelief. "Allie, we can save the bookstore."

"No. We can *try* to save the bookstore, but it would be a huge risk. I don't want you to lose your money, Liv. No way."

This is so not the reaction I expected that I don't know what to do. "But—"

"Liv, I love you to death. I'm so touched that you'd want to do this, but I just can't let you. And honestly, I'm done with the bookstore anyway. It's been such a struggle these past couple of years. It's time for me to do something else."

To my utter shock, tears sting my eyes. I hadn't known until this moment how much I'd been looking forward to this—not only finally being able to help a friend, but also becoming a legitimate business owner.

"Don't be upset, Liv." Allie leaps off the sofa and hurries over to hug me. "There are so many other things you can do with the money."

"I love the bookstore, Allie. You love the bookstore. How can you just give up?"

"I'm not giving up. Sometimes things have to end."

My stomach tightens. "What if you don't want them to end?"

"Then you try and start again," Allie says. "Fall seven times, get up eight, right?"

"But you don't even know what you're going to do next."

"I'll find something." She squeezes my arm. "You will too. Thank you for the offer, really. It means the world to me that you'd even consider doing such a thing. And you know I'd do anything for you, too."

She blows me a kiss and heads out the door. I take the tape out of the VCR and toss it onto a table, then go to finish getting ready for the day. I walk to the Historical Museum, battling back the disappointment over Allie's refusal.

Now what?

I can invest all the money in mutual funds, but even that wouldn't put me on a path toward actually working for something of my own.

I glance at my watch, quickening my pace when I realize I'm almost late for my shift. As I turn on Emerald Street the door of a coffeehouse opens and a woman steps onto the sidewalk.

I stop. So does she. We stare at each other.

Then rage floods my chest. I tighten my hands into fists to prevent myself from clawing her eyes out.

She ducks her head and turns away.

"Maggie." My voice is like barbed wire.

She hesitates, then turns to face me again. Even through my anger, I'm struck by how she looks both young and old at the same time—her hair is thick and curly, her skin unlined, but there's an ancient weariness in her eyes, as if life has already stripped her of youth and innocence.

My fingernails dig into my palms. "Why?"

She averts her gaze. "I'm telling the truth."

"You're not. You're lying. We both know it."

"Look, Mrs. West, you don't know what's been going on." Maggie lifts her chin, her eyes hardening. "I won't let your husband get away with ruining my life anymore."

"So you're going to try and ruin his by threatening him with a false charge?"

"A *false* charge?" she snaps. "You, of all people, should know it's not false."

"What the hell does that mean?"

"Think about it," she retorts. "I'm not supposed to talk to you about this."

"Why not? What am I going to do—run to the Office of Judicial Affairs and tell them you're lying? My husband has been telling them that since we first heard about this. How do you think screwing up his life is going to help you?"

Her jaw clenches. "By getting me out of King's University. Either the administration will accelerate my graduation to avoid a scandal, or I'll sue them for not protecting me from a lecherous professor. Either way, I'll get out and be done with it all."

"And you'll still have your father's money."

"You don't know what my father is like," Maggie snaps. "But you should have helped me when I asked you to talk to your husband about my thesis. Now it's too late."

"It's not too late for you to do the right thing."

She shakes her head, her shoulders hunching as she hurries away.

I watch her go, not knowing if I just made things worse.

CHAPTER FOUR

MARCH 17

I've stopped researching information about sexual harassment cases at universities because they never seem to end well. The professors often end up resigning, and if they don't, their reputations are tainted by the allegation.

Even if they're innocent of the charge, their names are splashed all over the Internet, attached to news stories about the case. Some of the professors are not innocent, I know, and their accusers are right to pursue justice, but that sure as hell isn't the situation with Maggie Hamilton.

"If you see her again, don't talk to her, Liv," Dean says,

after I've told him about my encounter with Maggie. "I don't want Edward Hamilton giving us a bunch of BS about stalking again."

I promise him I won't, but worries hover around me like a cloud in the days following my encounter with Maggie. My inheritance check arrives via courier, and I deposit it one afternoon before my shift at the bookstore.

After leaving the bank, I stop halfway down Poppy Street, across from a sage-green Victorian building with painted white shutters. The windows are shaded by the interior curtains. The wooden Matilda's Teapot sign, hanging from a post by the fence, has been replaced by a For Lease sign.

I cross the street and approach the house. I've passed by several times since the tearoom closed a few weeks ago, but I haven't paid much attention to it aside from wishing it was still open so I could stop in for a plate of chocolate crepes and a pot of Darjeeling tea.

A vinyl banner with the word *Closed* hangs over the windows. I walk up to the porch and peer into one of the first-floor windows.

"May I help you?"

I turn to see a robust woman in her mid-fifties climbing the front steps. She has a broad, friendly face and brown hair streaked with gray.

"Are you Matilda?" I ask, recognizing her from my visits to the tearoom.

"Matilda was my mother."

"Oh." I gesture to the window. "I wasn't snooping. Well, not much anyway. It's just that I used to love your place."

"That's nice to hear." She reaches to unhook the banner

from the window. "My mother opened the tearoom years ago, and I took over after she retired."

"The crepes were amazing," I tell her. "I'm sorry you had to close."

"Well, my husband died a couple of years ago and it just got to be too much work for one person," she explains. "I won't miss all the paperwork and headaches, but I will miss the customers. Could you get that corner? I can't quite reach it. I'm Marianne, by the way."

"Olivia. Everyone calls me Liv." I put my satchel down, pull a narrow bench over to the window, and step onto it to unfasten the banner.

"What's going to happen to the building?" I ask.

"I don't know yet. It's coded for retail and food service, so I'm hoping someone will put it to a similar use." She glances at me as we lower the banner to the porch. "Why? Are you interested in leasing it?"

The question catches me off guard. "Uh, no."

"Oh." Marianne almost seems disappointed.

"I'm not... it's just that I don't know anything about owning a—"

I stop and give myself a swift mental kick in the ass. So what if I don't know anything about owning a business? I can learn.

I don't know anything about being a mother either, but I've started to believe that someday, I could be a good one. I'd certainly give it everything I have.

"Well, I could... I suppose I'd consider it," I finally say.

Marianne looks up at the second floor of the building. "I'm afraid I wouldn't recommend reopening the tearoom. Business was going downhill a bit, and we had a reputation for catering to senior citizens, so we weren't popular with younger people. Would you like to come inside?"

"Okay."

We finish rolling up the banner. Marianne unlocks the front door and pushes it open. After she flicks on the lights, I can see that the interior is more dingy and worn than I remember. All the tables and chairs are stacked against one side of the room beside a pile of chintz tablecloths. The floral wallpaper is starting to peel, and a thin layer of dust has settled over everything.

I run my hand over the high, curved back of a chair. "Has anyone asked to lease the building?"

"I've had a few inquiries, but no applications yet."

"What kind of place would you like to see here?" I ask.

"I haven't really thought about it, Liv." Marianne looks around a bit wistfully. "My mother always just loved the fact that people enjoyed themselves here. She liked making customers happy, serving them good food. She never minded that some of them would stay for several hours, just chatting and drinking tea. In fact, she'd encourage it."

"Your mother would have gotten along great with my friend Allie," I remark. "Allie's the same way. A natural hostess. She owns the Happy Booker bookstore over on Emerald."

"Oh, yes. I saw there was a going-out-of-business sale."

A pang of sorrow hits me. "Allie lost the lease on the building. She tried everything to bring in new customers. Children's parties were her biggest events, but she never had much success despite all her planning and creativity…"

My voice trails off. Something flickers to life in the back of my mind.

"Do you have a business card?" I ask Marianne.

"There's probably one still back here." She goes behind the front counter and rummages around underneath the cash register. "I have a crew scheduled to come in next week and clear out the tables and things. Ah, here we are."

She retrieves a card and writes something on the back. "There's my cell phone number, if you'd like to discuss anything."

"Thanks." I glance around the restaurant again before Marianne and I exchange goodbyes.

I walk to Emerald Street and the bookstore. Allie is busy moving the remaining sale books to the front shelves.

"Hey, Allie, I understand why you need to let the bookstore go," I tell her, "but would you hear me out about something else?"

"Sure." Allie straightens and gives me her full attention.

"I was just over looking at Matilda's Teapot when the owner stopped by," I explain. "She seemed really nice. We started chatting, and she told me she doesn't have any plans for the building."

"That's a great place, isn't it? Like a big old dollhouse."

I try to ignore the nerves tightening my stomach again. "Allie, what if you and I rented the building and started a new business there?"

Allie blinks. "A new business? What kind of business?"

"It's coded for food service, so I was thinking of a café, but something unique and focused on children and families."

Allie leans her elbows on the counter. "Mirror Lake does have a ton of families, and there's a whole new bunch of them every summer during tourist season. A family café wouldn't lack for patrons. But there are also a million other restaurants and cafés in town."

"That's why we'd have to do something different. Something that would appeal to both locals and tourists."

"Like what?"

"Like a party place," I say. "Your children's book parties were always so creative and fun… what if we opened a place where kids could have themed birthday parties?"

"There are lots of kids' party places in town, not to mention in Rainwood and Forest Grove."

"Not like this… I don't think." Of course, I haven't done any research, so I go to the computer and do a quick Internet search. "Bouncy houses, sports parties, pizza places, karate parties. They don't offer the kind of parties that you could. Like that *Alice in Wonderland* birthday you had when you turned ten, with the Red Queen cake and Mad Hatter tea party."

"I couldn't even get kids to come to those at the bookstore when I offered them free cake and cookies."

"What if we combined it with another business, like a café?" I ask. "We both researched opening a café when we were looking into putting one in the bookstore, and I'm sure Marianne would give us advice or even help out. Maybe we could have a café that also offers birthday party packages."

Allie straightens, a gleam of interest finally appearing in her eyes. "That's not a bad idea."

"We could uphold the tradition of Matilda's Teapot by offering tea, but we could tailor the experience toward children and families," I say. "Like have whimsical plates and teapots, maybe Red Queen cupcakes and those rainbow cake-pops you had for the *Wizard of Oz* party…"

Allie and I look at each other for a minute. It's a good idea. We both know it.

"I have the money to invest now, Allie."

"*You* do," she says. "I don't. I'm maxed out on credit, and another loan isn't an option. I can't contribute to start-up costs."

"But you have a lot more experience than I do," I point out. "You know about expenses, taxes, insurance, hiring employees, payroll. I don't know any of that, but I'm a fast learner. If I contribute the money, you'd contribute the know-how."

"Brent could help us out with the logistics," Allie muses. "He was assistant manager at the Sugarloaf Hotel for three years, and now he's a manager at the Wildwood Inn. Plus he has two degrees in hotel and restaurant management."

The whole venture sounds both daunting and exciting. As Allie and I work for the rest of the afternoon, we exchange ideas about the café.

"I think we should do something like your *Alice in Wonderland* party," I say. "Put greenery around the front entrance so it's like a rabbit hole. Then we could have Queen of Hearts tarts and Cheshire Cat porridge… or if we combined it with the *Wizard of Oz,* we could have those sugar cookies you made with *Heart* and *Courage* iced onto them, and the lime-green punch…"

"That building does have two stories," Allie says. "We could have one theme upstairs and another downstairs. Then have one menu, but with different dishes from each theme."

"And we could offer birthday parties in one of the upstairs rooms so that they're separate from the everyday running of the place."

A palpable excitement flows between us.

"What'll we call it?" Allie asks.

A name pops into my head without effort, as if it has been there all along.

"The Wonderland Café," I say.

"I love it!" Allie claps her hands. "We'll have murals on the walls with scenes from the books, and we can paint the staircase to look like yellow bricks leading up to the *Wizard of Oz* section."

I can't help smiling at the way she's now talking about it as if it's something we're actually doing. The funny thing is that I can picture it too, envision how it would all look.

During my call with Dean that night, I take a breath and tell him about my ideas for turning Matilda's Teapot into a café and birthday party place.

"That's a great idea, Liv," he says. "I've never even heard of that kind of café, and the location of the tearoom is perfect to catch a family crowd."

Oh, my husband's voice. Better than chocolate, hot baths, café mochas, sunshine. Warms me from the inside out and everywhere in between. I curl beneath my quilt, pulling my knees up to my chest.

"I think it's a great idea too," I tell him.

"I'd only suggest that you make sure you have enough money not just to start up, but also maintain working capital for at least eight or nine months."

Ah, Professor West. Always practical. And usually right.

"What does Allie think?" he asks.

"She's excited about it, but we need to do a lot of work and research first. I don't even know how much it would take to get started, or if my inheritance is enough."

"I'll give you whatever else you need."

My stomach twists. "I know you would, but I really want to do this by myself."

"I don't mean I'd be a partner. I'd just give you the money."

"Dean, I don't want you to."

"Why not?"

"Because I need to figure it out *by myself*," I tell him. "And if you ride in like the cavalry to save me, that defeats the whole purpose."

"How is supporting you defeating a purpose?"

"I don't want to be indebted to you for a business. Do you realize that I have been financially dependent on you for everything?"

"That doesn't matter, Liv."

"It matters to me now." I can't keep a hint of impatience from my voice. "I thought it was all so blissful and comfortable, and it was easy to let you take care of everything. Even when I was looking for a job, there was no urgency about it because I knew you'd be there if I failed. Maybe that's why I never figured out what I'm good at. I haven't failed enough."

"You don't need to fail to figure that out. It takes time, not failure."

"Look, all I'm saying is that I appreciate the offer, but I can't take money from you. I won't. With this inheritance, I finally have the opportunity to start something on my own."

"Liv, everything I have is yours too. You're not taking anything from me."

"No, Dean. I need to do this *without you*."

The air between us vibrates with irritation. The pattern of my quilt blurs before my eyes. Once again, it would be so easy to surrender. Dean would give Allie and me whatever amount of money we need, we'd start our fanciful little business… and there would be a huge safety net beneath us no matter what went wrong.

Who wouldn't want to accept such an offer?

And how would I feel about myself if I did?

I straighten my spine and take a breath before speaking again.

"Thank you," I say. "And I don't mean to sound ungrateful. You know in the *Wizard of Oz* when Dorothy realizes at the end that the ruby slippers will bring her home? And Glinda the Good Witch of the North tells her that she had to learn for herself that she always had the power?"

"Uh, sure."

"It's like that."

"Okay." He sounds faintly confused.

I search my brain for something he can better relate to. "Or it's like King Arthur. He couldn't have become king if he hadn't had the strength to pull Excalibur from the stone, right?"

"Actually, evidence is that there were two swords," Dean says. "And there are a few different versions of that story, one from Geoffrey of Monmouth stating that the Lady of the Lake gave Arthur the sword after he ascended the throne."

I can't help smiling. My sexy, wonderful husband, a scholar to the core.

"Do you get my point at all, professor?" I ask.

He's silent for a moment. I almost hold my breath.

"I get it," he says, and now the tone of his voice indicates that he really does.

"Okay." I exhale slowly, my tension easing. "You know I love you like a bee loves honey."

"You know I can't wait to pollinate your flower."

I chuckle. "It's been a while since you have, huh?"

"Way too long, baby."

My heart tightens a little. Neither of us knows exactly how *much* longer it will be.

"Still there?" Dean asks.

"I'm here. I miss you."

"I miss you too, beauty."

I imagine him lying on his bed, one arm behind his head, his T-shirt stretched across his muscular chest. I shake off my brief sorrow and run a hand over my body.

"You know, I've been having such hot dreams about us," I remark.

"Am I still a gladiator in your dreams?"

"You've been all sorts of sexy, manly things." I close my eyes and settle deeper into the chair. "A knight, of course. A vampire."

"I'm sure I bit you."

"Uh huh." I slide a hand underneath my T-shirt to my breasts. "You've been a rock star, a cowboy, a firefighter... oh, that was a good one because you rescued me from a burning building, then couldn't take your hands off me... And once you were a half-naked genie—"

"A genie?"

"Mmm. You went up in smoke when I rubbed your lamp."

I don't know whether to be annoyed or amused when Dean starts laughing.

Over the next week, Allie and I continue to brainstorm ideas for the café as we finish emptying the bookstore. I call Marianne to set up a meeting so Allie can also see the interior of Matilda's Teapot.

"We were talking about murals." Allie spreads out her hands to frame the south wall. "Maybe we could paint a scene of the Mad Hatter tea party there. Curtains and tablecloths with patterns of cards on them. And if we do the *Wizard of Oz* upstairs, we could decorate the rooms according to the location. Like Emerald City, a Kansas farm, Munchkinland, and the witch's castle."

"You'll have to get inspections done, but the building itself is up to code," Marianne says. "And the kitchen is ready for cooking and customers, so it would be a matter of redecorating, establishing the menu, ordering new inventory, and working out a business plan."

I glance at her. "You told me you were sorry you had to retire, but that running the tearoom became too much for one person."

"That's true."

"Would you be interested in helping us do some planning?" I ask. "We could use your expertise."

"I'd love to. I can give you all the overhead costs and help you with permits and insurance. I can also put you in touch with my suppliers and even my former staff, if you'd like."

The three of us sit down at one of the tables. Allie gets out her notebook and I open my laptop.

"Oh, and a local magazine is doing a story on Matilda's Teapot and how it became an institution," Marianne continues. "If it works out with your idea, the reporter might include you in the story as the next business for the historic building. It's a magazine about women entrepreneurs, so it would be a great angle."

"Great publicity too," Allie remarks.

Though I'm excited at the idea of even being considered an entrepreneur, by the time we've figured out a budget for start-up expenses, I'm shell-shocked at how much it will all cost.

"If we get moving soon, we can start remodeling right away," Allie says as she and I walk back to the Happy Booker. "Even set a date for opening. The sooner we can open, the faster we can start turning a profit."

"Remodeling alone will be pricey."

"We can do a lot of that ourselves, like painting and stuff. And Brent knows a bunch of contractors who'd give us a good price."

"This is a huge undertaking."

"I know, but we have an awesome location, and with Marianne and Brent's help we'll have great management. And Marianne said her staff would probably love to come back. Some of them had been working for her for years, and they have a ton of experience."

"Who will run the kitchen?"

"Brent knows the woman who runs the kitchen over at the Sugarloaf Hotel," Allie says. "She has lots of contacts in the area. I'm sure she can recommend someone good. Oh, I was thinking we could serve shoestring fries and call it Scarecrow's Straw. Wouldn't that be fun?"

I should have known, I think, as I haul another box of books to the storage area. Aside from being an eternal optimist, once Allie sets her mind on something, she's like a bull-dog gnawing on a steak bone.

Well, more like a cocker spaniel nibbling at a dog treat, but she'll bite your ass if you try and take it away from her.

After turning over the numbers a hundred times and getting Brent's input, Allie and I hire an inspector for the building, and meet with a lawyer who explains and negotiates the lease terms.

Finally, before either of us loses courage, we agree to sign the lease. On the evening of March twenty-seventh, after we hang up the *Closed* sign at the Happy Booker for the last time, Allie locks the door and comes to the front counter where I'm putting on my coat.

"Hold on." She hurries into the office and returns carrying her things and a bottle of champagne.

"What's that for?" I ask.

"For us." Allie plunks the bottle on the counter and produces two plastic cups from her bag. "A celebration. One door closing, another one opening and all that."

"Good God, Allie, do you fart glitter?"

She bursts into laughter. "Pink and purple all the way."

I grin as she hands me the bottle to open. We pour the champagne, toast to the end of the Happy Booker and the beginning of the Wonderland Café. Allie locks up the store and pushes the keys back through the mail slot. We hug each other goodbye, agree to get together later in the week, and head home.

Now that the bookstore is officially closed, I'm even more nervous about the café venture. It was my idea, and I'm the one who asked Allie to be a partner. If it doesn't work out, the failure will lie on my shoulders.

And even though I told Dean that maybe I haven't failed enough, I certainly don't want to take a friend down with me if I do. On the other hand, Allie was right when she said we already have a great support system and location. *Failing* would actually take some work.

I shake off my lingering uncertainty as I walk into the foyer of our apartment building. I collect a few bills from the mailbox and go upstairs. There's a note taped to our front door. I stop.

Shock floods me. I stand there and try to process what the note means. Then my heart gives a wild leap, jolting me into action. I turn and hurry back downstairs to Avalon Street. The instant I step outside, I start to run.

CHAPTER FIVE

OLIVIA

I rush down the street on a wave of excitement, swerving to avoid pedestrians, my feet barely touching the sidewalk. My heart is spinning, leaping, twirling. Exhilaration dances through me like a million bubbles buoyed by the wind.

I have to force myself to slow and muster some calm as I approach the Wildwood Inn. One of the nicest hotels in Mirror Lake, the Wildwood is housed in a fancy building that sits on a tree-lined street overlooking the lake. A uniformed doorman greets me with a tip of his cap and opens the door.

I step into the hushed interior, which has been lovingly restored over the years with a polished oak staircase, nineteenth-century antiques, and stained-glass windows. Trying to appear composed even though my whole body is zinging with elation, I go to the front desk.

Allie's boyfriend, Brent, is working at one of the computers, wearing his *Manager* tag. He glances up and smiles at me.

"Hi, Liv."

"Hi." I stop, still struggling to catch my breath and settle my racing heart. "I was… there was a note… I mean, I think my…"

Brent turns and takes a key from the old-fashioned rack behind the counter.

"Firefly Cottage is one of our private cottages down by the lake," he says, extending the key to me. "Take the door leading to the garden and follow the path to the right. It's the third cottage on the left."

I manage to close my hand around the key.

"He's waiting for you." Brent gives me a wink and reaches for the phone. "I'll tell him you're on your way."

I go past the dining room to the back garden. Once I'm outside, I hurry over the flagstone paths toward the green-shuttered cottage tucked in a grove of trees. Light shines through the windows. An engraved sign over the door reads Firefly Cottage.

With a shaking hand, I unlock the door and push it open.

Dean.

I feel him the instant I step into the room. An intense crackle of energy arcs into me, soaring through my blood. A happiness like no other fills me, a deluge of colors almost overwhelming in depth and intensity.

He's standing on the other side of the room, his hands in his pockets, his dark hair brushed away from his forehead.

Dressed in charcoal-gray slacks and a navy shirt, the tan of his skin making his eyes more brilliant than ever, my husband is strikingly, heartrendingly beautiful. I can only stare at him, as if he's a mirage that will disappear if I blink.

Our eyes meet with a thousand sparks. And then he smiles that gorgeous smile that makes his eyes crease at the corners and takes away what little breath I have left. My knees get so weak I'm not sure I can stand much longer.

But, as it turns out, I don't have to. Because Dean crosses the room to me in a few long strides, wraps his arms around me, and lifts me clear off the ground. He pulls me against him, the length of his body pressed to mine, the heat of him flowing through his shirt and into me.

He tightens one arm around my waist and cups the back of my neck with the other. We stare at each other, his eyes dark and intense before his lips come down on mine in a kiss of fierce, tender possession.

And, just like that, I fall wildly in love with my husband all over again.

A flood of tears fills my eyes. I wind my arms around his shoulders and my legs around his waist, tears slipping down my cheeks even as our lips remain locked together. Emotion ripples around us, all the pent-up longing of our separation breaking open into a spiral of warmth and light.

Finally Dean eases back a few inches and rests his forehead against mine.

"Hey, beauty." His deep voice rolls over my skin.

"Welcome home, professor."

He lowers me down slowly, sliding my body against his. I press my face to the front of his shirt, inhaling the familiar scent of him as the area around my heart expands with love. We stand there forever, wrapped in each other again, our separation disappearing like a shadow lightened by sunshine.

I rub my cheek against his strong chest. "When did you get back?"

"Earlier today. Wanted it to be a surprise."

"Best surprise ever."

He presses his lips to the top of my head. A slight tension courses through him. "I have to leave again, but I've got about ten days. Came back to see you and also for a meeting."

I tighten my arms around his waist and don't respond. The unspoken implication of the *meeting* is clear enough, and I want nothing bad to invade our reunion.

I ease back to look at him. He puts his hand against my cheek, the tension fading as he brushes away the tears still tracking down my face.

"You have no idea how happy I am to see you," he says.

"Oh, I have an idea. Especially if it's half as happy as I am to see you."

"It's twice as happy. No, way more than that."

"Not possible."

He smiles, sliding his thumb across my lips, his gaze warm. Pleasure fills me at that look, so replete with love and tenderness that I'm reminded anew that together we can withstand anything.

Brushing his hand over my neck, Dean steps away and goes to the telephone. His gaze still on me, he picks up the phone and presses a button.

"About ready here," he says into the receiver.

I give him a puzzled look. He turns away and lowers his

voice. I take the opportunity to look around the room, which I haven't even noticed in my excitement. Firefly Cottage is a bright, airy place with maple furniture and a gleaming, hardwood floor. Ivory curtains hang from the windows, a handcrafted down quilt covers the bed, and there's even a little kitchen with stainless steel appliances and granite countertops.

I step to the French doors on the other side of the room, which lead to a private porch and a pathway to the shore of the lake. The sky is still light enough that I can see the water rippling in the wind, the mountains outlined against the horizon like a painting.

I turn at the sound of a knock on the front door, and Brent appears with a wheeled cart topped with silver-domed dishes. He grins at me again and sets up the dinner on a linen-covered table beside the windows.

He lights two candles, places a vase of roses on the windowsill, and uncorks a bottle of wine. He exchanges a few words with Dean and puts another covered plate and silver carafe on the kitchen counter.

After Brent leaves, Dean pulls a chair out from the table and gestures for me to sit down. I'm suddenly aware of how I must look—dressed in torn jeans and an old, button-down shirt, grubby from hauling boxes at the bookstore all day, not a speck of makeup on my face.

I run a hand self-consciously over my hair and search in my pocket for a rubber band. I wish I'd taken the time—and had the presence of mind—to at least have put on some lipstick before flying back to my husband.

"Sorry, I didn't even have a chance to brush my hair," I mumble.

"You're beautiful. You're my wish come true."

"Aw." I smile as that fluttering sensation warms my blood. "Good one."

He winks at me. "Don't put your hair up."

I toss the rubber band onto a nearby table, finger-combing the tangles out of my hair before I sit down. By the time Dean has uncovered the plates, I'm even more in love with him. King salmon, wild rice pilaf, grilled zucchini, eggplant, and peppers.

"Our first date dinner," I say. "At the White Rose."

"Hoped you'd remember." Dean pours two glasses of pinot noir and sits across from me. "Not bad with the courting you, huh?"

"On the contrary. All very good."

I'm so happy to be sitting across from him again that I'm not sure I can even eat anything. But the food is delicious, and we soon ease into a comfortable conversation about the Wonderland Café, a few local events in Mirror Lake, and the next phase of excavation for the archeological dig.

We keep glancing at each other as we eat, and several times Dean reaches across the table to brush a speck of rice off my lip or push my hair away from my forehead.

"I can't stop touching you," he says, his gaze tracking over my face. "You look incredible. I know you kept telling me you were okay, but I hated not being able to take care of you."

"I've done a pretty good job taking care of myself."

"You really have, Liv. I'm proud of you."

My heart fills with pleasure. It's like the satisfying click of a puzzle piece fitting into place. I reach over to squeeze his hand in silent thanks before we return to our dinners.

The candles are half-burned by the time we start eating slices of rich chocolate torte for dessert. When we've both finished, Dean pushes away from the table and comes around to my side.

He grasps my hands and tugs me to my feet. His expression fills with warmth as he gazes at me for a long minute.

"And now, my beauty," he says, placing his hands on either side of my face, "I'm going to kiss you like I've never kissed you before."

Oh…

Desire brews in his eyes as he lowers his head to press his mouth against mine. I melt, falling into him as if we've never been apart, as if we've never had any heartache between us. The years slip away, my entire being sparking with that thrilling anticipation of discovering the depths of our attraction.

I part my lips under his, my body swaying against him as his tongue slides into my mouth. Lust flames through me, scorching my blood. He tastes like chocolate, his breath warm and delicious.

The ache of longing from the past few weeks disappears into *this…* all heat and light. The world both spins and steadies around me, a cascade so thrilling because I know that no matter how far and wildly I fall, Dean will always be there to catch me.

He takes my face in his hands, lifting his head just far enough so he can trail kisses over my cheek to my ear, down to my neck, then back up to my lips again. Each touch of his mouth sends shivers raining through me. His body heat burns through his shirt, and I press closer, my nipples hardening against his chest. I can feel the urgency coiling in him, the hunger that has gone unsatisfied for too long.

We tumble onto the bed together. Dean curls his fingers around my wrists to pin my hands beside my head. He shifts halfway on top of me, putting his leg over my thighs as he lowers his head to kiss me again.

His body is powerful and hot, his chest a solid wall of muscle against my breasts. He deepens the kiss, licking my lower lip, claiming me again. Pleasure swirls through me, thought disappearing into the reminder of everything we are to each other.

Dean releases one of my wrists and moves his hand to the front of my shirt, slipping two buttons free to expose a deeper V of skin and the swell of my cleavage. My heart kicks into high gear at the sensation of his hand on my bare skin, his erection pressing against my thigh. I'm drowning in images of our naked bodies sliding together, my legs wrapped around his hips as he thrusts into me again and again...

I close my eyes as Dean kisses the hollow of my throat, his breath steaming against my skin. I grip the back of his shirt, eager to pull it from the waistband of his trousers and run my hands over his muscular back.

And then, unwelcome and sudden, a wave of stark worries filters through my haze of lust.

It's been at least twelve hours since I last showered... I'm wearing an old white bra that's been washed so many times it's gray... and, oh lord, when was the last time I shaved my legs...?

"You feel so damn good." His muffled whisper brushes against my skin as he trails a kiss lower. "I want to..."

Then a sense of restraint goes through him as he slows the explorations of his hands and mouth. He lifts his head to look at me, his hand resting loosely against my throat, his eyes filled with heat.

I reach up to brush his disheveled hair away from his forehead, stroking my palm over his cheek.

"What?" I whisper, still throbbing despite my concerns about my current neglect of personal care.

He shifts away from me with a groan, rolling onto his back. He throws his arm across his eyes. His chest heaves.

"Dean?"

"We're not going any further." His voice is rough.

"We're... we're not?"

"I'm stopping with a kiss tonight."

"What? Why?" I'm bewildered. Even with my hesitations, I'd just assumed he'd be pounding into me like a jackhammer by now.

My whole body goes weak at the thought, and inwardly I'm screaming, *"Oh God, yes, fuck me harder, faster... more... oh, please..."*

I squeeze my thighs together. I'm on the edge. I'm so far over the edge I'm about to go crashing over it into pure bliss.

Dean swears, scrubbing his hands over his face. "We're dating again, right? That means we're not having sex yet."

I push up to my elbows and stare at him. "At *all?*"

"Not *yet.* And I'm staying here at the hotel."

"For your whole visit?"

"Yeah."

I'm not sure whether to find this proposal sweet or disappointing. In addition to being so hot I'm about to go up in flames, I've also been having all sorts of sexy, romantic images of what we'd do together once he comes back home and my legs are shaved.

"So you're going to stay at a hotel because we're dating again?" I ask, convinced I misheard something.

"Like how it was when we first met."

I can't help smiling. That's what I wrote in my manifesto: *I will remember how it was when we first met.*

I shift onto my side to look at Dean. The candlelight flickers over his strong features, creating a pattern of light and shadow and emphasizing the golden flecks in his brown eyes. The lines of stress that once bracketed his mouth and eyes have eased, his tension replaced by the Dean who is sure of himself and his place in the world.

"What about all that sexy talking we did over the phone?" I ask.

"Doesn't count. We did that when we were dating, remember?"

"Oh, I remember." A flutter of pleasure goes through me at the thought of all the erotic things we did in those early months. "We did a lot more than that when we were dating."

Back then, I'd been both so nervous and so comfortable around him—unsettled by how much I wanted him, embarrassed by all the things I wanted to do with him, and yet never had I felt more like myself than when I was with him.

Now after our long separation, I desperately want him to come home, to be back with me where he belongs. And yet...

Dean turns his head to look at me with those eyes that can see right into the center of my heart. He knows exactly what I know—that as difficult as it is to stop ourselves, this new, restrained intimacy reminds us of the beginning. Of *our* beginning.

Though my whole body tingles at the thought of stretching out our anticipation, I can't help glancing at the impressive bulge in his trousers. I battle back a wild surge of desire. My fingers flex with the urge to slide my hand over his thigh, rub all that delicious hardness...

I swallow to ease the dryness in my throat. "Um, so when do we get to…"

Dean puts his big, warm hand against my cheek. "I'm taking you out tomorrow night for a special date. Courting you, like you wanted. And afterward, you're coming back here and spending the whole weekend with me. Just us. We're going to watch the sun set over the lake, order room service, take baths together, sit by the fire, and spend a lot of time fucking… fast and slow and good."

"Oh…" An ache of hot longing fills me. "I love you."

"I know." A gleam appears in his eyes, ratcheting my heartbeat up again. "But you're waiting for me this time, Mrs. West."

"I don't want to wait," I breathe, sinking toward him, desperate for the sensation of his mouth on mine, more of his intoxicating kisses that make my head spin and my body throb. "Dean, we've waited for so long… please, kiss me again…"

Lust flares in his eyes again. He grabs the back of my neck and pulls me toward him, crushing his lips to mine with a force that rockets desire through me. With a moan, I sink back against the bed, driving my fingers into his rumpled hair, my own hesitations slipping away like torn silk.

He tightens his grip on my nape and lifts away from me again, his breath hot against my mouth. "Not yet."

While I know that Dean has an immense amount of self-control and discipline, this is off the charts even for him. I slide my palm over the side of his neck, feeling the heavy beat of his pulse.

"You're sure?" I can hardly get the question past the heat filling my throat.

Dean lifts his hand and traces my lips, pushing his thumb

gently into my mouth. A groan rumbles through his chest when I close my lips around his thumb and suck.

"I promise," he whispers. "It'll be worth it."

I ease away to look at him. "You're really *really* sure?"

"Uh huh. I have a plan. I'm sticking to it."

"Oh, lord." Now it's my turn to groan. I flop back onto the bed and try to will my raging body under control as I stare at the ceiling. "A Professor Dean West *plan*. God help us all. Not even the immediate possibility of mind-blowing sex with his extremely horny and lascivious wife will deter Professor West from his *plan*."

He lowers his head to nip the side of my neck, lighting my skin with shivers.

"The *plan* involves two parts," he murmurs. "And part two is a weekend filled with raw, hard fucking. I'm first going to strip you naked and kiss every inch of your gorgeous body. Then I'll rub that sweet pussy of yours and make you come on my fingers before thrusting into you so deep you'll forget we were ever apart at all."

I can't take it. I'm sweating. I'm about to explode.

Dean pushes his groin against my hip before pulling away from me, a shudder coursing through him.

"But you need to go now," he mutters, the taut note in his voice betraying his razor-thin control. He pushes up from the bed with a wince of discomfort.

Even with this dictate of his, I'm beginning to realize he wouldn't care if my legs are as hairy as a Wookiee's. I'm beginning to think I wouldn't care either.

Not if he plunges that thick cock into me and pumps like a well-oiled machine while rubbing my clit and whispering all sorts of dirty things in that deep voice of his... *"Come on, baby, come all over my cock... gonna fuck you so hard, just the way you like it... squeeze your pussy... tighter..."*

I press my hands to my flaming cheeks. I'm in serious danger of flinging myself on him and pulling off his trousers. Sinking down onto his cock and writhing up and down until I scream.

I could do it. Right now. Not even Dean has enough self-control to resist my full-force seduction. Especially not when we're both burning so hot it's like high noon in the desert here. He wouldn't stand a chance.

On the other hand, the love of my life has a *plan* that involves the two of us alone after a long dry spell and over a month of romantic courting. And I have a bunch of sexy lingerie that he hasn't seen in person yet. If I manage to restrain myself now, I could be *ready* for him right at the cusp of this insanely erotic weekend he has planned.

"Yes, I... um, I'd better go," I whisper. I can't believe I just said that.

"Yeah." He rests his elbows on his knees and shoves his hands into his hair. His whole body is rigid.

"Okay." I manage to get to my feet. I feel like I'm swimming against a rip current, moving against an opposing force. I don't want to leave any more than I want to stop breathing. "I guess I'll... I'll go now."

"Okay." His voice is tight enough to snap.

"Okay." I step away from the bed, all slippery and tense between my legs. I might come just from walking home. I might come before I walk out the door.

I grab a glass of water from the table and down it in three swallows before I pick up my bag. "I'll see you tomorrow, then."

Dean pushes up from the bed and yanks open the door. As I cross to it, he steps forward, as if he's about to reach for me. Then he stops. Leans forward and presses a hard kiss on my mouth that makes my entire body flame. He lifts his head, his eyes dark as midnight.

"Go," he growls.

Somehow, incomprehensibly, I walk out the door.

CHAPTER SIX

DEAN

*S*he's gone. I pound my head against the closed door. She left less than a minute ago, and it's like someone is squeezing the air out of my lungs. I need that woman in order to breathe.

I slam the locks on the door. Chain and deadbolt. Have to lock myself in or I'll break out after her. I want to grab her and shove her up against the nearest wall. Rip her clothes off and fuck her until the earth trembles and the stars explode. Until the universe shatters.

I deserve a goddamn medal for my self-control. I can't think. My blood is on fire. My cock is so hard it's about to bust my fly open. And I just let my hot, sweet wife walk away from me. I *told* her to go.

I bang my head against the door again. *Fuck. Fuck. Fuck.*

I can still feel her. Smell her. Taste her.

I push away from the door and get my phone. My fingers flex. She'd run back if I called. She's as jacked up as I am. I know all her little gasps and squirms. I know how close she was. She'd have come from one flick of my finger on her clit. She'd have come *hard*.

With a groan, I throw the phone back onto the bed. Grab a towel from the bathroom before shoving my pants and boxers down. I've spent the last month jerking off every night like a fifteen-year-old. I've got it down to a damn science, but it's nothing compared to how it feels with Liv.

Right now it takes me about five seconds to come. Still not much relief. I want *her*.

After changing into pajama bottoms, I collapse on the bed. I'm still half-hard. I bury my face into the spot where Liv was. The pillow smells like her, fragrant and peachy.

Christ, I missed her. I'd had visions of our reunion—hot, sweaty, naked visions. Liv all damp and lusty, her breath catching in her throat the way it does when she gets too overwhelmed to speak. Squirming underneath me. Full, round breasts with those tight nipples that I want to suck until she begs me to fuck her…

I inhale a few breaths. I'd gotten the idea a week ago and spent the time before my return putting the plan into place. Five thousand miles away, it sounded romantic as hell to stay at a hotel while dating my beautiful wife again and planning a sexy weekend.

I groan. Don't know how long I lie there on the bed, trying

to figure out how I'm going to survive this. Even one day sounds like an eternity.

My phone rings. I shove up and grab it. Liv.

"Hi." Her voice is breathless.

My cock twitches again. I tighten my grip on the phone. "Hi."

"Just wanted to let you know I got home okay."

"Good. Thanks."

"I'm so glad you're back."

"Me too."

We both fall silent for a minute, the air thick between us.

"So, you never did finish telling me about that underground radar system," Liv finally remarks.

"The…"

"You mentioned it during dinner. The radar you might use on the dig."

"Uh… yeah." Wondering why she's interested now, I try to shift my brain to archeology and science. Maybe this will take my mind off the fact that I'm sleeping alone tonight. Again.

"I'm going to make a trip to a Cistercian monastery in France," I tell Liv. "Valmagne. They're doing some work with ground-penetrating radar. GPR."

"What does that do?"

"It's a noninvasive way of studying the structure before starting a more systematic excavation plan."

"How does it work?"

"The equipment reflects radar waves off subsurface features and transmits them back to a computer. So before excavation, you first get a geophysical map of a large area of land and whatever is buried underground."

"Impressive."

"It works well, but sometimes it's hard to get a clear image. The geophysicists have run into some problems in Valmagne because the limestone foundations of the monastery don't give a good dielectric contrast with the carbonate-derived soil. Now they're trying an enhanced processing system that's given them some good images of the subsurface of the church. They want my opinion on the possibility that Gothic piers were built over preexisting Romanesque foundations."

"Hmm…"

A thought suddenly hits me.

"Liv, are you touching yourself?"

"What?"

"You are, aren't you? You're masturbating while I talk about ground-penetrating radar."

"I most certainly am not. What kind of freak do you think I am?"

"You're my very hot, sexy freak." I can't help grinning, even as my prick starts to harden. An image flashes in my head—my wife splayed out on the sofa, her panties tangled around her thighs as she rubs her pussy.

"How close are you?" I ask.

"I am *not* touching myself."

"What're you doing, then?"

"Just… just sitting here. Listening."

"What if I told you I had to jerk off thirty seconds after you left?"

She inhales sharply. "You did?"

"Uh huh. Couldn't stop thinking about you. Wanted to rip your clothes off, kiss your gorgeous body all over, lick your nipples, bite your neck, then spread your legs so I could thrust into you and fuck you hard for a thousand days."

"God, Dean."

"But you're not touching yourself."

"Well, I am *now*."

Heat bolts through me. My cock swells into full hardness.

"Are you?" Liv whispers in my ear.

I push my pants down and grasp my erection. "I am now."

"Oh…" She lets out one of those breathy little sighs that fires my blood.

I tighten my fist on my shaft. "Tell me."

"Oh, Dean. I want you so badly. I missed you so much. And I love this return to the beginning, but… are you sure you want to wait one second more?"

"I'm sure I'm about to explode." My cock is starting to throb. I want Liv back where she was. "Uh, transept chapels. Spherical wave divergence. Gothic hemicycle piers."

She giggles. "Keep going."

"My sexy wife sitting on my cock. Riding me until we both come like rockets."

She sucks in another breath.

"Are you naked?" I ask.

"From the waist down. I have a camisole top on." She pauses. "Um, I just took a quick shower and shaved my legs."

I have no idea why she told me that, but I don't care. It's a crystal-clear picture. She's on the sofa in our living room. One bare leg over the arm of the sofa, the other foot on the floor. Spread open. Wet. Hungry. No bra. Hard nipples poking against her shirt. Eyes dark and heavy. Hair loose around her shoulders. Skin flushed pink. One hand between her legs.

"You know I fantasized about us," I say. "Did you?"

"Yes," she whispers.

"Tell me."

"I'd press my face into your pillow and get on my knees. Spread my legs and push my ass up."

I groan. There are few sights I like better than Liv's round ass slamming against me as I fuck her from behind.

"I'd reach down to rub my clit while imagining you all hot and hard behind me," she continues, her words punctuated by quick breaths. "Sometimes I'd grab another pillow and push it between my legs. Hump it while wishing it was your cock."

Damn. I squeeze my shaft, my balls aching. Pressure tightens my whole body.

"What're you doing now?" I ask.

"Playing with my nipples. Wishing you could lick them."

"Ah, fuck…" My blood boils. "Touch your pussy."

"Dean, I'm so wet. I almost creamed in my panties the second you kissed me."

"Do it now."

"Talk to me," she whispers. "The dirty stuff. If I can't have you yet, I want you to fuck me with your voice."

Christ. I will crawl over fire and broken glass for this woman.

I shut my eyes. She fills my vision. My mind. Every fucking part of me.

"Soon you're getting on your knees in front of me," I tell her. "Naked except for tight cotton panties that rub against your pussy. You're going to squeeze your pretty tits together so I can push my cock between them and fuck them. Thrusting into that hot, damp valley all the way up to your throat.

"I'll shoot hard all over you, like a goddamn geyser. My

come will drip off your nipples before I make you rub it in. Then you're going to lick my cock clean, swiping your tongue over the shaft and taking it all the way into your greedy mouth."

"Oh, my God, Dean…"

"Your clit will be throbbing, and you'll gasp and squirm and try to get yourself off, but I won't let you. Then you're going to turn around and bend over the arm of the sofa so I can pull your panties down and spank your gorgeous ass."

She moans. I'm about to shoot all over my hand, and I'm just warming up.

"You're going to spread your legs to show me your wet slit." The images flash in my brain like fire. "I'll let you finger yourself, but you won't be allowed to come. You'll writhe around, pleading with me, rubbing your nipples against the sofa cushion. You'll be so turned on your juices will drip down your thighs. Then I'm going to spank your ass until your cheeks are red and burning. You'll be gasping, hungry, begging for my cock."

"I want it. I want *you*…"

"I'll put my cock right at your slit and ease slowly inside you, watching my shaft disappear into your sweet, tight hole while you push backward and fuck yourself on me…"

"Oh, Dean, let me," Liv gasps. "I'm… I want to come. Please, I…"

"Do you see it?" I work my prick faster, the urgency at boiling point. "See yourself bent over the sofa, legs spread wide with my cock plunging in and out of you while your ass slaps against me and you tighten your pussy around my shaft… *fuck*."

I spurt all over my hand and stomach, an explosion of heat. Liv moans heavily against my ear. I see her shuddering, quaking, her thighs clamping around her hand as she works all the sensations from her clit.

The air fills with the rasp of our breathing. My heart pounds against my ribs.

"I…" Liv pulls in a breath. "I'm really enjoying dating you again."

I struggle to grab a coherent thought. "Just wait until I get you back here."

"But I *can't* wait." Though she groans the words, there's a smile in her voice. "You know I love you like peanut butter loves jelly."

"You know I can't wait to get you all sticky again."

Liv laughs. After we end the call, I lean back on the pillows and close my eyes. Though I'm still aching with the need to bury myself deep inside my wife, there's also a heavy sense of satisfaction. The feeling that I'm finally getting it right.

My proposal to Liv was the worst ever. In fact, it wasn't even a proposal. I knew she didn't care about extravagant gestures, which was a relief since I wasn't good at the romantic stuff. But even I could have done better than that.

The summer after my visiting professorship in Madison ended, nine months into our relationship, Liv and I drove to Pennsylvania, where my next job at the University of Pennsylvania was located. We had plans to continue our relationship long-distance until Liv graduated, and then we'd figure out our next step. En route to the university, we stopped in a small town with a dozen antique shops catering to tourists.

After lunch, we walked around town and visited a few of the cluttered shops. I was looking at some old camera equipment, and Liv was busy examining the contents of a glass case near the front.

I heard her talking to the owner, a friendly, middle-aged woman with a nametag that read Mrs. Bird. I wandered over to see what they were discussing.

"It's a cameo ring." Liv held out a silver ring topped with a delicate, carved silhouette of a woman with flowing hair.

"A unique one," Mrs. Bird added. "Late nineteenth century, rose gold, with a carved shell cameo. Undamaged, as you can see. Notice the detail on the woman's dress too, the open flower near her collar."

Liv slipped the ring onto her finger and spread out her hand. "My mother used to have something like this. It belonged to her mother, I think. I don't know what happened to it."

"Does it fit, Cinderella?" I asked.

Mrs. Bird smiled. Liv twisted the ring and nodded.

"How much is it?" she asked Mrs. Bird.

The owner glanced at the tag inside the counter. "Nine hundred dollars."

"Oh." Liv tugged the ring off. "It's lovely, but I'm afraid that's too much."

"We'll take it." I pulled out my wallet.

"Dean—"

"I haven't gotten you an engagement ring yet." The words just came out.

Liv stared at me. My stomach twisted.

"Uh, if you... if you want one, that is," I stammered. "An

engagement ring. I mean, if we… I… want to… you know. Get married."

Mrs. Bird chirped with excitement. Liv blinked. I started to sweat. I wanted Liv with a force that hurt, needed her like I needed air, loved her beyond reason. But not until that instant did I realize I couldn't imagine the rest of my life without her.

"Dean—"

"Ring it up, please." I handed Mrs. Bird my credit card.

"Oh, what a romantic gift!" Mrs. Bird fluttered over to run my card through the machine. "Congratulations to both of you."

Liv was quiet as I finished paying and Mrs. Bird packed up the ring in a little box. When we stepped back outside, Liv put her hand on my arm.

"It doesn't have to be an engagement ring," I said quickly. "It can just be a…" *Shit, what was another reason for a ring?* "A… friendship ring."

"Dean, I love you."

My heart stopped as I waited for the *"but."*

Liv smiled that beautiful smile that hit me in the middle of my chest every single time.

"And I would love to be your wife," she said.

But…?

She looked at me expectantly. I swallowed hard.

"But?" I asked.

"What?"

"You would love to be my wife, but… what?"

Liv looked baffled. "But nothing."

"You would love to be my wife, period?"

"Yes." A frown creased her forehead. "You do want us to get married, don't you?"

Jesus, West, pull it together.

Because I couldn't stammer out a sentence, I just grabbed her and hauled her against me. I planted a deep kiss on her that was probably indecent in public. Then I eased away to look into her brown eyes.

My girlfriend. My fiancée. My beauty.

I wanted her to be *my wife* as soon as possible, but I knew women had ideas about big weddings and fancy dresses. Though I didn't think Liv ever had, I asked her what kind of wedding she wanted.

"One that ends with us married," she said.

I thought I should do something extravagant to make up for my pitiful excuse of a proposal, so I contacted an old friend whose father owned a vineyard in the Loire. After a few months of making arrangements, Liv and I went to France in July and were married on the villa's terrace by the cleric of the local church.

The details are all fused together—like the parts of a brilliant, stained-glass window.

Ivy climbing up the stone walls of the villa. The Delacroix family sitting nearby. Endless sloping hills covered with grapevines. The family dog lounging in a patch of sunlight.

Liv walking toward me in a simple white dress, a few flowers threaded through her long hair. Breaking my heart with her beauty.

The soft clasp of her hands around mine.

Her smile, like a secret meant only for me.

Her voice, gentle and certain.

The intense, overwhelming love that almost brought me to my knees.

"I'm at your feet forever, Olivia Rose," I whispered the instant before our lips met. "I'll move heaven and earth to give you whatever you want, whatever you need."

"Oh, Dean." She pressed her hand to the side of my face. "All I need is you."

And then the kiss, a perfect harmony of the stars and planets that started my universe all over again.

CHAPTER SEVEN

OLIVIA

MARCH 28

I finally understand why Dorothy, Maria, Eliza, Gigi, and Sandy break out into song in the midst of going about their lives. Sometimes your heart gets so filled with emotions that words alone can't express them all. So you need singing and dancing, a philharmonic orchestra, and a full chorus backing you up. Because there is *that much* inside you.

Since I don't have an orchestra or chorus, and my dancing skills are decidedly lacking, I compensate by humming a little tune as I arrange croissants and brioche in baskets. It's just past dawn, and the air is filled with the rich, fragrant scents of coffee and fresh baked goods.

My husband is home… my husband is home… my beautiful, intensely hot husband is home…

And he has a sexy weekend planned that has me all fluttery with excitement. I couldn't be more in love with that man if I tried. I also couldn't be more stirred up at the thought of all the erotic things we're going to do, but I manage to contain my arousal beneath my anticipation.

The wait, I know, will be *so* worth it.

Still humming, I go through the swinging doors to the kitchen and get another tray of brioche. The owner of La Première Moisson is a gruff, older fellow from Lyons who thinks *"zee Ahmericans ruin zee good cuisine with zee fast food."*

The man does know how to make a spectacular croissant, though, so I forgive him his pretensions. Plus, he might be right about us.

"Hey, Gustave, do you know how to sing?" I ask him as I slide the tray of golden-brown bread onto the counter.

"Zing?" His brow furrows. You would think I'd just asked him if he knows how to yodel.

"Yeah. Like Edith Piaf." I clear my throat and warble, *"Je ne regrette rien…"*

Gustave looks as if I just spit in his vat of butter. I stop singing.

"Only curious." I dump the brioche into another basket.

"I do not zing." Gustave returns his attention to shaping baguettes. "Neither, apparently, do you, Oleevia."

I grin and head to the front counter with the basket. After getting the displays filled, I unlock the doors at seven and help the customers who come in for coffee and breakfast. It's busy for the next couple of hours, with hardly a lull until around nine.

When the crowd finally dwindles down a bit, I restock all the baskets with fresh pastries, clean the counters and floors, and get ready for the second morning rush.

I'm dipping almond cookies in chocolate when a familiar, deep voice rumbles over my skin.

"Medium coffee, please."

I turn, my heart leaping at the sight of Dean standing on the other side of the counter. His dark eyes crinkle with warmth as he looks at me, a smile tugging at his mouth. He looks gorgeous, all rumpled masculinity in a sweatshirt and jeans, his hair disheveled by the breeze. If I stepped close to him, I'd smell shaving cream and fresh spring air.

A thousand memories wash over me of those early days when he'd walk in the door of Jitter Beans and our eyes would meet with sparks of electricity. How wonderful to feel that happy excitement again.

"Coming right up." I turn to the coffee dispenser. "Room for cream in your coffee, sir?"

"No, thanks."

I pour the coffee and slide the cup across the counter. "Can I interest you in a fresh croissant or brioche?"

"Sure. You pick for me."

I select a buttery, chocolate croissant for him and slip it into a bag, then ring up the purchase.

"See how I'm moving up in the world?" I ask. "From Jitter Beans to La Première Moisson. Ooo la la."

"Indeed." He returns my smile, digging into his pocket for his wallet. "You always did have that *je ne sais quoi.*"

He glances behind him to ensure there's no one else in the shop, then leans across the counter to press his lips against mine. A hint of eucalyptus and fresh air fill my nose.

I fall into him, melting like sun-warmed honey. He cups my chin and angles my face to his in exactly the right way. I slide my hand around the back of his neck, rising up onto my tiptoes to increase the pressure of the kiss.

"You smell amazing." He trails his mouth across my cheek to nuzzle his nose against my hair, his lips seeking my ear. His voice is a husky whisper. "Just want to back you up against the wall, lift your skirt, and spread your pretty legs."

A shiver rocks me to my toes. "God, Dean."

"Every time you say that…" he pulls away with a soft mutter, "…my self-control slips a little more."

"God, Dean."

He laughs. I smile and reach out to tweak his nose.

A Gallic-sounding grunt breaks through my pleasure. Gustave approaches, bearing a tray of éclairs. He puts the tray on top of the cold case and glowers at me, jerking his thumb toward the éclairs.

"Consider it done, monsieur." I hurry to arrange the éclairs in lacy paper cups.

Gustave goes back to the kitchen. As he passes me, I swear I hear him humming "That's Amore" under his breath.

"Okay, I'm going." Dean steals one last, quick kiss before stepping back.

"Can you still come to the café this afternoon?"

"I'll be there around one. Just going to stop at the apartment to pick up some things. And we're on for tonight?"

"Of course." I think about my sexy lingerie and wonder

which set I should wear for him. Just the thought of his hot gaze raking over my half-naked, lace-clad body has me pressing my thighs together to ease the ache.

"I'll pick you up at six," Dean says.

"Where are we going?"

"McDonald's."

"Big spender."

"Only for you, baby." He winks at me and turns to go.

For a good half hour after he leaves, I can't stop smiling. The orchestra is already striking up a song.

"Well." Kelsey puts her hands on her hips and studies the main dining room of Matilda's Teapot. "With some redecorating, you'll be in great shape."

"We're starting the remodeling next week." I look at the spreadsheets and plans scattered over one of the tables. "It's a huge undertaking."

"Yeah. But Allie's right. You couldn't have a better location, and it sounds like she and Brent know what they're doing." Kelsey turns to pierce me with one of her perceptive looks. "The question is… how do you feel about all this?"

"Mostly excited," I tell her. "I've never done anything like it before, but I know it's a great idea. I love being in business with Allie, and I'm happy that I can finally contribute something of my own."

She's still watching me. "So what's the problem?"

"It's nerve-wracking. What if I just poured my entire inheritance into a new business and it fails? And what if I didn't calculate the costs of working capital correctly and we run out of money?"

Kelsey pushes a chair away from the table and straddles it, resting her arms across the back. "You could find another partner."

"Not one both Allie and I could trust as much as we trust each other. Dean offered to help financially, but he knows I'm trying to do this on my own and he would never ask to be a partner."

"What about me?" Kelsey asks.

"What about you?"

"What if I offered to be a partner?"

I lift my head. "What?"

"I'd be a partner in your business."

"Are you serious?"

"Am I ever *not* serious?"

"I can't let you do that."

"Why not?"

"It's a bad idea. Mixing business with friendship."

"You've never done it before. How do you know it's a bad idea?"

"Everyone says so."

"I don't listen to everyone."

I can only stare at her. Tears sting my eyes.

"Jesus, Liv," Kelsey mutters. "Don't *cry*. I'm offering you a partnership, not a kidney."

"Sorry." I grab a napkin and swipe my nose.

"Besides, you're doing this with Allie, and she's a friend, right?" Kelsey asks.

"I know, but you... you're more like..."

"Like what?"

"Well, like family." My heart clenches a little.

We both fall silent. Then Kelsey heaves a sigh.

"Okay, look. I'll say this only once." She digs her fingernail into a crack on the back of the chair. "I've never had a lot of close friends. I don't like it when people start wanting to know shit about me. It's annoying. But Dean's never been like that. Never made me feel like I have to apologize for anything. And when he married you, I thought he'd change, that things would be different. I was all revved up to dislike you."

"You were?" I can't even imagine withstanding the force of Kelsey March's dislike.

"Yeah," she says. "But you made it impossible. The first time I met you was in LA at the farmer's market. After Dean introduced us, you gave me this... this *Liv hug* and asked me to join you for crepes."

She shakes her head, as if I'd asked her to fly over the rainbow.

"Um... I like crepes," I say.

"Liv, I mean you just accepted everything, you know? Me. You never questioned my friendship with Dean. Never felt threatened by it. Not many people have figured out how to deal with me as fast as you did. Like you didn't miss a beat. And you made your husband better, which is saying something."

She shoves off the chair. "Okay, I'm done. That little speech will self-destruct in five seconds."

I know enough not to respond to any of that, but my heart fills with love and affection for Kelsey and her bad-ass self.

"So, we're finishing up the final numbers," I say, turning to the spreadsheet. "Can I get back to you next week?"

"Yeah. You and Allie figure out if you need me, and I'll see what I can do. Just don't get all mushy about it."

The sound of footsteps comes down the stairs, signaling Allie's approach.

"Liv, I really think that front room should be the witch's castle room," she remarks, "because it has that view of the mountains, and the witch's castle was surrounded by mountains. Hold on, let me grab my portfolio from the car and we can sketch out some ideas."

She hurries out the back door. I gather up all the spreadsheets, and Kelsey shrugs into her jacket just as the bell over the door rings. We turn to see a tall man in his mid-forties enter, shedding his coat and pulling a hand through his salt-and-pepper hair. He's dressed with casual elegance in khakis and a buttondown shirt.

"Can I help—" I start to say.

The back door bangs open, and Allie bustles in again. "Oh, hey, Dad."

Dad?

Kelsey and I watch in astonishment as Allie and the man exchange a bear hug.

"Thanks for coming," Allie says. "Did you meet Liv?"

"Not yet." The man extends his hand to me and smiles. "Max Lyons. Allie's father."

I shake his hand in disbelief, stunned by the fact that not only is he quite young to have a twenty-seven-year-old daughter, he doesn't look anything like I'd imagined.

From what Allie has told me, her father moved to one of the artsy neighborhoods on the other side of the lake, after Allie's mother died years ago. Allie hadn't wanted to ask him for more money to help with the bookstore or the café, and I'd assumed that was because he'd helped her out a lot already and didn't have much money himself. In fact, I'd pictured Max Lyons as a long-haired hippie who wears frayed jeans and smells faintly of pot.

I did not picture a man who looks as if he's just stepped from the pages of *GQ*.

"And this is Kelsey March," Allie tells her father. "She's a professor at the university."

"In which department?" Max Lyons asks, holding out his hand to Kelsey.

I can't believe it. My majestic friend is standing there as if she's just lost the ability to speak.

"Atmospheric sciences," I pipe up, giving Kelsey a quick poke in the side.

"Uh, yeah." She shakes Max's hand, then takes a step toward the door. "Weather forecasting. Nice meeting you."

"You too."

"I asked Dad if he could stop by and give us his opinion about the building," Allie tells me. "He's an architect."

"Oh." Now things finally fall into place. "Well, that's great."

"Come on." Allie tugs on Max's sleeve. "I'll tell you what we're planning for the upstairs rooms. Liv, could you call Marianne and ask if she can stop by?"

"Sure."

Kelsey and I walk to the front porch as I take out my cell and leave Marianne a quick voicemail.

Dean's car pulls up to the curb. My heart gives a welcome, familiar leap as he approaches, his black peacoat buttoned against the cold. In contrast to his rumpled appearance this morning, he's now wearing a tailored suit with a navy tie knotted at his throat. His thick, dark hair is brushed away from his forehead, emphasizing the masculine planes of his face.

Although I always love the sight of my handsome husband in full, distinguished-professor mode, now my pleasure is shadowed by a twinge of despair.

Dean brushes his lips across my cheek and turns to hug Kelsey.

"How long are you staying?" she asks, pulling her car keys from her pocket.

"Ten days."

"Racquetball tomorrow, then?"

My stomach twists. Dean and Kelsey often work out together at the university gym, but with him not allowed to be on campus now...

"No, I've got stuff to do," he tells her.

Kelsey glances at me, as if she senses something is up. Then she shrugs and goes down the steps to her car. I move closer to Dean, disliking the ever-present knowledge of what he has to contend with.

"When is the meeting?" I ask.

"Wednesday. I'm going into Forest Grove this afternoon to consult with a library board about their medieval manuscript collection."

"What's the Wednesday meeting about?"

"It's a mediation meeting, see if we can come to some resolution so the case won't go to the university board of trustees." Dean gives me a reassuring smile that doesn't ease the concern in his eyes. "Shouldn't be too bad."

He runs his hand over my hair and nods toward the café. "So tell me what you've got planned here."

Pulling open the door, he steps aside to let me precede him. He takes his coat off, tossing it over a chair before unbuttoning his suit jacket.

I stop and do a double-take. Beneath his jacket, he's wearing…

"Is that a *sweater vest?*" I ask in astonishment.

As if he's forgotten, Dean looks down at the navy, buttoned vest he's wearing over a gray shirt. "Yeah."

"Since when do you wear sweater vests?"

"Since the girl at the store told me it looked good."

I stare at him, struck by how a piece of clothing so dorky can make a man like Professor West look like… well, like *this*. With his hair burnished by the lights, the knot of his tie tucked against his collar, the sweater vest molding beautifully to his sculpted torso…

"That girl was right," I admit.

"So you like it?" he asks.

I lean closer and whisper, "Makes me want to rub my naked body all over you."

His eyes flare, and he strokes his thumb across my lips. "Hold that thought."

"Keep that vest. It's incredibly sexy on you."

"You're incredibly sexy on me too."

I smile and stand on tiptoe to kiss him. Before I can ease away from him, he plants his hand on the small of my back and tugs me closer. His eyes fill with that combination of heat and tenderness that I know so well and have missed so much.

He brushes his thumb across my lower lip, sending a burst of sparks over my skin. My breath catches in my throat as he crowds me up against the wall and lowers his mouth to mine in a hot, heavy kiss that scorches my veins with desire.

I can't help a small moan, my body going weak against the wall as Dean presses closer, his tongue seeking mine. I wind my hands around his neck, tucking my fingers into his hair as his kiss deepens and fills me with a thousand tiny fires. My sex throbs, my pulse kicking into gear. I fight the urge to slide my hands beneath his vest and unbutton his shirt, running my palms over the hard slopes of his chest—

"Ahem."

I break away from Dean so fast the back of my head thunks against the wall. He moves in front of me, all effortless composure, and turns to greet Allie.

"Hey, Allie."

"Well, well." Allie's voice brightens. "I didn't know you were back, Dean."

"Just for a few days."

Allie introduces Dean to her father, which gives me a chance to regain my own composure before I emerge from behind Dean's shoulder. Dean steps forward to talk to Max, as Allie approaches me with a sly grin.

"Sorry," I mutter with embarrassment.

"No worries," she replies, her eyes twinkling behind her glasses. "There's a reason I call him Professor Hottie, you know."

I pull Dean away from Max so I can give him a tour of the building and tell him all of our plans. He is gratifyingly impressed and supportive, though he doesn't offer any ideas of his own. On purpose, I know. He'll keep his word and stay out of it.

"It's fantastic, Liv," he tells me. "Sounds like you've thought of everything."

"We're trying." I hesitate. "But I've been worried about us having enough working capital. I mentioned it to Kelsey this afternoon, and she offered to partner with us."

"That's great."

"You're okay with that?"

"Why wouldn't I be?"

"Because I turned you down when you offered financial help. But a business partnership with Kelsey is different from me taking your money."

"Liv, you wouldn't be taking my money. Everything I own is yours too."

"But this is a business. I need to treat it like one. Which means partnership agreements and budgeting, and not taking money out of our personal accounts just because it would be the easiest thing to do."

Dean studies me for a second, then nods.

"Okay," he says. "I get it."

My slight anxiety eases. "Good. Thank you."

"Don't thank me." He shakes his head, faint amusement flashing in his eyes. "You're the one going into business with a pit viper."

I smile. "More like a pit bull, don't you think?"

"That too."

After we return downstairs, Dean and Max, to neither Allie's nor my surprise, begin talking about the history of architecture from the Coliseum to Frank Lloyd Wright. Their conversation then turns to the findings of the Altopascio dig, major-league spring training, a recent state senate bill, and finally this awesome bacon burger Max had at a new restaurant in Rainwood.

"How cute," Allie whispers to me, nodding to where Dean and Max are standing by the front counter. "They're BFFs already."

It is pretty cute watching these two tall, handsome men

discussing manly things. I think it's kind of hot, too, though I don't tell Allie that.

After another half hour, I walk with Dean back out to his car so he can head to Forest Grove.

He opens the car door, then turns to kiss me. His mouth, warm and firm, lingers on mine as he cups the side of my face in his palm. Before I can lose myself in his kiss again, he eases away to look at me.

"Six," he murmurs, his eyes darkening with heat. "Be ready for me."

"I am ready for you," I breathe, as shivers shoot through my veins and settle between my legs.

"Be *more* ready." He brushes his fingers across my cheek and turns to get into his car.

I watch him go, thinking all those medieval knights had nothing compared to the intense, sexy chivalry of Dean West.

CHAPTER EIGHT

Olivia

*W*hen I get home, there's a box wrapped in brown paper outside the front door. The name *Mrs. Olivia West* is scrawled in Dean's familiar handwriting. With a smile, I bring the box inside and lift off the lid to reveal a clutter of puzzle pieces.

I dump the pieces onto the floor and start putting the puzzle together. Halfway to completion, I know what it is. An upwelling of love and emotion fills me.

I lock the last piece of the puzzle into place and stare at the photograph of me and Dean on our honeymoon in front of the Saint-Chapelle chapel in Paris. I grab my phone to call him, but his voicemail picks up. A text message from him buzzes a few seconds later.

Forty-five minutes.

I hurry to shower and dress in a purple, flower-print bra and matching hiphuggers under a fitted slip. I zip myself into a black sheath dress with a lace overlay, taking extra care with my hair and makeup.

I open the front door when I hear the foyer door snap closed. I step onto the landing just as Dean looks up.

A sizzle of energy arcs between us. My pulse zings through my veins at the sight of him—tall and handsome in a navy suit beneath his black coat. His hair gleams in the foyer lights, and a smile curves his mouth as he walks up the stairs to me, extending a bouquet of a dozen perfect red roses.

"Thank you." I take the bouquet, the flowers' perfume filling the air.

"If I'd thought about it earlier, I'd have recited a poem or something too." Dean stops in front of me, his gaze filled with appreciation. "You're so damned beautiful."

"That's all the poetry I need." I stand on tiptoe to press my lips against his cheek. The scent of him slides into my blood—a hint of spicy aftershave mingling with the crisp night air.

"I love the puzzle," I tell him.

"Good. One day soon I'll take you to Paris again." He tilts his head toward the street. "Ready?"

"Let me put the flowers in water and get my coat." I gesture for him to come inside, while I go into the kitchen to find a vase.

After arranging the roses, I bring the bouquet into the living room. Dean is standing by the window, his hands in his pockets. The sight of him back in our apartment, right where he belongs, warms me down to my toes. With the town lights shining behind him, he's so breathtakingly handsome that my heart does a little flip of happiness at the knowledge that he's mine. All mine.

I set the vase on the coffee table and fuss a little more with the arrangement of the roses.

"Your peace lily bloomed," Dean says.

"What?" I glance up.

"Your peace lily." He tilts his head toward the open flower. "It's pretty."

I smile, pleased that he noticed. "It's the same kind of plant I gave you that first time I went to your place for dinner."

"I remember." Warmth brews in his eyes as he returns his gaze to me. "That plant thrived because you took care of it the whole year."

"And I thrived because you took care of me the whole year."

Dean looks at me for a minute, then shakes his head. "Ah, Liv…"

I go to slide my arms around his waist, loving the hard press of his body against mine. He takes my hips in his hands, a murmur of pleasure rumbling from his chest as our lips meet.

"Let's go, beauty," he whispers, trailing his lips to my neck. "If we don't leave now, my plan will be shot to hell."

I laugh and untangle myself from him. We get our coats and walk to his car, and I'm so caught up in being with him again, breathing the same air, feeling the warmth of his presence beside me, that it's a good half hour before I realize we're heading out of Mirror Lake and up into the mountains.

"Where are we going?" I ask.

"You'll see."

It's a cloudy, crisp evening with reddish clouds skimming the mountaintops. Dean guides the car over a narrow road toward a domed building sitting on the crest of a ridge.

"The observatory?" I don't quite get it. "What are we doing here?"

"Dating." He winks at me and offers me his arm.

With a smile, I slide my hand into the crook of his elbow as we walk toward the entrance to the building. There's a truck parked nearby, though I can't see the lettering on the side of it. Dean holds the door open for me, and we walk into the hushed silence of the lobby.

He pulls open the auditorium door, and all the breath escapes my lungs at the sight of the silent room lit by a million brilliant stars spread over the arched ceiling. Soft music plays from hidden speakers. It's a singular, private universe, the stars and planets contained within this space, and for this moment, it's all ours.

"How did you manage this?" I ask as Dean takes my hand and leads me to a cloth-covered table set up on the stage.

"Pulled a few strings," he replies. "Closest I could get to giving you the universe."

I smile. "Good one."

"Wait here."

A bouquet of spring flowers blooms on the table, which is set with china plates and wineglasses. A candle flickers, but the light can't compete with the illumination of the stars. Dean returns a few minutes later with two delicious-smelling filet mignon dinners from the catering truck parked outside.

And under the dome of our own private universe, we spend a lovely hour eating and talking. My eyes keep straying to Dean's mouth, the curve of his hand around his fork, the way the starlight glows off his hair.

I'm reminded anew of our very first date, which included our first kiss. Even now, my body tingles at the memory of the heat filling Dean's eyes as he'd taken my face so gently in his hands.

"I'm going to kiss you now," he'd whispered, a second before our lips touched in a kiss that spun me into a whirlwind of knowing I could love this man.

That one day… *I would.*

Never before had I been so certain of my own instincts, and that knowledge has brought us to now.

After dinner, Dean spreads out a blanket on the stage and we lie back to look up at the stars sprinkled like sugar across the sky. Dean points out all the constellations and starts talking about medieval cosmology and philosophy. His deep voice flows over me, and I ease closer to him so our bodies touch.

"I wish it could be like this forever," I whisper. "Just us and the stars."

A faint apprehension ripples between us because we know it can't be. Not with the threat to his career looming over us like smoke obscuring the sky.

But none of that can touch us here. It can't obscure the beauty of our reunion.

Dean pushes to his feet, extending a hand to help me up. A little shudder runs through me at the heat in his eyes. We gather our things and return to the parking lot.

"Now." Dean bends to nuzzle my neck right before opening the car door for me. "Come back with me. Be mine all over again."

There is nothing in the universe I want more. Everything inside me lights with anticipation as we return to the Wildwood Inn.

When the cottage door closes behind us, my heartbeat intensifies. It's been weeks of fraught, tense longing, our sexy phone calls no comparison to what we can create when we're in the same room. Arousal blooms inside me, filling my veins with fire.

Dean leans against the door, his gold-flecked eyes sweeping over me in a slow, easy appraisal that makes my breath catch. I'm half-expecting him to stalk toward me with all that restrained lust uncoiling, to grab me in a wild fervor... but instead he gestures for me to come to him.

"Come here, beauty," he says, his voice husky. "Give me what I've missed so much."

My pulse pounds as I approach him. He lifts his hands and settles them against the back of my neck, his fingers sliding into my hair. The gentle way he holds my head, his gaze never leaving mine, wraps me in the knowledge of how precious I am to him. Everything inside me softens as I look at the lines of his cheekbones, his black eyebrows, the way his eyelashes frame his eyes, the shape of his mouth.

He lowers his head, his lips touching mine in a kiss of infinite warmth and tenderness, and then we're both home again, back in the place of Liv and Dean, sparks lighting the air as we fall into the spiral of us.

Dean shifts his hands, angling my head so that he can settle his mouth securely against mine, parting my lips with his. My blood surges with a love that will never fade and a desire that has been denied too long. I slip my arms around his waist, feeling the heat of him through the material of his suit and my dress.

He murmurs something low in his throat, caressing the arch of my back and down to my hips. I nestle closer, light glowing inside me like a million fireflies as our kiss deepens. My heart pounds against his. It's everything we've both craved all these weeks—the movement of our lips pressed together, the grip of his hands on my hips, my breasts rubbing against his chest.

Dean lifts one hand to my neck again, pushing my hair aside so he can unzip my dress. I let the material slither over my shoulders and fall in a puddle at my feet. I'm wearing a fitted satin slip over my lingerie, and Dean's breath escapes in a rush as he slides his gaze over my body again.

"Beauty, you make me want to stop time so I can look at you forever," he whispers as he pulls me closer.

He cups my breasts, his thumbs flicking over my hardening nipples, and my sex clenches with growing urgency. I lift my face to his again, desperate for more of his exhilarating kisses, and then he tucks his arm beneath my legs and lifts me against him. I twine my arms around his neck, bringing our mouths together again as he takes a few strides to the bed and lowers me onto the feather-soft quilt.

For all our pent-up longing and sexy talk, for all my expectations that we would fall on each other in a crash of frenzied heat... a lovely sense of restraint winds through us both. Dean eases on top of me, our lips still locked together.

The weight of my husband's body, combined with the deliciousness of his kiss, envelops me in a warm, protective shelter. I run my hands over his back and part my legs so he can settle between them. His erection presses against my thigh, the sensation eliciting a new wave of lust.

Dean moves his lips across my cheek, his breath a hot trail to my ear. Tension rolls through his body as he tangles his fingers into the straps of my slip and pulls them off my shoulders. I shift to help him, thrilled by the way his gaze darkens as he stares at my breasts clad in the flowered purple bra.

He growls low in his throat with appreciation before moving to press his mouth against the swells of my breasts, tugging the slip down around my waist. The touch of his lips and hands on my bare skin fires my whole body with heat.

I spear my hands into his thick hair as he tugs at the top edges of my bra to expose my breasts. He groans and takes one nipple between his teeth, rolling his tongue around the areola. Sparks rain through my blood. With a gasp, I shift and arch to rub against his erection.

"Oh, Dean… Touch me, please…"

His response is muffled against my skin as he moves to kiss my neck, the hollow of my throat where my pulse beats. He tugs the slip off me and tosses it to the floor. When he eases his forefinger beneath my panties and into my slit, my body flames.

"Ah, fuck, Liv…" His voice is hoarse with desire. "Want you so bad…"

He shifts to lower his mouth to mine again. His cock is rock-hard, pushing against the front of his trousers. Desperate need floods me as he slides two fingers into my body and circles my clit with his thumb.

"Come on, beauty," he whispers against my mouth, his teeth closing gently on my lower lip.

I'm lost in the swirling, beautiful pleasure of his intoxicating kisses, his body pressed against mine, his fingers stroking me. I tighten my hands on his shirt, letting my head fall back as he eases another finger inside me. One more stroke and sensation bursts through me in an explosion of light, wrenching a cry from my throat.

Dean's voice is a low rumble against my ear, his muscles taut as he pulls at my panties and unhooks my bra. When I'm naked, his hot gaze moves over my body like the most fervent of touches. He lowers his head, and then he's kissing me everywhere, his lips gentle on my breasts, down to my belly, his tongue circling my navel as his hands glide over the curves of my waist and hips.

I melt, closing my eyes as sensation washes over my skin. I feel like flowers are blooming inside me, velvety petals stretching and spreading open in the golden warmth of the sun. I tangle one hand into Dean's hair, brushing it back from his forehead as he moves to press kisses against my other palm, over the pulse beating at my wrist, and up my arm to my shoulder. By the time he reaches my lips again, I'm tingling all over with fresh desire.

"Your turn," I whisper, pressing on his shoulders to urge him to lie back.

My heart races as I straddle his waist and unfasten his tie, pulling it off with one tug. I yank at his shirt, buttons popping off in my sudden haste to get him naked.

When his shirt is fully open, I sit back and drink in the sight of him, all the gorgeous details I've only seen in my dreams for the past few weeks—the slopes of his hard pecs, the ridges of his torso, the line of hair arrowing down and disappearing beneath the waistband of his trousers.

His eyes are hot as he watches me spread my hands over

his chest, his muscles rippling with the force of his breath. I trace all the lines of his abdomen, back up to his chest and over his shoulders, reacquainting myself with the map of my husband's body.

When my core begins to throb again, I move back on his thighs to unfasten his belt and trousers, releasing his thick, erect cock. I close my hand around his smooth shaft, running my fingers over the pulsing veins.

With a groan, Dean grasps my wrist. "Need to be inside you."

I ease back up the length of his body, pressing my fingers between my thighs, shivering as another explosion rocks my insides. He sheds his clothes and rolls me onto my back again.

"I need you inside me," I gasp and arch toward him. "Do you have a—"

A faint relief curls through me when he reaches for a condom from his wallet. I want *us* back again before we leave things up to chance, and I want us both to go into our future knowing exactly what we're doing.

The air around us loosens, releases, as if all the pain of recent months has been a messy, snarled ball of knots that is now, finally, unraveling into silken threads of lust and love. Wrapping us in our own personal intimacy, the place where everything is right.

I roll the condom onto him before he moves between my legs to align our bodies. Anticipation unleashes inside me. I grip his shoulders, weakening with need as his thick erection slides into me. And then, finally, we're joined together again, a key fitting into a lock, our bodies straining toward each other and our hearts beating in unison.

Our eyes meet, glittering with passion. My soul overflows with an emotion so complex and intricate that the ties holding it together seem both indestructible and as fragile as gossamer.

I pull him toward me, pressing my forehead to his. Our breath mingles between us, hot and rapid. He pulls back and presses forward again, filling me, stretching me.

"Oh…" I run my hands down his back, my whole body vibrating with pleasure. "You feel so good… I've missed you so much…"

He lowers his mouth to mine. Our lips crash together in a collision of urgency, muscles tensing and flexing. He braces his hands on either side of my head and thrusts again and again. Intense need takes over, and our world dissolves into a chaos of moans and gasps, the deep push of his cock into my body, the heat flaring through our blood.

I cry out his name, lifting my legs to hug his hips, tightening my inner flesh around his pulsing shaft as bliss cascades through me. I feel the pressure releasing through his body, the delicious increase in the pace of his thrusts, before he presses into me with a heavy groan.

Panting, Dean rolls over and takes me with him, pulling me against his chest. We sink into the exquisite afterglow together, my body pressed to his side, right into the space where I will always fit perfectly.

⁐

Since the world will, unfortunately, not stop revolving just because Dean and I are together again, I force myself to wake early the next morning for a shift at the bakery. I stop at home to change and pack a small travel bag, as I have no intention of leaving the cottage for the next couple of days.

Though I'm tired after last night, my body hums with happy energy, and I'm in an excellent, friendly mood as I help customers with their croissant and baguette choices.

Because Dean is... well, Professor West—a man with an ironclad work ethic who values company time—he doesn't send me any sexy emails or texts while I'm working, though on my break I find a note from him in my satchel:

I'm muffin without you, beauty

I smile and send him an email:

> *Anyone can be passionate, but it takes real lovers*
> *to be silly.*
> *—Rose Franken, author and playwright*

Anyone can love, but it takes Liv and Dean to love like THIS.
    —Olivia West, Dean's very hot and sexy lady

After I clock out at the bakery, I hurry to the museum in the hopes that I can finish my shift there early. It's a cool, sunny day, green grass pushing through the melting snow as spring makes its final big push to overtake winter.

As I approach the Historical Museum, I see Florence Wickham getting out of a car parked in front of the building.

A member of the Historical Society's board of directors, Florence is a white-haired, elegant lady in her seventies wearing a belted camelhair coat and delicate, diamond jewelry. She sees me and waves. I walk over to greet her.

I've been a little embarrassed around Florence ever since she caught me and Dean getting hot and heavy in a coat closet at the Historical Society's holiday party last December, but she seemed more envious than horrified by the act. I suppose the fact that she left us alone to finish indicated her tacit approval of our sexy escapade.

"Hello, Florence." I take her elbow to help her step over a slushy puddle by the curb. "Looks like spring is finally in the air."

"Nice, isn't it, dear?" She glances behind me. "Is your husband with you?"

"No, he's working at the moment."

"Oh. What a shame."

"Indeed it is."

I hold open the museum door for her and follow her inside. We walk past the exhibition rooms to the Historical Society offices at the back of the building.

"Is there a board meeting today?" I ask Florence, as we take off our coats and hang them on a rack in the hallway.

"Monday morning." Florence pats her hair into place. "We're discussing the fate of the Butterfly House, that old place over on Monarch Lane. It's in such an ideal location by the mountains, both overlooking the lake and close to town, that developers have been trying to purchase the land. Of course that means they would demolish the house."

"That would be terrible."

"Yes, it would," Florence says. "We've managed to prevent that so far because the house is historically important. It was bequeathed to the Society years ago, but unfortunately we can't afford to do anything with it."

She waves me into one of the offices, where a drafting table is covered with blueprints and photographs.

I pick up a black-and-white photo of the grand, old Butterfly House. It looks to be primarily an American Queen Anne-style building with a large front porch, decorated spandrels, and overhanging eaves. There's a balcony on the second floor, bay windows, and a polygonal tower rising from the front that makes it look like a fairytale castle.

"When was it built?" I ask.

"In 1890," Florence replies. "It was a beautiful place in its heyday."

"What's going to happen to it now?"

"We're starting a fund-raising campaign to try and restore it," Florence explains. "We thought we could open it for tours and such, but we're in a bind because of zoning laws. Also there's quite a bit of resistance to the idea of a site open to the public, since it's close to a residential neighborhood."

I pick up another recent photo of the Butterfly House that shows the extent of its disrepair—the front steps are decayed and overgrown with weeds, the door and porch scarred by graffiti, the windows boarded up, the shingles broken.

I'm suddenly reminded of a children's book I once read at Allie's store—*The Little House,* about a lovely cottage that began falling apart when no one was left to take care of it. And though I have a ton of stuff to do for the Wonderland Café, I find myself asking Florence if I can help.

"Oh, we would love to have your help, Olivia," she replies. "There's so much to do with researching the historical value of the home. Samantha told me you're writing the exhibition brochure, so perhaps you'd like to work on something about the Butterfly House's history?"

I agree, thinking I can do the work at home in the evenings. Florence and I spend the next hour going over all the photographs and documents that the Society has already collected pertaining to the house's history.

After I finish my museum shift, I finally get back to the Firefly Cottage close to three. I find Dean sitting out on the porch overlooking the lake.

My heart just *sings* at the sight of him, all rugged and handsome in faded jeans fitted to his long legs and a worn T-shirt beneath a long-sleeved flannel shirt. He extends his arms. I sit in his lap and burrow right up against him like a cat curling into its favorite patch of sunlight.

"Good day?" he asks, brushing his lips across my hair.

"Mmm. No work tomorrow, though, and Monday's my day off. I'm all yours for the next two days."

"You're all mine for the next two millennia."

He leans in to kiss me, and I lose myself easily in the moment. A light rain drives us back inside, which is entirely fine with both of us as we spend the rest of the afternoon watching a movie, making love, and reading. We order room service for dinner, though by the time we get to dessert, I'm starting to yawn.

"Long week," I say apologetically, as Dean nods toward the huge bed and tells me to call it an early night.

I crawl under the covers and fall asleep, waking only when Dean climbs in next to me a few hours later. I tuck myself against his side. After so much time away from my husband, just sleeping beside his strong body is arousing. My subconscious soon spins and twirls with a resurgence of hot dreams, mostly involving Dean in the guise of a sexy warrior intent upon ravishing me.

Heat slides through my body. I shift, imagining him all rough and commanding, fondling my breasts, his cock hard. I dream of straddling his thigh and writhing against him. In the fog of sleep, I hear myself moaning, feel his fingers rubbing my damp cleft, his breath on my neck. And though reality with my husband is always better than my dreams, I wake all warm and loose, even a little sweaty.

Leaving Dean to sleep, I take a shower and wrap myself in one of the fluffy hotel bathrobes before grabbing my brush and going back out to stand in front of the mirror over the dresser.

"What were you dreaming about?"

My brush tangles in my wet hair. I yank it out and turn to stare at Dean. He's lounging on the bed wearing only a pair of pajama bottoms and a rather smug expression.

I frown. "What do you mean?"

"You were having a major sex dream last night."

Oh, lord. The images flood back into my mind, pornographic and vivid. I clear my throat.

"I was not."

"Uh huh." He grins. "You were moaning and everything. Very lusty."

A blush heats my face. "I was not."

"Yeah, you were. Got me all hot too."

As much as I don't want to admit to actually acting on a sex dream, it would certainly explain why I woke up feeling really good.

"So what were you dreaming about?" Dean asks again.

I turn back to the mirror and continue dragging the brush through my hair. I can still see him in the mirror, watching me with that cat-ate-the-cream look.

"Stop it," I mutter.

"Don't you want to know what else you did?"

"I didn't do anything."

"Oh, you did something. You rode my thigh, then spread your legs so I could finger your pussy."

"Dean!" I turn to face him again, my pulse leaping. "Did I really do that?"

"Uh huh."

"You are such a liar."

His grin widens. I stride toward the bathroom. As I pass him, he bolts upright and reaches to grab me around the waist. With a shriek, I tumble onto the bed. He moves over me and straddles my thighs, locking his hands around my wrists and pinning them to either side of my head.

The look he's giving me—teasing but hot—is enough to

spike my arousal higher. I buck my hips upward half-heartedly to try and throw him off. His grip on my wrists tightens.

He leans down to press his lips against mine, his tongue doing a slow sweep of the inside of my mouth. He tastes like mint.

"What were you dreaming about?" he whispers.

I'm starting to melt. I try to strengthen my resistance. "None of your business."

"Come on, beauty." He presses kisses along my lower lip. "Were you dreaming about getting fucked in public?"

I shake my head. His erection is starting to poke against my belly.

"Or about being with a woman?" he asks.

That thought makes his cock swell hard.

I shake my head again.

He shifts his hips, pushing against me. Since I just got out of the shower, I'm naked beneath my robe. One tug at the belt and he'd be sliding his cock against my bare skin. I draw in a breath. My heart is thumping, especially with him straddling me and looming over me the way he is.

"So?" he asks. "What was it?"

I stare at the bulge in his flannel pajama pants. "You."

"Yeah?" He's still rubbing up against me. "What were we doing?"

A blush begins to creep up my neck. "Um, you know. Having sex."

He pauses and eyes me skeptically. "What kind of sex?"

"Regular… just regular sex." I try to keep my voice casual, but he's not buying it.

Dean sits back on my thighs and continues to look down at me.

"Your reaction was pretty hot for regular sex," he says.

"Well, you did say I was lusty," I remind him.

"Which is exactly why I don't believe you were having a dream about *regular sex.*"

He tugs at the knot on my bathrobe belt. I squirm and try to buck him off again. He pulls the knot loose and eases apart the flaps of my robe.

"Very nice." He gazes down at my damp skin—though I don't know if that's from the shower or if I'm starting to sweat.

Then he palms my breasts and runs his fingers across my hard nipples. His touch is light, gentle, and delicious. I press my legs together because I'm throbbing.

"Tell me." He trails his hand down to my belly button, then lower to brush my mons. "Tell me and I might let you come."

Oh, God. I'm helpless against that kind of talk, and he knows it.

"Dean."

"Uh huh. Where were we in your dream?"

"Um." My flush deepens. I twitch under his teasing touch. "On a… a ship."

He lifts an eyebrow. "A ship."

"Yeah. A… a pirate ship."

"A pirate ship." Dean stares at me before a glint of humor lights in his eyes. "And might I have been a pirate?"

I skirt my gaze from his and look at the ceiling. "You might have been, uh, the pirate captain."

He laughs, but it's so filled with affection and amusement that I can't be irritated. He leans down to kiss me again, his tongue stroking the corners of my lips. Desire rushes through me.

"The pirate captain, huh?" he says. "And what were you?"

"A captured maiden."

"And did I ravish you?"

"Totally."

He sits back and squeezes my breasts. "Tell me."

By now I'm getting so aroused I'll tell him anything if it means he'll give me an orgasm. I take a deep breath and shift underneath him, making sure his erection rubs against my belly again.

"You had me tied down in the... whatever it's called. The brig or something. Had my... my hands tied above my head."

"What were you wearing?"

"A long dress." I can't think straight with his fingers tweaking my nipples like that. "I can't remember why you captured me. I think you wanted my land or something. Maybe it was my house. Or maybe I owed you money for a—"

"Doesn't matter," Dean interrupts. "Get back to the ravishing."

"Well, you had me tied up down there, and then one night I heard you coming down the stairs. You threw open the door and stalked in, all angry and menacing. You untied my hands and ordered me to pull up my skirts."

"And did you?" His eyes are starting to get a little glazed with arousal, which makes me warm to the story.

"Uh huh. All the way up past my hips. Skirt and petticoats. Then you told me to pull down my drawers and turn around so you could see my ass. Next thing I knew you were standing right behind me. I could feel your breath on the back of my neck. Then you... you spanked me."

"I spanked you?"

"Several times. You were wearing leather gloves. It stung. Made my cheeks red. But it also made me wet." Now that my hands are free, I reach up to caress the bulge in his pants. "Then you told me to bend over a barrel."

"And you did."

"I did." I grasp the waistband of his pants and pull them down. When his large, beautiful cock springs free, I can't help sighing. "I knelt down on the cold stone floor and positioned myself over an oak barrel with my drawers down and my petticoats up. You told me to reach back and spread my…"

The blush fires my skin again. I can't help it.

"Spread your…" Dean prompts.

"Spread my pussy for you."

His cock pulses in my grip. The evidence of his reaction, his lust, has my blood burning.

"You did it," he says.

"While you watched," I add. Parts of the dream are still vivid, but other parts have faded with daylight. At this point, though, I don't care whether I dreamed it or am making it up on the spot. "Then I felt your hands skimming over my ass again, felt you kneeling behind me."

"I had my cock out, I'm sure." His gaze is hot on the movement of my hand on his shaft.

"Not yet," I say. "First you took my arms and lashed my wrists behind my back. I was completely helpless." At the gleam in his eye, I add, "And at your mercy. Then you took off your gloves and trailed a finger over my folds. Like you were testing how wet and ready I was."

His chest is heaving. "Then what?"

"You rubbed the head of your cock against my pussy."

I squirm. I want his hand between my legs. Shivers wash through me. He puts his hand over mine, indicating he wants my grip tighter. He sucks in a breath.

He looks gorgeous, all masculine and sweat-damp above me, his skin flushed, his thighs hugging my hips. I'm so turned on that one flick of his finger on my clit and I'd come like a rocket.

"Go on." His voice is strained.

"Then I felt you pushing inside me," I gasp, "and your hands gripped my ass which was still red and burning from the spanking. I felt you stretching me, filling me, but all I could see was darkness. My breasts pressed against the barrel, aching. I couldn't move my arms. Then you started thrusting, slapping against me, making my ass burn hotter.

"I was moaning and jerking against the barrel, astonished by the feeling of your cock sliding in and out of me. I couldn't stop my excitement, the urgency that drove higher and higher. I started pushing back against you, begging you to do it harder. Then you thrust so deep I felt it through my entire body, and that was it. I screamed and came all over your cock... oh!"

An orgasm pulses through Dean's cock like a wave. He grunts and pushes forward into my fist, spilling over my breasts and belly. It's a sight that has me gasping with need, but before I can say anything, he slides down and pushes my legs apart.

The instant his tongue swipes across my clit, I shatter. I clutch his head and moan as he closes his lips around me and urges every last sweet sensation from my body.

"Damn." He heaves in a breath and crawls up the bed to lie beside me. "Those are the kind of dreams you've been having while I'm gone?"

"Nice, huh?" Even so, the mention of him being *gone* elicits a twinge of sorrow.

I push it aside, snuggling into the warmth of the sheets and the heat of his skin. My pirate captain, my gladiator, my white knight. I rub my cheek against his bare chest and stretch.

"Hungry?" he asks, skimming his hand up and down my arm.

"A little."

He pushes out of bed, and I admire the muscular lines of his body as he tugs his pants up and goes to the kitchen. As the coffee brews, we dress and bundle up in our jackets, then take our coffee and toast out to the porch so we can watch the sun rise over the lake.

I squeeze myself into Dean's chair, half on his lap so I can stay pressed close to his lean, strong body. The coffee is hot, steam rising in whorls, the air cold, the sun streaked with red and gold. Whitecaps ripple the surface of the lake.

We stay out until the sun is hovering over the water, then we go back inside and sink deep into the whirlpool bath, soaping each other down until we're both breathless and wanting each other again.

I make him sit back this time, straddling his lap and easing his thick cock into me with one glide of my body. Then we're both panting and moaning, water splashing over the sides of the bath as I move faster and harder, and Dean grips my hips and pushes up into me. I come violently, squeezing his shaft inside me as some distant part of my mind wishes this would never end.

As the day progresses, that wish intensifies. We watch

a movie, leaf through some magazines, trade massages, play backgammon with a board that Dean finds in a cabinet by the bookshelf. We fool around, laugh, tickle each other, order room service, consider and quickly dismiss the idea of actually leaving the cottage.

I spend most of the day wearing Dean's sweater vest and nothing else. After dinner, I get dressed so I can do a little striptease for him in front of the fire—even though I forgot to bring along an extra set of sexy lingerie. Still the dance doesn't last long, as Dean growls his appreciation once before pulling me down on his lap and crushing his mouth to mine.

He fumbles with the clasp of my white bra, groaning at the sight of my bare breasts before hefting me into his arms and getting us both to the bed in three strides. I open my arms, feeling excited, happy, loved to the very center of my soul as my husband lowers himself on top of me and kisses me senseless.

CHAPTER NINE

Olivia

*A*fter weeks of wanting, hoping, needing, now finally… it's *us* again.

Spring flowers bloom from vases around the cottage, and a crackling fire burns off the chill in the air. Reddish clouds lace the mountaintops. The lake is a sheet of glass, but inside everything is coated in a golden light.

I roll over in the feather-soft bed, putting my hand out to find Dean. He's not there, but the sheets are warm from his body. I open my eyes and find him sitting in a chair by the French doors, dressed in unbuttoned jeans and a wrinkled white shirt.

He's twisting a loop of string between his fingers, his strong hands spread apart, the cuffs of his shirt pulled up to reveal his hair-roughened forearms, hard with muscle.

Warmth floods me. His thick hair, which has grown longer over the past few weeks, brushes the back of his collar. He's wearing his reading glasses, his forehead furrowed slightly in concentration.

He glances up and finds me watching him. A smile tugs at his mouth.

"Hello, Sleeping Beauty," he says, his voice a husky murmur that makes heat pool in my lower body.

I yawn and stretch, feeling my muscles lengthen deliciously. "What time is it?"

"Almost six. Coffee?"

"Not yet." I shift onto my belly and rest my chin on my hands. My mind is foggy with pleasure, my body still pulsing from the thorough fucking I received a few hours ago.

A shiver travels down my spine. This is it. This is the solution. And it's so easy. It's what we've both known all along—all we need is us. All we need is to be alone, cocooned again in our own private world where neither of us has to explain or overthink anything.

It's the place where we don't have to distinguish between Dean's need for control and my unending desire to give him everything. From the beginning, he has taken me places I didn't know existed, and he has always kept me safe. I'll follow him anywhere, and he knows it.

That will never change. And for the first time I realize… it doesn't have to.

Because the opposite is also true. Dean always has and always will follow me into unfamiliar territory, knowing that his heart is safe with me.

"Your plan worked," I whisper.

"Mmm." His gaze tracks over my body beneath the sheet. He untangles the string, then lifts his hand and makes a circling gesture with his forefinger.

My heart jolts. He puts the string and his glasses aside and pushes to standing. The sight of him coming toward me, all masculine grace and prowling heat, sends my pulse soaring.

Already hot with anticipation, I shift beneath the sheets so that my back is to him. I feel him stop beside the bed, grab a fistful of the sheet and pull it off. The cotton slithers over my body, cooler air brushing my naked skin. My breasts press into the mattress, and I bury my head against my crossed arms.

Dean settles his large palm against my ass, rubbing his hand in circles. A thousand quivers fall through me. I twist to look at him over my shoulder, my breath catching as his dark eyes meet mine. He's all disheveled masculinity, his muscles coiled with that taut, intense energy that has my heart racing.

I shift, wiggling my ass enticingly. I want that energy unleashed *on me.*

After another slow rub, he trails one finger down the cleft of my rear to where I'm already damp between my legs. I tuck my face against my arms again and surrender, feeling my whole body yield. Dean leans over me to press a kiss right below my left shoulder blade. Then he pushes himself between my legs, spreading my thighs wider as he probes me gently with his finger and circles my clit.

My blood flames. I start to push myself onto my knees, thinking this is what he wants. Still standing beside the bed, Dean grabs my hips and eases me back down. He tugs me closer so that my legs dangle off the side of the mattress. There's a rustling sound as he pulls off his jeans. I start to turn and look at him again, wanting to see his thick, erect cock…

"No." He puts his hand between my shoulder blades, urging me down again. "Don't move."

Excitement spirals through me. I curl my fists into the bed-covers, my heart pounding as I feel the hard knob of his sheathed erection against my folds. With a muffled groan, I try to push backward and impale myself on him. He gives a hoarse laugh, and in one movement, plunges into me so fast that I shriek.

"Dean!" I instinctively jerk forward against the sudden-ness of the impact and the tight, full sensation of his shaft.

"Don't move." Dean clutches my hips to keep me still, his breath rasping outward as he waits for me to adjust to his entry. He shifts, his sac pressed against my pussy, the hair of his legs abrading my inner thighs.

I part my lips to draw in air. Sweat breaks out on my fore-head. Dean lowers his full weight on top of my back, curling his hands around my wrists. He pins my arms to the bed. His flat belly presses against my ass, his legs tight against mine.

The muscular weight of him is overwhelming, pushing me into the bed, his cock throbbing inside me. I bury my face against the mattress. My legs already ache from being spread so wide apart. He tightens his grip on my wrists.

"Christ." He shifts, rubbing his stomach against my bottom. "So hot…"

He eases back and pushes forward again, entering me so deep my blood burns. I shift, trying to match his rhythm, but through my lust-drenched mind I realize there is no rhythm, not this time.

He pulls out of me and thrusts in at his own pace, surprising me with every move, every shift. His hands are steel bands around my wrists, his breath rasping against my shoulder, his chest a heavy weight against my back. I wiggle a little to rub my nipples on the sheet, easing some of the tingling ache, but I can hardly move beneath him. I'm overpowered, impaled, conquered.

Only when I stop trying to move does Dean settle into a rhythmic thrusting, his cock sliding in and out of me hard and fast. I struggle to take all of him, moans streaming from my throat as the air drenches with fire.

He fills me over and over, his stomach tight against my bottom and his groans hot on my skin. My whole body trembles, and before I can think past the fog of sensation, my arousal builds like a storm front.

I bite down on a corner of a pillow and squeeze my eyes shut as urgency spins like a whirlpool through me. Again and again, he pumps into me, the friction driving me to the edge, his thick, smooth shaft stretching me beyond what I've ever felt before.

"Dean." My voice almost breaks with strain.

He lifts his head, closing his teeth around my earlobe. "Tell me."

"I'm so close," I gasp.

"No." Still gripping my wrists, he eases his cock out of me. "I want dirty words coming from your pretty mouth."

"Dean, I…"

"Dirty." He trails his mouth from my ear to my shoulder and bites down gently on my skin. "Lewd. Raw."

I moan and turn my face against the bed again.

"Put your cock in me," I whisper. "Fuck me, please… I need to feel you again… need to feel you throbbing inside my pussy, need you to make me come, Dean, please…"

He eases partway into me again, slick and hot. I tighten my inner flesh around him. Explosions flare through my blood. I try to shift, rubbing my ass against his stomach. His breath rasps against my shoulder.

"I… I feel it." I can hardly speak past the heat in my throat. "I want… my clit aches, Dean… touch it, please, and I'll come all over your cock, I can't stand it anymore, fuck me and I'll do anything… anything…"

"I know you will," he whispers, scraping his teeth over my shoulder.

I strain against the pressure of his hands, but his grip on my wrists is inexorable. He fucks me again and again, so hard I lose all coherent thought as sensations overtake me. My body bounces against the bed, the sound of his flesh hitting mine filling my ears, the slick plunge of his cock driving me to the edge.

I rock my hips, aching to rub my clit, before he pushes his hand beneath me and splays his fingers over my core. Bliss shatters me at his first touch, and I convulse around his cock with a shriek.

When the sensations ebb, he pulls his hand away and eases back, clutching my ass as he pounds into me. My unending moans clash with his grunts, his thrusts so deep and fierce the earth seems to tremble.

I grab the sheets and press backward, my body aflame, as he pumps three times in succession and pulls out with a groan. Shivers rain through me as his warm seed spurts over my ass, and I look over my shoulder to watch him stroke his big cock, his sweaty chest heaving and his eyes half-closed with pleasure.

"Oh, fuck, Liv…" With another groan, he collapses on the bed beside me, reaching out to run his hand over my damp back. "I don't want to leave you again."

Through the haze of lingering desire, my chest constricts at the thought of him leaving *again.* Surely once was enough.

I shift to curl up against his side as our breathing calms. I'm painfully aware that today is Tuesday. I need to work. And tomorrow Dean needs to attend the Office of Judicial Affairs' mediation meeting.

I press a kiss to his shoulder and push myself to a sitting position. My body aches in a deliciously sore, pulsing way that I hope will last for a while. I want to be reminded of my husband every time I move.

We both get up and take our time showering and eating breakfast, as the cloud of reality sets in.

"I have to go," I say reluctantly, when I notice that it's almost eight. "I'm meeting Allie and Brent at the café to start remodeling."

Dean smiles, his eyes warming as he tugs at a lock of my hair. "Proud of you, lady."

I return his smile, pleased by his pride and my own ambition. We linger as long as we can, before I finally pull on my coat.

"What are you doing today?" I ask.

"Working from here, then meeting with Frances Hunter. We're going over to Rainwood this afternoon to deal with some conference stuff, but I'll be back before dinner."

"Can you come over then?"

"Of course." He winks at me. "That was my plan."

He slides his hands to my lower back and pulls me against him, settling our bodies together. I gaze at him, my beautiful knight, struck by how invincible he has always been, how powerful, how certain of his place in the world. Nothing and no one has ever defeated him.

That thought gives me a burst of courage and hope as I press a hand to his chest to feel his heartbeat.

"I'll come over around seven." He gives me a gentle kiss and turns me toward the door. "Call me when you're done at the café. I love you."

After I leave, still practically floating after the beauty of a weekend alone with my husband, I stop at our apartment to change into jeans and a T-shirt before going to the café.

The windows are partly open, a radio is blaring, and the whole place is in disarray. Brent has recruited some of his friends to help with the remodeling, and the floor is covered with drop cloths and torn wallpaper.

After greeting everyone, I grab a bottle of remover solution and start pulling off the old wallpaper. Later, Allie and I go to the hardware store to arrange for deliveries of paint, window trim, and flooring. In the afternoon, we meet with Rita Johnson, the magazine reporter who wants to write an article about the café.

It's a good feeling, even if it's still scary, this working toward something both new and risky.

The sky is starting to darken by the time I head home. I can't wait to see Dean again and tell him about the magazine article and our plans. Maybe he'll have a few more plans of his own too.

Anticipation fills me as I hurry across Avalon Street. I pull open the door of our building.

And stop.

A woman is sitting on the stairs, dressed in a leather jacket and jeans. Long, wheat-colored hair spills around her shoulders. Her blue eyes meet mine.

"Hello, Liv," my mother says.

PART II

CHAPTER TEN

OLIVIA

I have only one picture of me and my mother, and one of me and my father. I keep both photos in an envelope tucked between the pages of a tattered paperback copy of *A Tree Grows in Brooklyn.* I bought the book for a quarter at a used bookstore when my mother and I were living outside Seattle. The name *Lillian Weatherford* is written on the inside cover in large, looped penmanship. I've always liked her name.

Lillian Weatherford, whoever she was, has guarded my photos for the past twenty years.

The picture of my father was taken at Christmas when I was five. He and I are sitting next to the tree—a small fir covered with lights and artificial snow. He looks handsome, young, a smile on his face. His arm is around me, and I'm holding a white stuffed bear with a red ribbon around its neck. I look happy.

In the picture of me and my mother, we're in California. I'm thirteen years old. My mother and I are sitting beside a campfire, both of us smiling, our faces shiny and lit by the glow of the flames. We look alike, our hair pulled back in ponytails, our smiles almost identical. We look like mother and daughter.

I remember everything about this photo. I've shown it to Dean, of course, told him the story of where it was taken and who took it.

The man's name was North.

"North?" I repeated after he'd introduced himself.

"Short for Northern Star," he explained. "Parents thought I'd have a good, steady life with a name like that."

"Do you?" I asked.

"Life is always good," he replied with a shrug. "But rarely steady. Waves are always on the horizon."

He was a medium-height, bulky man with long, graying hair, a bushy beard, and an open, kind face. He wore old T-shirts, torn jeans, and ratty sandals, when he bothered with shoes at all. A few strands of his beard were tied into a braid and held with a tiny, red ribbon.

North lived and worked on a Northern California commune called Twelve Oaks, a fifty-acre farm near Santa Cruz that my mother had heard about through an LA acquaintance. We stopped there en route to Oregon—hoping for a free meal and bed for the night—and ended up staying for seven months.

It was a weird place, but I liked it. About fifty people and their children lived there, and they made their own soaps and grew organic herbs and vegetables—all of which they sold at farmer's markets and to local groceries.

"Heard you have rooms for visitors," my mother told North when we arrived, her car keys dangling from her slender fingers, wide sunglasses concealing half her face.

North nodded, glancing from her to me. I stayed by the car, my arms around my middle. We'd just come from the urban sprawl of Los Angeles with its brown-smudged air and clogged freeways, but I was trying hard not to hope that we'd stay for a while in this farmland right by the ocean.

"Visitors have to earn their stay," North told my mother.

"How?"

"Work in the kitchens or gardens. Help with laundry. Clean. Asha keeps the work schedule, so we can talk to her about it."

My mother crossed her arms. She was wearing a yellow skirt and a purple tank top studded with yellow flowers. Her long, wheat-colored hair fell in waves to her tanned, freckled shoulders.

"All right," she finally said, snapping her fingers at me. "Come on, Liv. Let's get settled. I need some rest after all that driving."

I dragged a suitcase from the trunk of the old car that had taken us so many hundreds of miles. North showed us a bedroom in the main house, then brought us to the kitchen where an older woman with frizzy, blond hair explained the work schedule.

"Liv can do that." My mother pointed at the column for gardening. "And cleaning in the kitchen, right?"

I nodded.

Asha wrote my name in the column. North looked at my mother.

"And you?" he asked.

"I'd prefer not to be outdoors."

"What are you good at?" North asked.

"She makes pretty jewelry," I put in.

"Well, maybe you can help out in the workshop." North nodded at Asha, who wrote my mother's name on the chart.

"We won't be here very long," my mother said.

"Doesn't mean you can't work," North replied.

North had been at Twelve Oaks for over a decade. He played the guitar, did macramé and woodwork, and was in charge of the commune's website. The day after we arrived, he took Crystal to his workshop and taught her how to use different tools and materials. He sold wooden bowls, signs, and decorations at art fairs and the farmer's market, so he was well-equipped to help Crystal with her jewelry making.

"He's nice," I ventured one morning when my mother and I were getting dressed. "Seems to know a lot."

Crystal shrugged, looking at herself in the mirror as she tied a purple scarf around her hair and applied lipstick.

"He's no different from the rest of them, Liv."

But he was. He was one of the few men who didn't seem interested in my mother sexually, and she didn't set out to try and seduce him. Maybe it was the environment of Twelve Oaks or the fact that she didn't have to sleep with him in order to stay… Whatever it was, I welcomed the change.

One afternoon when I was picking basil, North stopped by the garden and tossed me a flat, metal medallion, the size of a half-dollar, attached to a silver chain.

"What's this?" I caught it with both hands.

He squinted his eyes against the sun. "Read it."

The medallion had an inscription—*Fortes fortuna iuvat.*

"What does it mean?" I asked.

"Fortune favors the brave." North tilted his head. "Like it?"

Wariness coiled tight in my chest. I took a step away from him. Despite the fact that he was different, I'd had a shield up for a few years now, ever since a couple of perverts, my mother's so-called boyfriends, had messed with me.

"Uh, thanks," I said to North.

He studied me for a second. "You're like a turtle, you know?"

"A turtle?"

North thumped his chest. "Hard shell. Hiding. You been on the road long with your mama?"

"Since I was seven." I had no idea why I was telling him the truth.

"School?"

"I've been to a ton of schools."

"What'd you like most?"

"I don't know. English, I guess."

"Come on. Let's see where you're at." He tilted his head to the house where most of the commune members lived.

I wasn't really afraid, just because there were always people around and little risk that I'd ever be alone with North. My mother and I stayed in our own bedroom in the main house, where about a dozen other people lived. Bedrooms were private, but we shared the other living spaces and kitchen. Some members lived in small cabins dotted around the farm.

North nodded to the rough-hewn trestle table and took a stack of homeschooling workbooks from a shelf. Figuring I had nothing to lose, I did the work he gave me, then frowned at the look on his face.

"What?" I asked.

"You ought to know advanced algebra and geometry by now. Maybe even some precalculus."

I stared at him. With his shaggy hair and scraggly beard, he looked like he'd never set foot inside a classroom, let alone knew anything about mathematics.

"You know about that stuff?" I asked.

"Sure. I studied physics in college."

"You went to college?"

A wide grin flashed behind his beard. "You think I've been a hippie my whole life? Yeah, I went to college. MIT. Plasma physics was my thing."

I couldn't help laughing. "So how'd you get from plasma physics to organic gardening?"

He tugged at the tiny, beribboned braid in his beard. "Sometimes you end up on a different path than the one you started on, you know?"

I didn't, not really. I'd never started on a path by myself. I'd always just been dragged onto one.

North sat across from me at the table and opened a math workbook.

"So what made you take a different path?" I asked.

He shrugged. "Just life, Liv. No one's immune from anything."

"Are you sorry you left MIT?"

"No. Sorry about other things, though."

"Like what?" I knew I was prying, but I was curious. And North didn't seem to mind.

"I hurt people," he admitted. "Did a lot of hard living before I found Twelve Oaks. Drugs, drinking. Fights. Arrested a few times. Hit rock bottom when a girl and I partied too hard. I blacked out. She ended up in the hospital for alcohol poisoning. A doctor got me into a rehab program, and as soon as I was done I moved out here. Lived in Berkeley for a while before a friend told me about Twelve Oaks. Came here and never left."

"How long have you been here?" I asked.

"Twelve years, I think. Thirteen?"

I could see why he'd stayed for so long. It was a nice place. The fragrant smell of simmering marinara sauce came from the kitchen, along with the low hum of people talking. A woman sat sewing in front of the fireplace, and a few kids ran around outside, kicking a ball. Everyone seemed content, at ease.

Even my mother.

"So, look." North pushed the workbook toward me. "We'll start with basic concepts and equations. Work your way up."

I wasn't all that crazy about doing the work, but I knew I was behind most other kids my age when it came to education. And because I wanted to catch up, I agreed to meet with North every morning.

Some of the other kids in the commune attended public schools, but my mother didn't enroll me since the school year was almost over. The younger kids were homeschooled and worked in a cabin that had been set aside as a schoolroom.

The work wasn't always easy—North pushed me hard, even with things like trigonometric functions. He was a good teacher, patient and insistent even when I tried to claim it was all beyond my comprehension.

"Nothing's beyond your comprehension, Liv, not even the reaches of your own mind," he said.

I had no idea what he meant, but he was prone to statements like that. We studied in the morning, and I helped in the kitchen and gardens in the afternoon.

I got to know others in the commune. Greta, the woman with long braids and piercing blue eyes adorning her weathered face. Susan and Tim, a young couple with a new baby named Penny. Sam, Parker, Emily—seven-year-olds who surfed the Internet after making soaps and macramé baskets. Roger and Clara, teenagers around my age who'd lived at Twelve Oaks for five years.

My mother spent her nonwork shifts in North's shop. Whenever I went to find her, she was working on a new jewelry technique, or North was showing her how to use a special type of pliers or file. They sat next to each other at mealtime. She went with him to unload boxes for the farmer's market. He worked in the garden alongside her.

Not once did I see them touch each other. Not once did my mother spend the night away from our bedroom.

Near the barn, there was a stone-rimmed campfire and benches set up, and every night a couple of the men would build a fire. We sat around it, listening to people play various instruments, sing songs, tell stories.

I always sat silently, watching the flames, feeling the warmth around me.

One night I watched my mother. She sat on the other side of the fire. She looked different, younger. Her hair had grown even longer, and she usually wore it in a high ponytail to keep it out of the way. She hadn't worn much makeup since we'd come here.

North came to sit beside her, bending to say something

close to her ear. She laughed. It was a genuine laugh, unforced, and I felt it spread over me from across the fire.

In that instant, I never wanted to leave Twelve Oaks.

For several months, it was good. Then my mother saw the necklace North had given me. I'd put it in the nightstand drawer and almost forgotten about it. She found it when she was looking for her glasses.

"North gave this to you?" she asked, holding the disk flat in her palm.

"Yeah. A while ago. I can't remember what it means. The inscription. Something in Latin."

She had an odd look on her face. I didn't get it. I do now, but I didn't then. I just shrugged and returned to my book.

The following morning North and I were working on lessons as usual. He was explaining ratios in right triangles when my mother came in and sat beside me.

"Just thought I'd see what you're learning," she said.

I felt her watching me for the next few days. Felt that something was wrong, but I didn't know what. I hoped she wasn't planning for us to hit the road again.

"Come on, then. Test time." North thunked a book beside me as I sat drawing at the trestle table after dinner.

The kitchen had been cleaned and everyone was drifting outside toward the campfire. I made a face at the book.

"I hate tests."

"Never say you hate learning. It puts up a block." He rapped his knuckles against his head. "Makes it hard for the knowledge to get in."

I sighed, but pushed my drawings aside and opened a paper on which he'd written a bunch of equations. He left the room while I worked, then returned a half hour later to check the test. I sat there fidgeting.

Finally he wrote something at the top of the paper and pushed it back to me.

I stared at the blue circled number. "Ninety-four percent? Really?"

He grinned. "Really. See what you're capable of? You just have to believe you can do it."

He pushed his chair back and stood, then reached out to run his hand over the length of my hair. It didn't feel weird or remotely sexual—more like an approving, fatherly pat on the head.

"Nice job," he said. "We'll get started on pre-calc tomorrow."

He ambled out the door toward the campfire. I looked up and saw my mother standing in the kitchen doorway, staring at me. My heart hitched. I swore she was looking at me with hate.

❦

"What did you do with him?" My mother's question was low, simmering with anger. It was late, the campfire long died out, everyone in their bedrooms.

"Do with him?" I still didn't get it. As far as I'd always known, my mother's relationships with men were sexual, and there'd been no evidence that she had anything physical going on with North.

Her eyes narrowed. Her face had that hard look again, the one she hadn't worn in the months we'd been at Twelve Oaks.

"Don't play innocent with me, Liv. You think men haven't

noticed you're filling out? Why else would you walk around in shorts and T-shirts so tight your tits are visible?"

I stared at her in shock. My shorts came almost to my knees, and my T-shirts were baggy old things we'd gotten from Goodwill. And while I knew I was developing, I made a conscious effort not to draw attention to that fact.

"I… North's just teaching me algebra," I stammered.

"For *now.*"

"He's not a creep," I said.

"I know that," my mother snapped. "But throw yourself at him, and what's the man going to do?"

"You're wrong. I—"

"Turn around."

"What?"

"Turn around."

I had no idea what she was doing. I turned around. I heard her opening a drawer, then felt her grab my ponytail and yank my head back. I gasped. Pain spread across my skull.

"Crystal, what…"

"Shut up, Liv." She yanked harder, then I heard the sawing of scissors, the clipping as my hair fell away from my head.

"No!" I tried to pull away, but her fist tightened. Tears sprang to my eyes.

"Be still," she ordered.

I stilled. Felt myself cower, unable to resist the command. My heart shriveled.

She sawed fast, and the next thing I knew, the pressure released and she let me go. I spun to face her. She held the long coil of my hair in her fist, her expression still cold.

Tears rolled down my cheeks. I put my hand to the back

of my head, felt the shorn, tattered ends of hair close to my scalp.

"Now you'll learn something about vanity." She threw the ponytail at my feet and stalked out of the room.

I sank onto the bed and cried until my throat hurt. I didn't realize until then how much a part of me my hair was—how it both connected me to my mother and set me apart from her. Like her hair, mine was long, straight, and thick, but it was dark while hers was blond. For some reason, that distinction was very important.

When I finally dried my tears, I picked up the scissors and tried to even out the ragged mess my mother had left, but I only succeeded in making it worse.

Finally I threw all the cut hair into the trash and cried myself to sleep.

Everyone was shocked when they saw me the next morning. I mumbled something about my hair having been too much trouble, so I cut it off. After breakfast, I ducked outside to the garden. My mother was nowhere to be seen.

I was picking tomatoes when a baseball cap landed on the dirt in front of me. I looked up at North. He gestured to my hair.

"Thought your head might be cold."

My throat tightened. "Have you seen my mother?"

His expression closed off. He shook his head. I put the cap on and stood, brushing off my knees. I started back to the house when his voice stopped me.

"Hey, Liv."

I turned. He stood with his hands shoved into the pockets of his torn jeans, his bare feet dusted with dirt.

"You know where to find me, yeah?" he said. "If you need anything."

Dread curled in my chest. I blinked back tears.

"Yeah." I took a step away. "Thanks, North."

I hurried back to the house. The bedroom I shared with my mother was empty, all our stuff packed away. My dread intensified when I saw our car parked near the barn, my mother standing beside it.

She jerked her head toward the passenger seat. "Get in. We're done here."

"Wait."

We both turned at the sound of North's voice. He stopped in front of us.

"Goodbye, Crystal." He spoke in a distant tone to my mother.

She didn't respond. North looked at me, reaching out to hand me the picture of me and my mother beside the campfire.

"You take care, Liv."

I nodded. I pushed the photo into my pocket, where the medallion was safely tucked away. Other people came out to say goodbye, but my mother didn't let me linger. Within fifteen minutes we were on the road. I sat hunched against the passenger door, my arms tight around myself.

"You tried to sleep with him last night, didn't you?" My question came out bitter and sharp. It was the only weapon I had. "And he rejected you."

"Shut up, Liv."

I could almost see it—Crystal standing at the doorway of North's bedroom, all soft blond hair and creamy skin, her robe lowered just enough to show a hint of cleavage. But

North hadn't wanted her. Or if he had, not like that, not her sexuality, cold as a diamond beneath her beauty. Her humiliation must still be scorching her from the inside out.

Because everyone wanted my mother.

"You'd never be good enough for him," I said. "He turned you out like the whore you are, didn't he?"

She reached across the seat and slapped my face. I pressed my hand to my cheek. Tears stung my eyes. I knew then that I would leave my mother.

I will not be like you, I thought. *I will never be like you.*

CHAPTER ELEVEN

OLIVIA

"*C*an I come in?" my mother asks.

Her question breaks me from my shock. "What... what are you doing here?"

"I wanted to see you." She stands, running her hands over her thighs. "It's been a while."

"Yes, it has."

We look at each other for a second before Crystal picks up two bags on the bottom step. My hand shakes as I dig into my pocket for my keys and pass her on the stairs. I unlock the door and push it open, stepping aside to let her enter before me. She smells like lavender. Her favorite scent.

She drops her bag and a square, leather case on the floor, casting a glance around the apartment.

"Cute," she remarks. "Looks like a place you'd see in a magazine. How to make the most of a small space."

I follow her to the living room. I can't stop staring at her, some part of my brain registering the changes wrought by the past three years.

Her pale skin is uncreased by age, and she looks thinner, her pronounced cheekbones emphasizing her blue eyes framed by incredibly thick lashes. Her long hair is the color of wheat, streaked with red in the light, falling in waves around her shoulders. She's wearing jeans and a loose, floral-print blouse beneath a cream-colored leather jacket.

She's beautiful. She's always been beautiful. Slender like a dancer. Small-breasted, lithe. Though I'm a couple of inches shorter than she is, I'm heavier, curvier. Bigger.

Crystal is looking at me as if she's assessing me the way I am her.

"It's good to see you, Liv."

"Thanks."

"Where were you?" she asks.

"Working." I go into the kitchen and start to make a pot of coffee just to have something to do. "Where did you get in from?"

"Indianapolis." She follows me and leans against the door-jamb. "I was visiting some friends."

"You're still making jewelry?"

"Yes. I go to art fairs when I can but my car is on its last legs. I need to get it fixed soon." She glances around the kitchen. "So where's your husband?"

"He's…" *Shit.* I have no idea how to explain that Dean is staying in a hotel without sounding like we're having marital problems. "He's working too."

He's also coming over in close to an hour.

"He'll be here soon." I turn on the coffeepot. "Help yourself to whatever you want from the fridge. I'm going to take a shower."

I go into the bedroom and strip out of my clothes. Not even the hot spray of the shower eases the apprehension tensing my shoulders. I'd had tonight's outfit all planned, but I can't go out with Dean and leave my mother here alone. And certainly he can't come in and have the evening we'd both been hoping for.

I pull on a pair of jeans and a fleece shirt before returning to the living room.

Crystal is sitting on the sofa, rummaging through her bag. She takes an elastic band and winds her hair up into a long ponytail. Her movements are graceful and unconsciously elegant. Exactly the way I remember.

As a girl, I would watch in silence as my mother brushed and arranged her hair. Then when she'd leave, I would do the same thing with my own hair, looking in the mirror as I tried to copy her movements.

"So how long do you think you'll be in town?" I ask, attempting to keep my voice casual.

"A few days," she says. "Can I crash on your sofa?"

Crash on your sofa. Sometimes she'd ask a man that question when she was looking for a place to stay, but far more often than not, she didn't have to ask because they just invited her. And she didn't crash on their sofas… she always ended up in their beds.

"No," I tell her. "There's really not enough room here, as you pointed out."

"I don't take up much space." She eyes me with a touch of offense. "After all this time, you're seriously not going to let me stay?"

"Crystal, Dean lives here too. There's not enough room for the three of us." I don't think there's enough room in Mirror Lake for the three of us.

Dean and Crystal have only met once—for about an hour when we were living in LA. I'd heard from Aunt Stella that Crystal was staying in Riverside, so I contacted her to tell her I was married and ask if we could see her.

We met at a diner in Riverside for lunch. Though Dean already had an intense dislike for Crystal from the things I'd told him, he'd made an effort to be polite. Crystal was faintly hostile, annoyed that I hadn't told her I was getting married, and then defensive when I'd said I hadn't known where she was.

All in all, it hadn't gone well. Since then, Dean has not given a damn where Crystal is or what she's doing, as long as she stays far away from me.

I look at the clock. My stomach is tight.

"I'll help you find a hotel room, if you want," I tell her as I go to the door. "But you can't stay here."

I step onto the landing and close the door behind me before going downstairs. Not five minutes later, Dean crosses the street toward the building and opens the foyer door. Warmth fills his expression when he sees me, but his smile fades as he recognizes something is wrong.

"What?" he asks.

I grab his arm and lead him outside, where I know my

mother can't overhear us. My heart seizes with nervousness. I take a breath before speaking.

"Dean, my mother is here."

"What?" His eyes flash, his body stiffening with that protective instinct I know so well. "When did she arrive?"

"A couple of hours ago."

"What's she doing here?"

"She said she wanted to see me."

"Sure, after all these years, she wants to see you."

My stomach roils at the irritated tone in his voice. And, unexpectedly, I experience a surge of hurt at the implication that my mother does *not,* in fact, want to see me.

"Where is she?" Dean asks.

"Upstairs."

He reaches for the door. I grab his arm.

"Dean, don't."

"I want to talk to her." He yanks his arm from my grip and pulls open the door.

"No!" The word comes out like a bullet, surprising both of us.

He stops and turns to face me. I reach for his arm again. My heart is racing.

"I can handle it," I tell him. "She asked to stay here, but I told her she couldn't."

"Damned right she can't," he snaps. "How much money does she want to get the hell out of town?"

"She... she hasn't asked for any money."

"She will." His expression is set hard, all the warmth from just minutes ago dissolved into anger. "Give her whatever she wants, then tell her to go."

"Dean." I can't untangle the emotions spinning through me… lingering shock and confusion that my mother is here, and frustration that my husband is issuing dictates about what I should do.

"I can handle this myself," I say, my own voice hardening. "She's *my* mother. I don't need you to tell me what to do."

Irritation darkens his eyes. "Find a hotel room for her. I'll pay for it, since I doubt she can afford it. I don't want her near you."

"Dean! Stop it." Though I understand the root of his anger—God knows I've felt the same thing toward my mother over the years—I'm overcome by the need to keep him out of it, to prove to both him and myself that *I can handle it.*

I have a sudden flashback to the times I've witnessed Dean's rage toward people he views as a threat—his brother, Tyler Wilkes—and how everything leading up to those encounters and their aftermath almost broke us apart.

Fear stabs through me. Somehow, I manage to get myself between Dean and the door. I put my hands on his chest to keep him from pushing past me.

"Look, I'm going back upstairs," I tell him. "You go back to the hotel. It's getting late, so she might stay for one night, but that's it. I promise, I'll find a place for her to stay tomorrow."

His jaw clenches. "I'm coming home tomorrow."

Of course he is. He's going to swoop down and spread his eagle wings around me, even if I don't want to hide behind them anymore.

I'm struck by an unpleasant sense that how we both approach this new situation is critical. I curl my fingers into the lapels of Dean's coat and yank him toward me.

"Dean." My voice is stern and unwavering. "Look at me."

He does. His eyes are still glittering with anger and determination, his mouth compressed into a line. I use all my strength to give him a hard shake.

"Stop it," I snap. "Just stop it. I'm not a child anymore, and she can't hurt me the way she once did. Have you forgotten that I walked away from her when I was thirteen years old? I did that *by myself.* And you sure as hell are not coming home just because she's here, just so you can stand guard."

I take a breath and shake him again. "When you come home, professor, you're coming home for *me,* for *us.* You're coming home because you're back for good, and because home is where you belong. You are not coming home because you're angry and need to control everything. You are not coming home to shield me from a woman I've barely seen in sixteen years."

I push on his chest to make him step away. "Now you go back to the hotel and cool off. I'm going to go upstairs and talk to my mother. Don't you dare call me until tomorrow. In fact, just wait until I call you. Do you understand me?"

For a few seconds, he doesn't respond, doesn't even react aside from staring at me with that set expression. Finally, though, he nods. His jaw tightens at the same time, but it's a definite nod.

"Good." I move back toward the door. "Go. I'll talk to you tomorrow."

I wait until he turns and walks away, his stride long and rapid. Only when he disappears around the corner do I go back upstairs. A memory pushes at me of last December when I'd let Kelsey deal with an enraged Dean instead of doing it myself.

Not this time.

My heart is pounding hard as I go back into the apartment. Crystal is still in the living room, leafing through a magazine. She glances up.

"Was that your husband?"

"Yes. He had to leave again."

"He's not sleeping here?"

"No." I suddenly wonder why I even care what Crystal thinks of my relationship with Dean. I don't owe her any explanations. I don't owe her anything. "Actually, he's staying in a hotel down the street for a few days."

"Oh." She frowns, clearly coming to the obvious, though mistaken, conclusion. "So, what's the problem with me staying here then?"

"I don't think it's a good idea," I tell her. "That's the problem."

The *problem* is also that I'm pretty sure Dean was right when he said Crystal doesn't have the money for a hotel room.

I won't let Dean pay for one either, and I'm not too enthused about the idea of using my money, which is earmarked for the café. But I will if I have to.

"You can stay for one night," I tell Crystal. "Then you'll have to find another place to stay. There are a lot of hotels in town. I'll help you pay for one, if you need it."

"I don't want your money, Liv." She shoots me a look that seems to freeze the air between us. "Especially not so that you can kick me out of your house."

A reflexive protest rises in my throat that I'm not kicking her out, but I swallow it back down. Because I *am* sort of kicking her out.

"Look, you need to find another place to stay," I tell her. "That's it."

She shrugs, as if it makes no difference to her. I go to the bedroom and change into a nightshirt, then get some clean sheets and pillows from the closet. When I turn, I see her standing in the doorway watching me. I suddenly wish I'd put on my bathrobe.

"You've gained weight," she remarks.

"A little." No way will I tell her it's the last few pounds of my pregnancy weight that I still haven't quite shed.

"More than a little." Her gaze travels over my body through my nightshirt. "But it suits you. You have the kind of figure that would look disproportionate if you were too much slimmer."

I have no idea if she's complimenting me or slamming me. Or both.

"Uh… thanks?"

She smiles. "Sorry. I meant that you look good."

"So do you." I go into the living room and spread the sheets on the sofa. "There's an extra toothbrush and toothpaste in the bathroom drawer."

She goes into the bathroom, and I hear her moving around, the water running, drawers opening and closing, before she emerges in a thin cotton robe, her hair twisted into a loose knot at the nape of her neck.

I get out my old quilt and toss it onto the sofa. "So… I'm sorry about…"

I don't even know what to say. *Your mother? My grandmother? Elizabeth Winter?*

"Your mother," I finally say.

Crystal shrugs. "Hadn't seen her in well over twenty years. Didn't even know she was sick."

An uncharitable thought rises like pond scum in my mind. *Does Crystal know about the inheritance? Is that why she's here?*

I study her as she puts a few things back into her suitcase. Nothing on her face would indicate that her mother's death affected her in any way.

"You had no contact with her?" I ask carefully.

"Why would I want to? She threw me out when I got pregnant with you. Then she refused to take us in when I needed her help after we left your father."

"How did you hear that she'd died?" I ask.

"Stella. She had my last address and sent me a note. I'd assumed she told you too."

I make a noncommittal noise. I wonder if this means my mother never heard from Elizabeth Winter's lawyer.

I shift the topic of conversation, and we discuss our lives in a polite, cordial manner. Crystal asks about places Dean and I have lived, tells me where she's traveled and what she's been doing.

She spent a year in Seattle working at a jewelry store, and has lived in LA, Austin, and Denver. Albuquerque, Portland, San Francisco. She's worked in nightclubs, hair salons, clothing stores, yoga studios, food co-ops, florists. She's sold her jewelry at art fairs, beaches, craft shows, street festivals.

"Do you like it?" I ask. "Living that way?"

"Who wouldn't like that kind of freedom?"

Me, for one, though I don't bother telling her that. She already knows.

"What's in there?" I ask curiously, nodding to the black case by the sofa.

"My jewelry."

"Can I see some of it?"

A faint surprise flashes in her eyes. "You want to see my jewelry?"

"Sure."

She hefts the case onto the coffee table and unlocks it. She opens little compartments and drawers to show me dozens of pieces—gemstone necklaces, beaded earrings, shell brooches, dozens of the woven bracelets and anklets I remember from years ago.

"The detail work is beautiful." I study a blue-and-white bracelet woven in a crisscross pattern.

"I took a few classes, learned some new techniques."

I look at a necklace with wire-wrapped green stones and a brooch painted with the image of a flower. They're pretty, obviously done with care and more expertise than I can recall Crystal possessing.

"Aunt Stella once said you wanted to be a fashion designer."

My words come out unbidden, almost as if someone else had spoken them. I tighten my fist on the brooch and look at my mother.

She doesn't respond right away, but the edge of her jaw tenses. "So?"

"Is it true?"

"I wanted a lot of things, Liv." She puts a few earrings into a drawer and slams it shut. "Doesn't mean I got any of them."

I'm struck with the urge to apologize—I know her life didn't turn out the way she wanted because she got pregnant with me. But I can't apologize for having been born. I have to swallow hard to push the *I'm sorry* back down.

She continues putting the jewelry back in the case. "So what else has Stella said?"

"She said my... my father regretted how things turned out."

The words *my father* sound unfamiliar in my mouth. I don't talk about him at all. Don't think about him. He's a ghost, there and yet not there.

He was in my life for seven years—long enough for memories and images to bury themselves like seeds in my mind. But they never grew because Crystal was the sun, bright, hot, blinding. Whatever memories of my father I'd wanted to cling to withered under the force of her light.

Now, unexpectedly, they push through the dirt. There's a man with close-cropped hair and a youthful swagger. Tall and broad, a silver chain around his neck. He smelled of sawdust and sweat. Worked as a carpenter. He died in a car accident when I was eleven.

Crystal turns to put the bracelet away, slamming the little drawer closed.

"Your father should have regretted a lot of things," she says.

"Do you?" Again, it's like someone else is speaking.

"Jesus, Liv." Bitterness discolors her voice. "My whole life is a regret."

The next morning, after I tell Crystal about the Wonderland Café, she comes with me to see the building. I take her on a tour of the interior, telling her our plans for the lower-level *Alice in Wonderland* theme and the *Wizard of Oz* rooms upstairs.

"When you were a kid, you used to love places like this," she remarks, peering out the upstairs window at the view of the lake.

For some reason, the band around my heart loosens a

little at her remark. It's an odd comfort to realize that she remembers something about me when I was a child. Maybe I hadn't been as invisible to her as I'd so often felt.

"Hi, Liv." Allie's cheerful voice precedes her entrance into the room.

"Allie, this is my mother," I tell her. "Crystal Winter."

"Oh, I didn't know you were in town." Allie extends a hand to my mother. "Liv showed me your commercial a while ago."

My heart drops. Tension rolls through Crystal, straightening her spine.

"I didn't even know Liv had that tape," she remarks.

Allie glances at me with uncertainty, appearing to sense that this is forbidden territory. "Um, it was fun to watch."

"I'm sure it was," Crystal says.

"So, Allie, isn't Brent coming this morning?" I ask.

"He should be here any minute," she replies. "I'm going to finish up in the front room."

She gives me an apologetic glance before leaving. Crystal is still looking at me.

"I thought I got rid of that tape years ago," she says. "I distinctly remember throwing it away."

"I… I got it out of the trash." I'd been nine years old. Crystal had gone out for a singing gig at a nightclub, and I'd rummaged through greasy TV dinner trays to retrieve the tape from the garbage.

"Why did you do that?" she asks.

I have no idea. I didn't understand my mother. I just wanted *something* of her, even an old VHS tape of a cereal commercial. A cherub-faced blonde girl who looked so happy and seemed like she had a bright future.

"I wanted to keep it," I finally admit. "You can have it back, if you want."

"No." Her voice is chilly. "I don't want it."

A clutter of voices drifts up the staircase. I tilt my head toward the door.

"We should probably go," I suggest.

"I thought you needed to work."

"Yeah, but you don't want to hang around here."

"I can help out." She digs into her pocket for a rubber band and starts to tie her hair up in a ponytail. "Just tell me what to do."

That's a role reversal, if I've ever heard one. She was always the one who told *me* what to do. After suggesting that she help strip the wallpaper from the front room, I go back downstairs.

I step onto the porch and call Dean on my cell. He answers before the first ring ends, but to his credit he waits for me to bring up the subject of my mother.

"As soon as I'm done here, I'll call around and find a place for her to stay," I assure him.

His breath escapes on a sigh. "Okay. You call me if you need me, right?"

"Of course." My stomach knots. "What time is the meeting?"

"Three."

"Look, why don't I come to the Firefly Cottage tonight?" I ask. "I know we have stuff to talk about, and I want to hear about the meeting. No one will bother us there."

"What time?"

"Seven. But promise me you won't get all blustery and caveman, okay? Just be cool."

"As a cucumber, baby."

Though he forces a light tone and I laugh, the tension between us doesn't dissipate much. We discuss our plans for the day before I end the call, waving at Max Lyons who is crossing the street with a tray of takeout coffees.

"Trying to stay on your daughter's good side, huh?" I ask, holding the door open for him.

"You got it. She's like a piranha if you get on her bad side." He puts the coffees on a table and looks around at the disarray of the place. "Good start."

"The tearing down is always easier than the putting back together," I remark.

He smiles. "But the putting back together is always worth it."

We both glance up as Allie comes downstairs with her portfolio in hand, Crystal following.

"Liv, your mother was just telling me about her jewelry design," Allie says, and her worried expression elicits a wave of apprehension in me.

"I offered to help with the murals," Crystal explains. "Allie said you weren't sure what to do with the borders, or along the tops of the walls."

"Um, a few friends of mine are going to help too," Allie says. "Don't want there to be too many cooks or anything."

While I'm grateful that Allie is trying to provide me with an excuse to reject Crystal's offer, I give her a reassuring shake of my head. It's not Allie's job to play referee between me and my mother.

"That's nice of you," I tell Crystal. "We'd appreciate your help."

Allie moves to pick up one of the coffees, shooting me an

encouraging, *it'll be okay* smile. She introduces her father to Crystal before heading back upstairs.

Max steps forward to shake Crystal's hand, and I see him look at her with that purely male appreciation that she's so accustomed to receiving. She's beautiful with her long hair pulled back to reveal the elegant lines of her neck, wearing a soft, pastel pink T-shirt that stretches across her breasts and slender waist.

To my shock, my reaction is visceral, as my heart kicks into gear and my stomach tenses. That *look,* that blatant appreciation of her beauty, was always the beginning.

After that, the men would invite Crystal—and me, by extension—into their houses, trailers, apartments. I'd try to be invisible, try not to exist, try not to wonder how long we'd live with *this* man *this* time.

Inevitably Crystal would go into the man's bedroom with him, and I was alone and anxious in another strange place, unable to avoid hearing the moans and grunting as I waited for my mother to come back out again because she was all I had.

I turn away, grabbing a cup of coffee. I take a quick swallow, hoping the heat will burn off the anxiety icing my whole body.

I hurry into the other room, where Brent and his friends are working. I get a wallpaper stripper and start tearing off long strips of paper. Kelsey comes in through the back door, her arms loaded with catalogs of kitchen supplies.

"Marianne asked me to drop these off," she tells me. "And I took out a few ads for the head chef position, so you should expect applications soon."

"Great, thanks." I follow her to the front room, somehow calmer in her no-bullshit presence.

Crystal and Max are still talking, but they break apart when I step in to introduce Kelsey to my mother. Kelsey's eyes narrow behind her glasses, but her voice is pleasant as she and Crystal exchange greetings.

A rush of affection for Kelsey fills me. Like Allie, she doesn't know all the details of my relationship with Crystal or my childhood, but she knows it's both painful and complicated. For her, that's enough to be wary of my mother.

"So how long are you staying?" Kelsey asks.

"I don't know yet." Crystal reaches back to tighten the band around her ponytail, the movement arching her back just enough to press her breasts forward. "I just wanted to see Liv. My mother passed away recently, so I was thinking I should go to Phoenix and see about her house and belongings at some point. Sooner rather than later, I suppose, since Liv won't let me stay with her."

A hundred curses race through my head and heat my blood. Somehow I manage to keep the anger from my voice as I say, "You know how small our apartment is. There isn't room."

"I wasn't complaining, Liv," she replies. "I'm saying that if I don't find a place to stay, I'll have to leave. And I'd hate to do that so soon considering I just got here."

"I told you I'd help you pay for a hotel."

"I don't want to take your money. That's not why I came to visit you." She looks at me with something resembling disappointment. "But never mind. I'll figure something out."

She shrugs as if to say there's no help for it. A tense silence descends. I slide my gaze to Max Lyons. He's looking at my mother.

Of course he is. I know exactly what happens next. He'll

come to her rescue, pained by the thought of her having to leave Mirror Lake after she just arrived to visit her daughter.

He'll offer her a place to stay, and she'll be ever so grateful as she agrees to go home with him. She'll go into his house, into his bedroom, and in exchange she'll let him into her body, and she'll stay with him until she gets antsy or bored or just needs a change, and then she'll leave and find someone else.

If it were any other man, I wouldn't care.

But even though I don't know him well, Max Lyons is attached to my circle of friends, my life here in Mirror Lake, my new business, even my husband.

I still shouldn't care. He's an adult who can do whatever he wants. I have no right to be angry if he hooks up with my mother.

He begins speaking to her in a low voice. She nods, keeping a slight distance between them. She's never been explicitly sexy, never needed low-cut blouses or tight skirts. She's secure in her own skin, knows that she's beautiful, knows how much men desire her. She knows how to get what she wants by giving them what they want.

My throat aches suddenly. I see Kelsey watching Max and Crystal too. Her eyes are ice-blue behind her glasses. She turns and walks to the door.

"Hey, Liv, get those orders in to Marianne soon, okay?" Kelsey calls over her shoulder, letting the front door slam shut behind her.

"Crystal, we should get going," I say, interrupting her and Max's cozy chat. "I thought you might want to look around town for a while."

"Oh, sure." She glances down at her clothes. "Can we stop at the apartment so I can change?"

"Okay." I grab my satchel, tightening my hand on the strap as Crystal approaches me. Tension grips my shoulders. The scent of lavender fills my nose.

"I was just thinking it over," I tell her. "Maybe you can stay with me for a couple of days after all."

CHAPTER TWELVE

I beat up the heavy bag at a downtown gym this morning, but I'm still mad. I don't like Crystal Winter and never will. Not only did she fuck up Liv's childhood, she failed in the worst possible way to protect her own daughter.

Every time I think about it, rage heats my blood. Every time I think about the fact that she's *here*, that she could potentially hurt Liv again, I want to hit something. It's all the worse because I can't do anything about it. Because Liv doesn't want me to.

I force the thought aside. Try to redirect my anger. Everything seemed almost manageable when I was working on the dig and thinking of ways to court my wife again, but now I don't know what the hell to do.

I've been banned from setting foot on the King's University campus. I'm not even allowed to go to my office or the library. Ben Stafford, director of the university's Office of Judicial Affairs, set up this "phase one mediation meeting" in a private room in the basement of a downtown bank.

Feels like a goddamn prison. No windows. Fluorescent lights. Stale coffee.

Maggie Hamilton is sitting across from me, next to her father. Edward Hamilton is a big, gray-haired man who looks like he wants to leap across the table and rip me a new one.

Part of me wishes he'd try it so I'd have an excuse to fight back. My fists clench. Frances Hunter shoots me a warning look.

She told me I didn't need a lawyer yet, and Stafford advised not having one present at this stage of mediation. Though I agreed, I've contacted a man whose firm specializes in sexual harassment cases. Edward Hamilton is a lawyer, and he'll know exactly how to fuck with me. I need all the defense I can get.

After introductions and a summary of the charges, Ben Stafford starts in with questions.

"Miss Hamilton, you say you never established a thesis proposal topic when Jeffrey Butler was your advisor?"

Maggie shakes her head. She looks sweet and innocent in a green sweater and gold necklace, her blond hair loose around her shoulders. She hasn't looked at me since this meeting began. Hasn't looked at anyone, in fact.

"That's correct, Mr. Stafford," she says. "I did my coursework when Professor Butler was my advisor, but he retired before I could establish a thesis topic. So when Professor West took his place, I thought it would be easy enough to get started writing my thesis."

"But you claim Professor West has yet to approve your proposal."

"Yes, sir."

"What is the suggested topic, Miss Hamilton?"

Maggie blushes. The girl actually blushes. Apprehension digs into my shoulders.

"Well, Professor West suggested I write about Trotula of Salerno, who was a thirteenth-century female physician." Maggie rubs a finger on the table. "Professor West wanted me to research medieval views of women's sexuality."

Shit.

"When I first joined the King's faculty, you came to me with that topic," I say, unable to prevent the angry bite in my tone. "You said you'd done some research the previous summer."

"My daughter said that you insisted on it," Edward Hamilton snaps. "That you forced her to—"

"Quiet, please, both of you," Stafford interrupts. "Professor West, you'll have a chance to respond when it's your turn. Please remain quiet until I've finished questioning Miss Hamilton."

I sit back and try to inhale. My apprehension deepens.

"So, Miss Hamilton, you claim Professor West suggested the topic of medieval women's sexuality," Stafford says.

"Yes. I should have been suspicious, but it seemed interesting at first. Until he started suggesting that I read books about gynecology and menstruation... stuff I wasn't comfortable discussing with a male professor."

"Did you tell Professor West about your reservations?"

"No, because I was afraid he'd make me start the process

all over again. Then when he suggested that he'd only approve the proposal if I… if I submitted to him…" Her voice trails off plaintively.

The girl missed her calling. She should have been an actress.

"How did Professor West make that implication?" Stafford asks.

"He said that if I did what he wanted, he'd approve my proposal and we'd both be happy," she says. "Then he tried to kiss me."

I can't fucking stand this. Edward Hamilton looks like he's about to explode. Frances puts a warning hand on my arm.

"Professor West has suggested the opposite took place," Stafford says. "That you, in fact, offered sexual favors in exchange for his academic support."

Maggie shakes her head. "No, sir."

Stafford glances at me. "Can you explain what happened in your view, Professor West?"

"Miss Hamilton and I had had conflict over her proposal all summer," I explain. "She inappropriately approached my wife and asked for her help convincing me to approve her proposal. My wife told me about the encounter, and I confronted Miss Hamilton and told her she needed to change advisors. She was upset because she said changing advisors would mean she had to take her coursework all over again, and that would delay her graduation schedule."

"Would it?" Stafford asks.

"Yes, but that was her fault," I reply. "She had no right to approach my wife. Since Miss Hamilton was placed under my advisement, she has done no valuable research and taken none of my suggestions. So when I told her to change advisors, she got upset and asked me what it would take to get her proposal approved."

"And you interpreted that as an offer of sexual favors?"

"Yes."

"At any time did Miss Hamilton explicitly offer sexual favors to you?"

"Not explicitly, no, but the implication was clear."

"What was your response, Professor West?"

"I asked her to leave my office."

"Did you ever try to kiss her or touch her?"

"Never."

"Did you ever make sexual or inappropriate comments to her?"

"Never."

"Ever do that with another student?" Hamilton snaps at me.

"Mr. Hamilton, please," Stafford says. "I will ask the questions."

I stare at Hamilton from across the table. There's something weirdly triumphant in his expression that makes my stomach turn.

"I must tell you again, Mr. Stafford," Frances says, "that none of Professor West's other students have even hinted that his behavior has been anything but professional."

"I understand that, Professor Hunter, but it's my job to investigate every angle." Stafford consults his notes again. "Professor West..."

I hold up a hand to stop him, not taking my eyes off Edward Hamilton. "What did you mean by that question?"

Hamilton jerks his chin at Stafford. "Ask him."

Stafford sighs. "Mr. Hamilton..."

"Ask West about his wife," Hamilton orders.

Rage flashes through me. My fists clench.

"What about my wife?" I demand.

"Professor West, you stated that you never had a sexual relationship with a student," Stafford says.

"That's correct."

"But according to official records, your wife was a student when you were a professor at the University of Wisconsin."

My heart seizes. "Yes, but she wasn't my student."

Hamilton barks out a laugh, as if that makes no difference.

"She was *a* student, Professor West," Stafford says. "When did you begin a relationship with her?"

A sick sense of foreboding fills my throat. "I'm not talking about this."

"You'd damn well better talk about it," Hamilton says. "You have a precedent for screwing students, and if you think—"

I'm out of the chair in less than a second, rage blinding me as I reach for him, wanting to smash that smug expression off his face, shut him up. I hear Maggie's gasp, feel both Frances and Stafford grab my arms.

"Dean!" Frances snaps. "Sit down."

"Go on, do it," Hamilton tells me, his voice hard. "I'd love to hit you with an assault charge."

"Fuck you." I want to beat him until he bleeds.

"Dean, sit down!"

Somehow Frances's voice penetrates my rage. I sit down.

"Everyone, please calm down," Stafford orders, tapping his finger on a piece of paper. "Mr. Hamilton, if you and Miss Hamilton will sign your statements, I will continue this meeting alone with Professors West and Hunter."

Edward Hamilton glowers at me. For a second I don't care what I'm charged with if I can beat him to a bloody pulp. Then he gestures for Maggie to get her things and sign the paper.

As they do, Frances leans toward me to whisper, "Calm down right this second, Dean. If you don't, they'll have more ammunition against you and will just dig deeper. Is that what you want?"

I shake off her grip and take a breath. My heart is racing.

After the Hamiltons leave, Stafford sits back down and pins me with a look.

"How the fuck does Hamilton know about this?" I ask.

"He's looking into things on his own," Stafford explains, "which is within his rights as long as he doesn't impede the OJA investigation. I assure you I have not given him any information. Now when did you start a relationship with Olivia Winter, Professor West?"

I dig my fingers into my palms and try to block an image of Liv. "I'm not talking about this."

"*You'll* be impeding the investigation if you don't," Stafford warns me.

I shove away from the table and stalk to the other side of the room. I force the words out of my throat. Try not to think about her. Try not to remember.

"September," I finally say. "The year I started my visiting professorship."

"So right about the same time you started the job," Stafford says.

I sense Frances's sudden wariness.

"It wasn't against university policy." I battle another surge of anger. Sweat erupts on the back of my neck. "I checked, before I even asked Liv out. As long as a student isn't under a professor's authority and the relationship is consensual, it's not against regulations."

Stafford sighs. "I'm afraid that's not the point, Professor West."

"What *is* the fucking point?"

"The point is that Olivia Winter was a student," Stafford says. "You were a professor. And when I asked you in January if you'd ever had a sexual relationship with a student, you responded that you had not."

"The question implied a student *of mine,* which Liv was not." I want to throw something against the wall. "I have never had a sexual relationship with a student *of mine.*"

"Any other students, of yours or otherwise, that I should know about?" Stafford asks.

"No." *Goddammit.*

Stafford studies me for a minute before collecting his notes. "Well, this discovery has delayed things further, Professor West, and I'll have to include it in my report. I'd appreciate your cooperation if anything else relevant to this case comes to mind. I should have things wrapped up soon."

Provided we don't end up in front of the university's board of trustees.

Stafford says goodbye and heads out, closing the door behind him.

I try to breathe, but my chest is so tight it hurts. I can't stand the idea of Liv getting anywhere near this shitstorm. I'd hoped it would be over by now. Instead it's like a deadly virus that won't go away.

Frances is still glaring at me. "This isn't good, Dean."

Shut up, Frances.

"I didn't do anything wrong." I tug at the knot of my necktie. "There was never a goddamned thing inappropriate about my relationship with Liv."

"As Mr. Stafford said, that is not the point. Words are power, Dean, and the words *student* and *professor* and *relationship* do not go well together."

I stare at the empty whiteboard on the opposite wall. "I'll quit, Frances."

"Dean—"

"If it'll end this whole thing... I'll quit right now."

"That's as good as admitting guilt."

"I don't care."

"I think you do."

I turn to look at her. "Then what, Frances? I let that girl destroy my career?"

"You need to let the process play out."

"Bullshit. Her father will take me down, no matter what. You know it as well as I do. Now that he knows about *Liv,* for God's sake... I have no defense."

Which means all I can hope for is that Maggie will withdraw the accusation. And I have no idea what it would take for her to do that.

"Will the administration make a deal?" I ask Frances.

"No. That would look worse for them than having a professor accused of sexual harassment."

"Then what needs to happen?"

"When the OJA finishes their investigation, they'll determine if they have enough evidence to pursue the case. If they don't, they'll dismiss the charge."

"Which will never happen with Edward Hamilton breathing down their necks and considering a goddamned donation to the university. So I'm found guilty of something I didn't do and am fired from my job. Maggie returns to King's, gets her degree, then goes off to law school with her father's money."

Frances doesn't respond.

I am so screwed. I can't see any way out of this, except to quit before things get really bad. I'll liquidate all my assets and leave the country. Take my wife to live on a remote island with white-sand beaches and sapphire seas.

Right as she's launching a new business venture. Right when she's finally found something that she wants to do.

I grab my coat. Fight the rage and fear scorching my insides.

If Edward Hamilton gets anywhere near my wife…

"I'm sorry, Dean," Frances says.

I can only shake my head. I leave the office, pulling in a few breaths of cold air. The streets are almost dark, puddles of yellowish light pooling from the streetlamps.

I walk through downtown fast, trying to force away the sickening realization that I'm stuck in quicksand with no way out.

And now I'm dragging Liv down with me.

CHAPTER THIRTEEN

OLIVIA

*M*y mother is making herself comfortable in the apartment. Her lacy bras and panties are hung up in the bathroom to dry, and a beauty case rests on the counter. Long strands of blond hair weave through the bristles of my brush.

I yank them out with a comb and toss them in the trash before dragging the brush through my own hair. I peer at myself in the mirror, pinching my cheeks to add color to them. I put on a green sheath dress and low heels, grab my purse, and go into the living room.

Crystal's suitcase is open and overflowing with soft, pretty clothes. She'd told me she was going out for dinner—in the parlance of my childhood, that also meant "I'm going to find a club, maybe a man"—and I'm glad I don't have to explain my own plans for the evening.

I stop at an Italian restaurant and get some takeout before going to the Wildwood Inn. The instant Dean opens the cottage door, my heart plummets. Tension coils through him like wire, and his expression is set with a combination of anger and frustration that sears me through the soul.

I attempt a smile and hold up the paper bag.

"Takeout manicotti and salad. Our second-date dinner."

Dean takes the bag from me and sets up the containers on the table, though I'm not hungry. He doesn't move to sit down and eat either. My skin prickles with foreboding. A longing to return to our private weekend hits me in the chest so hard that I almost can't breathe.

Dean turns to face me. Restrained energy vibrates from him, his innate urge to do something stifled by the dictate that he can't do anything.

"Is your mother gone?" he asks.

I shake my head. A current ripples between us. Dean narrows his gaze.

"What?" he asks.

"Don't be mad."

"Oh, shit, Liv… *what?*"

I take a breath. "I offered to let her stay with me."

He stares at me. I approach and put my trembling hand on his chest. His heart is racing.

"Dean, I know it doesn't make sense to you, that you won't understand, but—"

"Why, because I'm such a caveman?" He shoves my hand

away and stalks to the other side of the room. "What won't I understand, Liv? That your mother is poison? That she hurt you? That you've spent your life struggling with everything you went through?"

"That I asked her to stay with me so that she won't poison my life any more than she already has."

"What the hell does that mean?"

"If she didn't stay with me, she'd end up at Max Lyons's house."

He blinks in disbelief. "When did Max Lyons become part of this?"

"He was at the café this morning. I know my mother, Dean. I know she'd end up with him."

"So let her. Why does it matter to you?"

"I don't want her getting involved with Allie's father. I know it sounds strange, but I don't want her insinuating her way into my circle of friends."

His mouth compresses. "You're right. I don't get it."

"I have a life that's mine, not hers. I don't want her to be part of it. And I don't expect her to stay much longer anyway. She never stays in one place very long."

Dean exhales a heavy breath. "I hate that she was the cause of everything you went through."

"But everything I went through led me directly to you."

And aside from my friends, I really don't want my mother getting near my husband. I'm suddenly relieved that he's leaving Mirror Lake again soon.

"Our marriage is what matters to me now, Dean." I take off my coat and toss it over a chair. "I want this whole mess with the OJA cleared up, and I want you back home where you belong."

He gazes at me for a moment before turning to pace across the room. Silence, tense with things unspoken, fills the space between us. Anxiety clutches my stomach.

Dean stops by the window and turns again, sliding his hands into his pockets. The sheer masculine beauty of him floods me with awe—the way his shirt stretches across his chest and shoulders, the swathe of hair falling across his forehead, those perceptive, intelligent eyes that conceal so many complex ideas.

"Liv." He shakes his head. "I…"

His voice fades. I curl my hand around the back of the chair. I sense a sudden tangle of thoughts in him, his struggle to figure out what to say.

Professor Dean West always knows what to say.

A bolt of fear hits me.

"Hey." I go to him again and put my hands around his waist. "Remember that fantastic make-out session we had a few weeks after we started dating?"

A smile tugs at his mouth. "I remember."

"We could do that now, given that we're dating again. Well, dating with benefits, anyway."

Dean closes his hands on my shoulders, darkness shadowing his expression. I spread my palms over his lower back and tuck my fingers beneath his belt. I step closer, closing the scant distance between us and pressing my body to his. I almost moan at the contact of his chest against my breasts.

"Liv." Restraint cords his forearms as he tightens his grip on me. "We need to talk."

I don't think that in the history of time anything good has followed those four words.

I move my hand to the back of his neck, spearing my fingers into his thick hair as I pull his mouth down to mine.

Our lips collide with sudden force, stopping his protest. Dean mutters something against my lips, his surrender swift as he slides his tongue into my mouth and pulls me even closer.

Longing and lust unfurl between us. I clutch his shirt, sinking into the whirlpool of pleasure evoked by the touch of our mouths. The world seems to right itself, settling into balance again. I skim my tongue against his, over his lower lip, my blood streaming with light.

"Sofa," I whisper.

I grab his arms and walk backward to the sofa in front of the fireplace, keeping my mouth pressed to his until we sink against the cushions together, the delicious weight of his body over mine. Arousal billows inside me, shocking and delighting me with its intensity.

I grip the back of Dean's neck and bite down on his lower lip in a way I know makes him hot. A groan rumbles in his chest. His erection presses heavy and thick against my hip. My body throbs in response.

I run my hands over his chest to the knot of his tie. With a few quick tugs, I pull it off and drop it to the floor then urge him back to me.

Our kiss eases into a lovely, teasing rhythm of lips and tongues. Gentle kisses, heated stroking. Dean curls his fingers into the material of my dress, a shudder of urgency vibrating through him. I force my mouth from his, our breathing hard.

"Take off my dress." I fumble to reach the zipper at the back.

His eyes darken with that lustful anticipation I know so well. I manage to get the zipper down a little, and Dean reaches behind me to yank it the rest of the way. I squirm to get the dress off my shoulders and push it to my waist.

"Oh, fuck..." Dean's eyes glaze over as he stares at my breasts.

"Nice, huh?" I look down at the emerald-green, push-up bra, which displays my cleavage to great advantage, the satin edge brushing my skin.

"I'm about to come already." Dean spreads his hands over the bra, rubbing his thumbs across my taut nipples.

A shiver races down my spine. "There's more."

I wiggle my hips to indicate he should pull my dress off. His hands tremble as he grabs the material and tugs it down my legs to reveal the matching panties. Then he sits back and stares at me. My heart racing, I push up to my elbows as his gaze strokes the length of my body.

"You are so damn sexy," he says.

The hoarse note in his voice makes me quiver. I sit up to unbutton his shirt and push it off, revealing the musculature of his shoulders and chest. I skim my hands over all those hard ridges, then move lower to take his erection in my palm.

"I want to make you come," I whisper.

He groans and sits back against the cushions. I unfasten his belt and trousers, pushing them to the floor as his cock springs hot and heavy into my hand. I kneel beside him on the sofa and bend to swipe my tongue over the head of his erection, pushing my lower body upward.

Less than a second later, Dean strokes his hand over my bottom, which is covered tightly by emerald-green silk and lace. I gasp as the heat of his palm burns through the thin material. He edges his finger into the satin border at my thigh.

Urgency coils inside me, a desperation made all the sharper

by the things left unspoken. I grasp the base of his cock and lower my head again to take him into my mouth. His breath escapes on a hiss, his other hand tangling in my hair.

The salty taste of him fills my mouth, his shaft throbbing against my tongue. My breasts press against his thigh, the material of my bra abrading my sensitive nipples. I sink my mouth lower over Dean's cock, rocking my hips as his finger probes deeper beneath my panties.

I draw him in even farther and press my tongue to the smooth underside. *Up, down, lick, stroke, kiss.* His thighs tense, his hand tightening in my hair.

"Liv, I'm…"

I slide my mouth upward and to the head of his cock, squeezing his shaft just as an orgasm shudders through him. I take a breath and suck him deep, swallowing the semen pulsing into my mouth. When the vibrations ease from his body, I pull back and start to sit up.

Dean presses his hand to my lower back. "Don't move."

My heart jolts with excitement. I brace my hands on the other side of his lap and arch my back, moaning when he eases another finger into my damp cleft. The constriction of the panties heightens my tension.

I dig my hands into the sofa cushion and strain toward the exquisite release of pleasure. Dean touches my folds in the way I love, circling his forefinger around my clit as he reaches beneath me with his other hand to pull down the cups of my bra and fondle my breasts.

I come within seconds, bucking against him as sparks explode through my nerves. He eases every last sensation from me before I sink across his lap and try to catch my breath. He runs his hand over the length of my body, rubbing circles over my ass.

I roll onto my back and look up at him—my beautiful husband with his gold-flecked eyes still dark with arousal, his chest glistening with a sheen of sweat. I brush my palm over his torso as the lovely afterglow descends.

"How many of these do you have?" Dean runs his finger along the edge of my bra.

"About half a dozen. Maybe I'll do a fashion show for you one day."

"If you do, I'll give you a really big tip."

I wiggle against his cock and grin. "Yeah, I'll bet you will."

He returns my grin and helps me to a sitting position. Sliding a hand to the back of my neck, he pulls me in for a deep and thorough kiss that makes me tingle all over again.

After we part, I climb off the sofa, aware of his gaze on my rear end as I walk to the bathroom. I grab one of his T-shirts from his open suitcase and use the bathroom, then pull the shirt on over my head.

Pushing my hair away from my face, I return to the main room. Dean is zipping up his trousers, and the instant I look at him, my heart sinks. That air of somberness is back, hovering over him like a cloud.

I stop halfway to the sofa. Dean pulls his shirt over his shoulders. Against reason, my pulse kicks into gear again at the sight of him all disheveled and sweaty, his white shirt open to reveal his gorgeous chest.

I pick up my discarded dress and toss it over a chair. Dean watches me. A shutter descends over his features.

I sit down on the sofa, twisting the little ring Dean sent

me from Italy around on my finger. I can't think of a way to stop whatever it is he's going to say.

"What?" I whisper.

"I need to talk to you about the meeting."

"Okay. What... what happened?"

He sighs and drags a hand through his hair. "When I started teaching at King's, Maggie Hamilton told me she wanted to write about Trotula of Salerno and women's history. Since Trotula was a physician, the research included stuff about women's sexuality. Now Maggie is saying I was the one who suggested it, that she wasn't comfortable with the subject... that kind of shit."

"Oh, no."

"Yeah." His jaw clenches. "And when I was gone, Ben Stafford looked into my past jobs and positions. He found out that you and I started dating when we were at the UW. So now he's questioning the ethics of our relationship."

Shock bolts through me. I sink back onto the sofa. "The *ethics* of it?"

"Professor and student, right?"

"But I wasn't your student! We didn't do anything against the rules."

"Doesn't seem to matter. You were a student, and I was a professor. Considering a student is making this claim... it doesn't look good."

A sick feeling rises into my throat. My early relationship with Dean is one of tangled, intense beauty. The idea that strangers could make it obscene because of a vindictive girl's lies...

I press my hands to my eyes.

"What's Stafford going to do?" I ask.

"I don't know. But Edward Hamilton knows about it too, and he's accusing me of having a history of getting involved with students. If he finds a way to use that against me, he will."

My stomach tightens. No one knows about our early relationship, the secrets we told, the games we played, the talks we had, the desire we explored. No one except us. That's the very reason it was both beautiful and dangerous, like a secret island where we were uncertain of rescue… until we saved each other.

Our island. Our love. Our marriage.

I hate the thought of strangers dissecting it all, probing for something immoral and wrong, with Dean and I forced to defend the very foundation of our relationship.

"Oh, Dean."

"I know. I'm sorry."

Twenty-four hours ago, I was so happy I would have whistled a merry tune, if I knew how to whistle. Now I'm all knotted up and blistering again.

We look at each other. We both feel it, the sharp invasion of the rest of the world into our space. He shoves his hands into his pockets. His shirt is still unbuttoned, his hair sticking damply to his forehead. Silence stretches taut between us. I search for and find a measure of courage.

"What if I went to Ben Stafford and told him the truth?" I push off the sofa and pace to the windows. "Before either Maggie or Edward Hamilton can spread more lies?"

"No." His refusal is fast and hard, tension stiffening his shoulders. "No way. You're not getting anywhere near this."

"But I could—"

"No, Liv. You stay out of it."

I struggle with conflicting emotions of relief and irritation. No, I don't *want* to talk to Ben Stafford about my relationship with Dean, but at the same time I would do anything to end this slander.

"Maybe it would help," I persist. "I could tell Stafford how careful you were about ensuring you didn't break any regulations, that you've always been completely professional with students and colleagues. Everything I'd say would vouch for your character, right? And no one knows you better than I do."

"You know me as your husband. You don't know me as a professor."

I blink in surprise. "What does that mean?"

"You don't know how I interact with my students." Dean turns away, dragging a hand through his messy hair. "You don't know if I could've said or done something wrong."

"Of course you haven't done anything wrong!"

"What was the subject of my last research paper?"

"What?"

"The last paper I submitted to the *Journal of Medieval Architecture.* What was the subject?"

"I—"

"You don't know," he says. "And you don't know because it's not important to you."

Shame and irritation twist inside me. "You think your work isn't important to me?"

"What was the subject of my last paper?" Dean repeats.

My heart does a strange descent into my stomach. He turns to face me, his expression unreadable.

"Look, I don't care, all right?" he says. "It doesn't matter to me that you don't know I wrote about the chapels of the

Notre-Dame Cathedral. There's no reason it should be important to you. But that also means you don't know what goes on in my lecture hall, in my office, during meetings…"

"I know how good you are at what you do. Isn't that enough?"

"Liv, *I* don't even know if I did something wrong! Maggie Hamilton is right, goddammit. I did suggest books on sexuality and female anatomy. That was her thesis topic. God knows I could've said a dozen things that anyone could interpret as harassment. I said things to her about views of sexuality, prostitution, and contraception in the Middle Ages. She probably still has emails from me. And if Stafford asks me that in a deposition, I have no defense."

"You do have a defense. Your career and reputation are your defense. Everything I'd tell Stafford would just reiterate the fact that you're honorable to the core." I pause, aware of the rising shame again. "Even if I don't know your theories on the Notre-Dame cathedral."

"Liv, I don't care about the damn cathedral." Dean rubs his hands over his face. "I'm warning you it could all get so much worse. And you're not going anywhere near Stafford because he could ask you questions you don't have an answer for."

"Dean, love of my life, he's investigating us now, right? I'll always have an answer about *us.*"

Dean gazes at me for a minute before approaching and settling his hands on my shoulders. I lean my forehead against his chest, feeling his tension.

"Please let me do this for you," I tell him. "For us. I want to prove that I can."

"You don't have to prove anything to me, Liv. You never have."

"But I want to prove it to myself."

I ease back to look at him and hold up my left hand. He places his palm against mine, and our wedding bands click together before we entwine our fingers. We both hold on tight.

"Pie love you, professor," I whisper. "Have faith in me, okay?"

"Ah, Liv." He presses his lips to my forehead. "I don't have faith in anyone but you."

∽

When I return to the apartment, my mother is in the living room, her head bent as she files her nails. A news program is on the TV, and the scent of coffee lingers in the air. She glances up when I enter.

"Where've you been?" she asks.

"With Dean. We had to talk."

"Talk?" Her gaze sweeps over me in one movement, and my breath shortens. If anyone knows the signs of post-sex, it's Crystal Winter.

I fight back the urge to blush. I had sex with my husband, not some random man I picked up at a grocery store while my daughter waited in the car.

Shit. A wave of old apprehension floods me. I drop my purse on a chair and head into the bathroom. I slam the door and get into the shower, hating the sense that I'm trying to wash the scent of Dean off my skin.

When I go back into the bedroom, Crystal is sitting on the bed cross-legged, one elbow resting on her knee.

"It's okay, Liv," she says. "Plenty of people have problems in their marriage. I did."

"I'm not having problems in my marriage, not that it would be your business if I were," I tell her. "I'm tired. I need some sleep."

"How long has he been gone?"

"He's not *gone.*" I grab a brush and drag it through my wet hair. "He left in February to work on an archeological dig in Italy. He's back for a few days to take care of some stuff and is staying in a hotel for personal reasons. He's leaving again on Monday. That's all there is to it."

"Well, I'm sorry he's leaving again," Crystal says, "but you can leave too, you know."

"I don't want to leave."

"I was thinking I should go to Phoenix soon, see about my mother's house and whatnot," she says. "You should come with me. A road trip, like old times."

God in heaven. Just the suggestion has my heart sinking and my brain flashing with images of hot, vinyl car seats, crumpled fast-food containers, the sun glinting off the windshield. A black strip of highway behind us. A strip of highway before us.

This is exactly the same thing Crystal wanted from me years ago. I'd been a senior in high school, still living with Aunt Stella in Castleford, when Crystal came to visit and asked me to go on the road with her again. I'd had a perfect excuse to decline—I needed to stay in Castleford and graduate because I was going to Fieldbrook College on a full merit scholarship the following fall.

And though that accomplishment had ended up shattering like glass around me, I know my answer to my mother will never change.

"I... I can't go with you." *Not to Phoenix. Not anywhere.* "I have work here."

"You're also separated from your husband."

"Dean and I are not separated."

She rolls her eyes. "This is why I never got married, Liv. Too much trouble. I refuse to let a man control me or my life. And maybe if you were on your own again, you'd figure that out too."

"Crystal." I take a breath and try to control the anger scorching my chest. "I'm not going anywhere with you. I can't."

"Can't or won't?"

"Both."

"Is it because he won't let you?"

"No! This has nothing to do with Dean. I won't go with you because I don't want to. I hated being on the road with you, Crystal. That's why I left. Why would I ever want to go back?"

"You will," she replies tartly. "When you realize you're delusional to think that marriage is better than freedom."

Crystal gets off the bed, her footsteps soundless across the carpet as she returns to the living room. I close the bedroom door and crawl under the covers, pushing her words out of my mind. I sink into a shallow and restless sleep before waking at dawn.

Crystal is still asleep when I get up to make coffee and start to put breakfast things out. For an hour, it's peaceful and quiet as I think about what we need to accomplish at the café today.

I hear Crystal rustling around as she wakes and goes into the bathroom. I pour a cup of coffee and put it on the table along with a pitcher of milk.

"Morning."

I turn to glance at my mother and stop. She's holding a pink box that makes my heart twist.

"Where… where did you get that?" I stammer.

"Bathroom cabinet. I was looking for tampons." She examines the pregnancy testing kit. "Are you pregnant?"

"No." A wave of dizziness hits me as I remember the reason Dean and I needed a test kit in the first place. "No… I… I just had a pregnancy scare a few months ago. Nothing happened."

"You're sure?" An odd stillness surrounds her.

"Of course I'm sure." I can feel her looking at my waistline. I think of the two newborn hats, soft as a cloud, one pink and one blue, both wrapped in a yellow-striped box beneath our bed. My throat constricts.

"Are you trying to have a baby?" Crystal asks.

I concentrate on unwrapping a loaf of bread. I don't know how to answer her question.

"I… maybe one day," I say.

She's still watching me. She knows. I can feel it, as if she has some maternal instinct about me now that she never had when I was younger.

"It was more than a scare, wasn't it?" she asks. "How far along were you?"

How does she know? How can she tell?

I can't lie, not about this. Not even to her. And what would be the point, anyway?

"Ten weeks," I tell her.

"When did it happen?"

"End of January."

"And your husband left right afterward?" Crystal asks.

"No, he did not leave right afterward." I crack an egg into a hot pan and watch it sizzle. "I really don't want to talk about this, Crystal."

She pours herself a cup of coffee and sits down. We're both silent as I bring my plate to the table. The air between us feels as fragile as a soap bubble.

With the overhead light on, Crystal's eyelashes make half-moon shadows on her cheekbones. She still has a sprinkle of freckles across her nose, which has always added to her youthful, wholesome beauty. I realize that my eyes are shaped like hers, just brown instead of blue. She meets my gaze.

The invisible soap bubble seems to pop, the current between us breaking.

"I know she left you a lot of money," Crystal says.

I poke at my toast. I shouldn't feel guilty, but I do.

"How did you find out?" I ask.

"I asked the lawyer for a copy of her will," she says. "My mother left me nothing, and she left you thousands of dollars. I'm sure she had a good laugh over that."

I can feel her watching me. We share a surname, Elizabeth, Crystal, and Olivia, all of us Winter women. Crystal had given me her last name rather than my father's because she'd wanted me to belong only to her.

"You didn't tell me about the inheritance," she says. "Why?"

"It didn't seem necessary."

"Did you think I'd be upset?"

"I don't know, Crystal. I've barely seen you in the past sixteen years. I didn't even know your mother. I get this letter that she's died and left me all this money, and then out of nowhere you show up on my doorstep... what *should* I think?"

"You shouldn't think what you obviously do." Her voice is getting chilly. "You think I want the money she left you."

"You've asked me for money before," I point out.

"I've asked you for help," she replies. "And I don't want *her* money. Not after what she did to both of us."

I wonder if that means she wants *my* money, not that I have much to give her.

"It doesn't matter, in any case," I say. "I've already invested most of it in the café, and the rest is set aside for working capital. It's all spoken for."

"Sounds like you put it to good use."

"And I don't have much else. I don't have access to Dean's money." Which is a lie, but she doesn't need to know that.

"Keeps you on a tight leash, does he?"

"No. I'm just telling you I don't have much money right now."

"I didn't come here to ask you for money, Liv."

"Why did you come here, then?"

"Because I wanted to see you. I thought we could… never mind."

We both fall silent. And beneath my frustration blooms the tiny hope that has been buried inside me for over fifteen years.

The hope that one day, Crystal Winter would be the kind of mother I'd always longed for. All those years I lived with Aunt Stella, battling the humiliation of what happened at Fieldbrook, struggling to start again, to get back on my feet… it was always there, this kernel of hope that Crystal would contact me, want to see me, apologize, ask to start again, confess that she missed me.

Again I feel her looking at me. Strange that her gaze is like a touch.

"Remember the Grand Canyon?" she asks.

The Grand Canyon. I search my mind. It's there, buried like a seed. A good memory. Bright. Warm. Peaceful.

We'd never been to the Grand Canyon before. It took us two days to get there from LA. We arrived at midnight and slept in a seedy motel room. Crystal woke me up when it was still dark outside.

"Dress warm," she said.

"What…"

"Come on."

I stumbled out of bed, figuring we were getting on the road again before rush hour started. I splashed water on my face, then dressed in jeans, a sweatshirt, and a heavy jacket. Crystal was waiting in the car when I emerged. She parked in one of the Canyon lots and got out. I followed without asking questions. I'd gotten used to that.

The sky was starting to lighten as we approached one of the ridges overlooking the canyon. Vast shadows coated the rocks. A few other jacket-clad tourists milled around with cameras and binoculars. I huddled on a bench, yawning and irritable.

Then the sun peeked over the horizon and the gray pallor of the canyon began to surrender to the light. I peered at the sky for a moment and went to join Crystal, who was standing at the edge of the rocks.

We stood together and watched the brilliant light paint the canyon. We watched color dance with the silhouettes. We watched rocks warm with gold, trees and shrubs reaching out to capture the crimson. We watched the sky and clouds burst with streaks of yellow and red and blue.

Neither of us spoke. We stood there for an hour. Just us and a sunrise.

"I went there once with my parents when I was a kid," Crystal tells me. "You were about ten when I took you. You've probably forgotten."

"No. I remember."

CHAPTER FOURTEEN

APRIL 5

"So what do you think?" The real-estate agent Nancy Walker enters the kitchen of the four-bedroom, 3,000-square-foot house.

I stare out the window at the backyard. Over the past few weeks, Nancy has emailed me listings of several houses on the market. I haven't responded to her messages until now. When Liv was pregnant, I'd looked for a house because I knew we'd need one. Then after the miscarriage...

Anger and fear swamp my chest. I take a breath and shove them aside before turning to face Nancy. "It's nice."

"Great school district, and walking distance to the park," she remarks.

"I'll talk to Liv about it."

"Okay. Don't wait too long if you want to make an offer, though. There are two more showings this afternoon already."

I thank her and head out to my car. There's a message on my phone from Liv that she's running late. We'd agreed to meet at Java Works after she's done at the café.

I park on Avalon Street and walk to the coffeehouse. As I cross in front of our apartment building, the door opens and Crystal Winter steps out.

Fuck.

I react on instinct, my fists clenching and every muscle in my body contracting in defense. She pauses to look inside her purse, then she glances up and meets my gaze. To my grim satisfaction, she wavers a little.

"Oh, hello, Dean. I thought you were gone already."

"When are you leaving?"

"Not sure yet. I've been enjoying the time with Liv, and helping out at her café." She puts on her sunglasses. "I might stay for the grand opening."

Dislike spears through me. I don't bother trying to suppress it. This woman hurt my wife in ways I can't comprehend. I'll never come close to forgiving her.

"Why did you come here?" I ask.

"To see my daughter, of course."

I wish I could believe her, for Liv's sake if nothing else.

"I know you don't believe me," she continues. "I don't know if Liv does either, but I've been hoping we can put all the crap behind us and move on."

An image of Liv appears in my head. I can almost feel it, her secret wish that it might be true. That maybe, somehow, Crystal can still be the kind of mother she has always wanted.

I step closer to Crystal.

"Look." I lower my voice. "I don't care if you want money. How much? I'll write you a check right now. But if you do one fucking thing to hurt Liv again, you'll regret it."

Crystal's eyes harden. "Your protective streak is all very touching, Dean, but trust me on this. Liv doesn't need it."

"You don't know what Liv needs."

She looks at me for a minute. "Why did you leave her after the miscarriage?"

My jaw tightens against a new wave of anger and guilt. Goddammit, but the woman knows how to hit a weak spot.

"Leave her alone, Crystal," I say through gritted teeth. "Just leave her the fuck alone."

She shrugs and turns to walk away.

I shake off my rage, inhaling a deep breath. I know my anger is exactly what Crystal wants, that she likes the idea of coming between me and Liv because…

The truth slams into me. Crystal doesn't want money. She wants *Liv*.

Unease twists in my gut.

I can't leave Mirror Lake again. Not now.

Pushing thoughts of Crystal out of my head, I yank open the door of Java Works and find an empty table. After getting a coffee, I distract myself with checking email. "Professor West?"

I glance up to see my grad students Jessica and Sam approaching from the back of the room. They stop beside my table.

"Hey, we didn't know you were back," Sam says.

"Good to see you both." I gesture for them to sit. "I'm leaving again on Monday. How's your work going?"

They sit down and give me updates about their research, and we talk about city planning and architecture. Within a few minutes, I can already feel the tension slide from my shoulders. Discussing medieval history with grad students is, at least, one thing I can still do well.

I look toward the door when it opens again, feeling Liv before I see her. She shoots me a smile, then pauses to order a coffee at the counter. She's wearing a blue skirt and sweater over a white blouse with a little collar. She looks like the sky.

Her hair is down, loose around her shoulders and messy from the wind. She pushes it back with one hand as she walks toward me. It's one of her sexiest moves—even more so because she's unaware of how beautiful she is.

I stand to pull out a chair for her.

"Sorry I'm late." She reaches up to press a kiss against my cheek. My head fills with her peaches scent.

"Oh, hey, Mrs. West."

"Hi, Jessica. Sam." Liv puts her satchel on an empty chair and sits down. "Nice to see you both again."

After exchanging small talk, Sam and Jessica get ready to leave. As they pick up their backpacks, Sam pauses.

"Uh, don't mean to pry, Professor West," he says, "but did Maggie Hamilton ever change advisors?"

Wariness floods me. "No. Why?"

Sam glances at Jessica. "She's been… well, she's been complaining to the other students about you."

"Has she?" I try to keep my voice even, though anger claws up my throat. "What's she been saying?"

"Just crap about you being unfair and too tough on her and showing favoritism," Jessica says. "The rest of us know it's not true, but it's kind of shitty, you know?"

I can feel Liv bristling. I wish Sam and Jessica had brought this up before my wife arrived. At least they don't seem to know anything about the sexual harassment charge, but it could only be a matter of time before Maggie spreads lies about that.

"Thanks for letting me know," I say.

"Sure." Sam pulls his backpack over his shoulders. "It's especially lousy that she's doing this when you're out of town and all."

They say goodbye and walk outside. I turn toward Liv, hating the dismay in her brown eyes. I change the subject to a far more pleasant one.

"The café," I say. "How's the remodeling going?"

"Really well. Did I tell you Brent is going to leave his job at the inn to be our general manager? He has a ton of great experience." Liv stirs a packet of sugar into her coffee. "What did you do this afternoon?"

"Looked at a house up in the Spring Hills neighborhood."

Surprise flashes in her eyes. "A house?"

"Nancy Walker emailed me about it, and since I'm in town…" I shrug. "Figured it wouldn't hurt to see it."

"I didn't know we were still looking for a house."

"I didn't either. Seems to make sense, though."

Total bullshit. Of course it makes no sense to look for a house when my career is in danger. I have no idea why I even bothered.

"But you're leaving again on Monday," Liv says.

"So?"

"So how can you buy a house now?"

"I didn't say I was buying a house. I said I looked at one."

She frowns in confusion. "So *why* did you look at one?"

For some reason, irritation grips me. "If you want to have a baby one day, Liv, we're not staying in that apartment. We're going to have a house with a big yard, in a good school district. I made the plans when you were pregnant, and I'm not changing them."

She blinks. "*That's* why you looked at a house? Because you want to follow through on the plans you made when I was pregnant?"

I sit back. My heart is pounding. I hate fear. Hate letting it control me.

"I just looked at it, Liv. I'm not making an offer."

"But one day you will?"

"One day we'll have to."

The admission settles in the air between us. Liv stares at me, as if she doesn't know what to make of that statement. I don't know either. She reaches across the table and puts her hand over mine.

"It's probably best if we wait to think about a house anyway," she finally says. "We don't know what's going to happen."

My shoulders tighten again. I can't stand the thought that my wife would ever doubt my ability to escape this harassment fuck-up alive.

Even if I doubt my own ability to do that.

"Come with me." Liv pushes her chair back and reaches for her satchel. "I want to show you something."

We go out to where her car is parked, and she gets in the driver's seat. It's nearing dusk, the sky holding a few reddish clouds, but the air is warm. Liv drives in the direction of the university, turns onto a street winding toward the mountains, and parks at the base of a dirt road.

"What's up here?" I ask as we get out.

"You'll see." Liv takes my camera case out of the trunk. "I found your camera in the closet. I didn't think you'd mind if I borrowed it."

"Not at all. But for what?"

"Come on."

We walk up the dirt road to where an old, abandoned house sits in a clearing. It's a huge, spectacularly irregular Queen Anne-style house with a polygonal tower, a wide front porch, and patterned siding. Reminds me of a once-beautiful actress who has been long forgotten. Half-surrounded by trees, the house overlooks a view of the lake and downtown.

"It's called the Butterfly House," Liv tells me. "The Historical Society is launching a campaign to save it, but it's been in limbo for a long time because of zoning laws. I'm helping with the campaign, and I wanted to take some pictures."

She tells me the history of the place as we circle the grounds. The house is a disaster. The gabled tower is punctured by broken windows, the doors boarded up, graffiti scrawled over the walls, the porch balustrade falling apart. Liv stops to take a picture of the back of the house.

"Have you been inside?" I ask.

"I don't have the key."

Ah, Liv. My good girl never had a typical rebellious phase. Neither did I really, though I got into some scrapes in high school and had some rowdy nights out with friends that involved seeking out deserted places to party.

Liv was different. She rebelled against her mother when she was thirteen years old. There's no way in hell Crystal Winter can manipulate her anymore. And I know I need to let Liv deal with her mother alone, even if *not* shielding my wife goes against every instinct I possess.

I watch Liv take a few more pictures of the house. I approach the side door and pull on a loose board nailed into the doorjamb.

"Dean, what are you doing?"

"Getting into the house. Don't you want to see what's inside?"

"Well, yes, but it's not our property."

I pry the board away from the nails. "This wood is so rotted it's about to fall off anyway."

"Dean." Her voice is worried as she approaches me. "Really. This is breaking and entering."

"You have a right to be here, don't you?" I pull harder on the board, and it yields with a screech of rusty nails. "You're doing research for the Historical Society."

"That doesn't mean I'm allowed to break in."

"You're not." I shoot her a grin. "I am."

I'm gratified when a faint smile appears on her face. I push the board aside to reveal a narrow hole in the door, edged with splintered wood.

"Come on, beauty." I peer through the hole into the darkness. "Let's live dangerously."

"Well, for us, I suppose this is about as dangerous as it gets," she mutters. "Dean, please be careful."

I push my way through the door, then extend a hand to help Liv through. We find ourselves in what was once the kitchen—now a mess of broken chairs, a rusted sink, and shattered tiles. A layer of dirt covers everything. Dust motes swim in the faint light.

Liv tightens her hand around mine as we walk into the other rooms. A musty smell clings to the air. The front rooms are no better than the kitchen—torn, filthy rugs, peeling wallpaper, pockets of mildew. Drop cloths cover some pieces of furniture. The fireplace is coated with soot. But even through the grime, the historic beauty of the place is evident in the decorative trim, the ceiling medallions, and paneled wainscot.

"Can you imagine how beautiful it once was?" Liv says.

"It's a shame no one took care of it." I let go of her hand to take the camera from her, then angle the lens and take a picture of the room.

We explore the other rooms on the lower floor, all in disrepair with broken plaster, scarred wooden floors, and a million cobwebs. I snap a few more pictures of cool, architectural details—crown molding, the arch of a door, a carved newel post—before we go upstairs.

There are five rooms on the second story, with windows overlooking each side of the house and half-filled with broken furniture. The walls are patched with slats of wood, the ceilings discolored with water damage.

"I can see why the Historical Society needs a huge fundraising effort for this," Liv says as she peers at a rusted light fixture. "It'll cost a fortune to renovate."

"It would be well worth it, though, if it were done right." I pause beside a door leading to a narrow staircase. "Let's see what's up here."

Liv follows me up to the tower that rises above the front

porch. She stops and sucks in a breath when we reach the top. It's an octagonal tower with windows on each side, cluttered with a few old chairs. Most of the windows are boarded up, but the one facing the lake is clear and unbroken.

"Wow." Liv crosses to look out the window. "This must have been amazing, once upon a time. You can see all the way past the lake to the other part of town. What a view."

I pause to take a picture of the cathedral ceiling. I examine the furniture, brushing the dust off a parlor chair that has a detailed engraving on the back.

"I can understand why medieval towers were used for defense," Liv continues. "You can see so far away."

"Sometimes they were used for other things too." I angle the camera for a picture of the chair. "Chapels, prisons, libraries."

"Cool place for a library."

I lower the camera just as Liv turns to face me. My heart slams against my chest. For a second, I can't speak. Can hardly breathe.

She blinks. "What's wrong?"

"Don't… don't move."

Sweet mother of God, my wife is beautiful.

At that exact moment, a reddish sunbeam shines through the window, painting Liv's skin with a rosy blush. Her dark hair is loose around her shoulders, and light weaves through all the thick strands. Behind her, the window glows and town lights sparkle against the expanse of the lake.

I may not be all that great at the romantic stuff, but sometimes the world sure gets it right.

I lift the camera again and focus the lens on Liv before snapping the shutter.

"Dean, I don't even have any lipstick on."

"You don't need any." I pause to check the picture. Even in the small window of the LCD display, it's incredible. "Stay right there."

Liv pulls her hands through her hair in an attempt to straighten it out. I take a few more pictures, zooming the lens in and then back again. I move to the side and keep photographing her, not wanting to miss any angle of the perfection that is my wife.

Finally, I lower the camera and just look at her.

"What are you going to do with all those pictures?" Liv asks.

"Plaster them on the ceiling like stars so I can look up at them at night."

"Aw." She smiles. "Good one."

I don't know how it is that this one woman can both bring me to my knees and make me feel like the greatest knight in history.

I click through the photos on the camera, pausing at one where a shadow falls across her neck and into the open V of her shirt.

A thought hits me like lightning. "Take your shirt off."

"What?"

I lift the camera again. "I want a picture of you with your shirt off."

"Me topless in an old tower?" Liv asks. "This sounds suspiciously like a rather kinky medieval fantasy, professor."

"Too bad I don't have any manacles, huh?"

She smiles again, but shakes her head. "Dean, I can't undress here."

"Why not? No one's around. I bet not many people even know about this place."

"Florence Wickham does."

"I guarantee you that Florence Wickham isn't going to break in through the side door and come up to the tower."

"I wouldn't put it past her," Liv mutters.

To ease Liv's mind, I shut the door leading to the staircase and turn the rusty lock. "Okay?"

She's watching me, wariness and… curiosity appearing in her brown eyes.

"Live dangerously," I suggest.

She lets out her breath and slowly sheds her sweater, tossing it over the back of a chair. My heart kicks into high gear when she reaches for the buttons of her blouse. She unfastens two buttons and glances at me.

"I don't have sexy lingerie on," she admits.

"Good." I don't want her in sexy lingerie. I want her exactly as she is.

Liv unfastens another button. Even from a short distance, I see her hands trembling. Warmth floods my chest. Finally she gets all the buttons undone and pulls the shirt off her shoulders.

Ah, God. Just the sight of her cleavage cupped by a plain white bra has my blood heating. I focus on adjusting the aperture setting.

"Now I'm kind of nervous," she tells me.

"Liv." I lift the camera and focus on her. "You have no reason to be nervous."

I snap the shutter. She fidgets at first, crossing her arms, winding a strand of hair around her finger, shifting from one foot to the other, but when I start to tell her how beautiful she is, she begins to relax.

A series of photos follows that I swear would win awards

in photography competitions, for no other reason than the fact that Liv is a subject like no other—all at once sexy, sweet, assured, shy, and captivating. The light changes as the sun descends, painting her in shadows.

I look at her again.

"Take it off." My voice is hoarse.

Liv's gaze shifts away from me. After a heart-stopping second, she reaches back to unfasten her bra. All the breath leaves my lungs at the sight of her naked breasts, her nipples hardening in the cooler air, her long hair falling to curtain them.

So fucking beautiful.

I try to pull my attention from my lust as I adjust the camera again and get back to taking pictures. At my instruction, Liv moves to different areas of the tower—against a boarded-up window, near the door, in the center of the room, beside a rocking chair—and does what I tell her to.

"Put your arms over your head… that's it…" *click click* "…now pull your hair back like you're going to put it in a ponytail…" *click click click* "…one hand on your hip, the other on the doorjamb… both hands behind you on the windowsill…" *click click* "perfect… so damn pretty…"

Then I lower the camera.

"Touch them," I tell her.

Liv's throat works with a swallow, but she runs her hands over her breasts, cups them in her palms, pinches her nipples. I can see her getting aroused, all those telltale signs I know so well—her breath is getting faster, her cheeks flushed, and her thighs tense as she presses her legs together.

By the time she slides one finger down the valley between her breasts, I'm rock-hard and aching to get my hands on her.

I force myself to focus on the camera and keep clicking the shutter.

Then, without my needing to ask, Liv unzips her skirt and steps out of it. Naked except for cotton underwear and her low-heeled shoes, she smiles at me, as if she knows quite well that the balance of power has shifted.

Which it has, since I'm at her mercy.

"You're killing me, lady," I mutter, changing the shutter speed.

"This was your idea," she reminds me. She runs her hand down her torso to her panties. "Do you still want me to touch myself?"

Holy fuck, do I ever.

"Do it," I tell her.

I click the shutter again, my pulse pounding as she eases her fingers into her underwear. A sigh escapes her. Then, half to my shock and half to my utmost pleasure, she hooks her fingers into her panties and tugs them halfway down her thighs.

I try and shift the discomfort of my erection, then snap a series of photos that I don't even need since this image of Liv is burned into my brain forever—naked except for her panties tangled around her thighs, her hand still easing down toward her slit, her hair a tumbled mess over her bare shoulders, her breasts so full and perfect. Arousal brewing in her eyes. I can feel it from across the room, pulsing through her like lava.

I lower the camera. I want her bad.

"I think..." I clear my throat. "I think the camera is running out of memory."

"Oh. I was hoping to get a few shots of you."

I shut the camera down before she can act on that. The

air is thick, hot. I want to pull her into my arms, feel her body crushing against mine, pliant and yielding.

"Dean."

I lift my gaze to hers. She's watching me, her breath still quick.

I can't stand it anymore. I put the camera down and cross to her in three steps. Grab her shoulders and haul her against me. Capture her sweet mouth and kiss her senseless.

She sucks in a breath, her body going all soft against me, her arms winding around my waist. Her full breasts press against my chest. I can feel her nipples clear through my sweatshirt. My head spins with the feel and taste of her.

She runs her hand down my stomach to my erection. The heat of her hand burns through my jeans. She steps back far enough to unfasten them, pulling them and my boxers down. When she closes her hand around my stiff cock and starts sinking to her knees, my head almost explodes.

"Wait." I yank my sweatshirt over my head and drop it onto the floor in front of her.

She shoots me a quick smile, adjusting the sweatshirt so she can kneel on it before she turns her attention to my cock. In one, easy movement, she has me in her mouth.

I tighten my hand on her hair. The sight of her kneeling in front of me, her lips and tongue working over my shaft, drives all thought from my brain. There's only her wet mouth and my blood pulsing. Tension builds like steam.

I grip the back of her neck. She slides her mouth off me and sits back, her chest heaving. I reach down to palm her gorgeous breasts, rubbing my fingers over her nipples in the way I know she likes. She lets out a sigh and pushes herself into my hands. I tug her to her feet and turn her toward one of the boarded-up windows.

"Hold on."

She grasps the windowsill and pushes her ass toward me. I tug her panties down her legs and pull them off.

"Jesus, Liv." My chest burns as I stare at the curve of her back, her round ass, her legs spread apart. "I'm going to come before I get inside you."

"Oh, don't," she breathes. "I want to feel you again…"

I rub my hand across her pretty ass. She gasps, spreading her legs wider. She's still wearing her heeled pumps. She's sexy as hell.

I trail one finger down to her slit. She moans. I ease a finger into her. Grasp my shaft with my other hand and squeeze. Pressure cords my spine. As much as I'd like to draw this out, I know I can't last much longer.

Liv lowers her head, her hand sliding between her legs to her clit. "Dean, please. I need you now."

I push my knee between her thighs to press them farther apart, then position my cock at her slit. One thrust into her tightness, and my blood goes into full boil. She groans, pressing one hand to the board and pushing backward again.

Heaven. Pure, sweet heaven.

I clutch her hips and shove into her again and again. Her ass slams against my stomach. Moans stream from her throat. The air is drenched with heat.

Part of me never wants this to end. I could do this forever, pumping into her, feeling her inner muscles clenching around my shaft, her body shaking as she takes the force of each thrust. I dig my fingers into her hips, wanting to drive us both to the edge.

"Dean, I'm… oh, God, don't stop." Liv moves her hand

up to play with her breasts, the other still braced against the window. "Oh, you feel so *good*."

I pump into her a few more times, then pull out. I grab her waist and tug her upright. She turns toward me, her hair falling into her face as she sinks against me for a hot kiss.

"Come here." I take my sweatshirt off the floor and toss it onto the parlor chair. After sitting down, I motion for Liv to come closer. Her gaze tracks down my chest to my rigid cock. I slide my hands to the backs of her thighs and turn her around.

She spreads her legs over my lap and reaches back to take hold of my shaft. In one smooth movement, she lowers herself onto me and starts to ride. The sight of her ass bouncing up and down on my thighs, her skin glistening with sweat and her hair sticking damply to her back... I'm on fire inside and out.

My body tenses with the effort of trying to retain control. Liv moves off me and turns, lowering her head for a kiss as she sinks onto my cock again. Now with her breasts right in front of me, her nipples hard as cherries...

"Oh, fuck, Liv..." With a groan, I pull out of her and let go, shooting with a volcanic force. I push my hand between her legs. One rub on her clit, and she gives a sharp cry as her body convulses over mine.

She gasps and falls against me, pressing her face to my shoulder. I run my hands over her smooth back. She's all soft, sweaty heat, her breath steaming against my skin, her body still trembling.

She shifts, pressing one hand to my cheek. She opens her mouth above mine and runs her tongue over my lower lip. Warmth rushes through me. She leans her forehead against mine.

"I'm going to miss you all over again, professor."

"I'll miss you too." Everything in me is fighting the idea

of leaving my wife again.I got it the first time, the idea that if I left Mirror Lake, I couldn't be accused of any new transgression that could screw things up even more.

But now? With the poisonous Crystal Winter in town? With Edward Hamilton accusing me of having a precedent of getting involved with students? With Stafford investigating my relationship with Liv?

What if he wants to know more about her? What if he digs into her past?

The thought of Stafford bringing *Liv's* history into this investigation sickens me with fear. And what the hell am I supposed to do about it from five thousand miles away?

"Hey." I pull in a breath to suppress the growing anger. "How about I figure out a way to stay here? I can—"

"Dean." Liv touches my face. "You have to go back. They're expecting you, and I… with my mother here, it's better if you're away."

A wave of frustration hits me. I don't want to be *away* from my wife. And I hate that she wants me to go.

"It's *better* if I'm away?" I repeat, unable to keep the irritation from my voice.

"You know it is." She eases off me, shaking her head. "Don't fight it again, Dean, please. You have to go back to Italy."

Tension floods me as I reach for my jeans. I pull them on and watch Liv as she slips into her underwear, her hair swinging in a curtain over her shoulder, her skin still damp.

My chest tightens. Somehow, always, everything is okay when it's just the two of us alone together. It's when we have to deal with the rest of the world that everything gets fucked up.

And I still have no idea what to do about it.

CHAPTER FIFTEEN

Olivia

April 11

*T*his time after Dean leaves Mirror Lake again, I'm almost relieved by the fact that he's away. Not because I want to be separated from him again, but because an ocean's distance between him and my mother is a good thing—especially when my mother hasn't yet given me any idea of how long she intends to stay.

I don't have much time to worry about her though, because between the café and my hours at the museum and library, I have a commitment every day. I have to quit my bakery job, which doesn't bother Gustave after we make plans to have him supply the café with croissants and brioche.

Marianne continues to help us with logistics, and with Brent as the café's general manager, we move toward our early June grand opening. Marianne brings us a million samples of curtain fabrics, glasses, tablecloths, and soon we're repainting the walls and installing a new subfloor.

I don't see much of my mother during the week after Dean leaves. We exist in a strained but not overtly hostile way, and she continues to help out with the painting at the café. She's never home in the evenings, as she goes out every night to clubs and bars, returning long after I'm asleep.

Though I talk to Dean at our usual time every night, safely ensconced in his office with the door locked, things are different than they were the first time. Now they're strained by the unspoken presence of my mother and the threat to our future hovering over us like smoke.

One night shortly after he's left, he reminds me that he didn't use a condom the evening we fooled around at the Butterfly House.

"I'm not pregnant," I tell him. "I started my period yesterday."

"Oh."

My heart thumps suddenly as I wait for more. *"Oh, good"? "Oh, too bad"? "Oh my God, let's try again"?*

There's nothing else. Just *"Oh."*

"I guess we got carried away," I say.

Even with all we've been through, I'm not surprised by this. We've had a rough time since last October, and we've both been trying to navigate this new territory between us. And in an old, gabled tower on a hill above Mirror Lake, isolated from discovery, wrapped in the intense sexiness of Dean photographing me naked… it's no wonder we lost ourselves in cascades of heat and unreality.

"So… what if I were pregnant?" I ask.

Dean is silent. My heart pounds.

"Then I'd buy a house," he finally says.

I can't help laughing, even as sudden tears sting my eyes. "But would you *want* to buy a house?"

Silence again. Then he says, "Do you remember that time we went to the Vilas Zoo in Madison?"

"We went lots of times."

"Yeah, but there was one time we went on a cold fall morning during the week," Dean says. "Lots of mothers there with babies and little kids in strollers. I was waiting for you near the gift shop, by that front gate that swings back and forth. When you came through the gate, you looked behind you to see if anyone was following.

"Then you held the gate open so a woman pushing a double-stroller could get through. There were two kids in the stroller, a boy and a girl, all bundled into jackets and hats. The woman stopped to say something to you, and then one of the kids started getting upset and crying. And as you were talking, you put your hand on his head, right on top of his fuzzy winter hat."

"I don't remember that," I say.

"I don't think you even realized you did it," Dean says. "But the kid settled down in about two seconds. Just like that. Stopped crying and waited for the stroller to get moving again. And I looked at you and thought, *She would be a great mother.*"

I can't speak. I don't think I can even contain my heart right now.

"But it's easy when it's just us, Liv, you know?" he continues. "That's why it's always been so damned good. And these past few months... half the time I want to take you to some tropical island where we can just lounge around naked eating bananas."

I smile through the tears still blurring my eyes. "We have a tropical island, Dean. It's called *our marriage.* And I'd be happy to lounge around naked eating bananas, if that's what you want."

"I want to be with you," he says. "That's all I've ever wanted. And I hate that things get screwed up every time... every time it's *not* just us anymore."

Now we're both silent. The air between us vibrates with tension. I sense an odd shift in those few seconds, as if he's the one seeking reassurance for once.

"Dean, having a child doesn't make our lives *not us,*" I say gently. "It makes our lives *more than us.*"

He doesn't respond. I can picture him lying on his bed, one hand behind his head, his gaze staring out the window, as if all the answers to the world can be found in the dawn light.

"I can think of a thousand reasons to say no," he says.

"Me too." I press a hand to my chest and close my eyes. "But if we look hard enough, we can always find a reason to say no. We can always find a reason to be afraid. So maybe it's time to stop looking and see what finds us instead."

We fall silent again. A very long time passes with nothing but the sound of our breath.

"I might not come out of this investigation alive," Dean says.

"Yes, you will. But I won't be waiting for you when you do."

"You won't?"

"No. I'll be at your side."

APRIL 21

The sound of my mother's laughter rings out from the front room of the second floor. She and Allie's friend Stacy have been working on painting the Wicked Witch's castle room for the past few days. I pause in my attempt to rip up a baseboard, trying to pretend that I'm not eavesdropping even though I totally am.

"It's a nice place," my mother is saying. "Small-townish, but with a good amount of stuff to do. I was there for about three months."

"I think it's so cool that you've traveled all over," Stacy replies. "The only place I've been is Tennessee to visit family."

"Liv never liked traveling," Crystal replies. "She didn't have an adventurous streak. She won't even come to Phoenix with me for a few days. I wanted her help finding out about my mother's house and stuff."

Stacy's response is drowned out by the sound of the radio turning on downstairs. I put down the crowbar and go to where Brent and a couple of other guys are starting to nail down the hardwood floor. I step onto the front porch and breathe in the fresh air.

Envy. That's what this ugly, gnawing feeling in my gut is. I've felt it before, every time people gravitated toward my mother, praised her, wanted her acceptance. It makes no sense that I should still feel this way, but there it is. My mother has always been at ease with so many people. Except me.

Of course, those people haven't had the history that Crystal and I do, but that doesn't make it any easier.

I leave the café earlier than I'd planned and spend a couple of extra hours at the Historical Museum working on my report about the Butterfly House. As I walk home, I call Kelsey on my cell.

"You doing anything tonight?" I ask.

"I've got a meeting about that meteorology conference in Japan I'm going to," she says. "Won't be home until late."

"Bummer."

"Why? What's going on?"

"Oh, you know. If it's not one thing, it's your mother."

She chuckles. "How long is she staying?"

"She said something about leaving next week. I just want her to be gone before Dean gets back."

"Which is when?"

"I'm not sure yet. A month, maybe." Though my heart aches at the idea of not seeing Dean for that long again, I can't shake my conviction that he is still safer in Italy.

"Okay, go to your meeting," I tell Kelsey. "Call me tomorrow."

"I will. Hitch up your big girl panties."

"I'm trying, but they give me a wedgie."

"I'll loan you some tweezers."

"With the size of my ass these days, I'll need pliers."

Kelsey laughs. We exchange goodbyes, and I stop to pick up takeout Chinese food before returning home. After leaving the boxes on the kitchen counter, I go into the living room.

Crystal is sitting on the sofa, writing something on a pad of paper. She rips the page off and hands it to me.

"Phone call from a lawyer," she says. "Asked for your husband."

My heart plummets. Written in Crystal's flowing handwriting is the name of the lawyer who specializes in sexual harassment cases.

"Thanks." I toss the paper onto the foyer table and go into the bedroom to change.

When I emerge in clean jeans and a T-shirt, Crystal is still sitting on the sofa. I go past her, aware of her following as I head for the kitchen.

"Liv."

"Not your business, Crystal."

"Why does he need a lawyer?"

"Dean has a lot of investments and stuff." I realize that's probably the wrong thing to say. "Never mind."

"Is the guy a divorce lawyer?"

"No! Of course not. Again, not that it's any of your business."

But I'm not stupid. One click of a mouse and she'd find out exactly what Sterling and Fox specializes in. I could deflect that discovery with bullshit about Dean needing a lawyer for employment reasons, but Crystal wouldn't buy it. I've visited the Sterling and Fox website. *Sexual harassment* is listed as their firm's primary area of practice.

I feel my mother watching me as I dump the Chinese food into bowls and take them to the table.

"If there's anything I don't regret," she says, "it's that I didn't marry your father. It would have been a mess to try and divorce him."

"Dean and I are not getting a divorce. And I'm not going to talk about it anymore."

Somewhat to my surprise, she doesn't press the issue. I eat a few bites before holing up in Dean's office to read for the rest of the evening. It's not until the following morning that I know Crystal knows. Sometimes I hate the Internet. Or at least, I wish I was a better liar.

"Is that why he's out of town?" she asks.

I shake my head and swallow a gulp of too-hot coffee.

"Is it a student?" she asks. "Or another professor?"

"None of your business."

"But it's *someone*," she says, and too late I realize that my response was a tacit acknowledgment that she got it right.

"It's no wonder something like this happened," Crystal remarks. "He's a handsome man, and with all those young, pretty students around—"

"Oh, for God's sake, Crystal, stop it," I snap. "Dean didn't do anything wrong. One of his students is upset that he wouldn't approve her thesis proposal, and she's using this charge as a weapon of revenge."

"That's what he told you?"

"That's what I know."

Her mouth compresses. "Jesus, Liv, he has you snowed, doesn't he?"

"No! Believe it or not, Crystal, there are good men in the world. And Dean is one of the best."

"You don't have to defend him. I know you don't want my opinion, but I've learned a lot about men over the years, and it seems to me like your husband isn't all that you think he is."

"You're right." My shoulders tense. "I don't want your opinion."

"He's the only man you've been with, right?"

I don't respond. Can't. How does she know that?

"I've known men like him," Crystal continues. "He's older than you. Way more experienced. Good-looking. Good talker. You met him when you were young and struggling with school and work. He has plenty of money and promised to take care of you. He gives you whatever you want, and in return you give him what *he* wants, right?"

I can't breathe past the tightness in my throat. "You don't know anything about it."

"I do know something about manipulative men who force you to do exactly what they want."

"Dean has never forced me to do anything."

"Of course you don't think so," Crystal replies. "A man like him would make you believe you're the center of his world. You think he'd never use you. But then you follow him wherever he goes, let him take care of you, while you keep him happy in the bedroom. He knows how good he has it. But you can't see the truth of it, which is that he's manipulating you."

My chest aches. Every cell in my body is fighting Crystal's ugly, twisted assessment of my marriage.

"You need to either shut up or get out." My voice, cold and knife-sharp, doesn't sound like my own.

"Don't get angry with me," she says. "I was young and naïve once too. That's exactly how I ended up pregnant with you. And it upsets me to think that my daughter, that thirteen-year-old girl who had one helluva backbone, has ended up with a sugar daddy and still nothing of her own."

Oh, shit.

I can deflect what she said about Dean and me. I know the truth of our marriage. I know the truth of my husband.

But this arrow flies past my defenses and hits me where I already hurt. And she knows it.

"All of what you're saying is bullshit," I tell her. "You were the one always looking for a man to take care of you. You're the one who still has nothing of your own."

"And yet you were always ranting about how you never wanted to end up like me."

Shit. Shit. Shit.

"I'm not like you," I retort. "I'm nothing like you. I own a business now, goddammit. I have a life here. I'm putting down roots. And if you're trying to make me doubt my marriage and my husband, good luck with that. Because I never will."

"I'm not trying to make you doubt anything, Liv. I can read the signs. The miscarriage, your husband being gone for so long, leaving you alone, this business with a lawyer... you're obviously having marital problems, and you're blind to what your marriage really is. I want you to see it and to know you still have a way out."

"You can't make me *see* anything. You don't even know me! I don't want your opinion or advice or anything, okay? And I sure as hell don't want a way out." I force myself to approach her. "You need to leave, Crystal. I don't want you here anymore."

She holds up her hands. "Okay, fine. But I'm worried about you. And the offer to come with me to Phoenix still stands. You just need to grow a spine."

An ice-cold shiver rattles through me. I know exactly what she's trying to do. She can't stand the thought that I have what she doesn't. And she wants me to believe all this shit she's throwing at me so I'll feel the need to escape with her again.

"Conversation's over," I tell her. "It's past time for you to find somewhere else to stay. Either start looking for a hotel room or leave for Phoenix now. You can't stay with me anymore."

I no longer care where she goes, as long as it's *away.* I go to the TV stand and grab the VHS tape that contains the video of Crystal's cereal commercial.

"And you can take this with you." I throw the tape on the coffee table, then stalk to the bedroom and slam the door so hard the hinges rattle.

CHAPTER SIXTEEN

DEAN

APRIL 22

"I don't want you to talk to her." I tighten my grip on the phone. Anger seethes in my gut. Just because I agreed to this doesn't mean I have to like it. On the contrary. I fucking hate it.

"Your wife actually saved me some time by contacting me first," Ben Stafford says on the other end of the phone. "I'd intended to call her soon to set up an appointment. I just need to ask her some basic questions to verify everything you've already told me."

"There's no way you can leave her out of it?"

"It's procedure, Professor West. When will you be back in town?"

"I don't know. I'm chairperson of a Medieval Studies conference that's taking place in July. I have to be back for that. I want to come back sooner."

"I've gotten pretty busy with several other cases, but I should have yours wrapped up well before the end of the semester so I can make my recommendation to the board."

Which could be even more of a disaster for me. I end the call and dial our home number, clenching my teeth when Crystal's voice comes over the line.

"Olivia West's residence," she says.

"It's Dean," I tell her. "Where is she?"

"At the café, I suppose. How's Italy?"

"Italian. Tell Liv I called."

"Of course," Crystal says. "Did she relay the message from the lawyer?"

My heart seizes. "What lawyer?"

"Sterling and Fox," she replies. "I took the call. I thought maybe Liv had contacted a divorce lawyer."

"No, goddammit." Though I hate letting Crystal get to me, the words *Liv* and *divorce* crash in my brain like missiles.

"Well, all evidence points to you having marital problems," Crystal continues, "but I saw that's not Sterling and Fox's area of specialty."

Cold foreboding prickles my skin. I want to hang up, but I can't. I need to know what she knows.

"What did he say?" I ask.

"Just asked for you to return his call." She pauses. "I imagine sexual harassment is like a rape charge for a man. No matter the outcome, the stigma never goes away. And Liv will have to deal with being married to a man whose reputation is ruined."

A red haze coats my vision. My voice drops to a dangerous level. "I want you out of my house. Away from my wife."

"*My* daughter," she says. "Look, I've been in… compromising positions before, Dean. I'm sure Liv has too. If you just—"

I hang up on her before my fury unleashes. My hand shakes as I try Liv's cell again. I could give a shit what Crystal Winter thinks of me. But if she knows what happened to Liv at Fieldbrook, if she uses it against her—

I throw the phone on the bed.

The arrows are flying at my wife from all directions. And I'm five thousand goddamned miles away.

I want to be back with Liv right now. I *need* to be. The urge to shield her from this shitstorm is visceral, instinctive. It's the only thing I can do.

Shoving aside my anger, I sit down and try to work for the next hour. I stare at a photo of Liv above my desk, one of the more modest pictures of her I'd taken at the Butterfly House.

I told her once that I'd move heaven and earth to give her whatever she wanted. I still would. I'll fight forever to give her all the things she never had as a child—love, safety, happiness, protection—but now there's something else, a desperate urge to give her a marriage filled with *more,* to give her things she didn't even know she wanted.

To give her a life beyond what either of us has ever expected.

Need boils inside me. I fumble for my phone again and push the speed dial button.

"Dean?" Liv's voice, breathless. "What time is it there?"

"Uh… eleven, I think. Where are you?"

"At home."

"Is your mother there?"

"No, she's out looking for another place to stay. She'll be gone before you get back."

"She wants you to leave with her, get on the road again."

"I'll never go anywhere with her, Dean, you know that."

"When did she find out about Sterling and Fox?"

Her breath catches. "Yesterday, but how did you—"

"She answered the phone when I called earlier."

"I'm sorry. I was at the grocery store."

"Why didn't you tell me she knows about the goddamned charge?"

"I didn't know she'd figured it out until this morning. What did she say to you, Dean?"

Liv will have to deal with being married to a man whose reputation is ruined…

My throat tightens. I can't push any words past it.

"Are you okay?" Liv asks.

No, I'm not okay. I'm not okay five thousand miles away from my wife. I'm not okay with my career and reputation hanging in the balance. I'm not okay with being powerless.

"Dean?"

"I need to be with you. I need to do something."

"I know you do."

"Liv."

"I'm here."

"Tell me you know this is all bullshit. That Maggie Hamilton is lying."

"Of course she's lying."

"You never thought it could be true?"

"What?"

"Not once did you wonder if it was possible?" My heart is suddenly pounding hard. "That I could have hit on a student?"

"No, of course not. Why would you ask me such a thing?"

"I've lied to you before."

"Oh, Dean, don't."

"How can you just trust that I'm telling you the fucking truth?"

"Because I know you, you ass! You're the man who looked up the university *rules* before you asked me out."

"Years ago."

"So, what, you think I'm suddenly going to doubt you *now?* After all we've been through?"

"It's happened before." I can't stop, have to get it out. "Other female students, professors… some of them have come on to me over the years."

"I know."

"You know?"

"Of course! You're so handsome, successful, intelligent, so… *you*. Women have always fallen over themselves for you, and I'm not so naïve to think they don't still flirt with you."

"I've never—"

"Dean." Her voice sharpens. "You don't even have to say it."

"Why do you just believe me?"

"*Because I know you.* I'm your girl, dammit."

Of course she is. That's an unbreakable, rock-solid truth.

"Dean, please. My mother has been trying in her insidious little way to convince me that there are cracks in our marriage, but—"

"What the fuck? What has she said to you?"

"Nothing that means anything. Nothing I *believe.* But this is why I knew you had to leave again. I need you to understand that I meant it when I said I could handle my mother alone. Just like I can handle talking to Ben Stafford. I know the truth. So don't you dare lose your faith in me or in us."

"I never will, but I can't stand this." My chest feels like stone. "I know what you've been telling me. I can't protect you from everything. I get it. But goddammit, Liv, I'm not supposed to be the one hurting you again."

"You're not! The only thing hurting me is that we have to be apart."

"Then I'm coming home."

"Dean, you—"

"I talked to Simon this morning about figuring out a way I can do the work from home. Maybe with one or two short trips to Altopascio. I'll make it work. I can't stay away from you until the end of July. I won't."

My heart hammers as I wait for her response. She was the one who wanted me to leave in the first place, convinced it would be good for me, for us. And I've been okay with going on the dig—been grateful for the job, even—and the dating thing Liv and I are doing has admittedly been fun.

But ultimately it all means that I'm away from my wife. When the only place I want to be is *with* her.

"Oh, Dean," Liv says. "You know I want you to come home. We *need* to be together, but—"

"No. There's no *but* in this conversation, Liv. I'm coming home."

"Frances told you to stay, that it was good for your career."

"I don't care what Frances said."

"She knows you're doing well there."

"Yeah, I'm doing well here." I shove off the bed and start to pace. "I'm doing well because I know how to work. But nothing I do here is going to make a damned bit of difference if I have to abandon you. And I'm sick of it. I'm sick of being away from you, not seeing you, talking to you only once a day, jerking off every night because I can't be with you… No. Fuck this, Liv. I've never hidden before. I'm not going to start now."

My chest heaves. I press a hand to the wall and suck in a hard breath.

"Liv."

Suspicious silence on the other end.

Oh shit.

"Liv, don't cry." I bang my forehead against the wall. "Please don't."

"I'm not." Her voice sounds thick. "Dean, please… look, I know it seems like nothing is within your control, but—"

"It doesn't *seem* that way," I interrupt. "It *is* that way. It's been that way since last fall when things got so fucked-up and I couldn't fix them. Then that mess with my parents, the miscarriage, this bogus charge against me, the suspension… Jesus, Liv. I told Frances I'd quit my job to stop this whole thing."

"You told her you'd *quit?*"

"What the fuck else can I do? Stafford's forcing me to sit on my ass until he finishes his investigation. You're getting dragged into this shitstorm right when you're starting a new business. And I can't give you anything, Liv, not even a guarantee that I'll still have my job next year. At least if I quit, I can stop it from getting worse."

"For God's sake, Dean, you've never quit anything in your

life. But you're going to let that girl force you out of a job that you love?"

"Damn right I will, if it'll—"

The words stop abruptly in my throat.

Silence vibrates.

"If it'll protect me," Liv finishes.

Goddammit.

Anger breaks inside me. I grip the phone harder.

"Look, I'm not going to apologize anymore," I snap. "Yes, I want to protect you. You're my wife. I'd fucking kill for you, Liv, and if that makes me a possessive bastard of a husband, then fine. That's what I am. I'm not going to change either. I love you too goddamned much."

"I know you do!" she cries. "I know you would. That's why it scares the crap out of me to think of you back in Mirror Lake before the investigation is over."

I stop. "What?"

"Dean, I wanted you to leave because I knew you wouldn't be able to stand doing nothing here, but I also…"

"What? You wanted to stand on your own, right? Well, you have. Now you still don't want me to come back?"

"No! That's not what I—"

"Not what you meant?" I stalk across the room. A thousand sharp edges cut into my chest. "What did you mean then, Liv? That I should stay away until it's convenient for you that I come back? That I should jerk off and talk dirty to you until you finally decide it's okay for us to be a married couple again? That you don't want me to come back because you need to do everything by yourself now?"

"Dean, would you shut up and listen to me?"

She's crying. My throat aches.

Is *that* it? Have I been stifling her so much that I can't see any other way? Is that why she insisted I leave? Does she really think she can't do anything with me near her?

I stare out the window. The courtyard blurs in front of my eyes.

Do I love my wife too much?

"Dean? Dean… are you there?"

"I'm here."

I'll always be here. She could rip me open, tear me apart, and I'd still crawl back to her. She's had me whipped since the day she stood in front of me on the sidewalk with her hair all windblown as she asked me about medieval knights.

And while I've been trying my damnedest to give her what she wants—I'd promised her I would—I can't stand the thought that she'd ever believe us being apart is a good thing.

I try to breathe. My heart is racing. The walls are closing in.

"I need you to listen to me, Dean."

"I am."

Liv takes a breath. "When I asked you to leave, when you left, yes, I knew it was a chance for me to stand on my own. And I have. But I also…"

"What?"

"I knew… I knew that if anything happened here, if Maggie started spreading rumors, if something got out about the charge, I knew you'd be safer if you were gone."

I sink onto the edge of the bed, all the wind knocked out of me.

"You—"

"I wanted you to be safe," Liv admits, her voice still thick.

"It was… it was the only way I could think of to protect you from anything bad that might happen here. And to keep you away from my mother. I told you I don't want her to poison my life any more than she already has, but more than anything I don't want her to poison *you*."

"She… she can't hurt me."

"She already has. You've always been angry with her for what she did to me, for what she *didn't* do. I just… I knew if you went back to Italy, she couldn't touch you. But because you are such a stubborn ass, I also knew you'd fight me tooth and nail if you thought my mother was the reason you had to leave again. *I* can handle her. But I don't want you to have to."

"Liv." I picture her all curled up in my office chair, hugging her knees to her chest, her hair sliding over her shoulders. I'm about to break in half.

"I'm here," she says.

"Okay." I shut my eyes. "Okay. I love you."

"I'm yours," Liv whispers. "I'll always be yours. You told me once that I became your world the minute you saw me. It was the same for me. I'll never forget it, Dean, the instant I looked up and saw you. Something opened in me, something I didn't even know existed. And then when you reached out to touch me… I couldn't believe how I was reacting, this intense, hot *pull*, like I already knew I belonged to you."

"Damn right you belong to me." My voice roughens. "You belong *with* me. I'm not doing this anymore. I'm not staying away from you. I need you, dammit."

"Oh, Dean." Liv's breath escapes on a rush. "Whatever you need from me, you know I'll give it to you. I'll do anything for you."

"Anything?"

"Anything."

"Then get ready for me. I'm coming home."

CHAPTER SEVENTEEN

Olivia

April 28

*M*y mother moves in with the owner of the auto repair shop after she takes her car in to be fixed. Our apartment seems lighter without her, and though she still comes to help at the café on occasion, we don't speak much after our argument.

I try not to think about the fact that she is very likely still here because she's feeling the loss of her own mother in ways she probably never comprehended. And all her futile attempts to convince me to come with her again are a sad way of easing the loss. I try not to think about the fact that I might even pity her.

The day before Dean is scheduled to return, I go to the university for my meeting with Ben Stafford of the Office of Judicial Affairs. He is a slender, bearded man with a long, narrow nose who reminds me a little of Inspector Clouseau. This is rather comforting, as I'd been having images of me sweating under hot interrogation lights.

"Can you please tell me when you first met Professor Dean West?" Mr. Stafford asks, after we're seated in his office.

"When I was a student at the University of Wisconsin."

"First year?"

"Yes, but it was my junior year. I was twenty-four. It was my first year as a transfer student."

"Your major?"

"Library sciences and literature."

"How did you meet Professor West?"

"I had some trouble with transfer credits and was at the registrar's office trying to work it out. He was there and offered to help."

Ben Stafford peers at me. "How did he offer to help?"

"He suggested I go to the professors directly and ask them to approve the credits. I did, and the problem was solved."

"When did you begin dating?"

"A few weeks later, after he came into the coffeehouse where I was working." I'm starting to get nervous, which seems silly since I'm just telling the truth. But I've never talked to anyone about how I met Dean, let alone our relationship, and it feels like I'm divulging our secrets.

I know there has always been a teaching dynamic to my relationship with Dean, mostly because of our different world experiences, not to mention his sexual confidence and history. But never has that dynamic been controlled by a sordid sense of power.

I take a drink of water and try to steady my shaking hands.

"Did you ever take a class with Professor West?" Stafford asks.

"No."

"Did you ever enroll in one?"

"No."

"Any Medieval Studies classes?"

"No."

He nods and makes a note on his legal pad. "Do you remember your first date?"

Seriously? How could I ever forget?

"Yes," I say. "Dean asked me to attend a lecture he was giving at a local museum. We had dinner afterward."

"At the time he asked you to attend the lecture, did Professor West make any implications about your class schedule or grades?"

"No."

"Did you discuss your academic work?"

"During the date, yes, but just casually. Like what classes I was taking, that sort of thing."

"Did you find it odd that a professor would ask a student out on a date?"

"No, because I wasn't his student. I knew it wasn't against university regulations."

"At any time did Professor West indicate that your response to his requests would affect your academic work?"

"Never."

Mr. Stafford scribbles notes again and asks more questions— how much did I know about Dean's classes, did I ever interact with any of his students, what was my level of involvement in his work.

The questions go on for about an hour before Stafford seems satisfied. He asks me to sign a form before reaching to turn off the recorder. As I put the pen down, I notice a small framed picture on the desk of Mr. Stafford, a blonde woman who must be his wife, and two young girls.

"Your daughters?" I ask, gesturing to the picture.

He nods with evident pride. "Emma and Nellie. They're seven and nine."

"You should bring them to the grand opening of our café," I suggest, taking a flyer from a folder inside my satchel. "It's at the beginning of June, and we're going to have all sorts of fun activities like face painting and a bouncy house. Lots of free food too."

"Sounds like fun." Stafford glances over the flyer as he walks me to the door. "I apologize again for having to involve you in this, Mrs. West, but you saved us some time by contacting me."

"I assume you also have to investigate Miss Hamilton's history as well." I turn to shake his hand. "To see if she's made such an accusation before?"

The second the words are out of my mouth, something jars loose in the back of my mind. I try to grab it as Stafford nods solemnly.

"We're covering all bases, Mrs. West, I assure you. As I told your husband, please don't try to contact or speak to Miss Hamilton. It's best for all involved if you communicate everything through the OJA."

We thank each other again before I leave the office and go outside.

What the hell am I trying to remember?

As I walk back to the parking lot, I think of the day last fall when Maggie Hamilton confronted me. She'd gotten angry and made a nasty comment about Dean expecting more from his female students than good scholarship.

What else did she say? Why do I feel like I'm missing something important?

I get out my cell phone and leave Dean a message telling him that Stafford was polite and respectful, and the meeting was fine.

After I hang up, I push aside thoughts of the investigation and focus on my happiness that Dean is coming home. Despite my belief that his time in Italy did us both good, I know that he's right, that the next step for us is learning how to handle all of this *together*.

I go to the café where Allie, Brent, and a few other friends are busy working. After greeting them, I head to a bathroom to change into ratty jeans and a T-shirt, then grab a paintbrush and get to work.

"Liv, that looks great." Allie comes into the room where I'm painting the window trim. "Brent is bringing in more paint for the murals tomorrow, and Marianne wants us to meet her at the restaurant supply place sometime this week to finalize our order."

"I'm free anytime after noon," I tell her. "Just let me know."

We discuss a few more business-related issues before I finish the windows and go out to pick up pizzas for everyone. After eating, I get back to painting until it starts to get dark.

"Liv, we gotta go," Allie shouts up the stairs.

"I'll stay and work for a couple more hours," I call. Dean will be back tomorrow morning, and I want to be at home when he arrives. "I'm almost done with this room."

"You shouldn't stay here alone, so come on. We'll finish it tomorrow."

Knowing she won't leave without me, I put my supplies away and head downstairs. I decline Allie and Brent's offer of a ride and walk home, enjoying the fresh air. Streetlamps are starting to twinkle over the sidewalks, and the sky is covered with reddish clouds.

I pick up the mail and go upstairs to the apartment. The instant I step into the foyer, my heart leaps.

And I *know.* I know without needing to see him that Dean is here.

Anticipation fills me. I drop my satchel and jacket and go inside. His travel bag is by the sofa. I hurry into the bedroom just as the bathroom door opens.

Dean steps out, naked except for a towel wrapped around his waist, his hair damp and his chest glistening with water droplets.

"Oh." I stop, my breath escaping on a rush. His masculine beauty strikes me right in the heart, flooding me with pleasure. "Hi."

His dark gaze sweeps over me from head to toe, a slow appraisal that has my pulse kicking into high gear. It's a touch, that look, sending a waterfall of shivers over me. A taut, leashed energy radiates from him. He hasn't shaved yet, and the coating of stubble over his jaw combined with the coiled tension of his powerful body and the intense look in his eyes...

I swallow to ease the dryness of my throat. "I... I was expecting you back tomorrow."

"You'd better expect me right now." His voice is edged with roughness, like a torn piece of paper.

He steps toward me, his muscles steeling. I can't move,

can only stand there staring at him as he approaches me with a determination that has my whole body zinging with eagerness. His gaze pins me to the spot. Urgency builds in me like steam, and I'm aching to let my own gaze slide down the sculpted muscles of his torso to the front of his towel…

But I don't—can't—look away from those gold-flecked eyes that have always watched me with heat, love, tenderness. I can't read them now, can't see anything beyond the fierce, contained resolve that vibrates from every fiber of his being. A combination of anticipation and excitement twirls through me.

Dean stops inches from me. Heat emanates from his damp skin. The delicious smells of soap and *him* sink into my blood, warming me from the inside out. A drop of water slides from his hair over his smooth shoulder, and I'm seized with the urge to follow the path with my tongue, to lick the strong column of his throat…

He plants both hands on the wall behind me, caging me between his arms. He presses closer, pushing me to retreat until my back hits the wall. And then I'm surrounded by him, engulfed by the heat of his body, his mouthwatering scent, the desire coursing through both of us.

I lift a hand to touch his face, running my fingers over the whiskered planes of his jaw, over his lips, down to the hollow of his throat. My heart races. His gaze never leaves mine.

He moves even closer and lowers his head. I part my lips to draw in a breath, desperate for a strong, possessive kiss that will overwhelm me with lust and eradicate any barriers still lingering between us.

He touches his lips to mine. Lightly, almost not there at all, but I feel it, feel *him,* and I curl my fingers into my palms against the growing ache of need. The contrast between the hard urgency of Dean's body and the restraint of his kiss is wildly exciting. The pulsing between my legs expands into a heavy throb.

Dean doesn't take his hands from the wall behind me as he lifts his head to look at me again. He motions with his head to my clothes.

"Take them off."

An intense surge of desire rockets through me. My hands shake. I unfasten my jeans and push them over my hips. Again, dammit, I'm not wearing my sexy lingerie. At least my legs are shaved this time, but I'd planned to meet him all pretty and perfumed-up, clad in my polka-dot panties and lace-edged bra...

I push my shoes off and wiggle quickly out of my jeans, kicking them aside. Dean nods at my T-shirt.

"And that."

I grasp the hem and yank the ragged shirt over my head. My nipples push against the stretched fabric of my bra. I unhook the front clasp and toss the bra on top of my discarded clothes.

Cooler air sensitizes my nipples, which ache with the need to be touched. My blood pounds. I want Dean to cup my breasts in his big hands and twist my nipples while kissing me so hard and deep I forget my own name.

His eyes burn with lust. He pushes his knee between my legs. My heart jolts with arousal. Beneath the towel, his thick erection presses against my belly. I swallow and lean my head back against the wall. Dean's lips brush mine, his tongue probing into my mouth, his chest rubbing against my taut nipples. Everything inside me softens and yields to him.

But his restraint is stretching my urgency to the breaking point. Sweat breaks out on my forehead. The core of my body is an unending pulse. I let my eyes close, breathe in the scent of him, and absorb the feeling of utter safety within the confines of his strong arms.

He moves his lips across my cheek, his breath hot. I'm trembling with need, and if I don't have something to hold on to, I'll slide to the floor. I run my hands over his arms to his shoulders. His muscles flex beneath my palms, and I'm seized by the urge to stroke down to his chest where I can trace all the slopes and planes of his sculpted torso…

"Dean, kiss me," I plead, when he runs his tongue slowly across my lower lip.

"Kiss you?" he whispers, his voice guttural with restraint. "Or fuck you?"

A wave of heat washes over me. "Both. Oh, please… both."

He doesn't. He trails his lips over my cheek again, down the side of my neck, his stubble scraping my skin. Tingles fall through me. I tighten my hands on his shoulders, a glow spreading in me like the rays of the sun.

He lifts his head again, his gaze tracking down to my bare breasts, my hard nipples. He shifts his hips, rubbing his cock against me. The friction of the towel combined with that hot bulge beneath it… a gasp catches in my throat. Then he grabs the knot of the towel and pulls it off, his erection springing up between us.

I melt, my knees weakening at the sight of his thick shaft. I can't stop myself from closing my hand around his cock and tracing the pulsing veins with my fingers. He mutters something under his breath, pushing his hips forward.

"Tighter," he orders hoarsely.

I increase my grip on him, running my thumb over the damp head of his cock in the way I know he likes. He pulls back and pushes forward again, fucking the vise of my fist. My breath burns through my chest, quivers centering in my lower body.

Dean puts his hand flat against my belly and slides it down between my legs, his forefinger pressing my clit through the cotton of my underwear. Electricity bursts in my veins. I sink back against the wall. Every cell in my body strains toward the intense, deep bliss that only he can give me.

I move both hands up to his shoulders and arch my hips into his touch. He shifts closer, his lips against mine, his finger probing deeper as his tongue does a hot, slow sweep of my mouth.

He eases his hand beneath my panties, and then he's inside me, stroking me with two fingers, his thumb circling my clit. Pressure builds in me like steam, scorching my blood. I surrender, clutching at him as the strain breaks and floods me with sensation. Dean captures my cry of pleasure, pressing one hand to the small of my back as vibrations shake me to the core.

Gasping, I sink against him, my heart pulsing as he strips off my underwear. Tension ripples through him, the beat of urgency that I know so well. He moves away only long enough to roll on a condom, then grabs my waist and pushes me back up against the wall.

His eyes are almost black, seething with heat. Before I can even take another breath, he hooks his arms beneath my thighs and lifts me off the ground, plunging his cock into me at the same instant. Another cry wrenches from my throat at the sensation of him filling me, stretching me. I can't move, can only grip his shoulders and hold on.

Sensation drenches me—the wall against my back, my legs spread over his arms, his shaft thrusting up and into me again and again, his deep groans vibrating against my skin. Our bodies slam together, the slick sound of fucking filling my ears, the scent of sex flooding my nose. My head falls back, my hair sticking to my damp skin.

His mouth crashes down on mine, and I open in near desperation, needing every part of him inside me, his breath, his voice, his body. Sudden tears sting my eyes, and his name breaks from me on a sob. My legs ache. I cling to him, feeling him plunge so deep, all the way to the center of me, his cock pulsing and throbbing.

He presses his forehead against mine, his chest heaving, his fingers digging into the undersides of my thighs. Sweat drips down his temple.

My body flares with a riotous combination of love and desire. I tighten my fingers into the muscles of his back as another orgasm rips through me, my sex clenching around his thick shaft. He thrusts again, the rhythm getting faster, even deeper, until a violent shudder racks his body. He groans, pushing forward, holding me against the wall.

Dean doesn't let go of me, doesn't release me. He puts his face against my shoulder, his breath rough. He lowers me slowly to the ground, but I'm shaking so hard that my knees buckle.

He tucks his hands beneath my knees again and lifts me against his chest, taking me a few steps to the bed. I wind my arms around his neck, bringing him down onto the bed with me.

He brushes my hair away from my forehead, stroking his

palm over my cheek. As our breathing slows, I curl up against his side and absorb the pleasure of us back in our bed together. His muscular arm is heavy around me. I rest my head on his chest, falling asleep to the rhythm of his heartbeat.

When I wake, my body loose, my blood still pulsing, I feel Dean's gaze on me. I look up into his eyes that are filled with a hundred emotions I can't define. I press my hand against his jaw, moving my palm up into his messy hair.

"Your paper on the Notre-Dame chapels was about the socio-economic context of their construction," I murmur. "You analyzed how the design of the chapels influenced their function and served as a standard model for French chapel architecture."

The line between his eyebrows eases. "You read my paper."

"I found all your articles in your filing cabinet." I shift and move my leg over him so that I'm straddling his thighs. His gaze goes to my naked breasts.

"You've written a ton of stuff, Professor West," I remark. "I even read your book on Romanesque cathedrals. I learned that Romanesque walls were very thick and… massive."

"Yeah?" He strokes the curves of my waist and around to my back.

His body is hot between my legs. I run my hands over his powerful chest, skimming my fingertips across the ridges of his abdomen. I lean down so that my hair falls in a curtain on either side of his face.

"I learned a lot about medieval architecture from you," I whisper, looking into his dark eyes.

"Like what?"

"All about groin vaults." I kiss his chin. "And drum columns."

"Mmm." He squeezes my ass.

"Elevated naves." I kiss his nose. "Enlarged piers." I kiss his cheek. "Structural members."

I trail my lips over his jaw to his ear and whisper, "Double bay systems."

"Baby, that is so fucking hot."

I giggle and squirm backward on his thighs, pressing my mouth to his neck, his smooth shoulders, the slopes of his chest. The sensation of his firm, taut skin and hard muscles has my own body responding with a surge of heat. I straddle one of his thighs and press my cleft against him. He groans, his hands flexing on my hips.

I move lower, spreading my hands over his stomach, until I can slide my lips over his cock and take him into my mouth.

"Oh, shit, Liv…" He tightens his hand in my hair as his erection swells in my mouth.

I love this, love the salty, male taste of him, feeling him harden, his muscles tensing beneath me. I lick his shaft, swirl my tongue around the tip, wrap my hand around the base. When I feel him straining toward me, I ease away to roll a condom onto him, then move back up to straddle him again.

His eyes seethe with lust as he clutches my waist to adjust my angle. I lower myself onto his cock, gasping at the sensation of him filling me, pulsing and hot. I brace my hands against his chest and ride him, our bodies thrusting, our breath rasping in the air. We fall into it at the same time, the overwhelming need and passion, the slick, easy way that we move together, the rhythm of us.

I lower myself onto him, my breasts rubbing against his chest. He tightens his grip on my hips as he pushes inside me, driving us both toward the explosive release that only we can create. When we're on the edge, he grabs the back of my neck and brings my mouth to his as bliss shatters us both.

CHAPTER EIGHTEEN

DEAN

*L*iv is still sleeping, half-buried under the covers, her hair spilling over the pillows. I bend to press a kiss against her cheek, breathe in her peachy scent.

I go into the kitchen to start the coffee, liking the familiarity of being back in our apartment. I haven't been here in weeks. Out of habit, I glance at the clock a few times, even though I have nowhere I need to be anytime soon.

Deflecting a stab of irritation, I take two mugs from the cupboard. I've never had nothing to do, nowhere to go. There have always been classes, work, lectures, research, meetings. As much as I hated being away from Liv, she was right when she told me I had to go to Altopascio or I'd go crazy just sitting around.

"Is it really almost seven?" Liv shuffles out of the bedroom in her nightshirt, rubbing one eye and yawning. "Why didn't you wake me?"

"I didn't know I should. You're never up before seven."

"These days I'm up by six," Liv says. "Got work to do. Oh, hey, look at you standing in our kitchen all shirtless and sexy."

I smile and extend my arms to her. She walks into them, burrowing against my chest, her body warm and soft. I press my mouth to her hair and tighten my arms around her. Exactly where we both belong.

To my unexpected pleasure, we fall into our old routine with ease, as if we've never been apart, as if I've been here all along. I pour the coffee, she sets the table, I make eggs, she gets out the bread for toasting and brushes up against me whenever she passes by.

Exactly the way it's supposed to be.

After breakfast, Liv gets ready and leaves for the day. I answer emails and phone calls about the Altopascio dig before going to meet Frances Hunter at a nearby coffeehouse.

"Sorry I'm late, Dean." Frances stops by the table, trying to balance a coffee, a wet umbrella, and her bag.

I stand to help her, and she mutters a few complaints about the rainy weather before settling in across from me.

"You look tired," she remarks.

"Jet lag."

"How's Liv?"

"Fine." Better than she's ever been, probably. That thought

eases my apprehension about what Frances might have to tell me this time.

"How's her café coming along?" Frances asks. "I read an article in a professional women's magazine about it."

"The article is out already?"

"The latest issue came out just a couple of days ago," Frances says. "It was a great article, all about the history of the building and the tearoom, and how Liv and some friends are turning it into a children's café."

My pride in my wife knows no bounds. I make a mental note to stop at the store and buy the magazine.

"Well." I pull my cup toward me. "All the more reason I need to put an end to this nightmare."

"Just a few more weeks, Dean," Frances says. "May twentieth."

"What about it?"

"That's when Ben Stafford will make his recommendation about the case." Frances removes the lid from her coffee and takes a sip. "If he determines there's enough evidence against you, he'll go to the board of trustees and recommend that they pursue the case. If not, he'll close the file."

"Then what happens?"

"Either you get formally suspended or you return to your job."

Her tone is so matter-of-fact—*either you get regular or decaf*—that I almost laugh.

"That's it?" I ask.

A smile cracks her face. "Easy, huh?"

"Christ, Frances." I shake my head and take a gulp of coffee. "With Hamilton like a fucking bloodhound… What if he keeps up with his own damned investigation?"

"I don't know." She shrugs. "Really, though, I don't imagine he'd discover anything that could be used against you. At least, nothing Ben Stafford wouldn't also know about. Unless there's something you haven't told us."

"Nothing relevant to this. I haven't done anything wrong."

"For what it's worth," Frances says, "the board of trustees is very impressed with your work on such a prestigious dig, not to mention your IHR grant and the conference. Even if Stafford does recommend further investigation, I'm certain the board will be... lenient. None of the board members want to lose you, Dean."

My jaw tightens. "But if this cluster-fuck gets turned over to them, everyone knows about it. And with Hamilton still dangling his donation to the law school in front of them... Forget it, Frances. I'm screwed."

She doesn't respond, but we both know it's the truth. Even if by some miracle I escape this alive, any confidentiality would be shattered. Faculty, students, administration... all of them would know that a female student accused me of harassing her.

And as much as I hate Crystal Winter, she was right about one thing. The stigma will never go away.

"Will Stafford interview my other students?" I ask.

"Not unless he recommends that the board pursues the case."

"Which we both know he will." I stare out the window. "This is a fucking nightmare, Frances."

"I know." She hesitates. "Look, if it's any consolation, your reviews are outstanding. I've no doubt every one of your students will vouch for your integrity."

Sure. While they're being asked questions like, *Has Professor Dean West ever made suggestive comments to you or touched you inappropriately?*

"There's not much recourse against a false claim of sexual harassment, Frances," I say. "Even my lawyer admitted that. The fallout is brutal."

She doesn't respond.

"Jessica Burke told me Maggie is spreading shit about me to the other students," I continue. My chest is tight. I have the sick, pervasive sense again that there's no way out of this. "It won't be long before something gets out about me harassing her, even if Stafford doesn't want the board involved."

"I'm sorry, Dean," Frances says.

Though I know she really is sorry, I also know there is nothing she can do.

I push away from the table. "Anything else?"

"No. Just hang in there." She looks down at her coffee, her face etched with lines of frustration and disappointment.

Guilt stabs me. Frances was the one who hired me. And now she's had to waste a ton of time and energy on this investigation. If it goes to the board, she'll take some heat too, not to mention having to be the one to explain it all to the rest of the history faculty and all the students.

As I pass her chair, I pause to put my hand on her shoulder. Apologies crowd my throat. Finally I manage to say, "Thank you."

She puts her hand on mine and nods. "Say hello to Liv for me, Dean."

Liv.

I have a sudden urge to see my wife. I say goodbye to Frances and head outside. The rain has stopped, sunlight breaking through the gray clouds and warming the spring air. I walk down Avalon Street and turn toward the café.

As I approach the Historical Museum, a white-haired lady in a pink suit and little hat crosses the sidewalk to the front steps. She pauses and peers at me with one of those *I know you* looks that elderly ladies often have.

"Nice afternoon," I offer.

"Yes, it is," she agrees. "Aren't you Olivia's husband?"

"I am." I extend my hand. "Dean West."

"Of course." She smiles as she closes her gloved hand around mine. "Florence Wickham. I'm on the Historical Society's board of directors. We met at last year's holiday party."

"I remember. It's nice to see you again."

"You too. I thought you were out of town."

"I was. I'm back now."

"Lovely. We adore Olivia, Dean. Her new café sounds just delightful."

"She and her partners are doing amazing work."

"I told her that my granddaughter is the assistant superintendent of the Rainwood school district," Florence informs me. "She has many contacts in the area with parent organizations, and she's very excited about the Wonderland Café. And even with all that work, Olivia has been so helpful with our Butterfly House campaign."

Heat slides through my veins at the memory of what Liv and I did at the Butterfly House. I return Florence's smile. "She's been enjoying the research."

"You're a historian, isn't that correct?" Florence tilts her head toward the museum doors. "Would you mind giving me your opinion on something?"

"Sure." I hold open the door for her, then follow her inside and back to the offices.

"We're trying to raise the money to restore the house to its original structure." Florence takes out a bunch of photos and documents and spreads them over a long table. "But we're having a terrible time with the zoning laws and such, which is hampering our fund-raising efforts. And because it's such a prime piece of land, we're worried the city will pressure us to sell it to a developer, who would demolish the house."

"That would be a shame."

"Yes. We want to apply for government grants, but we must emphasize the historical value of the home. That's what Olivia has been working on, and we're going to submit photographs as well. As a historian, what elements of the house itself would you consider most important?"

I pick up a photo and study it. "The architectural features that are most distinctive to the time period and house style. Like these decorated gables, the polygonal tower, the wraparound porch. And interior features like the wooden relief panels and plaster medallions."

Florence blinks. "We haven't been inside yet."

"Uh, I meant… I assume the house has features like that." I clear my throat. "Why haven't you been inside yet?"

"We need to thoroughly clean it, but we don't have the money or staffing." Florence shrugs. "That's the reason most things are delayed."

"I could help with clearing it out."

She glances at me. "You mean the interior?"

"Sure. I'd just need a dumpster. There's some furniture you might want to keep and restore, but there's also a lot of stuff from previous remodeling jobs that can be thrown away."

"How do you know that?"

Though this might get me in trouble, I admit, "Liv and I went into the house a few weeks ago. Just to look around."

"Oh." Florence looks intrigued. "And you say there's still furniture?"

"It's pretty much a mess," I tell her. "But if you want, I can start to go through it all. I'd be able to tell what's worth saving and what should be tossed. Then I can take pictures of the interior features that are historically important."

"Oh, how wonderful, Dean!" A smile breaks over her face, crinkling her eyes. "We would love for you to do that. I'm afraid we don't have the funds to pay you, but—"

"I'm volunteering," I say. "I'm on leave from the university this semester, so I'll be glad to have something to do."

Florence claps her hands in excitement and gives me a warm hug that smells like talcum powder.

"I'm heading to a board meeting right now," she says, gathering up the documents and photos. "I'll tell the other members about you. They'll be thrilled. We've been wanting to get started on the interior, but just haven't had the resources."

She pauses at the door. "Was Olivia able to locate the keys? I didn't think anyone had found out where they are yet."

"No, but I don't need the keys." Though I realize I'm admitting to breaking and entering, I suspect Florence won't mind. "There's a way to get in through the side door. I just have to squeeze through."

"Oh." She tugs one of her gloves up her wrist, eyeing me with speculation. "Well, you are quite the expert at squeezing into tight spaces, aren't you, Dean? Out of them too, I imagine."

She gives me a smile and a little wave before heading off.

I have no idea what she just meant by that, but then again I don't have much experience dealing with elderly ladies.

I take out my phone and text Liv that I'm heading up to the Butterfly House. I stop to get a toolkit and other supplies out of our storage garage, then drive to where the house sits on its huge parcel of land.

After shouldering my way in through the loose board at the side, I walk through the house again, studying the furniture, everything that needs to be fixed, picturing how it would look if it were all restored to its original glory.

Then I open the front door and get to work.

May 7

It takes one phone call. It's almost a relief, as if I've been waiting for the catalyst. The excuse I need to finally confront the thing that has gnawed at me for weeks.

It's a warm day, the trees and flowers flourishing, the sun bright. A few boats are out on the lake, the sails like giant bird wings. After working for a couple hours at the Butterfly House, I drive to the café with the intention of asking Liv if she wants to go to lunch.

The place looks phenomenal with new tables and chairs, the walls painted and murals almost done, the hardwood floor gleaming. I find Liv in the kitchen, going over some papers with a few people she'd introduced to me as the head chef and kitchen staff.

Liv gives me a quick smile and wave of hello, then turns

back to the discussion. I watch her, my heart thumping hard as it always does at the sight of her.

She looks different—more confident, in charge, as they talk about the stations, the ordering system, purchase specifications, and work flow.

I let out a breath, feeling something loosen inside me. This, I know, is exactly what Liv wanted. Even through all we've had to deal with, she's stood her ground, found a goal, and gotten it done. She's finally realized how strong she is and has proven it to herself.

When she sets the papers down and approaches me, I'm grinning like a fool.

Liv stops, amused. "Well, you look happy."

"Sure I'm happy. You're here, aren't you?"

"Aw." She smiles, giving me a little pinch on the arm. "Good one."

"Can I take you to lunch?"

"Of course. Just give me a sec."

We return to the main room, and Liv goes behind the front counter to her open laptop. I sit down at one of the chairs, which has upholstery covered with a playing card design in honor of *Alice in Wonderland,* and wait for Liv to finish typing on the computer.

The phone rings. Still looking at her computer, Liv answers it.

"Good afternoon, Wonderland Café."

She pauses. Something radiates from her suddenly that gets me to my feet. I cross the room in a few strides, tension clawing at me.

"Yes?" Liv says into the phone.

She turns, her gaze meeting mine. My instinct kicks into gear, and I'm reaching for the phone before I can think. Liv puts her hand up and steps back, the phone still pressed to her ear.

"What?" she says into the receiver, her skin paling. "No. I don't want to talk to him."

I go around the counter and grab the phone from her, knowing to my bones what this is about.

"This is Dean West," I tell the caller. "Who's this?"

"Um... I was speaking to Olivia West," replies a woman.

"This is her husband." My grip is about to break the phone. "Who is this?"

"This is Mary Frederick, assistant to Mr. Edward Hamilton. Mr. Hamilton would like to make an appointment to speak to Mrs. West about—"

I slam the phone down, anger flooding me, my heart hammering. Liv is watching me, wary now, her eyes dark with the realization of what that phone call means. Edward Hamilton is now a very real threat to her and possibly her new business.

"What does he want?" she asks.

"To get to me." *Through you.*

Edward Hamilton is an asshole, but he's not stupid. He figured out early on that Liv is the one guaranteed way he can scare me. That if he goes after her... I'll do whatever it takes to protect her.

Liv knows that too.

Her brown eyes fill with fear, pain, worry. A sharp ache cuts through my chest. And as my wife and I stand there in the Wonderland Café looking at each other, the decision solidifies inside me like ice.

I reach out to tuck a lock of Liv's hair behind her ear. Any excuse to touch her. Not that I need an excuse. Most of the time I touch her just because I want to. Because I can. Because she's mine.

"I need you to do something for me," I finally say.

"Anything."

"Don't change your mind. Don't tell me you want to talk to Hamilton and defend me or defend us. Not now. Not ever. I will go bat-shit crazy if I have to let you go to him."

She curls her hand around my wrist. My pulse beats against her fingers. She shakes her head.

"I won't," she promises. "I'd never talk to him about us."

"Okay." Relief melts away some of the ice.

"What if he…"

Her voice trails off, leaving a hundred questions unspoken. A seething anger snakes into my blood at the thought of what the answers could be.

"I'm going to deal with this." I tug my arm from Liv's grasp. "And you're going to let me."

If there is one certainty in the world, it's that my wife knows me. She knows that this is not a question, not a negotiation.

"What are you going to do?" she asks.

"I'm going to talk to him."

Liv nods, her expression clouding. "Please be careful."

"If his assistant calls again, hang up on her," I say.

"What if he calls?"

"He won't." I check the caller ID on the café phone, then take out my cell phone and program Hamilton's office number in. "I'll take care of this."

There's no other option. Not with Hamilton closing in.

Instead of taking Liv to lunch, I go home and make arrangements for the hour-and-a-half flight to Chicago the following day, with a return flight the same evening. I call Frances Hunter and keep the conversation short. Apologize. Don't listen to her protests. Thank her and apologize a second time.

Then I call Hamilton's office and tell his assistant when I'll be there.

The next morning, I say goodbye to my wife yet again.

The hot, sweet crush of her body against mine, a tangle of silky hair, the peach softness of her cheek, the press of her mouth.

She's all I'm thinking about as the flight lands in Chicago. She's all that matters. I catch a taxi from the airport, and the driver stops in front of a downtown high-rise. I grab my briefcase and go inside, taking the elevator to the twelfth floor.

Edward Hamilton's law office is filled with leather chairs and polished mahogany furniture. His receptionist greets me with a smile and offers coffee or tea.

"No, thank you."

"All right, follow me, please. Mr. Hamilton is waiting for you."

My teeth clench as I follow her into the room, the window overlooking the lake, the huge desk where Hamilton is sitting in his leather chair. He's on the phone, and he gestures the receptionist out of the room as his gaze meets mine.

"I'll call you back," he says into the receiver before dropping it back onto the cradle.

Hostility thickens the air. He points to a chair.

I set my briefcase down and remain standing. "I want you to leave my wife alone."

He eyes me narrowly, closing his hand around a pencil and tapping it on the desk. "I'm sure you do."

"She has nothing to do with this."

"Stafford thinks she does," Hamilton replies. "We have

evidence that you were involved with a student in the past. A student whom you seduced and later married."

My fists clench. Anger heats my insides.

"What do you want?" I ask.

"You know what I want," he says, pushing to stand up. "You fucked with my daughter, and I want you gone. She can't get anything done with you still at King's, and there's no way she can graduate with you there. If the board doesn't fire you, I'll beat you to a pulp myself."

Every muscle in my body tenses for a fight. I need one excuse, one goddamned opening...

Hamilton looks down at some papers on his desk.

"Your wife had a nervous breakdown, didn't she?" he asks. "Lost her merit scholarship at... Fieldbrook College in the first year. What exactly happened? Reports are that she dropped out for personal reasons, but there's a record that a psychologist had to—"

"You fucker."

I leap across the desk before I can think. Grab Hamilton by the throat and bring us both crashing to the floor behind the desk. My fist connects with his face. He grunts. I hit him again. My vision goes red.

"Mr. Hamilton!" The receptionist's voice penetrates my anger.

I land two more punches on Hamilton and pull back for a third when two security guards grab my arms and yank me off him.

I fight them, my blood replaced with rage, hating the restraint. *Don't stop me, you bastards. Let me kill him.* The guards are shouting. One of them wrestles me away. Hamilton climbs to his feet, wiping a trickle of blood from his mouth.

"Mr. Hamilton?" The receptionist hurries forward. "Are you all right?"

I push myself away from the guards, holding my hands up. My breath burns my chest. I stalk to the other side of the room.

"You want us to throw him out, sir?" one of the guards asks.

Hamilton heaves in a breath, his gaze cold on me as he shakes his head. "No."

"But, Mr. Hamilton, you—"

"Never mind, Mary." Hamilton waves a hand to the door. "Go away."

With a worried glance at me, Mary hurries from the room again. The guards hesitate before Hamilton snaps at them to get out.

"We'll be right outside," one of them says. They leave the room and shut the door behind them.

I clench my jaw. My shoulders are about to crack.

"How far do you want to take this, West?" Hamilton grabs a glass of water from his desk and takes a swallow. "You want me to charge you with assault and battery? Take it to court? Have it all dragged out in front of the board of trustees and student body? You know they'll call your wife in to testify."

Fear stabs through my anger. I shove aside thoughts of Liv.

Hamilton and I stare each other down like wolves looking for another opening to attack. Hatred seizes me as I walk back to him, my fists tight, my voice like stone.

"You leave my wife alone," I order. "You leave her the fuck *alone.* I hear that you're asking one goddamned thing about her, that you've tried to contact her, that you've *said her name,* and you're dead. I will fucking kill you, Hamilton."

"We can end this all right now," he replies with a shrug. "It's up to you."

I fight back a new wave of rage, grab my briefcase, and walk to the door. Outside, I drag in a few breaths of cold air.

I get a taxi and go to a computer services store where I can hook my laptop to a printer. I power up the laptop and open a document.

Don't think. Just type.

> *Dear Chancellor Radcliffe, Professor Hunter, and members of the Board of Trustees,*
>
> *I am writing to resign from my position as professor of Medieval Studies at King's University, effective immediately.*
>
> *Given the circumstances that have affected me both personally and professionally, it is in my best interest, as well as that of King's University and my students, that I leave the position.*
>
> *I have greatly enjoyed teaching at King's and regret this course of action tremendously. I will do whatever is necessary to facilitate the transition for my students.*
>
> *Please accept both my resignation and my heartfelt gratitude.*
>
> *Sincerely,*
> *Dean West*

CHAPTER NINETEEN

Dean

After signing and sending three hard copies of my resignation letter via certified mail, I have a few hours before my flight leaves tonight. I walk to the Art Institute of Chicago and look at Impressionist paintings, Greek vases, Japanese silk screens, German sculptures.

I take the stairs to the second floor and walk through the arms and armor collection. I stop in front of a full suit of plate armor dating to the sixteenth century. The steel breastplates are perforated for bolting a lance rest or reinforcing armor, the close helmet fronted by a pivoting visor. A knight would have worn the suit in the field or for a tournament.

My brain processes the facts, but I also wonder about the man who once wore the armor. It's the part of history I like the most—thinking about the people who lived, the knights who served their liege lords, the pledges and vows, the training in horsemanship, weapons, battle skills, hunting.

The chivalric code. Honor, loyalty, sacrifice, duty, faith. Ideals I learned about when I was a kid devouring the stories of Galahad, Lancelot, Arthur, and Gawain. Then at thirteen, when I told my brother he wasn't really my brother, I broke just about every tenet of that code.

I sit on a bench and take out my phone. I'd left a message earlier for Liv that I should be home by ten. I pull up an email window and type a message.

TO: My beauty
FR: The guy who loves you

I walked into Jitter Beans that morning in a hurry. Thinking of a hundred things. Lectures, office hours, a grant proposal deadline.

The world stopped when I saw you behind the counter. I had a flash of unreality. That it couldn't be you, Olivia R. Winter, the girl from three weeks earlier who'd taken my breath away.

But it was. You were explaining the difference between two kinds of coffee to a customer. I wanted him to get the hell away from you, and I was plotting some dark move when you glanced up and saw me.

> *You knocked my heart right out of my chest.*
> *Sent it up to the stars. I looked at you and thought,*
> *"I could fall in love with her."*
> *I didn't know that I already had.*
> *I'm going to kiss you for a long time tonight.*

I send the message and turn off my phone. Push to my feet. Study the knight again, the weapons and helmets. Sometimes not even all that steel armor was enough defense.

I leave the museum and spend the rest of the afternoon walking around downtown Chicago before catching a taxi to the airport. The tedious routine of travel is enough to dull my thoughts. An icy ball forms in my chest.

The flight is delayed, and I text Liv that I'll be late. After the hour and a half drive back to Mirror Lake, it's past midnight when I finally go into our apartment and push open the bedroom door.

The bedside lamp is on. Liv is half-curled under the covers, one hand still loosely holding a book, her body moving in the rhythm of sleep.

I set my briefcase down and go to take a shower. After pulling on a pair of pajama bottoms, I take the book from Liv's hand, glancing at the title. *A Tree Grows in Brooklyn.* She'd once told me how much she liked the heroine, a hardworking, imaginative girl who loves books and writing.

I put the book on the nightstand and climb into bed. The sheets are warm from Liv's body. I tuck myself against her, put my leg over her thighs, press my face into her hair. Tighten my arm around her. Breathe. Her fragrant smell fills my nose.

She shifts, wiggling back against me, settling her ass

against my groin. I feel her start to wake before she turns to face me. She's heavy-eyed, flushed with sleep.

"Oh, hi," she whispers, rubbing her cheek against my shoulder. "I was trying to wait up for you. Did you get my voicemails? What happ—"

I press my mouth to hers, stopping her words. A little moan catches in her throat. She shifts to wind her arms around my neck, parting her lips under mine, letting me in, pulling me closer. I close my eyes and sink into her. Tension fades, replaced by the spark of lust that fires my blood.

I run my hands over Liv's curves, tugging at the hem of her tank top, the waistband of her pants. Soft, she's always so soft, so warm, even more so when she's sleeping, as if she keeps an extra reserve of heat inside that only radiates from her when her defenses are down.

"How is it you're always so warm?" I bury my face in her neck, pressing my lips against her collarbone.

"Because of you," Liv murmurs, slipping her hands into my hair. "You drive away the cold and melt the ice. You've always made me *bloom*."

My chest constricts. I want to drown myself in her sweet goodness. The heat of her burns off my own lingering cold. Her mouth opens, her teeth scraping my lower lip, her tongue sliding over mine. Lust jolts through me, welcome, familiar. I push my hips against her, wanting her to feel the growing ridge of my cock.

She makes a throaty noise that echoes inside me. Everything else breaks apart. There's only her, only us, only the warmth of our bodies. I push my hands underneath her shirt, rubbing her smooth torso up to her full breasts.

She arches her back, pushing herself into my hands, her nipples hardening against my palms. I squeeze her breasts, stroke my fingers over the tight peaks, slide my hands into the hot crevice beneath them.

"Take my shirt off." Liv pulls her mouth from mine, her eyes darkening to the color of cocoa.

I grab her shirt and pull it over her head. Urgency floods me at the sight of her naked breasts, her nipples like berries. I hook my fingers into her waistband and tug her pants off, tossing them to the floor. Then I just look at her—my beautiful wife with her rounded hips, the slopes of her shoulders and waist, the dark curls between her legs, the curve of her stomach, the arch of her neck.

I move lower on the bed, pushing the sheets aside, getting between her legs. My erection pulses against the loose material of my pants. I put my hands on Liv's inner thighs, rubbing the tender flesh before easing her legs apart.

She sinks back against the pillows, watching me, her breathing quick and her face flushed with pleasure. She's already hot. I ease one finger into her, my blood pulsing as she moans and closes her inner flesh around me.

So easy. It's so easy with her. I know exactly what she likes, wants, needs. I circle my finger over her folds, rub the knot of her clit, push her legs farther apart before moving down to put my mouth on her.

"Dean!" She arches upward with a gasp.

I pause, inhale the scent of her, wait for her to settle. I press my hands against her hips and lick her with long, sweeping strokes that make her twist and buck up into my grasp. The taste of her fills my head. My cock throbs, and I shift to rub my groin against the bed.

"Oh, God…" Liv groans, running her hands up and down her body, squeezing her breasts. Tension vibrates through her. "So good…"

I move my hands back to grip her inner thighs and push my tongue inside her. She lets out a cry of pleasure, pulling her legs up to her hips, opening herself fully. Her cries become louder, a stream of pleasure that fills my ears and drowns out everything else.

She reaches down to grab my hair, twisting her body beneath me. When she comes, her whole body flexes and shakes, her hips curving upward, a groan tearing from her throat.

"Dean, oh… hurry, please…" She pulls me back up to her, her hands on the back of my neck as she crushes her mouth to mine.

She's all soft, yielding heat, her breasts pillowing against my chest. I get on top of her, pressing her into the bed as her curves surrender to my weight. I want to enfold her, surround her, consume her. She slides her hands down my back to tug at my pants.

"Take these off," she whispers, trailing her lips down to my shoulder.

I shove my pants off and grasp my aching shaft. Pressure floods me. My blood is on fire. Liv pushes to the side, her breath fast as she fumbles for the drawer of the nightstand.

I grab her wrist to stop her. Her breath catches in her throat, her eyes widening as she stares at me. The air thickens between us, drenched with heat and untold possibilities.

"I want to come inside you." My voice is rough.

Something flickers to life in her expression that I can't read, can't define. I press my mouth against her cheek, down to her neck, back up to her lips. She puts her hand on my chest, right in the middle, as if she wants to feel my heartbeat.

Everything inside me fills with *her*.

"Let me." I press my forehead to hers. My chest burns.

"Yes," Liv breathes, tenderness filling her brown eyes as she searches my gaze. "Of course, Dean, love of my life. *Yes.*"

She strokes her hands over my back and writhes beneath me, opening her legs, pulling me closer. Beneath the physical pleasure coursing through my blood, there's an immense shifting inside me, like the plates of the earth locking together.

Liv slides her hand down my abdomen and closes her hand around my cock. The touch of her fingers almost makes me come. Her breath is hot against my ear. I move again to position us both before surging into her tight channel with a groan. Sensation explodes through me. Liv winds her legs around my hips and her arms around my back, moans vibrating from her and into me as I ease out of her and push back in.

I want it to last forever, the clench of her pussy around my shaft, the hot dampness of her body beneath mine, the jostle of her breasts. I plunge into her again and again as lust fogs my brain and instinct takes over. My muscles tense and strain as I move faster, Liv's cries driving my own need higher.

I brace my hands on either side of her head, wanting to feel the full length of her against me. She parts her legs wider. Our gazes lock through the heavy air. Sweat trickles down my chest. I push into her again, reaching between us to put one hand over her pussy and circle her clit with my thumb.

I love this, love her all spread open for me, watching her get all twisty and desperate, her long fingers plucking her nipples, her hair sticking damply to her shoulders. Another flick on her clit, and she comes with a cry, her pussy rippling around my cock. I surge into her, my mouth coming down on hers—open, wet, hot.

Liv clutches my biceps and closes her teeth on my lower lip. My head spins with the feel of her, every part of me driving toward the base need to mark her, claim her, make her mine again.

"Take me," I whisper. "All of it."

"Yes."

She wraps her legs around mine, her fingers digging into my shoulders, her lips sliding over my jaw. Pressure cords my entire body. I thrust fully inside her as the pleasure explodes, shooting through me and into her with a flood.

"Dean, I... I feel it," Liv gasps. "Oh..."

I sink on top of her, my chest heaving with ragged breaths, my cock still inside her. A shudder courses through her. Tears fill her eyes. I put my hands on either side of her face and kiss her—her lips, her cheeks, her chin, her nose, her eyelids.

I ease aside and take her with me, pulling her halfway on top of me. She hides her face in the slope of my shoulder. Her tears dampen my skin. I stroke her back, her hair, breathing in the sweet smell of her.

She's trembling. Her heart beats against my chest in rhythm with mine. She rubs her damp face against my shoulder. My entire being fills again with the need to give her everything, to take care of her forever, to always prove how much I love her.

"Okay, beauty." I press my lips to her temple, tightening my arms around her. "Let's see what finds us."

CHAPTER TWENTY

OLIVIA

I wake with a start, my heart pounding. For a second, I can't remember why my body is pulsing, almost sore, why the sheets are twisted around my legs. Then I hear the sound of the coffee grinder, and suddenly it's a year ago, and I'm waking to the sound of my husband making coffee after we indulged in a night of hot, sweet sex.

I'll stumble to the kitchen where Dean will be dressed in a tailored suit with a gray shirt and striped tie, all distinguished-professor handsome as he gets ready for a day of lecturing about concentric castle architecture…

Then reality breaks into my almost desperate wish.

With a soft groan, I roll over and press my face into Dean's pillow. Breathe him in. Try not to think about the world encroaching into our space. Like weeds choking a garden of sunflowers.

No. I won't let them in. Not here. I can still feel Dean on top of me, his weight between my legs, his deep voice against my ear.

"I want to come inside you."

My inner thighs are still damp. I shiver. A million tangled emotions rise to the surface of my heart, but they are all eclipsed by pure, bright love.

I pull myself out of bed, heading into the bathroom to brush my teeth and splash water on my face. I shrug into my robe and go to the kitchen. Dean is leaning against the counter reading the paper, dressed only in his pajama bottoms, his hair messy and jaw unshaven.

I pause in the doorway to admire him, heat cascading through me as I gaze at his chest, his powerful arms corded with muscle, the hard slopes of his pecs, the ridges of his torso that I love to trace with my fingers.

His pants are slipping just enough to reveal the incredible V of his abdominal muscles arrowing toward his groin, and I imagine pressing my lips over them, following the path lower and lower…

"Ah, my marshmallow beauty."

I jerk my eyes up to his, my breathing a little short. "Um, what?"

Amused, he nods toward my heavily padded bathrobe.

Well, crap.

I finally own several lacy nighties and a matching silk robe, but instead of slipping into one of those and strutting out here all sexy-like, I shuffled out in my old padded robe with my hair a flyaway mess.

I give Dean a mild glare and try to pat my hair into place. Of course *he* gets to look all deliciously rumpled and effortlessly sexy.

He puts the paper down and approaches me, sliding his arms around my waist and pulling me against him. He pats his hands all over my thick robe.

"I know you're in here somewhere," he mutters with a frown.

I poke him in the chest. "You know, I might be naked under this robe."

"Yeah?" Intrigued, he looks me over. "Then let's see if I can figure out how to liberate your gorgeous nakedness from such confinement."

He presses his hips against me as his patting grows more aggressive, his hands moving down to tug at the belt of my robe. I consider maintaining my indignation over his teasing, then quickly dismiss the idea when he pulls the knot out of the belt and opens my robe.

He exhales a long breath of appreciation as he gazes at my naked body. That look alone makes my skin tingle and my nipples tighten.

"I could just lick you from head to toe," Dean says, his voice a throaty growl that ratchets my arousal up.

"I wish you would." I reach down to palm his groin, a thrill racing through me when his cock swells against my hand. The air between us charges with sparks as he lowers his head and captures my mouth in a kiss.

A moan escapes me as my body, still primed and hot from last night, responds with a surge of pleasure. Tension shudders through Dean, his cock pushing against my belly. He slides his hands up to my breasts, his lips locked to mine.

I fall into the whirlwind without hesitation, winding my arms around his neck and opening my mouth to his. I'm still wearing my open robe, and the contrast between the warm padding and the cool air coursing over the front of my body is wildly arousing.

Dean backs me up a few steps, then grips my ass and hauls me up onto the kitchen counter. I open my legs as he moves between them, his breath rasping against my neck. Heat flares. I push forward to rub my cleft against the hard bulge in his pajama pants, wrapping my legs around his hips.

A sudden fever lights the air. With another growl, he bites down on my lower lip, one hand holding me steady at the small of my back as he unfastens the drawstring of his pants and pushes them down.

I break away from him with a gasp, wanting to see the thick, rigid length of his erection. My heart hammers when he takes hold of the pulsing shaft and strokes from base to tip, rubbing his thumb over the damp head. My sex throbs in response to the quick movements of his hand, the rigidity of his muscles, the heat of his skin.

"God, Dean, now," I whisper, pulsing from the inside out.

He positions himself and pushes inside me, both of us staring down as his cock sinks into me, filling me, stretching me. I clutch him to steady myself, unable to move in my precarious position as he begins to thrust.

He grabs my ass and pulls me forward as he fucks me. I dig my fingers into his broad shoulders and hold on, thrilling in the sensations sparking through my blood. Our lips collide, his tongue pushing into my mouth, everything in me opening, surrendering to him.

He reaches down to spread his fingers over my clit, his shaft pulsing against my inner flesh, thrusting into me, and then I feel it again, the surge of semen as he shoots deep inside me. I press my face to his shoulder. He strokes me harder, his other hand spread over my back as pleasure erupts inside me.

Still quivering, I twine my arms and legs around him and hold on. I close my eyes and absorb the feeling of him still inside me, the semen dripping between my legs, the strain of my thighs around his hips. We slowly separate. I reach down and touch his slick cock, spreading the sticky fluid onto my fingers, over my belly.

As the sensations ease, Dean lifts me off the counter, wrapping his arms around me and pulling me against him. I press my face to his chest, inhaling the scent of his skin.

"Damn, woman," Dean mutters, sliding his lips down to my cheek. "Now my coffee's cold."

"Cold coffee, hot wife." I smile and give him a little pinch on the butt. "Told you this robe drives you wild with lust."

"What's *in* that robe drives me wild with lust," he responds, squeezing my breasts before easing away to tug my robe closed.

I fasten the belt, feeling all warm and loose as we heat up the coffee and get breakfast together. I sit at the table with a bowl of cereal, my gaze falling on the airline receipt he'd left for me yesterday with his flight information.

A chill prickles my skin suddenly. I put down my spoon, watching Dean as he approaches with his coffee and a plate of toast.

"So… how did it go yesterday?" I ask, trying to keep my

voice casual even though my stomach is knotting up with anxiety.

He doesn't respond. He pulls out a chair and sits down, his muscles rippling with tension. He doesn't look at me.

That scares me more than anything.

"Dean?"

"Later." He looks up, his eyes tender as he reaches across the table to rub his finger over my lower lip. "We'll talk about it later, okay? Right now, I just want... this."

I nod, needing to give him what he wants, even though my fear takes root. After breakfast, Dean goes into his office, and I let myself believe what I did first thing this morning—that it's just us, going through our day together, happy and content.

Rain begins to splash against the windows. Dean comes out of his office close to noon. I'm sitting on the sofa beneath my ragged quilt, reading a biography about a medieval author I found on one of his bookshelves. I set the book aside and look at him. Lines are etched around his eyes. A strain fills the air.

I push the quilt away so he can sit beside me. The sensation of his strong, muscular body next to mine is a comfort.

He leans forward, his elbows on his knees, his head bent. I can only stare at him, dread spreading black tendrils into my heart, my chest so tense that I struggle to pull in my next breath. I get to my knees on the sofa and put my hand on his thigh.

"Dean?"

"When we first met, I felt like I'd woken up," he says, his gaze on the floor. "Like everything before you had just been the prologue to my real life. I'd spent all those years waiting for you, not even knowing I was waiting, and then you were *there*. The second I saw you, I knew I'd do whatever it took to make you mine. But even when I did… it scared the hell out of me, being with you."

His confession from our first year together echoes in my head. *"You're the first woman who's ever made me afraid. Afraid of how good this is. Afraid it won't last. Scared to death of losing you."*

An ache of love spreads through my own apprehension. I turn my palm upward so we can twine our fingers together.

"I don't want to be afraid anymore," Dean says.

"You don't have to be," I tell him. "Not with me. You know how nervous I was when we first met, how I flinched when you touched me, how I ran from you when I realized how badly I wanted you. But you were so gentle, Dean, so warm and inviting, like this big, comfy quilt that I wanted to burrow into forever. And you wrapped yourself around me so tightly that you made my fear go away. I want to do that for you."

Dean tightens his hand on mine. I feel his wedding band pressing against my fingers. I stare at the lines of his profile, the way his hair tumbles over his forehead, the column of his throat.

"I resigned, Liv."

Not until he says the words do I realize I'd been half-expecting them. And yet they sear into me like a burn, filling my entire body with pain.

"No." My voice cracks.

Dean turns to face me, his eyes dark. "I know. I didn't tell you before I did it. Exactly what you've been asking me not to do. But this time, keeping it from you wasn't just my way of protecting you."

"Why… why didn't you tell me, then?"

"Because I wouldn't have been able to go through with

it if I had." He pushes to his feet and crosses to the window, staring out at the wet, gray light. "I wouldn't have been able to stand the look in your eyes. Knowing how much it would hurt you. I was… in a way, I was trying to protect myself. I couldn't weaken. Couldn't make it harder than it was."

I press my hands to my face. Anger and sorrow boil inside me. This can't happen to him. Not Dean. He's worked so hard. It'll kill him to lose the solid ground of academia and scholarship. It can't all crash down like this.

I try to stem the tears flooding my eyes as I cross the room and slip my arms around him from behind, fitting myself against him. Then I let the tears fall, soaking into his shirt, my body trembling against his.

"I'm sorry," he says.

I shake my head, swiping at my damp face. "I don't care that you didn't tell me, Dean. But I don't understand why you did this *now*. You don't even know yet if Stafford is going to pursue the case. And there's no evidence against you so how…"

My words fall away as the truth strikes me.

Of course.

My white knight. My beautiful, strong, brave husband who loves me more than I ever knew it was possible to be loved.

This man would give me the stars, the moon, the sun. He has slain monsters for me and alongside me. He's battled through dark, tangled woods with me because he has never once wavered in his belief that we are meant to be forever. He would do anything for me. For us.

He's a rare gift, my husband, perfect and flawed and completely, unreservedly mine.

I tighten my arms around him. Absorb his solid strength.

Press my body against his back. After a few minutes, the rhythm of my breath rises and falls in time with his.

I move around to face him, pressing my hand to the back of his neck to guide his face down to mine. Pain gleams in his eyes, but he allows me to bring our lips together.

"You promised you would kiss me for a long time," I whisper. "How about we start right now?"

Warmth lifts some of the darkness from his expression as he takes my face in his hands and settles his mouth over mine. A cascade of gentle shivers falls over me as we ease into the delicious rhythm of kissing that is both familiar and wonderfully new every single time. I part my lips under his, letting his tongue slide into my mouth.

He slips his hands around my waist and we move to the sofa. I push him backward and tumble on top of him, stretching myself over his strong body as our mouths join once again. He rubs his warm hands over my back. I ease my leg between his and fall into a swirl of pleasure.

There are no fireworks, no bells ringing, no collision of stars. The earth doesn't move. It's just us, Liv and Dean, kissing long and deep with our bodies pressed together and our hearts beating in unison. My curves yield to the hard planes of his chest, my hair falling on either side of his face to curtain us in our own private world.

Our lips move seamlessly, tongues stroking, breath mingling. I shift to kiss his cheek, his chin, my hands flexing on his arms. He tightens his fingers on the nape of my neck as he trails his lips to the hot hollow of my throat where my pulse flutters.

Everything inside me softens in response to his strength, his absolute, unwavering conviction that our marriage is worth any risk, any battle, any sacrifice. And I now know that all these years, my husband hasn't only been protecting me. He's been protecting this intense, precious bond we share that is more than desire, more than tenderness, more than adoration, more than love.

PART III

CHAPTER TWENTY-ONE

OLIVIA

Once upon a time, I lost sight of what it means to be brave. I forgot that's what Dean loves and admires about me, that he'd once said I was the one who showed him how to start a new life. I forgot about the thirteen-year-old girl who walked away from her mother. About the nineteen-year-old woman who braced herself against the world yet again after seeking safety at Twelve Oaks.

I had no plans when I dropped out of Fieldbrook College halfway through my first year, broken in the aftermath of a forced sexual encounter and horrible rumors. I'd lost everything I'd worked so hard for—my merit scholarship, my reputation, my future, my sense of self.

I only knew I needed to leave, to get on the road, and for a while I didn't care that I might end up like my mother.

I packed up my old hatchback and told Aunt Stella I was going to visit some friends. Though I had no destination in mind, I headed west, in the direction of the ocean, mountains, and sunsets. Only as I was driving did I remember there was one safe place in the world, so I kept going for two thousand miles until I reached Northern California.

I didn't even know who was at Twelve Oaks anymore, or if North was still there. In my effort to put my mother behind me, I'd cut all ties with my past. Yet as I drove through the winding roads of the Santa Cruz mountains, I knew I'd be welcomed by whoever lived at Twelve Oaks now.

The valley looked the same as it had when I was thirteen—low, rolling hills covered with thickets of grass and trees, the sloping cliffs that led to the half-moon curve of the beach. I walked down the drive leading to the big, central farmhouse of the commune.

My stomach knotted. Surrounded by benches, the fire-pit sat near the barn. I wondered if they all still gathered there after supper for conversation and guitar-playing.

"Help you, miss?" An older woman with short gray hair approached me from the garden.

"My name is Liv," I said, suddenly nervous. "I was… I stayed here once with my mother years ago."

"Oh." The wrinkles on her forehead eased a bit. "You need to talk to someone?"

"Yes." I wiped my palms on my jeans. "There was… when I was here, a man named North used to run the place. Is he still here?"

"Oh, sure. North's been around forever. Likely he's in his workshop now. You know where that is?"

"I remember. Thanks."

My nerves intensified as I walked toward the wooden building. I knocked on the door, then pulled it open when there was no response. The smells of sawdust and burnt wood filled my nose. I blinked to adjust my eyes. A big, male figure sat beside the window, his head bent as he chiseled a plank of wood.

He looked up as the sunlight lanced into the room.

"Hi, North. It's Liv. Liv Winter. I was—"

"Liv Winter? I'll be doggone." A smile split across his bearded face as he got up from the stool and approached me. "How many years has it been?"

"Six or seven," I said.

"I thought I'd never hear from you again."

Relief filled me, so swift and sudden that I was caught off guard. I hadn't realized until that instant how much I hoped he'd remember me. That I hadn't been forgotten.

He stopped in front of me, studying me in the dim light. "How are you, Liv?"

"I'm… I'm okay."

"Your mama with you?"

"No." My voice cracked. A wave of dizziness washed over me.

North's smile faded. He put a hand on my shoulder and steered me back outside, into the sunlight that smelled like the ocean. We sat on a wooden bench alongside the door of the workshop. I rested my elbows on my knees and breathed the cold, fresh air.

North didn't speak. We sat there for a long time. Finally I glanced at him. Sawdust coated his baggy shorts and T-shirt.

Gray streaks speared through his tangle of brown hair and bushy beard, and weathered lines radiated from the corners of his eyes. He still had a tiny braid on the left side of his beard, the strands knotted and tied at the end with a frayed, red ribbon.

I gestured to it. "You still have that."

He tugged at the braid. "Some things you keep."

"Why?" I'd never asked him before.

"Memories. Reminders of the good stuff. I had a daughter. She died when she was a baby." He rubbed the braid between his thumb and forefinger. "She had just enough hair to wear a red ribbon."

"I'm sorry." My throat tightened. "How is that the good stuff?"

"I had her for nine months. She'd hold my thumb. She always stopped crying when I picked her up. Bluest eyes you've ever seen. Some people don't get even that. If I don't look at it that way, it would have killed me years ago."

"Is that why you quit MIT?" I asked, knowing his daughter's death was the catalyst for his descent into hard living before he found Twelve Oaks.

"Yeah." North tugged at the braid again. "Sometimes it takes a while, but eventually you learn which way is up, you know?"

I didn't know, but I wanted to. I hoped maybe one day I would.

We fell silent again. I stared at the ground and clasped my hands together.

"You finish school?" he asked.

"Graduated from high school."

"Good for you. Any plans?"

"Not yet. I… I was in college, but had to leave." Words

crowded my throat. I took a breath. "Some… some bad stuff happened to me, North."

He didn't ask what. Didn't seem to expect a confession. Instead he rubbed his braid again and stared out at the artichoke field.

"You want to stay here?" he asked.

Tears stung my eyes. "Can I?"

"We keep a couple of rooms open for visitors. They're unoccupied now. One of them's yours, if you want it."

"I want it."

"Okay, then. You remember Asha? She writes up the work schedule, so talk to her and figure out where you can help. She's probably in the kitchen."

He pushed to his feet. "Welcome back, Liv."

I thought I would leave Twelve Oaks in a few weeks, but I stayed for over a year. I lived in a small bedroom at the back of the main house and spent my mornings working in the vegetable garden and my afternoons learning how to make soap or helping North with his woodwork. I boxed up herbs and vegetables for the weekly farmer's market and spent ten hours a week in the commune's library cataloging their collection.

I spent as much time as I could in the garden, digging my bare hands into the dirt, killing insects, picking tomatoes. I started a flower garden in a little patch of earth between the main house and the barn, and within a couple of months I'd created a colorful blanket of geraniums, petunias, pansies, and lantanas. I began to think I might stay at Twelve Oaks forever.

One day I was working at the downtown Santa Cruz farmer's market. North and I were at the Twelve Oaks booth selling our home-grown, organic produce. Vegetable stands, food trucks, bakeries, and florists all lined the street, and crowds of people strolled around sampling strawberries, peaches, honey, cinnamon rolls.

Stepping out of the flow of traffic, two young women stopped beside the Twelve Oaks booth. Both were slender and pretty, one with straight blond hair and the other with a short ponytail. They had backpacks around their shoulders and held little cups of sorbet.

"If I declare a major now, I'll be able to do the education abroad program my junior year," the girl with the ponytail remarked.

"The tropical biology project is in Costa Rica," the blonde said. "I'd love to do that. Don't you also have to do a field study abroad?"

I moved closer, listening to them talk about sociology majors and curricula before they shifted into a conversation about a mutual friend who had a new boyfriend. The ponytail girl glanced up to where I was standing.

"Hi." I cleared my throat. "Would you like to try a sample of our vine-ripened tomatoes?"

"Sure." The girl took a tomato from the basket I extended. "What's your major?"

The question startled me until I remembered I was wearing a UCSC T-shirt that had once belonged to a Twelve Oaks resident.

"I'm not a student," I admitted.

"Oh. Wow, these tomatoes are really good." She reached for another one. "We should get some and make a salad for Emily's dinner party tomorrow night."

They conferred over the vegetables and bought a few baskets. After handing them their change, I watched them disappear into the crowd with their backpacks and cloth shopping bags.

I looked at North. He was sitting behind the lettuce bins, munching on a samosa.

"You could go back," he said.

I shook my head. "Not to Fieldbrook. And I can't afford tuition anywhere else."

"So you go to community college for a few years. Get your general ed out of the way, then transfer to a university."

It was a scary thought. Any thought beyond staying at Twelve Oaks forever was scary.

"Liv."

I looked at him.

"Don't hide," North said.

"I'm not."

"You remember I told you once you were like a turtle?" North asked.

"Yes."

"I don't think turtles have very interesting lives."

"What's that supposed to mean?"

"It's okay to have a hard shell," North said. "Not okay to hide in it when you're so young."

"You've been at Twelve Oaks for twenty years now," I reminded him, my tone defensive. "Isn't that hiding?"

"I lived a lot before I came here," he said.

"So have I." Pain tightened my throat.

North settled a hand on my shoulder. "Sometimes you have to go through the crap to find the good stuff, you know? Shit makes the flowers grow."

I couldn't help smiling past a wash of tears.

"And based on that garden of yours, Liv," North continued, "you do know how to make flowers grow."

I rolled my eyes. "Thank you, O Wise and Profound One."

He gave me one of his rare grins and tweaked my earlobe. "Find out who you are and what you want, Liv. That's all I'm saying. Now go restock the tomatoes."

I did. And I thought about what he said. I didn't come to any immediate conclusions or make any plans, but as summer eased into fall and the commune's children began returning to school, with some of the older teenagers going off to college, I had that old, all-too-familiar sense of getting left behind.

I wrote to Aunt Stella and asked if I could come back for a few months while I got enrolled at a community college. Maybe, just maybe, I could try again.

One afternoon North and I went to the deserted beach. We sat on the coarse sand, cold salty wind whipping around us, low waves spilling against the shore. North looked out at the ocean, the sand peppered with driftwood and seaweed.

"Try not to come back," he said. "I want to hear from you, but don't write too often."

I didn't have to ask why North wanted me to make a clean break. He knew that the only way I'd move forward again was if I no longer had a place to hide. I knew that too, even though my heart constricted at the thought of never seeing Twelve Oaks again.

"I'm scared," I confessed.

"Yeah."

I picked up a piece of driftwood and brushed the bits of sand from it. We sat in silence for a long time.

"You're lucky, you know," North said.

"How?"

"It's your name, a part of you. The reminder of what you should do. What we all should do. It's both the easiest and hardest thing in the world."

I shrugged, chalking that statement up to another of North's weird philosophical remarks. Two weeks later, after I'd packed up my car and said goodbye to everyone at Twelve Oaks, I hugged North and tried not to cry.

"I'm going to miss you," I said.

"Nah." He patted the back of my head. "Go on."

Even so, his voice got a little choked up as he gave me directions to get back on the highway. He stepped away, watching me start the car and drive toward the gate surrounding the property. When I looked into the rearview mirror, I saw him raise both his hands in farewell.

I drove away from Twelve Oaks past fog-shrouded hills, the blue-gray swath of the ocean, gnarled cypress trees. Toward the highway, the unknown, my future once again. And then I finally understood.

Olivia… Liv… Live.

CHAPTER TWENTY-TWO

Dean

May 15

"*I*'m so mad I could spit." Frances Hunter glares at me from the doorway of my office, her arms crossed and her eyes blazing.

I take a few more books from the shelf and put them in a box. Because my home office is small, I've kept most of my academic stuff at King's for the past few years. Books line the walls, the filing cabinet is stuffed with papers, and there are a million articles, office supplies, souvenirs. Even a plant that Liv once gave me to *"liven up the place because really, Dean, it's like a mausoleum in here."*

"Would you please reconsider this foolishness?" Frances snaps.

I take the framed photo of Liv from my desk and put it in the box along with a few of her drawings that I'd stuck to my computer.

"The chancellor has my resignation letter, Frances."

"I'll tell him it was a horrible mistake, that you were hit on the head and wrote that letter when you weren't thinking straight."

I stop to look at her. Affection and regret both twist inside me.

"I'm sorry, Frances. I had to end it."

"Along with your *career?*"

I shrug. "I'll find something else. You'll give me a great recommendation, right?"

Frances glowers at me. "I'm not giving you any recommendation. I'll be damned if some other university gets to have you when I can't."

"Now you just sound jealous."

"I *am* jealous. I hired you. If I hadn't, King's would never have gotten the benefit of all your renown. You started the Medieval Studies program! I knew I should have pushed harder to get you fast-tracked for tenure."

"Not even tenure could have saved me from this," I tell her, which is the plain truth. I'm not sure anything could have saved me from this.

"Stop clearing out your office," Frances orders. "You're on faculty until your resignation goes into effect."

"I said it was effective immediately."

"You need to give me a chance to explain things to the board," Frances says. "They're upset that King's is losing the prestige of having you on faculty, but I want to tell them that this isn't your choice, that—"

I hold up a hand to stop her. "It is my choice. And I'd make the same choice again, if I had to. Maggie Hamilton withdrew the complaint, and Stafford is writing his final report. He doesn't have to make any recommendation to the board. It's over."

"And one of the best historians in the country is out of a job based on a lie," Frances says.

I heft the box onto the floor and look at her again. "You never told me you knew it was a lie."

"Of course it was a lie, for God's sake, Dean," she replies tartly. "I'm not stupid. I have to be the voice of reason when there's a conflict between a student and a professor, but I know Maggie Hamilton doesn't deserve to be here. I've never approved of the way she was admitted to King's. The only reason she's lasted this long is that Jeffrey Butler went easy on her. If he hadn't retired, she might even have finished her thesis by now."

Something flickers in the back of my mind. I replay that last conversation with Maggie in my office. *"Your predecessor wasn't above allowing a student a little extra credit,"* she'd said. *"I'm sure you're not either."*

"Why did Jeffrey Butler retire?" I ask.

"He wanted to spend his time on research and consulting rather than teaching."

"But he wasn't at retirement age."

"No, he took early retirement." Frances frowns. "Why?"

I shake my head. "No reason."

"That wasn't a *no reason* question."

"Just wondering why he went easy on Maggie."

"Jeffrey was always more interested in his own work than

that of his students," Frances says. "And now Susan Chalmers is stuck with Maggie Hamilton. And I'll tell you, Susan is not happy about it. Don't be surprised if she throws rotten eggs at your car."

I have to chuckle at the image of the dowdy ancient history professor egging my car.

"Will you at least stay on until the conference is over?" Frances asks. "There is no way we can host it without you. We'll announce that your resignation is effective at the end of the conference. That will also give us more time to begin the search for a new professor."

"Agreed." It won't be all that easy to run the conference with everyone knowing I've resigned, but at least no one knows why.

"You'll come out of the conference with a dozen job offers too," Frances mutters. "And I don't want to hear about any of them."

"You won't."

"Good." Frances heaves a sigh as she watches me put another empty box on my desk. "You've talked to everyone you need to talk to?"

I nod. I've spent the past few days making phone calls and sending emails, telling my colleagues and students about my resignation. Their responses ranged from shock to disbelief, and with me unable to adequately explain the reason behind my decision, I left all of them confused and hurt.

That, more than anything, stabs me with regret.

"I have a meeting with my grad students in half an hour," I say.

"All right, Dean. I'll be in touch about the transition. The press release goes out this afternoon, saying you want to pursue other opportunities."

"Thanks, Frances."

"You know where to find me if you need anything."

She pivots on her heel and strides down the corridor to her office. I keep packing up my stuff, setting filled boxes on the floor. Then I take a stack of file folders from my desk and walk down the hall to the meeting room.

My seven grad students are already there waiting, their heavy backpacks and satchels on the table, their voices low in the hushed air. When I step in, they fall silent and turn to face me.

I falter. Stop in the doorway. I can't stand their looks of bewilderment and uncertainty.

All of these kids have worked so damned hard. They're bright, motivated, resourceful, dedicated. Jessica is supposed to defend her dissertation this summer. Kevin just started his thesis. Sam is still waiting for my notes on his first chapter.

I pull out a chair and sit down. They're all still watching me. Waiting.

"I want…" I have to pause and clear my throat before continuing. "I want you all to know that I'm leaving King's because I have to. Not because I want to. There's personal business that I can't get into, but the reasons have nothing to do with my colleagues or you."

"Is this why you took the semester off?" Sam asks.

"Yes. I'm going back to Italy for a short trip in June, but for the most part I'm staying in Mirror Lake now."

"You're not moving away?"

"No. My wife…" Something sticks in my throat again.

I swallow hard. "My wife is opening a business here, and we have no plans to move."

"What are you going to do, then?" Jessica asks.

"Finish my work on the dig. Help facilitate the transition to a new Medieval Studies professor. Edit my next book."

"What about the conference?" Anne asks.

"I agreed to stay on as chairperson. Nothing about it will change."

There's silence for a minute before Jessica makes a noise of irritation.

"This sucks," she mutters, shooting me a glare. "You're the best professor in this department. The best professor at *King's*. I started my dissertation the year you were hired. And now I'm supposed to finish it without you? What the hell?"

Guilt claws at me. I hate the look of betrayal in her eyes. Jessica was my first student at King's. She and I have worked on her research from the beginning.

"I'm not going to abandon any of you," I tell her. "Jessica, I'll do whatever I can to see your dissertation through. And the rest of you too. Whatever the administration lets me do, I will. Read your work, help with research, facilitate the transition to the new professor. You all have my email and phone number. You can contact me any time."

A couple of the students nod, but Jessica won't meet my gaze. She stares out the window, her arms folded and mouth tight.

"I'm sorry." Because there's nothing else I can say, I push my chair back. "It's been an honor and a pleasure working with all of you. Please know that my door is always open to you."

I return the folders of their work to them, grab my briefcase, and take the stairs out of the building to the quad.

I inhale a few deep breaths before getting out my cell. Liv responds before the first ring ends.

"Hi," she says. "Are you okay? How did it go?"

"As Jessica would say, it sucked," I mutter.

"Oh, Dean. I'm sorry."

"Yeah, well, it's over. I just hope it doesn't affect their work in any way. They know I'll help however I can."

"Of course they know that. Are you still at the university? Can you come over to the café?"

"I'm going to stop at home and change. Thought I'd go do some work on the Butterfly House."

"Okay. You call me if you need me."

"I always need you."

"Likewise." The smile in her voice eases some of my regret.

I end the call and take another breath. Spring is at its peak now, the trees full of green leaves, the sky etched with white clouds. Students trudge across the quad with backpacks and paper cups of coffee, their heads bent, earbud wires trailing over their shoulders.

No question I'm going to miss it. I've always been at home in academia, at universities, in lecture halls and classrooms. Teaching has always been the one thing I know how to do well.

My phone buzzes with a voicemail. I access it and listen.

"Professor West, my name is Louise Butler," says a woman. "I'm a curator at the Clearview Art Institute. I used to be married to Jeffrey Butler. I heard through the grapevine that you're planning to resign from King's. If possible, I'd like to speak with you. It's important."

During the week following my resignation announcement, I field phone calls and emails from faculty members, staff, former colleagues, advisors, as well as several universities and museums asking if I'm looking for another position yet.

Though the professional interest is gratifying, I'm not leaving the area any time soon, no matter how prestigious the job. Liv has spent the past few years moving with me for visiting professorships and postdoc positions, and there's no way I'm uprooting her again. Especially not since she now owns a business.

I don't return Louise Butler's call. The whole farce is over with, and I suspect she's not contacting me about a job inquiry.

When the initial furor wanes a little, I call my father in California. I haven't told him anything about this, knowing he'll be disappointed, but resigning from my job isn't something I can hide.

"Why did you do it?" he asks. "Did they deny you tenure?"

"No. I'm not up for tenure yet."

I stare at the wall of our living room. I've always been the good son. No, the perfect son. I've tried hard to be. I'd thought it was like building a castle or a fortress—an indestructible image of perfection reinforced by the successful West family, my renowned career, accolades, the IHR grant, countless publications.

Now I realize that I'd built a house of cards that could collapse with one breath.

"I had some legal trouble," I finally say, and then I just

tell my father everything. He's spent the past twenty-five years thinking I'm the ideal son. Time to tell him there's no such thing.

He's quiet as I relay the whole mess—Maggie Hamilton's charge, the investigation, my unofficial suspension, the reason I went to Italy, Edward Hamilton's possible donation to the university law building, his threats against Liv.

All the reasons the battle was lost before I even had a chance to fight.

"Do you have a lawyer?" my father asks.

"Yeah, but I can't have this dragged into court. If anyone knows about it, I'm done. At least by resigning, I can leave with my reputation intact."

To reassure him, I tell him about the other institutions who have already contacted me about potential jobs. This news mollifies him a little, though by mutual agreement we agree not to tell my mother until everything is settled.

When I get off the phone, I listen to another message from Louise Butler. My curiosity finally wins out, and I return her call.

She asks to meet me in person, so the next day I make the three-hour drive to Clearview, figuring I have nothing to lose except time. We sit in the corner booth of a downtown deli, and the mysteriousness of our meeting makes me feel vaguely like a spy in a war movie.

"They had an affair." Louise Butler is a slender woman in her mid-forties who has a tight, compressed look about her. "Maggie Hamilton and Jeffrey."

Though I'm not surprised to hear this, I am surprised that Louise is so blunt about it.

"Since Jeffrey was her advisor, an affair would have been against university regulations," I say, for lack of knowing how else to respond.

Louise nods. "Of course it was. Not only that, it ruined my family."

"I'm sorry." But again, I'm not surprised. I know all about how affairs can ruin a family. I take a swallow of coffee, shoving aside an unexpected thought of my brother.

"We have children, Dr. West," Louise continues. "Their lives were wrecked because of the affair and the terrible divorce that followed. That girl destroyed us."

"It sounds like Jeffrey was equally culpable."

"Oh, I know. But she was the one who instigated the whole thing."

"What whole thing?"

"Maggie claimed that Jeffrey had promised to divorce me and marry her," Louise says. "When he didn't, she took her revenge by sending me videos they'd taken of their... sexual activities, and threatening to charge him with abuse. Jeffrey got scared that she'd go to the university administration with them, so he took early retirement before she could ruin his career. I divorced him shortly afterward and moved my children out of the area so we could try to start again. But the damage to my family was already done."

"Why are you telling me this?" I ask.

"When I heard that you were resigning from King's after just a few years, I checked to see if Maggie Hamilton was still a student. And when I found out she was, I suspected she might be responsible for your resignation."

"I wasn't having an affair with her," I say. "She filed a false allegation of sexual harassment against me. I couldn't risk the investigation going to the board and becoming public."

"I'm sorry, Dr. West." Louise sits back, her mouth tightening. "I don't trust Maggie Hamilton to let the whole issue drop. And if this comes to light, if she blames Jeffrey and drags him into it, my children will—"

She stops and shakes her head, her eyes flashing with hurt and anger. "That little home-wrecker has destroyed enough lives as it is."

"Maggie Hamilton doesn't have enough power to destroy my life," I tell her. "She and her father just forced me out of a job."

"Edward Hamilton." Bitterness threads Louise's voice. "I know all about him too. Maggie was scared her father would find out about the affair, especially after she realized Jeffrey wasn't going to marry her."

"She does seem… controlled by her father."

"He's even more of a threat than she is," Louise says. "And I swear to God, Dr. West, I will do anything to keep them from hurting my family again."

Though I have a feeling Louise Butler is motivated more by revenge on Maggie Hamilton than concern for my career, I thank her for telling me all this.

"The Hamiltons need to be stopped." She picks up her purse and slides out of the booth. "Both of them."

After she's gone, I head out to my car and drive back to Mirror Lake. I stop at the Wonderland Café, my defenses kicking into gear when I see Crystal Winter on the front porch.

"Thought you'd be gone by now," I tell her.

"I'm waiting for my car to be repaired."

"Seems to be taking a while."

Crystal shrugs. "I heard you resigned from your job. Because of that girl, I assume."

I stop to look at her. "It wouldn't have happened, Crystal, whether I resigned or not. Liv would never have gone anywhere with you."

"You don't know that."

"Yes, I do. Your daughter is stronger than you'll ever be. She's never run away from anything."

Before she can speak again, I go past her into the café. I find Liv upstairs in the Wicked Witch's Castle room, which is painted silver and black with black-topped tables and crystal-ball lights, high-backed chairs, and a mural of a dark mountain landscape with silhouettes of flying monkeys against a full moon.

Liv is arranging a display of a black witch's hat surrounded by a pool of acrylic water. She turns at the sound of my footsteps, and her smile washes away the unpleasantness of the afternoon.

"How did it go?" she asks, lifting her face for a kiss. "What did she say?"

We sit down, and I tell her everything Louise Butler told me about Maggie Hamilton and Jeffrey Butler's affair.

"That's what I was trying to remember," Liv says. "Last fall when Maggie confronted me, she said something about Jeffrey Butler liking female students, and not in a professional way."

"I guess she liked him too, if Louise Butler is telling the truth."

"Can we tell Ben Stafford about this?" Liv asks.

I shrug. "Yeah, but I don't know that it would do any good. They can't kick Maggie out of the university for having had an affair. Jeffrey Butler is already retired. Stafford won't pursue the case just because Butler's ex-wife has it out for Maggie. And I sure as hell don't want him to."

Liv frowns. "It's just so unfair. I hate that Maggie wins."

"She doesn't win." I put my hands on her knees. "No one who lies like that *wins*."

The creases on Liv's forehead ease a little. Something loosens inside me, like a knot untangling.

"Do you remember that time when we talked about keys?" I ask.

"Of course. You said everyone has a key to unlocking their secrets." Liv covers my hands with hers. "And you've always been mine."

I turn my palms upward so we can twine our fingers together.

"On our second date, you said that string figures and medieval knights were my keys," I say. "It's funny, but until you said that I didn't realize I still remembered the chivalric code that I'd learned about when I was a kid. Honor, trust, loyalty. I wanted to prove to you that I could uphold those ideals. That I was worthy."

She tightens her hands on mine. "You've proven that over and over, Dean."

"No." I shake my head. "Not always. But maybe it's not about upholding some perfect code. Maybe it's just about doing your best."

And I know I've done that. I haven't been able to protect Liv from so many things, but at least now I've blocked the storm. I've stopped Hamilton from destroying my reputation, dredging up my wife's past, attacking us. I've battled the monsters away from our island.

Finally.

CHAPTER TWENTY-THREE

Olivia

May 26

"*I* know, right?" Allie shakes her head at me in astonishment, her red curls tumbling around her face. "The brochures went like *that*."

She snaps her fingers, pleased with the success of our pre-grand-opening advertising campaign. We've contacted all the local media, sent out press kits, printed coupons, and set up a website. The head chef, Jan, is working overtime organizing the kitchen, Marianne is retraining the staff, and Allie and I are finishing the details of the interior design. We're almost ready.

"When's Kelsey getting back?" Allie asks.

"Thursday." I check my calendar, remembering that Dean is going to pick Kelsey up from the airport when she gets back from her combination vacation and meteorology conference in Japan. I write a note to myself to make a special dinner that night so Kelsey can join us her first night home.

After conferring with Allie about our schedule, I take my laptop and go through the kitchen, where manager Brent is talking to the kitchen staff.

A ripple of excitement fills me whenever I walk through the café and hear the noise, the chatter, the sound of things *happening.*

I pause where Crystal is painting a border on the walls close to the ceiling. She's been working on and off for the past few weeks, and though I haven't seen much of her since she moved out of the apartment, I'm constantly aware of her presence.

"It looks great," I tell her, which is the truth. The diamond-shaped border matches the playing-card motif throughout the lower floor of the café.

I've discovered that my mother is more talented than I knew, which both surprises me and makes me a little sad. I can't help wondering what she could have become, if her life had been different.

"Is your car fixed yet?" I ask.

"Almost." She wipes a drop of paint from the wall. "They had to order some part. I guess they're waiting for it to come in. Are you leaving for the day?"

"I'm going to distribute some flyers."

"I'll come with you. Can you wait ten minutes?"

"Okay. I'll be on the porch."

I get a stack of flyers and go outside just as Dean crosses

the street from his parked car. Dressed in old jeans, a sweat-shirt, and work boots, he looks both comfortable and worker-guy sexy. He's looking in the opposite direction, his stride long and confident as he approaches the café.

My heart does its usual *my husband is here!* twirl, but beyond that I'm struck by the looseness of Dean's posture, the relaxed set of his shoulders. He looks at ease, almost untroubled.

He turns his head, his gaze meeting mine. He gives me that gorgeous, hint-of-wicked grin that makes my breath catch and my body hum.

"Hi." He climbs the steps to me and brushes a kiss across my mouth. "You busy for lunch?"

"Only if you're offering to take me out." I eye the streaks of dirt covering his sweatshirt. "Nowhere fancy, I assume."

"I was working up at the Butterfly House and got hungry."

"So you thought of me?"

He leans closer to me and murmurs, "I always think of you when I get hungry."

I smile and rub my nose against his. "How's the work going?"

"Got a whole room full of furniture to go through," Dean says. "I found a mantel clock that looks like it might be made of rosewood. I told Florence I'd get in touch with some museum curators and send them pictures. See if they can give us an idea of provenance."

My heart fills at the undercurrent of enthusiasm in his voice, the evidence that he hasn't let the loss of his job deter him from his love of all things historical.

It's been over two weeks since he sent in his resignation letter, and though he's still working on the Words and Images conference from home, he only goes to campus to meet with students and help facilitate the transition.

"I have my last shift at the museum this afternoon," I say. "Do you want me to tell Florence anything about the Butterfly House, if I see her?"

"For some reason, she told me to be sure and check the closets." Dean scratches his head and shrugs. "You can tell her I did that this morning, but didn't find anything very interesting."

"Not like she did," I mutter.

"Huh?"

"I'll tell her," I assure him solemnly.

The front door squeaks open, and Crystal steps onto the porch. An instant freeze coats the air when she and Dean see each other. I put my hand gently on Dean's arm.

"Why don't I just meet you later for dinner at home?" I ask. "We need to distribute some flyers, then I have my museum shift."

He nods, his gaze still on Crystal as he steps back to let us both pass.

"Allie said he quit his job," she remarks as we walk down the street.

"Long story," I reply, keeping my voice casual even though my neck tenses with irritation.

"Classic story," she says. "But it sounds like he did the right thing. No sense letting something like that go to court, when he'd be screwed no matter what happened."

Though I don't like Crystal knowing anything about this, even I can admit that she's right. We distribute flyers to a few downtown stores and coffeehouses, then stop by the Chamber of Commerce to arrange for an announcement on their website.

We're heading toward a toy store when I glance across the street and see Maggie Hamilton walking on the opposite sidewalk. My chest fills with anger. I quicken my pace and duck into an alley so she won't see me, so I won't have to look at her…

"Mrs. West!"

I stop and turn, my hands tightening on the stack of flyers I'm holding. Crystal is a few feet away, watching Maggie as she hurries into the alley after us.

"What do you want?" I ask.

Maggie glances from me to Crystal, her mouth compressing. "How did you get that video? How did *he?*"

"What video?"

"You know exactly what video." She steps forward. Her eyes flash with a hint of panic that I recognize all too well. "I got the email this morning. That coward sent it anonymously, but I know it was from your husband. I swear to God, if he threatens me with that video, my father will kill him."

Unease roils inside me. "Dean won't threaten you with anything, Maggie. He did exactly what you wanted, right? He'll be done with King's after the conference."

"He'd better be. We know about you and him, Mrs. West. I doubt you were the first student he seduced."

I can only shake my head. Though I still hate the implication that my relationship with Dean is somehow immoral, I know the truth of my husband and our marriage. I know the truth of us.

"So someone sent you an incriminating video of you and Jeffrey Butler, is that it?" I ask Maggie. "My guess is that it was his ex-wife."

Maggie pales. Unexpected pity twists in my gut. With the

lines of stress around her eyes and mouth, the sharp jut of her cheekbones, she no longer looks young—instead, she looks hollowed-out, like an empty shell.

"I can't…" She steps back, her panic deepening. "Jeffrey told me he destroyed all the videos. I know Ben Stafford talked to him, but Jeffrey didn't tell him anything. He never would."

"I don't think it was him," I tell her. "His ex-wife said you sent her the videos after Jeffrey refused to divorce her and marry you."

Maggie just stares at me.

"Well, that was stupid," Crystal remarks.

My mother's voice almost startles me, as if I'd forgotten she's standing right there. Crystal crosses her arms, her blue gaze narrowing on Maggie.

"Sex videos, right?" she snaps. "You sent them to the guy's ex-wife? What kind of idiot are you?"

Maggie swings her gaze from Crystal to me and back again. "I—"

"Yeah, I know," Crystal continues. "You're a young, stupid idiot who really believed that some guy would actually divorce his wife and marry you. Who was he, Liv?"

"Um… the professor who preceded Dean at King's." I'm about as stunned by Crystal's sudden wrath as Maggie is. "He… he retired."

"Oh, for God's sake." Crystal steps forward, getting into Maggie's space and forcing the girl to retreat against the building. "You really thought an old married professor would screw up his life for you? You never figured out that you were just a piece of ass to him?"

"I loved him!" Maggie cries, tears filling her eyes.

"Sure you did," Crystal retorts. "And he said he was in love with you, right? Did he tell you that while you were stripping for him or while he was filming himself fucking you?"

Maggie starts to cry in earnest, her shoulders shaking. I put my hand on Crystal's arm, feeling the anger tightening her muscles.

"Face it, Maggie," she says, her voice cold. "The bastard used you, and you made things worse by trying to get revenge when you found out he wasn't the hero you wanted."

"You don't know anything about it!" Maggie wipes her runny nose, her eyes glinting with fury.

"I do know something about manipulative bastards who want to use you," Crystal replies. "Men who sweet-talk you while secretly thinking you're a piece of trash. But I learned early on how to turn the tables, to get what I wanted from them. If this guy seduced you into—"

"He didn't!" Maggie snaps. "I was the one who started it. I knew I wasn't good enough to be in the grad program. I couldn't understand all the stupid theories and methodologies. But I *had* to get my masters, and I'm... well, men have always liked me, so I approached Jeffrey and... it started."

She swipes at a tear. "But then I started falling in love with him. He made me feel special. So when he tried to break it off and told me he couldn't be my advisor anymore... I just snapped. If I was going down, then I was taking him with me."

"So you broke up his marriage, and for what?" Crystal asks. "Nothing, right? And when Dean West wouldn't play the same game, you found another way to threaten him. What the fuck is the matter with you?"

My heart is hammering. Though I find it hard to believe

that my mother would ever defend my husband, the stark truth of her statement echoes in the narrow alley like the ringing of a bell.

"If I were you, I'd be less worried about your father finding out about this mess than the entire freaking community," Crystal continues. "One click of a mouse, and that video will end up on countless porn sites. Then what'll happen to you?"

Maggie stares at her. Crystal's arms are crossed, her eyes blue fire. Her skin is flushed with anger, her jaw tight, her hair escaping the clip holding it away from her face.

For the first time in my life I experience an actual sense of sympathy toward my mother. Because I have the sudden, wrenching suspicion that she knows exactly how Maggie Hamilton feels.

"I'm not worried about what will happen to me." Maggie straightens, scrubbing at her eyes as a resolve seems to strengthen her spine. "My father would never believe I did anything wrong."

"What about everyone else?" I ask. "What about you?"

She blinks, as if no one has ever asked her that question. "What about me?"

"You haven't wanted to do anything your father has demanded of you," I remind her. "You've gone along with it because you need his money, because you don't know what else to do. But isn't it about time you figured it out?"

"I don't need your advice," Maggie retorts. "I've never had a choice about what to do."

"Of course you have a choice," I say. "No one knows better than I do that you have a choice."

I feel Crystal's sudden tension. I don't look at her.

"You can stay," I tell Maggie, "and be controlled by your father. Or you can leave and start your own life. A new life."

Just like I did.

"Yeah, right." Maggie's expression hardens, as if my words are ricocheting off her. "Is that what your husband is trying to do with his stupid resignation? You think that will get him off the hook?"

She backs toward the street, her eyes flashing from Crystal to me.

"My father will destroy you, Mrs. West, if you or your husband threaten me again," she snaps. "And you'd damn well better hope he doesn't find out about this."

She turns and stalks away. A hush falls in the air.

"You don't reason with a girl like that," Crystal says. "She'll make the same mistakes until she realizes she's fucking up her own life."

My stomach twists. "Why did you tell her all that?"

"Because I know what it's like to be used, and I learned my lesson." Crystal turns to face me, still rigid with anger. "But you wouldn't know about that, would you?"

I stare at her, my heart racing.

"Oh, I've learned lessons, Crystal. Hard ones."

"Sure. How *not* to be like your mother."

The years suddenly flash in my mind like a filmstrip. Liv the good girl, the straight-A student, the mouse who barely dated, who kept her head down and did what she was told, who didn't cause trouble, who was still a virgin at twenty-four. The girl who struggled for so long just to feel normal.

No. Nothing like Crystal Winter at all.

"I get it." I have to swallow hard past the constriction in my throat. "I've been humiliated too. I made bad choices that backlashed in ways that almost ruined me. I had to drop out of Fieldbrook because of what happened to me. I broke right in half. And it took me a while, but I finally learned there's no limit to the number of times you can start again."

"Oh, please." Crystal turns away from me and starts walking.

"There's not even a limit for you, Crystal," I call after her, but she doesn't break her stride, and I don't even know if she heard me.

CHAPTER TWENTY-FOUR

DEAN

I've taken down all the boards covering the windows on the first floor of the house. The glass is cracked and filthy, but some sunlight and air now circulate around the rooms. Most of the furniture deserves a second look, so I've moved it all into the front room for later study.

I'm fixing the hinges on the front door when a car pulls up. I stop and approach, extending my hand as Max Lyons gets out of the driver's seat.

"Thanks for stopping by," I tell him as we shake hands. "I wanted your opinion on the building. The Historical Society is trying to have it declared a historical site, but so far they haven't had much luck."

"Allie told me," Max says. "She said Liv was working on a campaign to save the house."

"Unfortunately, it sounds like that will take more money and resources than the Society has."

"Too bad." Max looks up at the house. "I did a paper on this place when I was a grad student. Have a soft spot for it."

"Is it salvageable?"

"Maybe." He shrugs. "The Historical Society will have to do a structural analysis. It'll take a lot of money to restore it."

We walk around the building. Max talks about the masonry and weathering, the roof pitch, the slate shingles, the original architecture compared to later remodeling.

"Do you want me to come back and write up a report?" he asks as we return to his car. "I know a structural engineer who can do the analysis, if needed."

"That would be great, thanks. I'm here…" *Every day now* "…a lot, so have them call my cell."

He programs my number into his phone just as another car rumbles up the drive, tires digging into the dirt road.

Shit.

Kelsey comes to an abrupt halt, getting out of the car and slamming the door. Max takes a step backward. Kelsey stalks toward me, her eyes flashing behind her glasses.

I hold up my hands in defense. "You told me you were coming back on Thursday. I was going to pick you up at the airport."

"I left the conference early to deal with a department screw-up," she snaps. "I got a ride back with a colleague. What the fuck, Dean?"

"I wanted to tell you in person."

"Well, I found out from the university paper." Kelsey's narrow gaze slants to Max. "What are you doing here?"

"Getting in the way, apparently," Max replies.

"Then you should leave," Kelsey says tartly.

Max gives me a look that says, *Good luck with this one, buddy.* Then he gets in his car and maneuvers back down the driveway.

"Kelsey, I'm sorry," I say. "I didn't want to tell you over the phone. I had a whole speech planned for when I picked you up at the airport."

She crosses her arms, vibrating with anger. "So tell me now."

"I had to resign because the Office of Judicial Affairs was investigating a sexual harassment charge against me."

She blinks. "That's a joke, right?"

I shake my head.

Her face drains of color. "You're going to have to explain this in great detail."

We sit down on one of the porch steps, and I tell her the whole story, starting with my rejection of Maggie Hamilton's thesis proposal.

"I couldn't tell you," I say. "The OJA kept it confidential, and we weren't supposed to talk to anyone about it."

"Dean, this is totally fucked-up. You can't resign because some little bitch lied about you."

"I already did," I tell her. "And it wasn't just because of the lie. Edward Hamilton was going after Liv. I'd…"

There's no telling what I'd do. And Kelsey knows it.

She shakes her head. "Well, shit."

"Yeah."

"How's Liv?"

"Upset, but… she gets it. Hardest part was telling her and my students."

We sit in silence for a while. A few birds chirp in the trees. Finally Kelsey squeezes my arm and shoves off the step.

"Racquetball tomorrow afternoon?" she asks. "I guess you have plenty of time on your hands now."

I almost smile. "Yeah, sure."

"Okay." She takes a few steps before turning back to face me. "Hey, it's horrible. I'm sorry. I wish there was… well, it bites the big one."

"Yes, it does. But…" I rest my elbows on my knees and look past her to the view of downtown, the clear blue lake. "It's kind of okay, Kels, you know? Like I did the right thing. I protected Liv. My reputation is intact. I'll finish my work on the dig. I can still do independent study work, write my book. I'll get another job one day."

"But you still hate that you were forced into it."

"I hate that it's affecting my students, but it would have been worse if they'd had to deal with the investigation and been asked if I harassed them. My colleagues too. My whole reputation, my life, would have been shot to hell if this all went public, resignation or not. And then if Liv… well."

I stare at the lake. "I'd do anything for her, Kelsey. Anything. It's insane how much I love her. And losing my job is nothing compared to… to *her*."

"I know. She feels the same way about you." Kelsey studies me for a minute. "Hey, remember when I kissed you last fall?"

"How can I forget?" I mutter. "It's like a bad horror movie. *The Attack of the Venomous Pit Viper*."

A grin cracks her face. "You know, when I told Liv about it, she laughed."

"Of course she did. It was so bad it was funny."

"My point," Kelsey continues dryly, "is that she didn't freak out like most women would have. It wouldn't have occurred to her to be threatened by that. Even though she had a shitty time as a kid, and her mother is a head case, Liv just… she knows you. She knows me. It's kind of amazing that she has this… I don't know… total *trust* in the people she loves."

"Yeah. It is kind of amazing."

"I've always wished I was a little more like her." Kelsey backs up a few steps. "But don't tell her I said that. She'd start crying."

"She wouldn't… well, okay. She probably would."

Kelsey grins and gets into her car.

After she's gone, I work for another hour before heading home. Liv is making teriyaki chicken for dinner, and the sight of her bustling around our little kitchen is a reminder that everything is still the way it's supposed to be.

Over dinner, she tells me about the encounter she and Crystal had with Maggie Hamilton. I'm less concerned about Maggie than I am about Edward Hamilton, though I'm not surprised Louise Butler found a way to threaten Maggie.

"I guess Maggie learned a tough lesson," Liv says.

"Ironic that she might've learned it from your mother."

Liv shakes her head, a shadow passing across her face. "My mother did graduate from the school of hard knocks."

"Hey." I rub my hand down her back. "You've handled this whole situation with your mother beautifully."

Liv arches an eyebrow at me in amusement. "Is that your way of admitting you were wrong?"

"I'd never admit such a thing."

She leans over to kiss my chin. "Well, you are my Mr. Right."

After dinner, Liv settles in to watch TV, and I go into my office to work. Even having handed in my resignation, I'm still a scholar with papers to review and edit. Life changes, but history doesn't.

I study an article about Chaucer and the concept of fate as a wheel of fortune. The wheel appears throughout medieval literature and art, often in stained-glass windows and illuminated manuscripts. The wheel spins you into either luck or misfortune, all set beforehand.

And though I never believed in love as a predetermined fate, even I had to admit it was a stroke of luck when, five years ago, I happened to walk into the coffeehouse where Olivia R. Winter worked.

After the day we'd met at the registrar's office, I thought I'd never see her again.

And when I did, I knew I wouldn't let her go. Fate, luck, or nothing.

Liv has always been the one part of my life I got right. Everything fit with her, like sliding a button into a button-hole. I knew I wanted her. Knew I'd wait for her as long as she needed me to. I knew it would be so easy to love her.

And even now, I have to wonder if fate, the medieval *rota fortunae,* was somehow involved.

I shut down my computer and put my books away. It's almost midnight. The noise of a comedy program comes from the TV. I push away from my desk and go into the living room.

All thoughts of medieval literature disappear at the sight of my pretty wife. Liv is curled up on the sofa, her hands tucked beneath her head. Her curved body moves with the rhythm of sleep. Her shirt has ridden up to expose the pale expanse of her stomach.

I turn off the TV, then pause to brush a few strands of hair away from Liv's forehead. On our second date, I'd been unable to stop myself from tugging her hair out of its ponytail so I could finally see it tumble over her shoulders. I wanted to touch her hair so badly my fingers hurt.

Now I get to touch it whenever I want, which is often. I slide my fingers through the thick strands, easing them away from her neck. She shifts. I realize she's not wearing a bra beneath her T-shirt. I move a hand down to her breast. She sighs and arches into my hand, her taut nipple poking against my palm. My prick twitches. Liv's tongue darts out to lick her lips. She shifts again, rubbing her legs together.

Ah, Christ. Liv doesn't have discreet sex dreams. She gets into them, twisting and writhing and letting out little moans that make me hard in an instant. She fidgets again, slipping one hand between her legs. I tweak her nipple, then skim my fingers into the warm crevice beneath her breast. She's sweating a little, strands of hair sticking to her neck, her skin flushed pink.

I consider waking her up, telling her to push her gorgeous breasts together so I can press my cock between them because, fuck, I'm starting to hurt. I yank on the button-fly of my jeans to relieve some of the pressure.

At that instant, Liv opens her eyes. She jerks her gaze up to my bulging crotch. Then she sucks in a breath and looks at me. Her brown eyes are glazed with sleep and arousal. I pull on the remaining buttons and shove my jeans and boxers down.

"Oh, God, Dean." Liv groans and reaches for my erection. "Give it to me."

I grasp a fistful of her hair and nudge my cock past her parted lips. Hot tension floods me the instant her beautiful mouth closes around me. Her tongue swirls and licks in exactly the right way, her hand pumping up and down the shaft. The pressure starts to build hard and fast, and I have to pull away before I can't control it any longer.

I grab her T-shirt and yank it over her head. Her breasts bounce with the movement, the hard-tipped globes making my mouth water. She rubs her hands over them, her slender fingers twisting her nipples, then down to slither out of her sweatpants.

When she's naked and flushed all over, lust bolts through me at the sight of her rounded curves and damp skin. I push a hand between her thighs and almost come. She's so hot, so wet. I slide a finger into her and work it back and forth.

"Dean." Before I've thrust more than three times, she comes, her legs clamping around me, her fingers twisting into my shirt. "I can't get enough... please..."

She never has to beg, but it's sexy as hell when she does. I back away and sit in an easy chair. My cock juts upward, and I have to fight the urge to stroke it. Liv rises on her elbow and stares at me, her eyes hot.

"Come and fuck me," I tell her.

She lets out a little moan that goes straight to my blood. Pushing herself off the sofa, she walks over to straddle my lap. She reaches down to position us both and then with one, mind-blowing plunge, she sinks onto my shaft.

I clutch her hips when she starts to move. I won't last long, not with her tight as a glove and her muscles so pliable. Not with her breasts bouncing in front of me, moans streaming from her throat, her ass slamming down on my thighs.

She braces one hand on my shoulder and uses the other to play with her nipples. Her breath comes faster, her hair falling over her face with the increasing force of her movements.

"Dean," she gasps, digging her fingers into my shoulder. "Touch them."

I palm her breasts as she supports herself with her other hand. Her muscles tighten with strain, and I'm sweating with the effort of withholding my orgasm. One twist of her nipples and she comes again with a shriek, convulsing around my shaft.

Before I can thrust upward, she slides off and moves back on my thighs. She grasps my cock, her gaze rapt on the movement of her own hand. A few strokes in and I can't hold it anymore, pushing up into her grip as I shoot all over her hand.

"Oh, fuck." Still gasping, Liv rubs her palm over her belly and sinks against my heaving chest. "That was amazing."

I stroke her smooth, damp back as her breathing begins to slow. "So what was this dream about?"

She doesn't respond, which makes me grin.

"Come on, beauty," I cajole, moving my hands to her gorgeous ass. "Was I a pirate captain again?"

She presses her face against my shoulder and shakes her head. I squeeze her ass.

"A swashbuckler?" I ask. "A king? A superhero?"

She shakes her head again. I can almost feel her blush against my skin.

"What then?" I slip a finger into her pussy just to make her squirm. She does. And moans.

"A knight?" I ask.

"No."

"Then what?" I work my finger a little harder. She shifts her hips to accommodate me.

"None of your business," she mumbles.

"Uh huh. What do you do when I'm not around during one of your hot dreams?" I swear her blush gets warmer.

"Left to your own devices, aren't you?" I circle my thumb around her clit. She shivers. "Seems only fair that you should tell me what you're dreaming about when I'm around to help you get off."

"All right, fine." She pushes up to glower at me. "You were an elf."

I'm so surprised that I stop touching her. "An elf?"

Her cheeks redden again. "Yes."

"Like with pointy ears and a funny hat?" I can't help grinning. "That's what got you so hot?"

She shoves at my chest. "No, not with pointy ears and a funny hat."

"Then what?"

"You were like a *Lord of the Rings* elf. You know, with a leather vest and tight pants and a bow and arrow."

"What were you?" I ask.

"I was a… a fairy."

"A fairy." This is increasingly promising. "Like Tinker Bell?"

"Not exactly. I did have wings, though. Jeweled slippers. I was wearing a white gown with a golden belt." She pauses. "And nothing underneath."

Nice.

Even though it takes some persuading to get Liv to tell me about her erotic dreams, the result is well worth the effort. Not to mention that she always warms to the story after her initial reluctance, likely embellishing it with extra details.

"So what'd we do?" I ask.

"Well, there was a war going on between the elves and the fairies over possession of the forest," she says. "I lived in a peaceful village with my fairy brethren…"

"Your fairy *brethren?*"

She swats my shoulder. "Yes. And you were out marauding with a troop of warrior elves, trying to take over the forest district by district."

"Uh huh."

"You saw me one afternoon when you were out hunting. I was picking flowers next to a lake. It was a really hot day, so I waded into the water to cool off. You were hiding behind a tree when you saw me getting all wet."

"And I got hard."

"Not right away because you were watching my pet deer."

Sometimes it takes Liv a while to get to the good stuff.

"You had a pet deer," I say.

"Yes. Its name was Clover."

"When did we have sex?"

Liv arches an eyebrow. "I thought you wanted me to tell you about my dream."

"Yeah, but maybe without so much backstory."

She sighs as if I'd said I wanted to read the Cliff's Notes version of a literary masterpiece.

"My pet deer," she says pointedly, "was named Clover. You wanted to bring her back to your camp for dinner. But when you moved to raise your bow and arrow, you stepped on a twig. Both Clover and I heard the noise. She ran off into the forest, and I hurried to try and find my gown, which I'd left on the shore."

"You were naked?"

"Of course I was naked. I was in the lake, remember?"

"Why were you naked in the forest if there was a threat of marauding elves?" *Two can play at this game.*

"I told you," Liv says. "I lived in a peaceful fairy district."

"But if warrior elves were taking over the forest district by district, you should've known about the danger and not gone skinny-dipping in the lake."

Liv folds her arms over her chest and frowns. She's trying for annoyance, but the position of her arms pushes her breasts up and out and makes her look damn sexy.

I want to lick her nipples. Instead I force my gaze back to her face.

"Okay," I say. "So maybe there was a treaty between the fairies and the elves that they'd leave your district alone. So you thought you were safe."

Her expression clears. "Yeah, that's good. I mean... um, something like that. Anyway, I was hurrying to the shore when you stepped out from behind the trees. You pointed an arrow at me and told me not to move. Then you realized I was naked."

"Took me a while."

"The sun was at a weird angle, so you couldn't really see at first. Then when you came closer, I grabbed my gown and held it in front of my wet body. You said you had to take me back to your camp. When I refused, you asked what I'd do to earn my release."

She stares at my mouth and settles back on my thighs. I shift so my erection slides against her pussy.

"What'd you say?" I ask.

"That I… um, that I'd do whatever it took. I had to get back to my village."

"Had to find your pet deer."

"Yeah." She lifts a hand and rubs her thumb across my lower lip. "So I said I'd do whatever you wanted. I was already… aroused, you know, being naked and in the water with the sun hot on my skin. And then you were there, all big and imposing with this tight leather vest and long hair…"

"Long hair?"

"You were an elf." She wiggles a little against my thigh. A jolt of heat goes directly to my cock. "You pulled my gown away so you could stare at my naked body, all glistening with water droplets. The sight of me made you crazy with lust."

She slides her hand down my chest to my stiffening prick. Her breasts move as she takes a breath.

"Then what?" My voice is getting hoarse.

"Then you ordered me to press my breasts together because you wanted to fuck my cleavage."

"And you did."

"Sank to my knees before you'd even finished giving me the order," Liv whispers.

My gaze goes to her full, round breasts which I actually haven't fucked in some time. I groan at the thought, shifting to ease what is again turning into an almost painful erection. My cock swells against Liv's hand.

Her eyes widen. "Nice recovery."

"Nice dream."

I figure my elven-self and her fairy-self both got off good and hard, but I'm no longer interested in the details. I reach up to fondle one of her breasts, running my thumb over the peak.

"Get on your knees."

She shifts to the floor, easing herself between my legs. I lift her other breast and push my cock between them.

"Oh, God, Dean…"

"Do it."

Liv cups her breasts and rubs them over my erection, her skin growing slick and shiny, her chest heaving against the underside of my shaft. Enveloped in her pillowy softness, I lean back and let her work herself over me, rubbing, stroking, squeezing. After a few minutes she lowers her head and licks the tip as I push upward.

Pressure tightens the base of my spine. I put my hand on the back of Liv's neck. She shifts to the side. I grasp her around the waist and bring us both to the floor. She wraps her legs around me, arching her hips as I plunge into her.

It takes longer this time, a slow and powerful fucking that makes me grit my teeth as the pressure builds. Liv clutches my forearms and moans, her body rolling and quivering with every thrust. I could watch her for hours, feel this forever, but the urgency spirals out of control. I sink deep inside her as she convulses around me, and then there's nothing but pleasure.

Easy. It's so easy to be with her, my lusty fairy, my beautiful wife. Wanting her is like breathing. Needing her is in my blood. And loving her will always be the beat of my heart.

CHAPTER TWENTY-FIVE

Olivia

June 7

A crowd of parents and children bustle around the gabled front porch of the Wonderland Café. The house has been repainted a fresh hunter-green with white trim, and the whimsical sign is guarded by a white rabbit wearing a monocle.

In honor of the grand opening, there is a bouncy house at the side of the building with inflatable hot-air balloons tethered to the roof. Actors dressed as *Alice in Wonderland* and *Wizard of Oz* characters wander around with samples of cakes and cookies. There's a face-painting station, a balloon sculptor, and a couple of musicians playing catchy songs.

Inside the café, the air shimmers with excitement and children's voices. Clatter rises from the kitchen as Jan and her staff get out orders of soufflés, sandwiches, Rainbow Fruit Pizzas, Flying Monkey Bread, Scarecrow Straw, and plenty of Cheshire Cat cupcakes and edible teacups.

Marianne and several of the former Matilda's Teapot staff bustle around seating people and recommending things from our tea menu, while Allie and I help expedite the food, and Brent ensures everything is running smoothly.

The place looks incredible with Allie's detailed murals covering the walls, a painted yellow-brick staircase, new light fixtures and bright, airy colors. Greenery adorns the front door, and guests are offered the choice of sitting in one of the Oz rooms upstairs or Wonderland downstairs.

It's everything I'd hoped it would be, everything Allie and I had envisioned.

"One Wicked Witch's Hat, made to order." I place a dish in front of a pigtailed little girl. She grins at the chocolate-dipped sugar cone upside down on a scoop of ice cream.

"Are you booking for your birthday party packages yet?" her mother asks me. "This would be a great place to have a party, especially in winter."

"We certainly are. I'll get you a copy of our party brochure so you can see all the options."

I get her one of the brochures, then check on a couple of other customers before going outside, where a crowd is enjoying the festivities. I shade my eyes from the sun as I see Ben Stafford by the face-painting booth with his daughters. Crystal is there too, wandering around with a man whom I don't recognize.

I approach Kelsey at the ring-toss booth, amused to see that she has a daisy painted on her cheek.

"It's fantastic, Liv," she says, after we exchange a hug. "You and Allie have done amazing work."

I smile, both pleased and proud. "We couldn't have done it without your help."

"Yeah, you could have." Kelsey nudges me with her elbow. "Where's Dean?"

"On his way. The guy who was supposed to drop off some bubble-blowing machines had a problem with his car, so Dean went to pick them up."

"Can I get a picture, ladies?" Rita Johnson, the magazine reporter who wrote the article about the transformation of Matilda's Teapot to the Wonderland Café, stops beside us.

Kelsey and I both smile into her camera as she snaps a few pictures.

"I've talked to a few of the parents, and they're thrilled to have a place like this in town," Rita says, studying the photo in the LCD window. "Looks like you're going to be a big success."

"I hope so. Did you try the Red Queen cake?"

"I've tried everything." Rita shoots me a grin and heads toward one of the food stations. "It's delicious. Think I'll try it all a second time too."

After doing a quick check to ensure all the servers have enough samples, I turn to go back inside.

A sense of alarm, of impending danger, hits me suddenly. My gaze lands on a big, gray-haired man who is coming toward the café. His face is set with anger, his stride long. My chest constricts. I know to my bones that this is Edward Hamilton.

I start for the steps, wanting to prevent him from getting near the café, but he reaches the porch and stops.

"Olivia West?" he asks.

Cold prickles my skin, and a black tendril of dread begins to snake around my heart. I force myself to approach him.

"I'm Olivia West. May I help you?"

He looks down at me. I dig my fingernails into my palms and meet his steely gaze.

"Where's your husband?" he asks.

Oh God.

"Mr. Hamilton, if you'd like to talk, we can go…"

"You can go to hell," he snaps.

Anxiety spears me. My breathing is getting too fast.

"This is not the—" I stop.

Behind Edward Hamilton, standing on the sidewalk, is his daughter Maggie. A bubble of rage bursts inside me. Our gazes clash across the space.

"You need to leave, Mr. Hamilton," I say. "Both of you."

"What the fuck gives you the right to slander my daughter?"

"I don't know what you're talking about."

"The hell you don't." He moves closer, a vein throbbing in his forehead. "My daughter and I both got an anonymous email with some crap about Maggie and another professor. That's bullshit. West is the one guilty of that, as you well know. And he can't hide behind anonymity like a fucking coward."

I'm starting to shake. I retreat to get him out of my field of vision, but my back hits the side of the porch. I'm half-aware of people starting to look in our direction. I pray the music is loud enough to drown out Edward Hamilton's voice.

"If you don't leave right now," I tell him, "I'll call the police."

"You do that, little girl. Get the police involved on your opening day, all these kids around. What a great story, huh?"

My fear is turning into outright horror as I realize Edward Hamilton has figured out that I have no way to defend myself, not here. Not now.

"What… what do you want?" I stammer.

"Where is that fucker husband of yours?"

"He's—"

"Right here."

Dean's deep, measured voice floods me with relief. I draw in a breath and shift my gaze to where he's standing a short distance away. His body is lined with tension, his eyes burning as he looks at Hamilton.

"Get away from my wife," he orders.

Hamilton turns to glare at him. "You want to take this up, West? You couldn't leave it alone?"

"We ended it." Dean steps closer, his fists clenching. "It's over. Now get the hell out of here."

"You trash my daughter, you're dead." Hamilton strides toward him, extending his finger. "Who else has that email?"

"I didn't send you any email."

"Liar."

Dean holds up his hands in a gesture of surrender, though he's gotten between me and Hamilton. "Look, you want to talk? Let's go. We'll take this somewhere else."

"The fuck we will." Hamilton's voice booms over the crowd.

Behind him, a few parents are pulling their children away from the café. Kelsey strides toward us, frowning. The music dies as more people turn toward the commotion.

"What's going on?" Kelsey stops near me, her sharp gaze scanning all of us.

"Nothing." Dean shakes his head at her, his voice tight with warning. "Mr. Hamilton is leaving."

Hamilton backs up a few steps, and for a second I think he really is leaving. Then he turns to Maggie.

"Tell them," he orders. "Tell them all what this guy did to you. Intimidation, harassment, trying to force you to sleep with him."

"No!" I can't stop the denial, anger flooding me. "Maggie is the liar! She was failing, and instead of actually *working,* she accused—"

"Your husband is a goddamned pervert who preys on students, Mrs. West," Hamilton shouts at me.

"Shut up, Hamilton." Dean's voice is dangerously low.

Allie comes out onto the porch, her forehead creased with confusion, with Brent right behind her. Kelsey taps at her smartphone and holds it to her ear.

"I will take you down further than I already have." Hamilton heaves in a breath, his eyes blazing as he stabs his forefinger into Dean's chest. "You think you can accuse my daughter of wrongdoing when *you're* the one fucking with your students?"

Gasps rise from the crowd. Panic fills my chest. More people take their children's hands and hurry them away. I rush forward to get to Dean. Kelsey grabs my arm and yanks me to a halt. My breath burns my throat. I struggle to twist my arm from her grip.

"Let me go."

"Careful, Liv." She's watching Dean, her eyes narrowed.

"It's about time everyone knows what a scumbag you are," Hamilton snaps at Dean.

"Leave. Now." Dean's muscles bunch with anger as he closes in on Hamilton, forcing him to the sidewalk.

Hamilton stops near Maggie, who is standing with her arms closed around her body. Her expression is set as she scans the crowd, her gaze landing on me. A wave of anger passes between us. Hamilton gets in front of Dean again, and then they're close enough that the air pulls tight with hatred.

"You did it with her, didn't you?" Hamilton gives Dean a shove, then points his finger at me. "Poor girl had a nervous breakdown after some college scandal, and you knew you could fuck her into—"

No!

Dean's rage explodes like a supernova. His body is a blur as he attacks Hamilton, tackling him and crashing them both to the ground. Maggie screams. Hamilton hits the sidewalk, a curse erupting from him.

Dean straddles him and lashes out, rage firing every muscle as he grabs Hamilton's neck with one hand and slams his face with the other. Blood spurts. I yank my arm from Kelsey and run forward, my heart pounding. Brent pushes past me and races toward the two enraged men.

"Dean, stop!" I scream.

A flood of horrified gasps rise from the crowd. People rush away. Children twist toward their parents, some of them starting to cry. Other customers come out onto the porch, faces wide-eyed with curiosity and shock.

Brent and a couple of other men try to grab Dean and yank him off Hamilton. Before they can, Hamilton rises and lands a few punches. Dean pulls himself away from Brent and lunges at Hamilton. They go down shouting, fists flying. Dean gets the upper hand and hits Hamilton again and again.

The wail of a police siren pierces the air. The crowd scatters as the car slows and comes to an abrupt halt. Two officers leap out, hands on their guns.

"Break it up!" one of them yells.

It takes three men to haul Dean off Edward Hamilton. Blazing with rage, Dean fights them off and breaks free, going for Hamilton again. One of the officers tackles him, forcing him to the ground. A second police car comes to a stop at the curb.

I watch in horror as Dean struggles to free himself, his eyes black with fury. The officer yanks his arms back and slaps handcuffs on him.

"Well, shit," Kelsey mutters beside me.

My face is hot, damp with tears, my chest aching. Panic encroaches again, the black cloud spreading over my whole body. I grope for Kelsey's arm to have something to hold on to and count to five as I breathe.

When my vision clears, I see Dean standing beside the police car, sweaty and angry, his face set hard as he nods abruptly in response to the officer's questions. Edward Hamilton is talking to two other officers, gesticulating wildly and pointing accusing fingers at Dean.

I can't look at Kelsey. I can't turn around to see Allie and Brent or Ben Stafford or my mother. I don't want to see the few people still lingering, watching my husband get handcuffed and arrested.

I wipe my face on my sleeve and walk toward Dean. I feel

Maggie Hamilton watching me, feel the triumph radiating from her.

Dean lifts his head. At first, he just looks at me, as if he'd forgotten I was there. Then his gaze scans the café, the abandoned grounds, the people still staring.

I stop in front of him and put my hand on his chest. His heartbeat races against my palm, his anger still burning.

"You're Mrs. West?" the officer asks.

I nod, my eyes still locked with Dean's. "Olivia West. I'm Dean's wife."

"We need to take him to the station, Mrs. West. Officer Randall will need your statement as well, and those of other witnesses."

A shout comes from near the other police car. I turn to see Edward Hamilton bolting toward Dean again. The only thought that registers in my brain is that Dean is handcuffed and Hamilton is barreling toward him like a battering ram.

I step forward into the space between them, shouts of warning ringing in my ears, Dean a blur in the corner of my vision. Hamilton slams into me. I hit the ground, my skull cracking against the sidewalk, pain shooting through me.

My mother's face appears in front of me. Noise fills my head.

A bright red balloon, broken from its anchor, floats above the street.

CHAPTER TWENTY-SIX

Olivia

"Am I what?" I feel like the nurse is speaking a foreign language.

"Pregnant," she replies, a touch impatiently. "Or is there a *possibility* that you are pregnant?"

"Uh… well, I guess… I mean, yes. There is a possibility. That I am. Pregnant."

The realization is a shock to my system.

"We'll do a blood test to find out," the nurse says.

She asks me more questions before telling me they'll have a bed for me shortly. After I register, a phlebotomist draws blood from my arm, I change into a hospital gown, and am directed to a bed.

I press a hand to my belly and take a deep breath. I'd had visions of discovering a pregnancy the usual way—by peeing on a stick in the privacy of my own bathroom—then telling Dean over a romantic, candlelit dinner.

Instead I'm in the ER with a splitting headache, fluorescent lights glaring from overhead, no-nonsense nurses firing questions at me, and a husband who is currently in a holding cell at the Mirror Lake police station.

Which, admittedly, is more like the police station in *The Andy Griffith Show* than *NYPD Blue,* but still…

Before the doctor arrives, I fumble for the phone to call Kelsey.

"Oh, for God's sake, Liv, he's like a caged tiger in there," she tells me. "He's furious that they wouldn't let him go with you to the hospital. The officer said he won't release him until Dean calms down, but you know what a stubborn ass he is. Dean, not the officer."

"Can I talk to him?" I ask.

"They're not letting him talk to anyone," Kelsey says. "What about you? Are you okay?"

"They're running more tests, but everything looks good. Where are the Hamiltons?"

"No idea about the girl. They held Hamilton for a while, but let him go."

"How much longer before Dean is released?"

"He's been processed, and they're willing to release him on his own recognizance since they verified all his info, but first they want him to dial it down a notch. Or ten. I'm just sitting here waiting for him. I'll bring him over as soon as I can."

I end the call as the doctor returns and conducts a thorough exam. He tells me I don't appear to have a concussion, but he'll do an MRI to make certain. As he's telling me about the MRI procedure, the nurse returns with the lab report.

"Your hCG levels indicate that you're pregnant, Mrs. West," the doctor tells me, studying the papers. "You didn't know?"

Since I can't speak past the constriction in my throat, I just shake my head.

"Though chances are your accident didn't harm the fetus, we'll do an ultrasound and connect you to a fetal monitor to assess the viability of the pregnancy," the doctor says, and the businesslike tone of his voice as well as the words *viability of the pregnancy* bring up a wave of old fear.

A bustle of activity follows. Allie, Crystal, and Marianne come in from the waiting room to see how I'm doing. The nurse shoos them out before bringing in the ultrasound machine and setting up for the exam.

When she turns to the machine, I grab my phone again. "Kelsey, you need to get him over here."

"They're letting him go since they need the cell for a couple of drunk college kids," she tells me. "He's getting his wallet and phone returned to him right now. He still has steam coming out of his ears. We should be there in about fifteen minutes. I told him you're okay."

"Kelsey. Hurry."

"On our way."

After getting off the phone, I sit back and watch the clock. Minutes pass. I'm not about to tell the doctor to hold off on the ultrasound, but the nurse tells me I need to drink more water before they can conduct the exam.

I down another glass of water, my stomach zinging with

nerves. I wait. I look at the clock again. The second hand ticks. *Hurry, hurry…*

"Liv?" Dean's voice breaks through my anxiety.

My heart leaps as he runs into the room, his eyes burning with concern, a bruise marring his unshaven jaw, his shirt torn and stained with blood. He careens to a halt beside my bed, his chest heaving.

"You're okay?" He grabs my shoulders, looking me over, his voice tight. "Are you okay? Goddammit, I almost lost my mind when they wouldn't let me come with you, and then they stuck me in a damn cell—"

"Because you were disturbing the peace." Kelsey hurries into the room after him. "And if you don't calm down here, they'll throw you out again. Is that what you want?"

Dean inhales and makes a visible effort to regain control of himself. He tightens his hands on my shoulders.

"Liv, are you okay?"

"Yes. Take another breath."

He does. Behind him, Kelsey scans the room, her sharp gaze stopping on the ultrasound machine. Her eyes widen a little behind her glasses. She gives me a questioning *does he know?* look. I shake my head.

Kelsey gets a chair and shoves it behind Dean.

"You'll want to sit down for this one, Professor Marvel." She backs away, shooting me a smile. "Aunt Kelsey's orders."

She turns and leaves the room. I squeeze Dean's arm.

"She's right," I tell him. "Sit down."

He sits, dragging a hand through his hair. "Liv, I'm so sorry I—"

"Hey. Be quiet. I have something to tell you."

"What?" Concern darkens his eyes again.

"Last February, I stopped at a baby boutique downtown," I explain.

He blinks. "Oh."

"I bought two cotton baby hats, one pink and one blue. They're wrapped in a box under our bed."

Dean searches my gaze. I grip his arm harder.

"We're going to need one of those hats in about seven or eight months," I tell him.

Shock registers in his expression. Before he can get a word out, the doctor and nurse return.

"Ready, Mrs. West?" the doctor asks, setting a clipboard beside my bed. "I'll do the ultrasound first, then hook you up to the fetal monitor."

All the color drains from Dean's face. I grab his hand, my own apprehension kicking into gear again. Our eyes meet, and a thousand hopes, fears, and wishes pass between us.

"You and me, professor," I whisper.

He leans closer to me, putting his other hand against my cheek. "You and me, beauty."

He straightens when the doctor approaches to prep me for the exam. Dean doesn't release my hand. Silence descends as the doctor spreads gel over the wand and starts a slow scan of my belly. My heart is racing. We watch the monitor.

For a second, there's nothing. Even the nurse seems to be holding her breath.

Then a grainy swath of black and gray appears on the screen, a light flashing rhythmically.

"There it is," the doctor says, sounding pleased. "A baby with a heartbeat."

The screen blurs in front of my eyes. I blink hard because I don't want to miss this. It's a little, peanut-shaped blob on the screen. The light continues to flash as it bounces around. A baby with a heartbeat.

"Want to hear it?" The doctor flips a switch on the computer, and a thumping noise fills the air. "One-twenty beats per minute. Looks good and sounds good."

Dean presses his hand to my hair. He's watching the screen. I can't read his expression.

The doctor is talking again, but I'm only half-listening. After I hear that I'm about six weeks along and everything looks normal, my entire body loosens with relief. The doctor inputs the data into the computer and tells me he wants to keep me overnight for observation.

Dean and I look at each other. He reaches out to put his warm hand against my neck, right where my pulse beats. He smiles that beautiful smile that makes his eyes crinkle at the corners and fills my heart to overflowing. And then there just aren't any words.

The hospital seems quiet the following morning as I get ready for Dean to come and pick me up. After the doctor conducts another exam and proclaims me "all set to go home," I dress in my clothes from the previous day and wait for the nurse to come with the discharge papers.

"Hello, Liv."

I look up at the sound of my mother's voice. She's standing by the door, beautiful as ever with her silky gold hair, dressed in a floral wraparound skirt and a peasant blouse with an embroidered design on the bodice.

"Hi, Crystal."

"They said I could see you since I'm family," she tells me. "Everything's okay?"

The lingering tightness in my chest loosens even more. "Everything's okay."

"You got your wish, I guess," she remarks.

I can only nod, thinking of that little bouncing ball on the ultrasound screen whose heartbeat echoed my own.

"I remember when I found out I was pregnant with you," Crystal continues. "Scariest day of my life."

Something twinges beneath my heart. She'd been alone when she found out about me, and shortly afterward her parents would kick her out of the house.

I press a hand to my belly. I think of going home to our Avalon Street apartment with its blue-and-white curtains, overstuffed chairs, seascape paintings and photographs of me and my husband. Dean's office lined with books, my desk beside the windows with a view of the sky-blue lake, the little white table where we have breakfast together every morning.

"I came to tell you that I'm leaving," Crystal says.

"Oh. Where are you going to go?"

"Phoenix, I guess. Maybe head up to Las Vegas."

"What will you do?"

"What I've always done."

I know what that means. She'll find places to stay, men to stay with. She'll sell her jewelry, find odd jobs, meet people and then leave again.

"Thanks for your help at the café," I say. There is an odd tightness in my throat.

Crystal moves closer to me. The smell of lavender clings to the air around her. Fresh, clean, a mixture of floral and musk. That scent was the only solid ground I had in all the places we lived. In dismal motel rooms, squalid apartments, strangers' houses... whenever I smelled lavender, I knew my mother was near.

And because I had no one else, I *needed* her to be near me.

Behind her, someone else approaches the doorway. Dean pauses, his hand on the doorjamb, taking in the scene with one glance.

And then they're both in my vision, both facing me—my mother and my husband. My past and my present. The one who hurt me, and the one who helped me heal.

"So, good luck, Liv," Crystal says, and I don't think she knows Dean is there. "I really did want you to come with me. I did want to help you."

"I don't need your help, Crystal."

I remember what she said to Maggie Hamilton. Remember all the men Crystal went through because they were the only way she knew how to get what she wanted. I wish she'd found a different way. I wish she'd find one now.

"It's like I told that girl," Crystal continues. "I know something about manipulative men, so be careful about thinking your husband is all that you want him to be."

I meet Dean's dark gaze. I feel the tension going through him, his urge to rush forward, to move between us, to shield me. He takes a step, his eyes never leaving mine, and then he stops.

I shift my gaze from Dean to Crystal. A wellspring of

strength rises in me. I needed my mother once, back when I was uncertain and scared.

I don't need her anymore.

"Dean is my world, Crystal. He helped me get back the life I lost. You will never make me doubt him."

As I look at her, I realize why she thought she could come between me and my husband, why she tried to convince me to leave him and go with her again, why she thought I could forget all that happened.

She doesn't know anything about love.

Not like me. Not like Dean.

I put my hand on my stomach again. I know, I *know,* that another kind of love awaits me and my husband… a love that will be both exhilarating and frightening, rich beyond measure. A love that will both encompass us and extend beyond us.

Neither Dean nor I have ever experienced a love like that from anyone except each other. Only together did we create *this*—an island of warmth and light, a haven of devotion, a place where we are both always safe and unreservedly loved.

I feel my mother studying me, assessing me.

"Putting all your trust in one man is stupid, Liv," she says. "And I never wanted you to be a coward."

"I've never *been* a coward," I tell her. "That's the reason I left you. Besides, you always said you'd have had such a better life if it weren't for me. But you made your own choices. You hit the road running and never looked back. And you took me with you."

"I had to," she replies curtly. "Your father was a lying, cheating bastard. My mother was a self-centered bitch who wouldn't help her own daughter. I had to leave. You think I had a choice?"

"I think we always have a choice. That's why I left you,

because I wanted to make my own choices. I didn't want to live like that anymore."

"And you ended up living a repressed life with Stella before you had to drop out of college, right?"

"No. I ended up married to a man who showed me exactly what it feels like to be loved."

"Oh, for God's sake, Liv. You never even knew how lucky you were. You never appreciated anything I did for you."

"Because you never did anything for me," I retort. A barbed-wire flashback threatens. I rip it apart, crush it to dust. "You didn't even protect me when perverts tried to mess with me. Instead you said it was my fault."

"I never—"

"Yes, you did." Old anger boils in my chest. I feel Dean's simultaneous flash of rage, but still he doesn't move forward. I fix my gaze on my mother.

"You even accused me of leading North on because you were jealous of our friendship," I remind her. "You blamed me for everything, Crystal. Maybe if you hadn't, you'd have learned that you could have had a different life. One that you really wanted."

A heavy, strained silence falls. My mother stares at me. For the first time ever, I see the fatigue in her eyes, the lines edging her mouth.

"You were the coward, Crystal," I say. "Not me. I started a new life on my own."

"You didn't start anything," she replies, her voice tight. "I'm the one who got us away from your father. I'm the one who saved us both."

"You didn't save me. I saved myself."

"All you did was run away."

"No." I shake my head, knowing the truth to my very bones. "It's not running away if you're running *toward* something."

And always, no matter what happened, I've always run in the right direction—to Aunt Stella's, college, Twelve Oaks, North, my future, Dean.

As I look at my mother, I realize that she's the one who has always run away. Because she has never had anything or anyone to run toward.

"Crystal, I've learned so much," I tell her, and for the first time ever I truly hope that my mother will one day find the ground beneath her feet, and the peace that has eluded her for so long. "And I promise you, putting down roots doesn't mean you're trapped or stifled or even… *ordinary.* It just means that you've finally figured out where home is."

For what seems like forever, we look at each other. I see her eyes that are shaped like mine, her hair that is as long and straight as mine. I remember the picture North took of us as Crystal and I sat beside a campfire together and smiled.

"Good luck," I finally say.

She nods, her gaze still on me.

"Well." She takes a step back toward the door. "I guess it was impressive, the way you stepped in front of that Hamilton bastard yesterday. Maybe you didn't lose that backbone after all."

"Maybe in some ways, I got it from you," I admit.

A faint smile crosses Crystal's face before she turns to the door. She falters for a second when her gaze clashes with Dean's. They stare at each other, hostility sparking in the air. Dean moves aside to let her pass.

Then my mother walks away from me, past my husband,

her posture ramrod straight. The fading sound of her heels clicking on the linoleum takes all the breath from my body. I sink onto the edge of the bed.

An immense freedom and relief flood me, like water spilling over a dry plant. For so long, I have trembled on the unstable, dangerous ground of my past, confused by all the twisting roads, shadowed by oppressive queens, flying monkeys, and wicked witches.

I haven't known if I would ever truly escape, uncertain of my own assertion that I'm strong enough to defeat the darkness by myself. That I do know what it takes to find my way home again, that I've always known the power of the ruby slippers and the path back to the rabbit hole. I've always known which way is *up*.

Dean gets on his knees in front of me. He reaches out, his fingers brushing the sleeve of my shirt.

"You," he says, "are heroic."

I look into his eyes filled with a hundred emotions I can't begin to define, but overshadowing them all is the singular love, both fierce and tender, that has always been like the moon for me. A brilliant light in the darkness, ever-present, constant. Forever.

He reaches into the pocket of his jeans, then takes my hand and puts a silver chain in my palm. My breath catches as I stare at the brass disk. *Fortune favors the brave.*

"I… I almost forgot you had this," I whisper.

"I kept it safe for you." Dean rests his hands on my knees. "Just like you asked me to."

I close my fingers around the necklace, feel the weight of the pendant pressing against my palm. Dean stands and reaches to help me to my feet.

"Come on, beauty. Let's go home."

CHAPTER TWENTY-SEVEN

DEAN

JUNE 12

"*D*id you get any prison tattoos?" Kelsey strides up the driveway of the Butterfly House, her expression a combination of amusement and concern.

I pull up the sleeve of my shirt to show her a scratch on my forearm from the fight with Hamilton.

"It's a dagger," I tell her.

"Pretty hot, tough guy." Kelsey drops her bag and sits beside me on the front porch. "Where's Liv?"

"On her way." I twist a loop of string between my palms to make a row of triangles.

"So… a baby, huh?" Kelsey asks.

My heart thumps. "How did you know?"

"I'm smart, remember? I figured it out."

I twist the string again. "She had a miscarriage in January."

"She told me. I'm sorry." Kelsey hesitates. "I guess it's scary then, huh?"

Yeah, it's scary. Lots of things are scary.

"You okay?" she asks. "I mean, without the job and all…"

"I can live without my job, Kelsey." I untangle the string and shove it into my pocket. "I figured I'd get another one someday. But the reason I resigned in the first place was to end it all, to prevent it from getting out and hurting Liv."

"She's not hurt, Dean. The doctor said she's fine."

"It's not just that."

"I know."

It's the public embarrassment, the fact that everyone now knows what happened, Edward Hamilton's threat to press charges, the complete ruin of the café's grand opening…

I couldn't have fucked it all up any more if I'd tried.

Though Allie, Brent, Marianne, and everyone else at the café have said the whole disaster wasn't my fault and have rallied to get things going again, I feel completely responsible for how it all went down.

I've insisted on covering the lost profits and operating expenses until the café gets back on its feet, but that hasn't been enough to turn public perception around yet.

And once again, I don't know how to fix it.

Kelsey and I look up at the sound of a car coming to a stop. Liv gets out of the driver's seat, and my entire being floods with pleasure at the sight of her in a polka-dot skirt and white blouse, her ponytail swinging.

I approach the car and open the passenger side door to help Florence Wickham out.

"Oh, thank you, Dean." Florence peers up at the Butterfly House and sighs. "I wish we had more community support for this place. I can't thank you enough for your help, even with all you've been through."

I try not to wince. The news about the Wonderland Café's disastrous grand opening has spread through town, and I can only hope the bad publicity doesn't hurt Liv or Allie too much.

"I heard all about it," Florence tells me, shaking her head. "That horrific fight you were in."

"I… uh, I didn't do anything wrong," I say, feeling the sudden urge to reassure this sweet, elderly lady that I'm still respectable.

Florence blinks at me in surprise. "Oh, Dean, of course you didn't do anything wrong! A man like you only does everything *right*. Isn't that so, Olivia?"

Liv nods solemnly. A current of amusement that I don't understand passes between her and Florence.

"Of course you're a model citizen, Dean." Florence reaches out to pat my arm.

She pauses, lifts an eyebrow, then slides her hand up to give my biceps a little squeeze.

"Oh my." She clears her throat, tightening her grip on me as we walk toward the house. "Well, as I was telling Olivia on the drive up, my granddaughter is the superintendent of the Rainwood school district, and she is just thrilled about the café. She's eager to help turn things back in your favor."

AWAKEN									373

"We'd welcome any help, believe me," Liv says.

She introduces Kelsey to Florence, and we go into the house so Florence can see the progress I've made on the interior. After touring the rooms, I step onto the front porch when my phone rings.

"Professor West? This is Ben Stafford of the Office of Judicial Affairs."

My heart drops. "Yes?"

"I wanted to let you know that you'll be receiving an official summons from the King's University board of trustees tomorrow," Stafford says. "In light of recent events, the board is required to investigate and determine if any university rules have been breached."

"I see."

"Also you are still a faculty member pending your resignation," Stafford continues. "Therefore you must be held accountable for your actions and subject to disciplinary proceedings."

"What are the possible consequences?"

"Sanctions include a formal letter of reprimand, suspension, or dismissal."

I don't care about being dismissed because my resignation is effective next month. I don't care about being suspended either. I don't like the idea of a letter of reprimand that will go in my permanent file, but I can live with it if I have to.

I exhale a breath. "Okay. It's a formality, right?"

"Er, well... no," Stafford says.

"Then what?"

"This is a public disciplinary hearing, Professor West. The investigative report will go on public record. And anyone can attend."

His slight emphasis on the word *anyone* is enough. *Anyone* can include Maggie and Edward Hamilton. *Hearing* means Liv might be asked to testify. *Investigate* means all the bullshit about my alleged harassment of a student will go public anyway.

"And my reputation is shot to hell," I say.

Shit. So much for all those inquiries from museums and other universities about the next stage of my career.

"Should I bring my lawyer?" I ask.

"I'd advise against it," Stafford replies. "The board tends to look upon a legal team as evidence of guilt, or at least an attempt to stonewall an investigation."

"So I just have to sit there and take it?"

"You'll have the opportunity to defend your actions, Professor West," Stafford assures me, though not even he can make it sound like that will do any good.

⟡

JUNE 16

The King's University board of trustees convenes in the main hall of the oldest building on campus, a brick-and-tile building modeled after Italian basilica architecture.

Liv and I go into the main meeting hall. A long, polished wood table sits at the head of the room, lined on one side with nine leather chairs. Another table with a microphone on a stand faces it, in front of the spectator seats.

We sit on a bench behind the table with the microphone. Because we're so early, there's no one else here yet. Liv takes my hand.

Once upon a time, I wouldn't have wanted her here. I'd have wanted to keep her away from the ugliness of it, handle things on my own, fix it for her.

Now I can't imagine her *not* being here.

I look at her. She's watching me, her expression serious, but her eyes warm. She's wearing a gray suit, her hair pulled back, little pearl earrings. The cameo engagement ring I'd gotten at that antique shop encircles her finger beside her wedding band. I have a sudden rush of regret that I never gave my wife the proposal she deserved.

The click of the door opening breaks through my thoughts. People begin to enter the room. Liv tightens her hand around mine.

It's okay. She's okay. Our baby is okay. I can handle anything if I know that.

Voices and noise fill the air as people sit down. I'd thought Frances Hunter would be here by now. The more the seats fill with spectators, the more tension grips my shoulders.

My one last hope was that not many people would show up to watch my downfall. So much for that hope. A half hour before the proceedings start, the room is full. My stomach turns at the thought of all these people hearing that I was accused of sexually harassing a student.

The hum of voices, rustling papers and backpacks, rise behind me. There's no sign of Edward Hamilton, but Maggie comes through the side door, her face pinched and her mouth set in a determined line.

When everyone is seated, the nine members of the board of trustees file into the room, all looking stern and duty-bound. I turn, trying to find Frances, the sheer number of people making me nervous. I see Kelsey in the front row, and she gives me a nod of encouragement.

After the trustees sit down and confer, Chancellor Radcliffe calls the hearing to order and begins with an account of my arrest.

"As a member of this faculty, Professor West," he says, "you are upheld to a code of conduct that you have publicly violated. You also stand accused of ethically questionable conduct which we will further investigate. You may deliver a preliminary statement in your defense, if you wish."

I detach my hand from Liv's and move to the microphone. Take a folded piece of paper from my pocket and open it.

"My name is Dean West, professor of Medieval Studies, PhD *summa cum laude,* Harvard University. I have…" My throat tightens. I pause and swallow hard.

"I have spent my adult life in the pursuit of knowledge and education. I believe strongly in academic freedom and hold both myself and my students to the highest standards of scholarship. I have never once violated the educational process or the trust and authority placed in me as a faculty member at any institution. It has been my honor to represent King's University and to work with the outstanding students and faculty here. I would—"

"Excuse me, Professor West."

We all turn. Frances Hunter strides down the center of the room from the main entrance. In a tailored, dark green suit, her hair steely gray, she looks like a general marching into battle. She stops beside me, shouldering me out of the way to reach the microphone.

"Chancellor Radcliffe, I apologize for interrupting," she

says, "but I must inform you that one of the scheduled witnesses will not be appearing at today's proceedings."

Radcliffe peers at her over the tops of his glasses. "Who, Professor Hunter?"

"Miss Hamilton's father, Edward Hamilton."

"What?" Maggie rises from her seat, paling. "How do you know? What happened?"

Frances shoots her a scathing look and returns her attention to the chancellor.

"We received word that Mr. Hamilton has left town and returned to Chicago," Frances continues, "in light of our discovery that Miss Hamilton's academic progress at King's was severely compromised under the advisement of Professor Jeffrey Butler."

Maggie gasps. The crowd stirs. Radcliffe frowns.

"To what are you referring, Professor Hunter?" he asks.

"Miss Hamilton allegedly had an affair with Professor Butler." Frances sounds almost triumphant. "Given that he was her advisor, it was a breach of university regulations on both their parts. Miss Hamilton has very poor academic credentials, and appears to have attempted to find another way to graduate from King's."

"That's not true!" Maggie cries, turning to point an accusing finger at me. "He's the one who has stopped me from finishing my thesis because he wanted—"

"I wanted you to do your work," I interrupt.

"Excuse me, Chancellor."

We all turn again as there is another rustle from the crowd, one of the spectators standing. Ben Stafford pushes past a row of people to reach the microphone, nudging Frances aside.

"Ben Stafford, Office of Judicial Affairs," he says. "I must unequivocally state that any case or claim from Miss Hamilton involving Professor West was determined by me personally to be entirely unfounded."

"We know, Mr. Stafford," Radcliffe replies. "Our purpose here is—"

"I understand that this hearing is intended for further investigation," Stafford interrupts, "but given Miss Hamilton's poor academic record and her relationship with Jeffrey Butler, it's clear that she was motivated by revenge toward Professor West. Therefore, may I please request that the board *dismiss and permanently close* their investigation of such a case?"

Behind me, I hear Liv's intake of breath. Under my locked defenses, a faint flicker of hope comes to life.

"I would further suggest," Frances adds, slanting another narrow glance at Maggie, "that we no longer devalue King's University by allowing Miss Hamilton to remain a student here. She is responsible for this entire fiasco. If she does not withdraw from the university herself, I strongly recommend that the board consider expelling her."

Maggie takes a step back, her eyes darting from Frances to me to the board, as if she's a trapped animal seeking escape. Radcliffe and the other board members exchange glances.

"And," Frances adds, "I'm quite certain the faculty and students of the Department of History would provide statements about Miss Hamilton's conduct and lack of academic ability. Perhaps Jeffrey Butler would too."

Maggie goes sheet-white. "He was my advisor! He would never say anything against me. And my father has donated buckets of money to this university, so if you think—"

"What I think," Frances replies tartly, "is that you are a spoiled little girl and a liar who never deserved to be admitted to King's University."

A stunned silence falls over the room. The board members shift in their seats and reach out to cover their microphones as they lean toward each other with low whispers.

Maggie's face goes red with anger and shame.

"I'll sue you," she snaps, whirling to glare at me. "All of you. None of you protected me from a professor who tried to blackmail me into sleeping with him!"

"Is that what Jeffrey Butler did?" Frances asks, smoothly deflecting the attention away from me. "Interesting that there is video evidence suggesting otherwise."

Now the crowd stirs with a few gasps of horrified amusement.

Maggie backs up, gripping her bag. "That's a lie."

"If you want to sue, then we'll ask the Office of Judicial Affairs to investigate further," Frances snaps. "Is that what you want? You can't hide behind your father anymore. As a matter of fact, you don't have anywhere to hide."

Maggie backs up another step, her bag clutched to her chest like a shield. And then, with a strange flash of fear, her gaze darts over the crowd and lands on the person sitting behind me.

I move forward instinctively to put myself between Maggie and Liv, to protect Liv from whatever venom Maggie might spit at her. Then I stop and turn to look at my wife.

Liv is watching Maggie, her expression calm but her eyes dark with a combination of anger and pity. Exactly the way she had looked at her mother.

The air seems to crack between Liv and Maggie. Then

Maggie whirls on her heel and hurries from the room, slamming the door behind her. Hushed whispers rise.

All the breath escapes my lungs. Liv looks at me and nods toward the board members and Frances. I turn back to them and try to refocus.

"All right," Radcliffe says, his voice loud and somewhat irritated. "We will address the matter of Miss Hamilton at a later date, as clearly some questions need to be answered. Now the issue at hand is Professor West's misconduct and possible crime. You were recently arrested, Professor West, is that correct?"

"Yes, sir."

"For disorderly conduct and fighting?"

"Yes, sir."

"Excuse me, Chancellor." Kelsey stands and pushes her way toward the microphone. "Kelsey March, associate professor, Department of Atmospheric Sciences."

Radcliffe sighs. "Yes, Professor March?"

"I was present at the time of the incident, Chancellor," Kelsey says. "It was the opening of Mrs. Olivia West's café, and if I might say, it was a lovely event before Edward Hamilton's assault on Professor West ruined it for everyone."

"Professor West was assaulted?" one of the other board members asks.

"Violently." Kelsey nods. "We all witnessed it. Verbal abuse, then a physical attack. It's a wonder Professor West didn't sustain more serious trauma."

"Is that true, Professor West?" Radcliffe asks me.

"Uh… there was yelling and fighting, yes, sir."

"And Edward Hamilton incited the fight by attacking Professor West first," Kelsey adds. "Everyone saw it."

I look at her in surprise. Even though my mind had been black with rage that day, I'm pretty sure I attacked Hamilton first in a full-body tackle.

Then I remember that he poked me in the chest before the real fight began. Though I don't know if anyone can really define that as an *attack,* I am suddenly and intensely grateful to Kelsey.

"The facts," Radcliffe continues, glaring at us all from beneath his heavy eyebrows, "are that Professor West has had difficulty with Maggie Hamilton for the duration of his employment at King's University, which culminated in a very public and violent—"

A sudden noise arises from the back of the room, the main door clicking open. A rustle of people enters. We all turn to see what the commotion is about.

I can only stare as at least forty of my students file into the room, backpacks slung over their shoulders, and march down the central aisle to stand in front of the board. There are so many of them that I'm edged out of the way and wind up near the side exit door.

"Excuse me, Chancellor Radcliffe." Jessica Burke pushes her way to the front of the crowd to reach the microphone.

The chancellor rolls his eyes. "Yes, miss?"

"My name is Jessica Burke. I'm one of Professor Dean West's PhD students. We're all students of Professor West's, both graduate and undergraduates."

She indicates her compatriots, several of whom wave at the board members.

"May I speak, Chancellor?" Jessica asks.

"It appears you already have, Miss Burke," Radcliffe replies dryly.

"Thank you." Jessica clears her throat and unfolds a piece of paper. "We are here to stand in full support of Professor Dean West. As students who were admitted to King's University based on our academic excellence, we can unequivocally state that Professor West is an outstanding scholar, mentor, advisor, and teacher. He has challenged us in our scholarship, guided us in our research, and believes in our ability to be both strong, innovative students and citizens of the world."

I feel a few of the students glance at me. My throat is so tight it hurts.

"Is Professor West guilty of a crime?" Jessica asks, her gaze sweeping over the board members. "The answer is yes."

The crowd stirs with murmurs of surprise.

"Professor West is guilty of blackmail when he insists his students turn in their best work before he'll give them a good grade.

"Professor West is guilty of insider trading when he puts students in touch with his colleagues in the United States and Europe so they can expand their research skills and be considered for career positions.

"Professor West is guilty of plagiarism when he copies his personal articles and quotes critical papers to help his students with their research.

"Professor West is guilty of fraud when he expects his students to know all the facets of history, yet only tests us on some of the material.

"And all of Professor West's students agree that he is most assuredly guilty of boring us to death when he gets started talking about the economic history of Cistercian monasteries," Jessica adds.

Appreciative laughter rises from the crowd. I look at Liv, who is swiping her eyes with a tissue.

"But as far as we are concerned, all professors should be guilty of such crimes," Jessica concludes. "Professor West is a true scholar, a supportive and innovative mentor whom we all admire and respect beyond measure. And if anyone… *anyone*… believes that Professor West is not an immense asset to this university and the community… that would be the real crime."

Jessica steps back from the microphone. The group of students begins to applaud, a resounding noise that grows to a thunderous pitch when the rest of the crowd gets to their feet and joins in.

I close my fingers around the back of a chair. The room is a blur.

"Order!" Radcliffe shouts, banging his fist on the table. "Order, please!"

The crowd quiets down, people resuming their seats under Radcliffe's glare.

"Thank you, Miss Burke," Radcliffe says curtly. "Now I will confer with my colleagues in private before coming to a resolution."

After he announces a short break, I approach my students to extend thanks that will never be enough and gratitude that is boundless. I shake Stafford's hand and hug Kelsey. It's a half hour later when the board members return, and Radcliffe orders everyone to be seated.

I sit down next to Liv, who has composed herself after a crying jag that left her red-eyed, blotchy-faced, and smiling from ear to ear.

"This hearing was convened in order to investigate Professor

Dean West's misconduct," Radcliffe says, shooting me a glare. "In order to protect both our faculty and students, it is critical that we take accusations of wrongdoing very seriously and carry out thorough investigations."

The room grows quiet.

"However," Radcliffe continues, "Mr. Stafford of the Office of Judicial Affairs, a dedicated man who is approaching his fifteenth year of employment at King's, has spent a great deal of time investigating the matter. And given the development with Miss Hamilton, the board of trustees is fully prepared to accept Mr. Stafford's recommendation and permanently close any such case against Professor West."

The tightness in my shoulders loosens. Applause begins to echo against the walls of the room. Radcliffe slams his hand on the table.

"Quiet, please," he orders. "I am not finished. Professor West must account for his arrest by issuing a public apology and stating that the incident had nothing to do with King's University."

He shoots me a glare. I nod in agreement.

"Also," Radcliffe continues, "in light of the students' testimony... such as it was... and the fact that the members of the board were sorry to receive Professor West's letter of resignation in the first place, we would ask that he reconsider leaving King's University and remain in his position as professor of Medieval Studies in the Department of History."

Disbelief fills me. Cheers erupt from the crowd. Radcliffe holds up his hand for silence again.

"With the understanding, Professor West," he adds, still glaring at me, "that you will report to the board of trustees once a month for the next year so that we can supervise your conduct."

Kelsey pushes the microphone at me. I stand and approach the table.

"Understood, Chancellor," I say, my voice hoarse.

"You have two days to rescind your resignation, Professor West," Radcliffe says. "This hearing is officially concluded. Thank you all for your time and... so-called attention."

Noise fills the hall as the spectators push to their feet, voices rising in animated chatter. A wall of people closes between me and Liv. I spend the next hour thanking people and accepting their congratulations.

"We just heard about Jeffrey Butler and Maggie, with some unpleasant video evidence," Frances murmurs to me when the crowd disperses. "Her father has declined to press assault charges against you because he's scared shitless of the publicity. Pardon my French."

"So it's over?"

"It's over." She squeezes my arm. "Welcome back, Dean."

"Thank you, Frances. For everything."

After the hall is almost empty, I finally turn to my wife. She's waiting on the bench, and her smile is like the sunrise.

"I knew it," she says, coming to hug me. "I knew it couldn't end any other way, not for you."

Only when my arms close around her am I able to take a deep breath.

"Are you all right?" I ask, resting my hand on her stomach.

"I'm exhilarated. Thrilled. Proud of you and proud that I was right."

I look at her brown eyes, the thick frame of her eyelashes,

the curve of her cheekbones and shape of her mouth. All those details that I treasure like air. Our history together flashes through my mind, and the truth falls into place.

"All these years, I've been wrong," I tell her.

"About what?" Liv asks.

"I'm not afraid when I'm with you. I never have been. In fact, being with you gives me a courage I didn't know I had. You show me what I can be."

"No. I just know what you *are*."

I lower my head to kiss her, feeling that shift inside me again, the great settling of the earth's plates, the stars and planets rotating in harmony with a thousand feelings. Gratitude, hope, happiness, surrender. Peace.

And there is a distinct sense of freedom, like whatever bonds lashed me to the ground have suddenly broken. I feel lighter.

I tighten my arms around Liv, knowing that in years to come I'll have to *let go* in ways I've never imagined. And somehow, that will be okay because my wife will always anchor my heart.

CHAPTER TWENTY-EIGHT

Olivia

June 25

*A*fter my white knight won the battle of his career, he won another battle against his fear of leaving me alone. Though he grumbled like a bear the entire time, he got on the plane a few days ago and returned to Altopascio to finish his consultation work before the Words and Images conference starts.

As we did before, we exchange emails several times a day, and as my pregnancy progresses uneventfully, I always assure Dean that everything is fine.

And it is.

Frances Hunter told us that Maggie Hamilton withdrew

from the university and left town, apparently without even telling her father. After the news about the affair and the videos spread, Edward Hamilton revoked his support for the King's law school building and cut all remaining ties to the university. While that means a loss of his donorship, the board of trustees and the faculty are immensely relieved to have avoided a scandal.

The reporter Rita Johnson helped shift public perception with an editorial article about the Wonderland Café, in which she condemned Edward Hamilton for his aggression during an opening day event that was intended for children and families.

Allie and I continue to brainstorm ideas to jumpstart the café's business, and we've planned a bunch of different events for the coming months—puppet shows, free kids' meals, cooking classes, craft parties, tea parties, costume parties. Florence Wickham's granddaughter Margery comes into the café one morning, bubbling with excitement.

"I've distributed all the information to our district's PTO presidents and several other parenting organizations," she tells me and Allie. "Believe me, you get all those mothers on your side, and you'll be a smashing success in no time. Your timing couldn't be better either, with summer approaching."

Our friends give us a huge outpouring of support, bringing in family members, children, and grandchildren. When more people learn about our themed birthday party offerings, Marianne tells me that we're starting to book parties all the way into September.

And every morning when I walk into the Wonderland Café where my friends are, when I smell the fresh croissants and soufflés, hear the chatter of voices, I know why Dorothy and Alice were so determined to leave Oz and Wonderland and find their way home. *Home* really is where your heart's desire lives.

Ten days before Dean is scheduled to return from Altopascio, Kelsey drives me to the airport.

"Sure you don't want me to come with you?" she asks as she pulls up to the curb.

"No, but thanks." I reach across the seat to hug her. "I need to do this one alone."

"Okay. Don't forget to call when you get in."

I go into the terminal and check in for my flight. Trying to ignore my nerves, I go through security and board the plane.

The flight is thankfully routine, and I have only a mild case of morning sickness that wanes shortly after the plane lands at the San Jose airport. I email both Kelsey and Dean to let them know I've arrived safely, then retrieve my bag and stand in another line to rent a car.

After consulting my map, I get on Highway 280 and follow the signs to Highway 17, which leads over a winding mountain road to Santa Cruz.

I make my way to the Pacific Coast Highway, where the ocean stretches out in a white-capped platter of blue and gray. The cold, salt-scented breeze drifts into the interior of my car. It's early afternoon, and the fog is fading away under the warmth of the sun.

By the time I find Twelve Oaks again, I'm filled with more emotions than I can untangle—nervousness, excitement, fear. I park at the gate and walk down the stretch of dirt road. A young man approaches me.

"I used to live here," I explain after introducing myself. "I'm looking for North."

"He's working over at the farmer's market," the guy says. "You want to wait?"

My heart skips a beat. I hadn't even known if North was still here.

"No, thanks. I'll find him."

I go back to downtown Santa Cruz and find a parking space not far from Pacific Avenue. Pedestrians stroll along the sidewalk. The farmer's market is a sea of people and white tents, voices rising into the air, the sound of a steel band carried on the breeze.

I maneuver through the crowd, looking at the vendor signs. When I find the Twelve Oaks tent, I stop a distance away. My heart is pounding.

North is busy talking to a customer, pointing at a box of heirloom tomatoes. He looks almost the same—more gray in his hair and beard, a little heavier, but I swear he's wearing the same jeans and T-shirt from ten years ago. And he still has a braid in his beard, tied with a little red ribbon.

I wait for the cluster of people to disperse before approaching the tent.

"Free samples of strawberries," North says, gesturing to the bowls on the counter.

"Hi, North."

He looks at me and blinks. For a second, I'm afraid he doesn't remember me. Then that old, familiar grin breaks out through his beard.

"Get over here, Liv," he says.

I go around the counter to hug him, tears stinging my

eyes as his arms tighten around me in an embrace of pure warmth and affection. When we part, he holds my shoulders and looks at me, shaking his head.

"I'll be damned. I thought I told you not to come back."

"You did. But I've learned that sometimes it's okay not to listen to people."

He chuckles. "True enough. Hold on."

He gestures to a couple of guys who are unpacking boxes from the truck and tells them to take care of things for a while. We get two iced coffees and find a place to sit away from the crowd.

"I've thought about you a lot," I tell him. "Wanted to email or write, but I remembered what you said."

"Yeah. I was glad that you moved on." North tugs at the braid in his beard. "So tell me now."

I tell him everything I did after I left Twelve Oaks ten years ago. Community college, working retail, transferring to the University of Wisconsin. Library sciences, literature, Jitter Beans, Mirror Lake, the Historical Museum. The Wonderland Café.

"When I was at the University of Wisconsin, I met a man who teaches medieval history," I say. "He's my husband now."

"He's a good guy?"

"The best." My throat tightens with emotion. "He really knows how to love me."

"Good."

"How's everything here?"

North tells me about the seed business, the changes in the commune, the people who have come and gone, their new expansion into making furniture and hammocks.

By the time we're finished talking, the sun has started its descent and several of the farmer's market vendors are packing up their stuff.

"You want to stay?" North asks.

Part of me does. I'd love to spend a few nights back at Twelve Oaks, enjoying the salty air, wandering the gardens, joining the group for dinner and the nightly campfire.

But I shake my head. "I booked a hotel room a few blocks from the beach."

"What are you in town for?"

"To see you."

"You came back just to see me?"

"You did so much for me, North. More than I can even explain."

He shakes his head, looking away for an instant before gruffly patting my shoulder. "I didn't do anything, Liv. You did."

"I just wanted to tell you that everything turned out…" My throat closes over. "Everything turned out better than I could have imagined."

"I'm really glad to know that."

We throw our cups into the recycling bin and walk back to the Twelve Oaks tent. I help pack up the remaining vegetables, handmade soaps and lotions, while North and the other guys dismantle the tent.

When the truck is loaded up, I approach North and dig into my pocket. I pull out the necklace he gave me.

"Remember this?"

He takes it in his hand and nods. "Long time ago."

"It helped me a lot. The reminder. It took me a long time to learn it was true, though."

"At least you learned," he says, putting the necklace back in my palm. "Some people never do. Always knew you were a good student."

He pulls open the door of the truck and gestures to the passenger seat. "You're sure?"

"I'm sure. Thank you, North. For everything."

"Great to see you again, Liv. You know where to find me."

"Always."

I take a step back and lift a hand in farewell. My heart fills with gratitude for this gruff, honest man who pointed me toward a road that led directly to *now.*

"When are you heading back?" North asks.

"Friday."

"So soon, huh?"

"Yes." I smile at him. "I have a life to live."

⟡

A week after my brief trip to California, I drive to the airport again. This time, it's to meet my husband on his return from Italy. Dean had emailed me that he would take a taxi from the airport, but no way am I waiting an extra two hours to see him come home.

For good.

Not "for better" or "for worse."

For good.

Dean's flight is scheduled to get in at six in the evening, and I arrive at the airport an hour early. I find an empty bench at the gate exit and sit down. By the time the plane lands, I'm jittery with excitement.

After what seems like an interminable wait, tired-looking passengers clutching bags and carry-ons begin to disembark. I stand up, searching the crowd. A few minutes later, a tingle ripples over my skin.

He walks past the open doors, my beautiful, dark-haired husband who would stand out in a crowd of Greek gods. He looks incredible in faded jeans and a rugby shirt, his face dusted with rough stubble. His hair is a little longer, curling over his ears, and I'm struck with a visceral memory of seeing him for the first time and experiencing that intense, hot pull of attraction.

I feel that rush again, uncoiling in my blood, but this time—more powerfully—my heart surges with joy and love. Dean doesn't see me as he starts down the stairs, but when he reaches the bottom, he looks up.

His glance passes right over me. He starts to turn toward the baggage claim area.

Then he stops. He turns back, his gaze colliding with mine.

For the first time, I don't run and leap into his arms, although the urge to do so is almost overwhelming. Instead I smile and approach him, holding out my hands.

"Welcome back, love of my life."

He stares at me, stunned, his hands closing warm and strong around mine.

"Liv."

"Hi."

"What are you doing here?"

"I came to bring you home."

He's still staring at me. He clears his throat. "You... uh, you cut your hair."

"I did." I turn to show him the back of my short, sleek haircut, which falls just below my ears in gentle waves. "Well, Kelsey's stylist cut it for me. Do you like it?"

"Very Betty Rubble."

I grin and turn back to face him. He still looks faintly dumbfounded. It's kind of cute.

"It'll grow back, professor." I pat his chest. "I promise."

"You're beautiful." Dean finally breaks out of his stupor and untangles one of his hands from mine. He reaches out to curl a lock of my hair around his forefinger, giving it a gentle tug. "As long as I can still do this, I like it."

He moves to grasp my waist and guide me away from the few remaining passengers. We edge behind an advertising display sign before Dean lowers his head to mine. He tucks his hands into my hair, angling my head in the exact right way, and captures my lips with his.

It's a lovely kiss that fills me with pleasure. I spread my hands over his chest, feeling the heat of his body through his shirt, the closeness of him sending shivers clear down to my toes. Our lips fit together seamlessly, that familiar sense of belonging wrapping around us both.

Dean lifts his head, his eyes tender as he spreads his hand gently across my belly.

"How are you?" he asks.

I wind my arms around his neck and rub my cheek against his. "Never better."

After another few stolen kisses, we hurry to get Dean's suitcase from baggage claim and drive home, both of us eager to return to the island of us again.

We spent the next few days settling back into our routine

and catching up with each other. One afternoon several days after his return, Dean comes out of his office looking rather stunned.

"I just talked to Frances Hunter," he tells me. "She said she recommended to the board of trustees that I get fast-tracked for tenure."

"Oh, Dean." Happiness and pride flood me. "That's wonderful."

"She also said the chancellor got a call from a man who's interested in donating to the new law school building at King's."

"Not... not Edward Hamilton."

"No." Dean shakes his head. "Justice Richard West from California. Frances wanted to know if I'm related to him."

It's enough to make us both realize that maybe some family bonds really are unbreakable.

And so things settle into place. For the next few weeks, Dean delivers lectures, organizes Jessica Burke's PhD defense, guides his students' research, and is as confident and in control as... well, all those powerful kings of legend. He contacts the real-estate agent Nancy about houses on the market and keeps an eye out for potential properties.

And because my husband is a scholar extraordinaire, he researches every last detail and makes plans for our upcoming parenthood. As he starts lists of everything we'll need for the baby, his vocabulary becomes an amusing mixture of medieval and baby-related terms: *Cistercian, onesie, crenellation, binky, scriptorium, exersaucer.*

The Words and Images conference is a resounding success, leading to a slate of new offers from universities and institutions trying to lure Dean away from King's. We meet his ex-wife

Helen for dinner one night, a nice evening that gives Dean a final sense of closure.

Summer arrives with wild, happy fervor. Sailboats float on Mirror Lake like lily pads, and both tourists and locals crowd the coffeehouses and cafés, including Wonderland. My blissfully normal pregnancy progresses without incident. By the time I ease into my second trimester, my libido kicks back into force, and Dean and I return to the pleasure of our lusty sex life.

And I just love the way my husband loves me. His kisses are like whipped cream melting into hot apple pie, like ripe, red cherries, and dark chocolate swirled with peppermint. I never dreamed that my response to Dean could be even more intense, but one brush of his mouth is enough to flood me with immediate desire. We seek each other out almost every night, both to satisfy our erotic cravings and to immerse ourselves in intimacy.

One evening I find him stretched out on the bed wearing only his boxers and his reading glasses, his forehead furrowed in concentration as he grades papers for his summer lecture course. Just the sight of my handsome professor lights a fire inside me. After a moment of admiring his rumpled hair and muscular chest, I climb onto the bed beside him. He pushes the papers aside and reaches for me with a smile, lust already brewing in his eyes.

The moment Dean's lips touch mine, a warm, scrumptious feeling blooms inside me. He takes my face in his hands, deepening the kiss, tracing the line of my lips. I press my thighs together to ease the ache cascading through my lower body. I open my mouth and surrender to the sweep of his tongue. A moan catches in my throat as I spread my hands over the muscles of his chest.

Though Dean is especially gentle with me these days, his

hunger for me burns hotter than ever. He unfastens the buttons of my shirt and pushes it off my shoulders, his eyes filling with both heat and tenderness. My heartbeat quickens as I shrug out of my bra and toss it aside, already desperate for his touch.

I'm rounder everywhere, my waist flaring to wide hips, my belly a distinct swell, my breasts full and sensitive. Dean's breath escapes on a rush of pleasure as he palms my breasts, rubbing his thumbs across my nipples before he bends to capture one between his lips. A shock of lust jolts through me.

With a gasp, I arch against him, my knees weakening as he licks one nipple while rolling and pinching the other between his fingers. His thick hair brushes my bare skin, an exquisite tickling that sensitizes my whole body.

"Now," I whisper, clutching at his shoulders.

He lifts his head, fondling my new curves with a growl of pure appreciation before pulling me against him. Our mouths lock together again, hot and deep. We tumble into the pillows, and I wrap my arms around him, kissing his neck, feeling his hands sliding smoothly across my body.

He takes off my pants and underwear, his gaze intense as he moves away to shed his boxers. I moan at the sight of his thick, stiff cock, so blatant and tempting that my sex tenses with the urge to have him plunge deep inside me.

I part my legs, moving back into a more comfortable position, tightening in readiness for his delicious penetration. He slides his hands to my inner thighs, pushing them apart, his shaft rubbing against my folds in a slick, easy rhythm that makes my blood burn.

I stroke my hands over my body, dipping my fingers into my cleft and back up my rounded belly to my breasts. My nipples are achingly sensitive, and one light twist drives my urgency higher. Dean's chest heaves as he pushes his cock into me slowly, watching the pulsing shaft disappear into my slit, his hands on my spread knees.

Even saturated with lust, he's careful not to lower himself on top of me, which means I have the pleasure of gazing at the gorgeous expanse of his body, the sweat-slick muscles of his shoulders and arms tight with strain, the heated expression on his face.

My body shifts and bounces as his thrusts increase in pace, his shaft filling me repeatedly as I arch my hips to meet every hard entry. We fall into the rhythm together, the rhythm of us, all damp skin, flexing muscles, gripping hands.

When bliss crashes over me, I clutch the bedcovers as Dean presses his fingers against my clit, his deep voice murmuring husky words of pleasure. My body is still vibrating when he moves his hands to my hips and plunges inside me with his own powerful release.

With a groan, he rolls to the side and pulls me closer, his breath stirring the tendrils of hair at my temple. I tuck myself against him, absorbing the slow ebbing of sensations.

As my mind clears from the fog of desire, I become aware of a nagging worry that took root during my many hours of researching before-and-after pregnancy issues. I push up to one elbow and look at Dean, who is lying there with his eyes closed, all sweaty, disheveled, and content.

"Hey, Dean?"

"Hey, Liv."

"Are you worried about having a baby?"

He opens his eyes. "You mean the labor and delivery?"

"No, I mean…" I twist a corner of the sheet. "Well, last

fall you said you didn't want anything to change between us. But of course with a baby, it will. And, you know, things will change sexually…"

Dean shifts to face me. To my surprise, a smile tugs at his mouth.

"Liv, you turn me on like no woman ever has," he says. "You always will. And sure things are going to change, but we'll work it out. Haven't we always worked it out before?"

Have we ever.

"Okay. I was just… you know. Wondering."

He's still looking at me. "You don't think I'm going to pressure you into anything before you're ready, do you?"

"No, of course not. But what if it's weeks and weeks?"

"Then we'll wait weeks and weeks." He shrugs. "Liv, I love having sex with you but I'm not a complete jackass."

"You're not?"

He reaches up to tweak my nose. "This is how it's going to go down, Mrs. West. After the kid is born, we're going to wait as long as necessary to have sex again. Months, if we have to. Until we're *both* ready. Then we're going to figure things out day by day. If something's bugging you, you're going to tell me. We're hiring a babysitter at least twice a month so I can take you out. We're getting a lock on our bedroom door so the kid can't walk in on us when we're doing it.

"There will be lots of kissing," he continues. "I will stare lustfully at you when you walk past me and often try to cop a feel. This in no way will obligate you to have sex with me, but if you want to I'll rock your world. And when the kid goes to college, all bets are off and you and I are going to get naked and dirty in every room of the house. In the middle of the day."

Since I'm speechless, I just sink against him, soft and melting. He folds himself around me in his enveloping, protective way, wrapping us both in the knowledge of all that we are to each other now and all that we will ever be.

⌒⌒

"See you tomorrow, Liv."

Allie and I wave at each other as we leave the Wonderland Café one Sunday evening in July. The sun has started its slow descent, and Avalon Street is crowded with people sitting at the sidewalk cafés, wandering along the lake paths, and window shopping. I walk home, enjoying the warm air and the breeze drifting in from the lake.

I go up the stairs to our apartment, pausing at the sight of a note taped to the door.

Butterfly House

Warmth fills me. Though I know Dean isn't luring me to the Butterfly House for a sexy encounter—he's too mindful of my pregnancy these days to pursue me anywhere except in the bedroom—I hurry inside to shower and change. Whatever my husband has planned, I'm not showing up all grubby after a day's work.

As I drive toward Monarch Lane, I wonder if Dean has the same idea I've been thinking about for the past couple of weeks. I pull into the driveway and get out of the car, my breath catching at the sight of the huge, ramshackle house. Though it's still mostly boarded up and overgrown with weeds, right now it looks like a dream.

Tiny white lights shine like fireflies from several trees around the house. Lush, potted plants and flowers bloom along the walkway leading to the front porch, which is draped in a waterfall of twinkling lights. With the sunset casting a reddish glow over the sky, and the lake and town spread beneath the mountains... it's a picture right out of a much beloved, classic fairy tale.

Except this fairy tale belongs only to us.

A tingle rains down my spine at the sight of a certain handsome prince standing on the front porch. My heart rate intensifies as Dean approaches me, a smile curving his mouth. Dressed in charcoal-colored trousers, a navy shirt, and a blue-and-gray striped tie, he radiates that distinct air of *sexy, brilliant professor* that quickens my blood.

He stops in front of me, his eyes warm. A tangible crackle of awareness fills the space between us.

"Hi," I breathe, my whole being flooded with both pleasure and astonishment. "This is beautiful."

"So are you." Dean brushes a kiss across my lips before extending his arm to me.

I slip my hand into the crook of his arm as we walk along the broken flagstones to the porch.

"You fixed the steps," I remark, pausing to look at the repairs he's completed. "And the balustrade. It looks wonderful."

"It's just a temporary fix," Dean says. "They'll have to be replaced eventually."

I let my gaze follow the roof of the porch to the tower where Dean once took pictures of me before things got downright hot. A little shiver runs through me at the memory.

"What did you ever do with those pictures?" I ask.

"I printed out the ones of you fully clothed," he says. "I have a couple of them in my wallet and one in my office. I deleted the others."

"Really? Why?"

"I don't need prints of them." He pulls me closer, his eyes darkening with heat as he taps his temple with his forefinger. "I've got every one of those pictures locked up here where only I can see them."

A wave of pleasure surges beneath my heart as I lean toward my husband like a flower stem bending to the wind.

"I think we have the same idea about this house," I whisper.

"What idea is that?" He slides his hands around to the small of my back.

"The one about buying it."

"Buying it?"

I ease back to look at him, realizing suddenly that he has no idea what I'm talking about.

"Isn't that why you asked me to meet you here?" I ask. "Didn't you talk to Florence Wickham?"

"I haven't talked to Florence since last week." A faint confusion furrows his brow. "Why?"

"She told me that developers are starting to ask about the property again," I explain. "Once they found out the Historical Society couldn't raise the funds to save it, they realized they could swoop right in. Of course they'd just raze the house and make it a commercial site."

"That would be a damn shame."

"That's why I was wondering..." I take a breath and rest my hand on the swell of my belly. "What do you think of us buying the house?"

"Us?" Dean repeats. "You and me?"

I smile. "Last I heard, *us* is definitely you and me."

"Why do you want us to buy it?"

"I thought we could renovate it and eventually live here." I look up at the house again, all the lights twinkling around it. "The location is amazing, and with the right care and attention, the house could be beautiful again. I know it'll take a ton of work and money, but saving and restoring an old house... it feels like something we should do."

And I know to the center of my heart that Dean and I were meant to bring this place back to its original glory.

"You're the perfect person to make sure the details are all historically accurate, and to preserve the integrity of the original building," I continue. "And I'd love to find out about the furniture and decorating. We could stay in the apartment with the baby for the next year or so until we get it all done."

Dean is still quiet, his gaze traveling over the front of the house. I can almost see the thoughts and assessments shifting through his mind.

"We'd just have to make a plan," I tell him. "Preferably a *Professor Dean West plan.*"

Dean turns to smile at me, his eyes crinkling at the corners, and my heart gives a leap of pure happiness.

"It's a great idea, Liv," he says. "I'd love to restore this house and live here with you."

"I'd love it too." I twine my arms around his neck and stand on tiptoe to kiss him. "When I saw your note, I thought you had the exact same idea."

"I do now." He rubs his nose against mine. "But I actually asked you here for another reason. Do you remember what day it is?"

"July… oh my God." I press my hands to my cheeks, shock diluting my pleasure. "I did not forget our anniversary."

"I think you did."

"Oh, Dean. I'm so sorry."

"Don't be." He gently tugs a lock of my hair. "We've had a lot going on, and I was kind of hoping you'd forget anyway. I wanted to surprise you."

He takes my arm and guides me up the steps to the porch where white lights fall around us like a curtain of stars. The sun is a halo of reddish-gold behind the mountains, and the town lights shine through the dusk.

Dean tightens his hand on mine, his dark eyes fixing on me with that singular intensity that shuts the rest of the world out. My heart flutters with anticipation.

"Liv, I think…" Dean pauses and clears his throat. "I think you know everything there is to know. You know that I fell hard for you the first time I saw you. You know that nothing on earth could have kept me from following you that day, and that I had to struggle not to touch you when we stood there on the sidewalk. You know you were the prettiest girl I'd ever seen. That you always will be. You know I went to Jitter Beans every morning in the hopes of seeing you again.

"You know I looked up the university rules before I asked you out, and that I spent hours coming up with the idea of seducing you with library call numbers. You know you're the sweetest, sexiest woman in history."

My entire body warms with love, and I smile through the tears blurring my eyes.

"You know I'll always fight for you," Dean continues. "That I'll always protect you and always want to give you everything. You know you're the one who showed me the meaning of bravery. You know you make my heart pound every time I see you, and that you drive me crazy with your insistence that I put the cereal boxes back in alphabetical order."

I laugh, thinking it's to his credit that he actually makes an effort to do that.

"And," Dean says, his deep voice washing over me like the sun, "you know you'll always be my beauty."

I fumble for a tissue from my purse to swipe my eyes. I do know all that. I've known since the day we met, like a tiny seed was planted right in the center of my heart and has blossomed over the years into a thousand flowers.

"But there are a few things you don't know." Dean reaches up with his other hand to brush a tear off my cheek. "You don't know that I never dared to believe a woman like you existed in the world, much less that you'd ever love me or let me love you. You don't know that you fulfilled a million secret wishes I didn't even realize I had.

"You don't know that I started believing in impossible things after I met you. Maybe a person could slide down a rainbow or taste the clouds or count to infinity. Why not, if there was Liv in the world? The stars shone brighter, the colors of the world became more vivid, everything was clearer, happier, *better.* All because of you."

"You'd better stop, professor." I scrub my eyes again and disentangle my hand from his so I can press my palm against his chest. "I'm a pregnant woman who is about to end up on the floor from sheer excess of emotion."

Dean smiles and then, to my surprise, he goes down on one knee in front of me. I wipe away my tears again.

"Olivia West," Dean says. "My best friend, my wife, my girl, my key to everything good, my beauty. Will you marry me?"

"Will I…" I swallow past the tightness in my throat. "You… you're proposing to me?"

"I'm proposing to you."

"This is why you asked me to meet you here?"

"This is why."

"But—"

"I never asked you to marry me," Dean says.

I blink. "What?"

"When we were at that antique shop." Dean rises to his feet and settles his hands on my shoulders. "I bought you the cameo ring, but I never asked you to marry me."

"You didn't?"

He shakes his head.

I think back to that day when I'd stood at the counter as Dean pulled out his wallet and said he hadn't bought me an engagement ring yet. I remember being a little confused by his disbelief when I'd said I would love to be his wife, but I'd been so flooded with exhilaration and love that I hadn't even noticed he didn't actually ask the question.

"Well," I finally say, "it's a good thing I read between the lines then, isn't it?"

"A very good thing," Dean agrees, amusement lighting his eyes. "But you deserve a real proposal, so I'm asking you now. Will you marry me?"

"Oh!" I realize I haven't even responded yet. I clutch Dean's hands as an immense happiness and excitement course through me. "Of course, love of my life. I'll marry you over and over again, until the end of time. Yes. *Yes.*"

A smile breaks over Dean's face as he hauls me against him in one of those enveloping, tight hugs that secures the world beneath us and presses our heartbeats together.

"Give me a kiss, beauty," he murmurs.

He cups the back of my head as I reach up to press my lips against his. My soul sprouts wings that lift me through the air, twirling and spinning.

When we ease away from each other, Dean reaches into his pocket. I wipe the lingering tears from my cheeks as he extends a small box. Inside is a silver band engraved with two keys and the words *Liv and Dean.*

Dean takes the ring from me and slips it onto my finger alongside my wedding band. I look from the ring to him, overwhelmed by the immensity of the love between us and its power to banish our fear.

"It's amazing, isn't it?" I say. "That we found each other and *flew* in love. How strong we are together, how much more we've become because we know how to love each other. How so much has changed…"

Dean is looking at me as if I'm the answer to all the questions in the world.

"Some things will never change, Liv," he says. "We'll always fall asleep and wake up together. I'll always make you coffee in the morning and tease you about your bathrobe. We'll always love each other to distraction, argue, hold hands, and kiss an awful lot. And I promise you that no matter what, we'll always have *us*."

I smile at him. I know this to the center of my soul. Like milk and cookies, pencil and paper, the moon and stars, please and thank you, movies and popcorn… Dean and I belong together.

We lift our left hands at the same time and place our palms together. Our wedding bands click softly as we entwine our fingers.

"You and me, professor."

"You and me, beauty."

He gathers me into his arms, strong as steel and warm as sunlight. I press my face against his chest, filled with a lovely sensation of coming home to the man whose heart I will keep forever safe. The man who understands all my strengths and flaws, who warms me from the inside out, who knows how to silence the noise of the world so all we can hear is us.

My husband and I will always be two people living one life of perfect imperfection. We'll always live here, in the place of Liv and Dean, where problems are solved and locks are opened.

A place of infinite love, persistence, tenderness, passion, acceptance, and forgiveness. A place where wishes are granted, dreams come true, and stories have happy endings—not because of fate or magic, but because we love each other so hard and so well.

EPILOGUE

*P*ink and red hearts, adhesive cupcakes, and smiling snowmen plaster the windows of the shops lining Avalon Street. Our curtains frame a view of white-capped mountains and skaters gliding across the ice-covered surface of the lake. Children walk with their parents along the street, stopping to play in the snow piled at the curbs. University students trundle past with backpacks slung over their shoulders and paper cups of coffee clutched in their hands.

Dean comes out of his office, looking deliciously rumpled in faded jeans and a King's University sweatshirt, his hair all disheveled and his jaw covered with that day-old stubble that I always find so sexy.

His eyes warm with affection as he approaches me. He kisses my forehead as his hand comes to rest gently on the five-day-old baby sleeping in my arms.

"Want me to put him in the bassinet?" Dean whispers.

Since I need to use the bathroom, I nod and shift Nicholas's weight, soft and cuddly as a bird in a nest of cotton. Dean moves to take Nicholas from me, cradling the bundle of blankets and baby close to his chest.

My heart fills with a wild tenderness as I look at them, my husband and our son, both dark-haired and dark-eyed, already knowing that they are the best of friends. A now-familiar expression of wonder crosses Dean's face as he looks at Nicholas, then he returns to his office where the baby's bassinet is set up right beside his desk.

After using the bathroom, I head into the kitchen to make a pot of tea.

"Go sit down." Dean comes up behind me, giving me a gentle pat on the rear. "I'll get it."

I return to my overstuffed chair beside the window, and Dean soon comes in with the tea and a plate of the Wonderland Café's popular *Home, Heart,* and *Courage* cookies, which he sets on a table beside me.

"Anything else you need?" he asks.

I reach up to squeeze his hand. "Just you."

"You always have me." He rests one hand along the back of my chair and bends to press his mouth against mine. I lean in for a longer kiss, feeling that melted-honey sensation slide through my blood.

"I picked something up for you earlier." Dean moves away from me, his palm lingering against my cheek.

He goes into the bedroom and returns with a big, white box topped with a red bow. He places the box on my lap and sits on the coffee table across from me.

I tug the lid off the box and separate the red tissue paper inside. I run my hand over a swath of thick material. As Dean takes the cloth out and unfolds it, my breath catches in my throat.

"A quilt?" I ask. "You got me a new quilt?"

"The Wickham sisters and I have been conspiring about it for months," he tells me. "Florence's sister Ruth is a quilt-maker, and when I told her what I wanted, she got right to work. She just finished it this morning. She said it's called an heirloom memory quilt."

I can only stare at the quilt. Each square is beautifully sewn with images and words that encompass my life.

The Wonderland Café sign, the University of Wisconsin logo, library call numbers, a book stitched with the title *A Tree Grows in Brooklyn,* Alice in Wonderland, the yellow brick road. A hot-air balloon, the Jitter Beans coffeehouse sign, a peace lily, apple pie, the Eiffel Tower, a patch from Dean's old San Francisco Giants T-shirt, a baby wearing a blue cap, ruby slippers, a cameo silhouette, the Butterfly House, a knight on horseback. And around the border, twelve squares stitched with twelve oak trees.

"Oh, Dean."

"Not bad, huh?" He looks pleased.

"I love you so much."

"I love you, Liv." He slides his hand through my hair, tucking a lock behind my ear. "More than anything. More than life."

He's a blur through my tears, but when I wipe my eyes, I see him watching me with a depth of emotion I can't even begin to fathom. I know because I feel it too, a million colors that fill my heart to overflowing.

I gesture for Dean to sit in the chair with me. He does, gently lifting me onto his lap. I press my face to his chest and sink into the warmth of him. He tightens his arms around me, surrounding me with his ever-present strength and devotion that will see us through anything.

Happy. That's what all the colors distill into. I am so happy.

Even though the unknowns are as innumerable as seashells scattered on a beach, the knowns are clear as glass and infinitely more powerful. Now, finally, I feel like Dean and I have reached the shore at the end of a long ocean voyage.

After exploring distant lands, battling unforeseen threats, learning how to navigate rough waters and emerge from storms, we have both come safely home together, fatigued but exhilarated.

I settle against my husband's chest, into his arms, as he pulls the quilt over my legs and we watch the bustle of Avalon Street outside the window.

We're here again. We've always been here, in our own private world, the space that belongs only to us. We've never left.

I run my hand over the quilt, knowing that one day our son will learn about this patchwork history that has shaped my life, all the people and places who have made me the woman I am now.

One day I'll tell our son about my own mother and father. I'll tell him about the grandmother I never knew who unknowingly helped me find my own path. I'll tell him about the warmhearted people who lived on a California commune, about the boy who taught me how to ride a bike, about beaches and the Grand Canyon at sunrise. I'll tell our son that sometimes people aren't kind but most of the time they are, and you should give them a chance to prove themselves.

I'll tell him about the day his father came to my rescue at the university, the day Allie jumped out at me in a scary apple-tree costume, the day I won Kelsey over with a hug and a plate of crepes. I'll tell him about the aunt who took me in when I needed her help, and a man named Northern Star who reminded me that living takes courage.

I'll tell our son to be the type of man his father is—a man of intelligence and talent, yes, but more importantly a man of deep kindness, loyalty, strength, and integrity. A man who slays monsters for the woman he loves and stands by her side when she needs to slay them by herself. A man who doesn't give up, who believes in chivalry and codes of honor. A man who knows what it means to both love and be loved.

There are so many important lessons I've learned in my journey to *now*. Trust your instincts, follow your bliss, make plans, work hard, learn to let things go. Don't be late. Remember that fortune favors the brave. *Live.* If you need to run, try and run toward something. Study for tests. Laugh at silly cartoons. Be organized. If you fall seven times, get up eight. Always carry an extra pen. Believe you can do everything. Find your key.

And the most valuable lesson I've learned will forever live in my heart, right beside my husband. Love the one who proves to you that *happily ever after* is only the beginning.

ABOUT THE AUTHOR

*U*SA *Today* bestselling author Nina Lane writes hot, sexy romances and spicy erotica. Originally from California, she loves traveling and thinks St. Petersburg, Russia is a city everyone should visit at least once. Nina also spent many years in graduate school studying art history and library sciences. Although she would go back for another degree if she could because she's that much of a bookworm, she now lives the happy life of a full-time writer. Nina's novel *Allure*, Book Two in the *Spiral of Bliss* series, is a *USA Today* bestseller, and *The Erotic Dark* hit #1 on Amazon's Erotica Bestseller list.

Find out about Nina's latest news and books
at www.ninalane.com or join her on
Facebook at www.facebook.com/NinaLaneAuthor
and Twitter at www.twitter.com/NinaLaneAuthor

ACKNOWLEDGEMENTS

I started writing Liv and Dean's story alone, and I am both honored and humbled by the number of people who have not only joined me on the journey, but supported and cheered me on to the finish line.

This trilogy would not be what it is without the editorial expertise of Kelly Harms Wimmer of Word Bird Editorial, who has helped me improve both my storytelling and writing abilities. Thank you to Jessa Slade of Red Circle Ink, and to Deborah Nemeth for incredibly thorough and thoughtful critiques. Martha Trachtenberg, you have my eternal gratitude for your meticulous editing of the entire Spiral of Bliss trilogy.

Victoria Colotta of VMC Art & Design has elevated the

Spiral of Bliss books to the level of art with her beautiful interiors and cover designs. Thank you, Victoria, for your talent, patience, perseverance, collaboration and for never acting like I'm a neurotic nutcase (even though we both know the truth).

My right-here-at-home friends and critique partners are one of my most valuable assets. Rachel Berens-VanHeest and Melody Marshall, thank you a million times over for all the very perceptive editing and story help, not to mention the much-needed reassurance. Bobbi Dumas, I love being able to always count on both your plotting skills and inexhaustible enthusiasm. Our monthly meetings are one of my greatest joys.

Thank you so much, Michelle Eck, Karen Seager-Everett, and Rosette Doyle of Literati Author Services for the Spiral of Bliss tours and cover reveals. You took Liv and Dean right over the rainbow with your professionalism and marketing expertise, and I am exceptionally fortunate to have you in my corner.

Jen Berg and Baba, I owe you both a huge debt of gratitude: Jen, for adoring Liv and Dean from the very beginning and for being such an insightful reader and steadfast champion, and Baba, for your unfaltering support, your very good manners, and for telling me exactly what I needed to fix. I'm so grateful to you both for your humor, honesty, and friendship.

Yesi Cavazos, Maria D., Patti, Michelle Eck, and Debbie Kagan, your opinions mean the world to me, and I'm beyond thankful not only for your love of Liv and Dean but for helping me stay true to their essences. Thank you all so much for your time and your ideas, which shaped this story in ways I never would have been able to achieve alone. I can't wait to meet you all and hug you in person.

Thank you to my longtime writing amie Sylvie Ouellette,

to Soraya Naomi for your editing acumen, and to Cathy Yardley for helping me navigate the course of Liv and Dean's journey.

I owe everlasting gratitude to all the bloggers and readers who have taken Liv and Dean's story to heart and helped me share it with the world.

I am especially indebted to Gitte and Jenny of TotallyBooked Blog, Aestas Book Blog, Michelle and Karen of Literati Literature Lovers, Bridget of My Secret Romance, Vilma's Book Blog, Becs of Sinfully Sexy Book Reviews, Milasy and Lisa of The Rock Stars of Romance, Jessy's Book Club, Trisha of Devoured Words, Sheri of Reading DelightZ, Sandy of The Reading Café, Cindy of the Book Enthusiast, and Tammy of Reviews by Tammy and Kim.

And a very special thank you to everyone who has participated in the Spiral of Bliss blog tours and cover reveals. I am so grateful for your support.

Gigantic thanks-with-confetti-and-lots-of-hugs to my beloved family for putting up with me being at my computer far more often than not, even when everything else falls by the wayside.

All of you have strengthened me with the confidence and courage I needed to give Liv and Dean the story they deserve. Thank you so much.

Liv and Dean's passionate journey began in
AROUSE, Book One in the *Spiral of Bliss* series.

"*One day I'm going to touch you in a thousand different ways and show you how to touch me,*" he said.

And he did.

Struggling with a tormented past, undergraduate Olivia Winter once led a practical but isolated life. Then she met Professor Dean West, a brilliant scholar of medieval history who melted Liv's inhibitions and taught her the meaning of both love and erotic pleasure.

But after three years of a blissful, lusty marriage, Liv and Dean now face a crisis that threatens everything they believe about each other. And when dark secrets and temptations rise to the surface, the fallout might break them apart forever.

Liv and Dean's passionate journey continues in
ALLURE, Book Two in the *Spiral of Bliss* series.

"*We* both want this so badly. I can feel it resonating between us like the hot pull of our first attraction, tangible and intense."

After lies and betrayal almost destroy their marriage, Dean and Olivia West reignite their blissful passion. The medieval history professor and his cherished wife are determined to fix their mistakes and fall madly in love all over again.

Then a family crisis forces Dean back into a feud with his parents and siblings, dredging up guilt over a painful family secret. Liv and Dean have battled obstacles together before, but with bitter family conflicts now endangering their fragile intimacy, they soon must struggle with events that could damage them in ways they had never imagined.

Also by Nina Lane

The #1 bestselling novel about a woman's
intense journey into submission

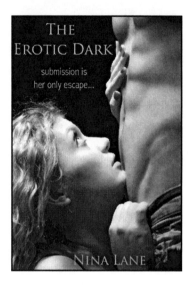

Submission is her only escape… and punishment takes many
forms. Seeking escape from her criminal past, a desperate
woman enslaves herself to a dark trio of men who own an
antiquated Louisiana plantation. Known only as Lydia, she
becomes controlled by three very different men—malicious
Preston, inflexible Kruin, and gentle Gabriel, all of whom
introduce her to a world in which the lines between pleasure,
pain, and shame are irrevocably blurred.

The plantation becomes both Lydia's haven and her prison
as she surrenders to the desires of her unholy trinity. Lydia's submission is fraught with tension and hunger, but what happens
when the outside world enters her dark, anonymous sanctuary?

CPSIA information can be obtained at www.ICGtesting.com
Printed in the USA
BVOW07s1844200114

342476BV00001B/41/P

9 780988 715882